THE
RENTED MULE

THE
RENTED
MULE

A NOVEL

BOBBY COLE

THOMAS & MERCER

Published by Thomas & Mercer, Seattle

www.apub.com

ISBN-13: 9781477808603
ISBN-10: 1477808604

This book is dedicated to all of my friends
and family in Montgomery, Alabama.
It was a fine place to grow up.

*The hands of the witnesses must be the first in
putting him to death, and then the hands of all the people.
You must purge the evil from among you.*

DEUTERONOMY 17:7 NIV

CHAPTER 1
1ST FRIDAY

Cooper Dixon was gently roused from an exhaustive sleep by the warm hand running down the top of his bare leg. Lying on his side, he blinked several times to adjust his eyes. With blurred vision, Cooper could see the dim glow of the alarm clock in the pitch black. 3:33 a.m. A sudden wave of anxiety washed over him as he tried to remember where he was. His business required that he travel frequently, and he often awoke in the middle of the night, confused. The major difference this time was the warm inviting hand, tenderly touching him. Cooper feigned being asleep, enjoying the gentle touch. He rolled over and eased his hand down her bare back and then slowly across her firm thighs. His touch was warmly received. She responded, hungrily. Pushing him back over, her dark hair spilled onto his face as she climbed on top, passionately kissing his neck. He could hear, "Cooper, Cooper."

"Cooper!" a raspy, older female voice yelled. "Your wife's on hold! Do you hear me? I said, Kelly's on hold."

Cooper slightly raised his head from his arm and looked around his office. He exhaled deeply and tried to focus.

"Ugh . . . yes ma'am, put her through."

The electronic ringing of the telephone helped transport Cooper back to the agony of his daily life. This was the second time in two weeks that he had fallen asleep at his desk. Passed out is a better description. Exhaustion was setting in with a vengeance. He leaned forward to activate the speakerphone.

"Hello," he answered, and then cleared his throat.

"Am I on speakerphone?" asked Cooper's wife, instantly agitated.

"Yep," he said, letting out another deep breath.

"Pick up, dammit!" she snapped.

Cooper grudgingly raised the handset.

"Yes, dear?" He asked with no small amount of sarcasm.

"Cut the crap, Cooper! I need you to run some errands. I don't have the time. Millie's blood pressure's botherin' her, so she didn't show up, again," Kelly said with urgency. *She must be tired from a long day shopping, he thought.*

"Is she okay? Do I need to go check on her?" he asked as he leaned forward.

As the longtime family housekeeper, Millie was getting up in years. She had helped raise Cooper, and he considered her family.

"No, she says she's all right, she always is. You gotta run some errands."

"Fine. What do ya need?" he asked, unenthusiastically, picking up a pen. He loathed running errands.

"Get the dry cleaning. There should be six shirts and two dresses. Be sure and count them, and pick up two bottles of good red wine. Then I need you to get the party trays from the country club. They're expecting you. I have the planning meeting tonight here at the house for Alexandra Von Wyle's daughter's bridal tea next month. I happily agreed to host this tea, which will be the biggest social event of the year. Everybody who is anybody will be here, including the editor of *Southern Living* magazine, and it will be at *my* house. I'm so excited. Oh yeah . . . get yourself and Ben something to eat . . . I'm not gonna dirty the kitchen, and there isn't much here to eat anyway," she explained excitedly.

Cooper exhaled deeply. "Does this deal gotta be so extravagant?"

"You don't have any idea about these things. Let me handle them, okay? Now hurry home. There's still a lot of things I need you to help with in order to have the house ready by seven," she added.

"What about Piper?"

"She's spending the night with a friend. Don't be late."

"Okay, fine. Bye," he replied and hung up the phone before she could give him any more instructions. He knew this event was going to eventually turn into a big headache for him. *Lots of yard work, maybe some remodeling. Some rich blue blood gets engaged, and I get a month of grief, complete with an inch-high stack of bills.*

Cooper stared out the window and then down at his desk calendar and realized for the second time that it was a beautiful late August Friday afternoon and he was stuck. Stuck at work. Stuck with an unhappy wife. The only positive was that Piper and Ben were full of excitement that the new school year had started. He knew they weren't typical kids and he loved them for it, but he dreaded going home. His life and wife were driving him crazy. Things weren't exactly going as planned.

For most of his thirty-six years, he had done the right things. He cruised through high school, struggled through college at Auburn, and managed to marry his college sweetheart. They had two great kids. Ben at eight was so much fun. Cooper coached his baseball team, and Ben loved to hunt and fish, so they spent a lot of time together. Piper was a teenager, and he could easily see her growing need for independence. Everyone had warned him about the stage she was about to enter, and he dreaded it. Cooper had already decided she wasn't dating until she was twenty-one. Not really, but it made her nuts to hear him say it. The kids were by far the best things in his life; they're what drove him to be successful. Like most parents, he would do anything for them.

Cooper's perception was that Kelly had changed since the kids were born; she had gone from being his lover to being a mother. He realized that this was a natural progression, but nonetheless, he missed the old days. Kelly had moved on to her motherly and social duties and never looked back at Cooper, except for funding. She could spend everything he made, oftentimes before he ever made it. She had an image that she wanted to maintain, and Cooper was her ticket.

When they met at college, Kelly was simple and genuine. She was from a small town in Bullock County, Alabama, where her dad grew tomato plant seedlings and she helped after school and during breaks. Now, she spent all of her energy trying to be the socialite hostess for Montgomery's elite. Cooper missed the modest small-town girl he'd fallen in love with and often wished that they lived in a quaint little town, without all the societal distractions. Feeling frustrated and tired of arguing all of the time, he woke up earlier, stayed later at work, and basically buried himself in his career.

Cooper Dixon was an owner of a successful ad design group in Montgomery, Alabama, called the Tower Advertising Agency. Actually, he owned only 30 percent, while a college buddy by the name of Gates Ballenger owned the remaining percentage.

Gates came from old Montgomery money. His father had reluctantly loaned the young men the money to start the business, knowing that Gates needed Cooper's sales skills to make it viable.

They formed a limited liability corporation with Gates having a controlling interest, which was of paramount importance to him; Cooper had a piece, but all of the daily headaches. Not paying attention to the formalities, Cooper considered himself an equal partner and did significantly more than his 30 percent of the work. Kelly Dixon got one of the things she wanted—the status that accompanied being married to a successful, independent business owner. Even Gates's two ex-wives were pleased with the arrangement.

Cooper would have been happy with a small office, in an old home rezoned for business, tucked quietly in a neighborhood, but Gates and Kelly insisted that they have a prominent address downtown in the prestigious RSA Tower. Their offices were on the eighth floor and cost more per month than Cooper cared to consider. He did, however, enjoy his view of the Alabama River and the baseball complex for the city's minor league team. Now, realizing he should have pushed for a larger ownership share and an equal vote in the key business decisions, Cooper stayed frustrated but worked harder and longer hours than ever.

Gates was city slick, always scheming something. Cooper hadn't really been bothered by this trait until the last few years of their working relationship.

Just recently, Gates had successfully lobbied a local bank to purchase the Tower Agency and the sale was near completion, pending the final year-end numbers. The buyer had been very pleased with the agency's campaigns for the bank and was looking to diversify its holdings. The bank was willing to pay—cash—four times the agency's earnings. Gates was really pressuring Cooper to increase monthly ARs, suggesting they take clients who they never would have handled before. Cooper didn't want to sell, but he didn't have any choice. This company had been his life for almost ten years, and their twelve employees had been more loyal than family. Kelly wanted to sell simply because Cooper stood to walk away with almost a million dollars and hopefully a cushy monthly retainer for at least the next twelve months. It was not enough for Cooper to retire on, but not a bad payday either. Cooper secretly wanted the money too. He had a dream.

Gates was focused on nothing but the money, and it was making Cooper crazy. He had all but abandoned Cooper during the last two months as he positioned the agency for the big sale.

Cooper stood and then walked over to the small refrigerator he had in the corner of his office. It contained a dozen or so small six-ounce bottles of Mexican-made Coca-Colas that Cooper regularly imported through a friend. Popping off the cap, a tired and frustrated Cooper sat down on the corner of his desk and stared blankly out the window, thinking about the property he wanted to buy, his Promised Land.

The property was perfect. It was exactly what he had always wanted with seven hundred rolling acres of hardwoods and old-growth pines mixed with some hay fields. It was a turkey hunter's heaven. He dreamed of building a cabin overlooking a pond and managing the property for wildlife—his true life's passion. It would be his retreat from the daily pressures, plus it was a solid investment. He had an option on the property to hold it until he could put the financing together, if he could, which was a big if. The option was about to expire, and he cringed knowing he would have to tell Kelly soon. *Tell her or ask her,* he wondered. Either way it wasn't going to be pleasant. The money from the sale of the agency would make it work though, if he could invest it before she spent it.

Gazing down at the snaking Alabama River, he wondered about the woman in his dream. Since she wasn't Kelly, his subconscious was playing with fire, fueled by several months of her increasingly intense comments and glances, making his vivid imagination run wild. It had surprised him and even felt good to have been the recipient of such attention. She made him pay more attention to how he dressed and acted. She made him feel young and alive. He wondered if she was just flirting or actually wanted more. *Wishful thinking.* The thought made him smile.

Cooper switched off the lights in his office as he headed out to complete his ubiquitous honey-do list.

CHAPTER 2

Stretching her legs, Brooke Layton eased her tanned feet through the sand until her toes popped up into the bright afternoon sunshine. She noticed her toenails needed painting. Upstairs in the condo, she had a bottle of hot pink nail polish. She planned on painting them later that night, after she and her son returned from playing miniature golf. Leaning her head back on her lounge chair, Brooke tried to relax, but kept wondering what her life would be like if her father had not lost his fortune. It would certainly be more comfortable than being a working, single mother.

The sky was an intense blue with an occasional white puffy cloud blocking the sun. The sand was sugar white, and the water was calm and foamy green as it lapped lazily at the beach. Brooke couldn't really afford to go to the beach this weekend, but her son Grayson had begged, and she gave in without much resistance. She had borrowed a friend's beach condo for a much-needed long weekend.

She slowly rubbed suntan oil on her arms and legs, paying careful attention to her upper thighs—*they never seem to get enough sun.* Just a few chairs away, a middle-aged wife sharply elbowed her husband for enjoying the scene just a little too much.

Brooke tried to take care of herself and was constantly dieting and exercising in an effort to stay in shape. She dressed to accentuate her assets. The shapely brunette had always enjoyed men staring. Brooke had a certain electric attraction about her. But you would never know that behind the dark sunglasses, the outwardly confident Brooke Layton was deeply frustrated with her life. It was missing something, and she knew all too well what it was.

From the beginning, Brooke had tried admirably to make the marriage work. She had read books and magazines, wanting to believe they could have a perfect marriage. Since the first night of their honeymoon, she sensed something wasn't right and that something really important was absent. The longer their marriage dragged on, the more apparent her husband's true colors became, and she realized that marrying him had been a colossal mistake. Staying married was an even bigger screw-up. After four years they divorced in what was a bloody legal mess. Four and a half years later, the chaos continued, leaving her in a constant state of raging emotions.

She held her head high and made no apologies for ending the marriage. Her sole focus was her son and his welfare. She felt that she could handle anything. *Almost anything,* she thought.

The problem was that her ex-husband had never accepted the divorce and hadn't moved on with his life. He hadn't even thought of moving on. He regularly stalked her, but was smart enough not to cross any legal lines . . . or at least ones that she would notice. At first he wanted nothing to do with their son, but in the last few years he had petitioned the courts for joint custody, mostly just to harass Brooke. So, now, every other weekend Brooke had to see him and he did his best to upset Grayson in some demented, desperate attempt to work his way back into her life.

Only Brooke knew the truth of her ex's dangerous side. She was certain that he was a sociopath, and he displayed symptoms of various mental disorders: bipolar, split personality, and last but certainly not least was multiple personality disorder. He had eventually admitted to her that he required medication after she threatened to club him with a tee ball bat.

He seemed to be getting worse. Unfortunately, Brooke couldn't prove it, and with his high-priced team of lawyers, he was winning battles. Brooke's guts knotted every time she was forced to allow visitation with Grayson. She smiled at the thought that she was mentally prepared to kill him if she had to, and then looking around, she wondered how many of these other women were thinking about killing their exes. *Probably most.*

Brooke had met "Mr. Wrong" while home from college over Christmas break. She was attending the University of Montevallo, pursuing a fine arts degree. He was handsome and affable . . . back then. It was at a Montgomery popular college bar that they were introduced. They ended up talking for a couple of hours about politics and world issues. Brooke wasn't, however, instantly attracted to him. He was a little too arrogant for her tastes. But after she returned to school, he would call and even sent yellow roses, which surprised her because they were her favorite and she hadn't told him. He was relentless but subtle in his pursuit and eventually charmed his way into her heart.

She now knew the truth. Her ex-husband had preyed on her from day one. The prospects of being married to her and her certain inheritable fortune were too much for him to resist. So she didn't stand a chance against his keen psychological manipulations. While very vulnerable, struggling with the death of her mother, he intensified his efforts to worm his way into her life. His devious plan worked. And then by cutting slits into the reservoirs of his condoms, he impregnated Brooke. Finally, against the advice of friends and family, she agreed to marry him.

When Brooke thought back on it all, she could see how it happened. He found out she was real-estate developer G. James Layton's daughter and instantly saw dollar signs; in fact, he had admitted as much. Brooke didn't know anyone who knew him at the time and ended up falling for every one of his lies and stories. The reality was that the long-distance romance prevented them from spending enough time together for her to really get to know him at all. He was simply one of life's pitfalls that every girl is warned about as she starts dating.

When he found out Brooke's father was near bankruptcy and, therefore, he hadn't married into an actual fortune, he began to chase every young thing in a tight skirt that crossed his path. He also oftentimes became violent. When she finally summoned the courage to mention divorce, he went ballistic. Brooke feared for her and Grayson's safety. She began to wonder if she would ever be free again.

Brooke wanted a good man in her life, although she had proven to herself that she was self-reliant. Still, she desperately sought someone to take care of her; someone financially sound, who could be a positive role model for Grayson. *Someone like Cooper Dixon,* she thought.

She'd been infatuated with Cooper for some time. But since he was married and didn't seem to notice her sly advances, she'd begun to reconsider her plans. Sitting on her beach towel, she glanced at her watch, which read 5:30 p.m.

That meant Cooper was probably on his way home. *Home to his wife.*

In frustration, she folded her arms across her knees and closed her eyes to daydream of better times ahead. *The good ones are always taken. But is he REALLY happy?*

Brooke opened her eyes to see her eight-year-old son walking up. He sat down and then stared up at an airplane pulling a banner that advertised "All You Can Eat Crabs." She had followed his gaze and thought just how adorable he was. All boy, and by far the best thing that had ever happened to her.

"Mom . . . I'm bored," he said, with a deep exhaling breath while kicking sand.

"Whaddaya wanna do?" she asked, pulling down her black sunglasses so that she could clearly see him.

"I wanna go fishin', like those people," Grayson said, pointing at a father and son casting into the surf.

Always one for adventure, Brooke said, "Let's go," as she jumped up and began gathering her beach accoutrements.

"But, Mom . . . I don't have a fishin' pole," he whined, turning out the palms of his hands.

"Well, we'll go buy one. Actually, we'll buy two, so I can fish as well," Brooke replied enthusiastically, while hiding her concern over her credit cards' balances.

"But you can't bait your hook, and I'm really not that good with shrimp yet," Grayson replied with an honest smile. "But Grampa's teachin' me," he quickly added.

"Okay, then. Looks like we'll just have to help each other. Go on inside and get ready. I'll be right there." Brooke believed that she could find someone to help them if necessary; and if not, she'd figure it out. She had fished with her father growing up and remembered the basics.

"Thanks, Mom!" Grayson exclaimed as he took off running across the warm white sand.

Brooke slowly stuffed her suntan lotion, towel, and Kindle into her beach bag while she watched Grayson racing toward the condo. Sliding her feet into her flip-flops, she hoped that he would continue for years to listen and trust her. She knew that was his best protection from his father's influence.

As she picked up her cell phone, she thought of Cooper and tried to come up with an excuse to call this late on a Friday afternoon. Finally, she said aloud, "What the hell," and punched in his cell number from memory.

She listened to it ring several times and almost broke the connection when he answered, "Hello?"

"Hey, Cooper. It's Brooke. I just wanted to let you know that I finished those art boards. I'll have them ready to view Monday," she explained happily.

"Great! I've made some progress on the project myself. Is that a seagull? Are you at the beach?"

"Yep. Took the day off, but I finished your boards first . . . of course. Gulf Shores is so beautiful," she said, and then took a sip of bottled water.

"I wish I were there. I mean . . . I need a break," he clumsily replied.

"You should get away; life's too short not to enjoy each day. At any rate, I just called to say the boards look really good. After I go fishin' with my son, and then eat, and probably play a round or two of miniature golf, I'll finish the whole presentation. You'll love it," she continued, twisting the cap onto the bottle and placing it inside her bag.

"That sounds like fun. More fun than I had at the office all day."

"You really need to take some time off . . . maybe you could go fishin' for a few days. That would be relaxin', wouldn't it?"

"Yeah, sure it would. But I've got too much going on at the office," he replied, intrigued by her suggestion.

"Go catch some fish. The office and everything you've got goin' on will be there when you get back, but you'll be recharged and feel better when you do."

"I know. I should. You're right. But I can't," Cooper acknowledged, wondering if he meant that he couldn't go fishing or that he shouldn't be thinking about her the way that he was.

"Okay, well, look, I gotta go. I'll bring the boards Monday. Call if you need me." Brooke hung up quickly, strategically cutting short the conversation, hoping to leave him wanting just a little more. He made her feel sixteen again.

Into dead space, Cooper said, "Great. Thanks, Brooke."

He stared at the phone for a moment, not believing that the woman of his daydream had just called. That alone would make his evening bearable. He sighed as he drove to the local grocery store in search of clear plastic forks while only a three hours' drive away was a woman who seemed very interested in having a relationship with him. She looked at him in a manner that he hadn't experienced in a long time. And he was experiencing emotions and thoughts that he had never considered possible. On top of everything, she was about to go fishing. He lived to fish.

Brooke stared at the crystal clear Gulf and yearned for things to be different. After several minutes she gracefully gathered her belongings, slipped on a beach robe that matched her bag, and walked toward the condominium, totally unaware that she was being watched.

CHAPTER 3

He was having a rough day. Sitting at his desk, Gates was overwhelmed by all the work that he needed to finish. Gates loathed any details and particularly paperwork. He decided to delegate this pile of mind-numbing documents to Cooper: *let him deal with it.*

Realizing that his hand was shaking, he went over to his door to check that it was locked, and then quickly opened a small wooden humidor to pull out a metallic cigar tube. He opened it carefully. Inside was a small baggie of coke. *I just need a little bump before this phone call*, he thought.

Gates poured a small amount onto his credenza and used a credit card to break up the clumps and then define the line. He rolled up a dollar bill and snorted the powder. The worried man closed his reddened eyes and pinched his nostrils as his body reacted to the sudden rush. He didn't think he was addicted. He only needed it to help get through the pressure of selling the business. There was much more at stake, however, and the stress was taking its toll on him.

Gates Albert Ballenger, III, almost always had everything he ever wanted and usually got it with little or no effort—the best schools, the best clothes, the best cars . . . and sometimes the best-looking women. His college days, of course, were a monument to mediocrity. And then later in life controlling a successful business didn't offer much satisfaction either since it never occurred to him that his lack of contentment was proportional to the amount of energy he didn't put into it. The company was successful in spite of Gates and was attributable to the efforts of others, namely Cooper, whom Gates was slowly beginning to despise.

Gates's second wife had recently left him and with alimony for two and the child-support payments for one, he was being eaten alive, financially. *Either I'm attracted to the wrong women or they're attracted to me. I'm not sure*, he thought.

One thing was abundantly clear: women paid very close attention to his money, or what they thought was his money.

As a kid, his father had allowed him to drink bourbon with him. His dad had thought it was cool to introduce Gates to his world this way, having no idea that Gates had been drinking since he was twelve. Shortly after his father's introduction to whiskey and "outside women," the no-longer deniable troubles with Gates began. By seventeen, he had experienced more than most twenty-five-year-olds, and he searched hard for anything that would give him a thrill.

Gates found nirvana in gambling. It first started at the dog track just east of Montgomery. Gates loved the thrill of betting and a custom-made false ID allowed the high schooler to walk right in. One week Gates would be up five grand, and the next he would be down ten. Soon he befriended a local greyhound trainer and tried to fix races to help his percentages. After a bad misunderstanding and a loss of over $20,000 in one weekend, the trainer's dogs mysteriously died and Gates barely missed an extended stay in juvenile detention. If the judge hadn't been his father's hunting buddy, Gates wouldn't have graduated with his class, he would have been pressing license plates.

Gates's father began to wonder if he had really helped his son when getting him out of a number of embarrassing situations. He couldn't shake the fact that his son coldly killed the dogs and then beat the trainer so badly that he ended up in a body cast. For whatever reason—a father's unconditional love or his desire to avoid societal humiliation—he always kept his son from behind bars.

The gambling bug never left Gates. He bet on everything. Horses, basketball, baseball, but his favorite was football. He was addicted to point spreads, the over/under, and he searched far and wide for his next tip. He listened to sports talk radio and did research online, all to not much avail, and the last three years found him paying more and more juice to his bookie. Gates was a loser. He lacked discipline, which coupled with a gambling problem was a recipe for disaster. The last tally showed him owing just over $1 million, with interest compounding daily. Nobody knew, but everyone had his or her suspicions. Gates's father had to cut him off. The ex-wives' relentlessly pursued their cut of his net worth. All of this was making Gates's extravagant lifestyle almost impossible to maintain.

He was a genius at showing the bankers that he was making money, the Internal Revenue Service that he was not, and his equally curious ex-wives that there wasn't any more blood in the turnip. What he could not do was manage his bookie. The guy was hot-tempered, hungry for payment, and growing anxious. Gates was constantly begging for more time. Now it appeared that he had only one option. If he could sell the business, he could satisfy most of his debts;

and if he could doctor the books, he could get even more money away from Cooper. He had to. Gates was terrified of his bookie; he knew he had pushed the limit with him. Gates was scared and backed into a corner.

He sat down at his desk and stared at the phone. He quickly dialed the number from memory and listened with trepidation as it rang.

"Hey, man. It's Gates . . . uh, how you doin'?"

"When you gonna pay me?" a gruff voice responded.

"That's why I'm callin' . . . to let you know . . . I got a meetin' with the bank next week, and I should have a firm sale date then."

Gates waited for a reply. He heard a cigarette lighter close and Mitchell blowing out a deep breath of smoke.

"That's good. I'm gettin' tired of waitin'. This is draggin' on way too freakin' long. You know I got a business to run. I got expenses."

"I understand, but I should know exactly what we'll get and a target date to close, I swear," explained Gates, trying not to sound terrified.

Mitchell Holmes ran a multistate booking outfit. To appear legitimate, he controlled several businesses through which he laundered money. On any given weekend during football season, he had hundreds of thousands of dollars crossing his books. Because several high-profile law enforcement officers placed bets with him regularly and watched his back at the local level, he felt very well insulated—nearly bulletproof.

"We? You've never said *we* before. Who exactly is *we*?"

"My partner, Cooper, gets a cut," Gates replied, wishing not to explain every detail.

"You gonna get enough to pay me, Gates? You never said anything before about havin' to pay out to a partner."

"I'll know soon. It should be enough. It'll be close."

"What's his name again?"

"Cooper. Cooper Dixon."

"Get rid of him," Mitchell said as he exhaled a lung full of smoke.

"I can't do that . . . how can I do that?"

Gates had every intention of cooking up some general administrative expenses to inflate his take of the sale, but never dreamed of killing Cooper, although he had planned to screw him out of a sizable chunk of his share of the sale. Gates nervously rubbed his nostrils.

"Listen, you little shit, I want all my money, and I don't care how you get it. You got that? Do I need to help you? Because I think I do. I can make things happen real fast, you know," Mitchell Holmes said coldly, implying everything that Gates feared.

"I hear what you're sayin'. Just give me a few more days. I swear I'll call as soon as I know the details."

"I want all of it. All of it. Ya hear me?" Mitchell instructed and then hung up.

"I know. I know," Gates said into dead air; then he returned the handset to the cradle and thought about Mitchell's comments. *Cooper's share is the answer to all my problems.*

Wearily, Gates leaned back in his chair and stared out the window at the State Capitol. The giant domed building was built in 1851. Many significant events had occurred there including the formation of the Confederate States of America and the end of Dr. Martin Luther King's historic Selma to Montgomery march. Gates wondered what gave the building the strength to endure over 150 years. *I know that I don't have that kinda strength, but maybe if I do somethin' dramatic, I can turn the tables.*

CHAPTER 4

After finishing off a dozen hot chicken wings, the waitress brought a third beer. He ogled her chest and drummed the table with his hands as she cleaned up his mess. She was accustomed to guys staring at her orange shorts and tight white top, but this freak really made her uncomfortable. There was something peculiar and very unnerving about the way he leered.

"Are those beauties *real*?" he asked, gawking at her chest.

She didn't respond.

"Hey, don't ignore me! I'm a payin' customer."

"What do you think?" she fired back angrily.

"Let me feel 'em, so I'll have a better idea."

"Look me in the eye."

He did, expectantly.

She said, "Not in this lifetime, asshole!" and then she turned and quickly walked away to alert the manager.

He chuckled and took a long pull of the cold beer. Setting the bottle on the table, he glanced at his watch and realized it was time to leave. He had a very important business appointment at ten o'clock. He checked the tab that the manager brought to the table. He dropped bills on the table, leaving a $1.37 tip.

As he walked across the street to his BMW, he pressed the unlock button and the lights flashed. Sitting in the car, he ran his fingers through his hair and thought about the chaos he was about to set in motion. He looked at himself in the rearview mirror and smiled. *This is some serious shit, and I've planned every detail. It's flawless. It's freakin' brilliant!*

He cranked the car and then adjusted the radio, stopping on an old Eagle's song. He pulled onto Highway 182, headed east to the infamous Flora-Bama—a beach bar sitting atop the state lines of Florida and Alabama. As he drove, he recalled the instructions he had been given. He was to sit at the end of the bar at exactly ten o'clock and light one match every minute until he was approached. Checking his pockets, he felt the book of matches and an envelope with $10,000 in one hundred dollar bills. Reaching under his seat, he pulled out his hammerless Smith & Wesson .38 revolver.

When he parked his car in the crowded parking lot, he untucked his navy blue golf shirt to hide the bulges in his pockets. His khaki shorts and boat shoes matched what half the crowd would be wearing. The other half would be bikers or wannabes. Although preppy, he appeared average, and he hoped very forgettable. Smiling boldly at himself in the rearview mirror, he brimmed with excitement.

"Let's do this," he said aloud as he walked toward the neon signs and the loud, rowdy crowd that was already spilling outside.

He paid the cover charge and then headed toward the back, deep into the crowded bar. Hot women were everywhere, dancing and having a great time. As he worked his way through the mob, he tried not to get too distracted by the tanned scenery. He became anxious when he spotted a big, burly guy with a blue jean vest and tattoos covering his arms sitting at the far end of the bar—his conceit evaporating at the sight of the huge muscular biker. He was going to have to ask the mountain to move.

"Hey, man. I need that seat . . . if you don't mind."

The big dude didn't acknowledge him.

"I'll make it worth your trouble," he yelled over the music.

Still no response.

"Look, if I buy you a beer, will you let me sit there?" he asked loudly, and again he was met with zero acknowledgement. He glanced at his Rolex but couldn't see the hands well enough to tell the time. Growing anxious, he held his left wrist toward a neon beer light and saw that he had less than five minutes.

"Okay, dude . . . look . . . this is my final offer," he almost screamed as he grabbed his wallet out of his back pocket. "Here's a hundred. All you gotta do is let me sit right there. Okay?"

"Make it two and you gotta deal," the big guy mumbled loud enough to be heard and then took a huge swallow of cold beer.

Gritting his teeth and looking at his Rolex, he realized that this was wasting time and decided it was just another business expense.

"Okay. Here. Take it. Now, can I sit down?" He was practically begging. He took another quick but futile glance at his watch.

The enormous man grabbed the money and then his beer and with a grunt pushed his way into the crowd.

Relief flooded him as he quickly sat down, nervously exhaling. His buddy could get him anything for the right price; they had worked several past deals and had formed a fast alliance based solely on cash and results.

He lit a match and held it in front of his face while it burned. Very few people even looked at him. As the second match burned brightly, he glanced around to see if anyone was paying attention.

The female bartender noticed and placed an ashtray and a bar napkin in front of him, asking, "Whattaya have?"

Wondering if this was part of the plan, he thought for the correct answer and when nothing came to mind, he just said, "Coors Light."

She nodded, reached into the cooler, grabbed and opened the bottle, and then sat it on the napkin and walked off. He laid a twenty next to the bottle.

He lit a third match, held it with his right hand and drank his beer using his left.

A tipsy blonde walked over and blew out the match, and then started singing "Happy Birthday" to him . . . until he finally convinced her to stop. She stared into his eyes and smiled. He admired her skintight cut-off blue jeans and equally tight white tank top as he returned the smile, but he was too edgy about his meeting to successfully flirt.

He lit a fourth match and held it up. And so it went.

While holding up the seventh and continuing to keep an eye on the blonde, the biker came back and laid a note in front of him.

"Read it and burn it," he mumbled as he leaned over the bar and grabbed a brown bottle from the beer box. "Put it on his tab," he instructed the bartender pointing a massive finger at the nervous guy lighting matches and then disappeared into the crowd.

Excited that he made contact, he turned over the napkin and read the scribbled instructions.

The person he was supposed to meet was across the street at Zeke's Marina on the boat *Mo' Money*. He reread the instructions before laying the crumpled note in the ashtray. He dropped a burning match on top, watching it slowly incinerate. Never thinking about his tab, he stood to leave and then with a sudden rush of paranoia quickly started pushing his way toward the exit. He glanced at the energetic blonde dancing alone and wondered if she was undercover. Innate cockiness overrode suspicion, so he determined that she had just found him attractive. He winked.

"Happy Birthday!" she yelled loud enough to be heard over everyone in the bar, singing along to Lynyrd Skynyrd's "Sweet Home Alabama."

He mouthed, "I'll be back," holding up one finger, signaling that he wouldn't be gone too long.

He was excited, and this was just as he expected. A professional criminal wouldn't talk shop in a crowded bar where someone could hear his conversation. *Nice form*, he thought.

He pulled his BMW into the marina's parking lot, and as he walked away, he locked the doors with his key fob. He heard the *chirp, chirp*. Heading toward the large fishing boats, he checked his pockets for his necessities.

The piers were long deserted. All the boats were washed down and ready for the next day's activities. The crews were most likely drinking at the Flora-Bama or at some less touristy watering hole. At the end of the longest pier, he saw a gaudy yellow cigarette-type boat. Almost halfway down the pier, he could see the name *Mo' Money* painted on its transom. He slowly walked to where she was moored. Looking around carefully, he didn't see anyone on board. He despised boats unless someone else owned them. They were black holes that floated on water rather than in space.

"Hello . . . I'm the Client," he called toward the boat.

"Yo, man, shut the hell up with that 'Client' shit!" The voice came from behind him. He jumped and then wheeled around to see the silhouette of a huge man standing on the back of another large boat.

"I got the note," he volunteered, not really knowing what to say but compelled to fill the silence.

After a long moment, "Pat him down," came from the big shadow of a man.

Another much smaller guy appeared and searched the Client with an electronic wand, after frisking him. He found the revolver and took it, but failed to find any form of active or passive surveillance.

"He's clean now, Dog," the small man said as he stepped back onto the boat. He emptied the cartridges into the water and tossed the gun back to its owner.

"What the hell did ya think you was gonna do with that piece?" the big man asked.

"It's for protection," the Client sheepishly replied as he slid the gun into his pocket.

"Bring another gun to a meet and you'll need a proctologist to find it! You feel me?"

"Yeah, uh . . . uh . . . I . . . I hear . . . I mean, yeah, I feel ya," the Client stammered.

"Good. Now where's my down payment?"

"Right here. I got it right here. See?" he said, nervously pulling it out of his pocket.

The big man stepped off the boat onto the pier; it creaked under his weight. "Good. What's the job? Give me the details."

Pausing to gather his thoughts, the Client glanced around and said, "I wanna have a woman kidnapped and held for a week or so. It's simple. I can tell you *all* about her, when would be a good time to grab her, and I even got ya a place to hide her. It'll be more like babysittin'. It'll be the easiest money you ever made . . . much easier than your normal business."

Before the Client realized it, the big man snatched him off the dock by his shirt collar. Holding him in the air, at his eye level, the big guy said through gritted teeth, "Get this straight, you don't know shit about my bidness or me . . . and if I *ever* hear of you sayin' otherwise, I'm gonna hunt you down and you ain't gonna like what I do to you. You hear me?!"

Consumed with fear, the Client couldn't speak. He just nodded several times.

The big man dropped him. "Now, gimme the rest."

"Yeah . . . ah . . . well, it's like this, it's . . . I wanna frame her husband for it, plant some evidence that makes it look like . . . you know . . . like that he's behind it. Basically, I wanna ruin him . . . and I . . . I want that son of a bitch to suffer. That's really the most important part of this deal. I want him in a *world* of hurt."

"That's cool, but my fee don't include poppin' nobody. We straight on that?"

The Client nodded, knowing that he, personally, would do any of the heavy lifting. "You don't hafta. That's not your job," he said with a malevolent smile.

"So, Homey, what's this dude done to deserve my attention?" The huge man asked, sitting down on a dock box.

"It doesn't really matter, does it?" the Client asked, regaining some of his arrogance. He sat down, across from the big man, on another fiberglass dock box.

The big guy paused as he took a hard, thorough look at the Client and then said, "Not as long as you got the cash, and don't even think about playin' me." He grinned, exposing a shiny gold tooth.

"Not a problem," the Client said confidently.

The Client stood and raised the envelope filled with cash, waving it, "I only deal in green!" He was again enjoying being who he thought he was.

"Lower your voice and sit your ass down," the big man hissed.

The Client quickly dropped back down, his head hanging. He mumbled, "Okay. I'm sorry. Well, uh . . . well . . . then. What should I do with this?"

"Give it to him," the big man said, motioning to his smaller companion.

After inspecting the envelope's contents, the small guy said, "It's good, Dog."

The big man then tossed the Client a small cell phone and said, "Keep it *on* and with you all the time. Don't lose it. My number's programmed as speed dial number one. Only call me from that phone."

"What's your name?" the Client asked excitedly.

"Mad Dog."

After a moment, Mad Dog continued, "Let's get this straight. I call the shots. I'm in charge. *Me!* Ya, feel me?"

"No problem, Mister Mad Dog. I'm only interested in results, and you come highly recommended, so I'm good with it."

"One last thing. You can't back out. There ain't no refunds. I get all my fee once this gets started. Am I clear?"

"Absolutely. You da man!"

Quivering with excitement, the Client went on to carefully explain the details of the job and the players involved. Then they negotiated the remaining balance of the fee, which the Client had no intention of paying.

The Client left the meeting exhilarated, feeling powerful.

He started his car and turned up the radio. Shifting into drive, his mind drifted to the drunken blonde at the bar. *Ya know . . . I think I just will let her give me a birthday present.*

CHAPTER 5

Cooper completed the honey-do list with little enthusiasm and then headed home. He had purchased wine—although it wasn't too expensive—clear plastic tableware, the party trays from the country club, and then he'd picked up the dry cleaning but had forgotten to count the shirts.

When he rolled into his driveway in his dark green four-wheel-drive Ram pickup truck, he could see Kelly giving instructions to a landscaper. As the huge garage door opened, he could see that Kelly's red Volvo was parked in the center, taking up both parking slots. He parked and quickly carried everything inside. He knew that he should be involved in whatever discussion was occurring outside in what he knew deep down would be a vain attempt at damage control. Landscaping was outrageously expensive. As he walked past the den, he noticed that something was different. Stopping to look back, he realized that his two prized deer-head mounts were gone and had been replaced with gold-framed floral prints. He groaned and then headed outside.

Kelly was rapidly explaining how she wanted the yard to be transformed: azaleas here, crape myrtles there, and a brick sitting area with a fountain in the corner. The landscaper frantically made notes on an iPad.

"Kelly? Kelly? I need to speak to you. It's important," Cooper implored as he walked hurriedly across the manicured lawn.

Kelly was infuriated that Cooper had interrupted her, but nonetheless excused herself from the landscaper and walked toward her husband. "Dammit, Cooper, I don't have time for your crap right now."

"What are you doing? We haven't discussed additional landscapin'. The yard looks fine! It was professionally landscaped just three years ago, when we bought this house," Cooper exclaimed in frustration.

"Look, you don't want me to be embarrassed. I have everybody that's anybody coming here for this tea, and I *will* make a good impression."

Cooper let out a deep breath, trying to keep his composure. The landscaper busied himself placing orange flagging on the shrubs he planned to remove.

"What you wanna do will cost several thousands of dollars. Just how do you expect that we pay for it?"

"When we sell the agency, we'll have plenty of money," she answered as if he had just asked the most idiotic question she had ever heard.

"That's crazy! We may not even get to sell it. The wheels may run off at any point," he answered, hoping that he could get through to her, but knowing it was futile.

"Gates says it's a done deal," she replied, looking around the yard, not really paying attention to Cooper.

Ben rode up on his bicycle. Cooper didn't want him to hear them arguing tonight since in the past year or so the kids had witnessed frequent disagreements between them and had sensed the strain in their relationship. The small blond-headed youngster was excited to see his dad and ran over, attacking Cooper's right leg.

"What happened to my deer heads?" Cooper asked as nonchalantly as possible; then he grabbed Ben, tossing him over his shoulder and then sitting him down on the grass.

"I told Mom you'd be mad," Ben quickly interjected.

"He gets mad anytime I wanna spend money," Kelly spouted harshly and gave Cooper the eye.

"I guess Mrs. Von Wyle doesn't approve of deer mounts?"

"She sure doesn't have any in her home," Kelly replied, folding her arms across her chest.

"That's her place. This is ours. And it oughta reflect who we are. Us. I live here, too, by the way." Cooper extended his arms to accentuate his point. "In case you didn't know, they got a huntin' camp, and it's full of mounts. Mr. Von Wyle hunts all over the world."

"Cooper hunny . . . it's just till this tea's over." Kelly laid it on thick, smiling, knowing that the changes would be permanent.

Cooper shook his head. "I suppose you'll want to do some remodelin', too, if we can get it done in time?"

"No. Just a little redecoratin'. Cooper, I swear you're gonna embarrass me," she said, looking around for any neighbors watching. "This discussion's over."

"This is unbelievable . . . you're . . . you are just unfreakin' believable!"

Cooper picked up Ben again and then noticed the next-door neighbor on the other side of the hedge a few yards away. Cooper shook his head and plodded toward the house carrying Ben on his shoulders.

Let her have her little party. Hell, she can fix up the house too. Whadda I care? I'll have my Promised Land . . . I hope.

CHAPTER 6
1ST SUNDAY

Clarence Armstrong, also known as Mad Dog, called a meeting at the Pink Pony Pub on the beach in Gulf Shores, Alabama, to discuss the plan with his eclectic criminal team.

They all arrived before the lunch crowd and had the place basically to themselves. It was a lazy Sunday late morning and, typically, no one seemed in a rush to do much of anything. Clarence ordered two plates of steamed shrimp with twin baked potatoes.

Weighing in at a muscular 260 pounds, it was obvious that Clarence didn't miss many meals. He was unbelievably strong and had played two seasons for Mississippi State as outside linebacker.

Clarence, clearly physically talented, with one of the highest GPAs on the football team, knew how to use his head and his muscles. He made significant cash writing term papers for other athletes and students. However, he had been devastated to learn that he was too slow physically to play pro ball and thereby wouldn't collect a big paycheck.

His Fifteen Minutes of Fame came during an ESPN Thursday night football game. After making a bone-crushing tackle on a quarterback—that could be heard in the cheap seats—he was picked up by a television camera microphone asking the dazed opponent about his grade point average. The announcers joked about it the rest of the night.

After graduating college and moving back home to the Gulf Coast, Clarence knew that he couldn't tolerate a standard eight-to-five job. He eventually met several members of the biggest local drug network, which exposed him to outstanding opportunities for making large sums of cash, fast.

Clarence quickly evolved from a drug runner to a criminal mastermind. He was well suited for intimidating people and had developed a reputation for productivity and creative crimes. He understood global economics, the Dow Jones, market trends, as well as how to thoroughly plan crimes. His attention to detail amazed everyone. Clarence successfully collected debts, hauled drugs, and brazenly robbed high-end jewelers, targeting gemstones, expensive watches, and precious metals. He became more cunning and daring as each job's take got richer. As soon as he experienced steady financial success, he recruited two team members with varying talents. At thirty-one, Clarence was doing very well. He worked hard and smart.

He was wearing his usual outfit of black sweatpants and a black T-shirt. Around his neck hung two heavy gold necklaces, and attached at the waist of his pants was a brand-new hi-tech smartphone that kept him connected to his world. He implored his crew to refer to him as Mad Dog. He felt Clarence didn't fit his persona.

His right hand was James Raymond Washington, a skinny black man he called "Jesse Ray." This trade school dropout was an electronics genius who weighed 130 pounds soaking wet. Jesse Ray was a self-taught computer hacker and understood alarm systems better than most system designers.

Jesse Ray had secured for the group cell phones that never had bills associated with them. Once a month he hacked into the cellular company's billing service to show the accounts paid in full. Clarence was amazed and wouldn't make a move without Jesse Ray. Between "jobs" with Clarence, Jesse Ray worked e-mail, credit card, and identity scams. He kept apprised of the latest technology—not reported by the mainstream mass media—through several obscure Deep Web sources. Clarence and Jesse Ray had met at the local Radio Shack and hit it off immediately. Fashion wasn't high on Jesse Ray's priority list. Loose-fitting jeans and T-shirts were all he ever wore. He ordered fried snapper with extra hush puppies.

Clarence's left hand was a twenty-six-year-old physically fit, attractive female with sandy blonde hair who started her criminal career as a pickpocket. She could think fast, talk sweet, and get herself into and out of most anything. She was tough as nails, cool under pressure, and yet as feminine as the situation and circumstances demanded. They relied on her to run interference, recon jobs, assist in logistical planning, and to be the ultimate distraction when needed.

No one ever suspected Jenny Johnson of being capable of doing anything wrong. She was a huge asset to the small team. Jenny ordered a grilled chicken Caesar salad and water. Her attire for the day was a tight-fitting pink tank top, khaki cargo shorts, and flip-flops. She turned heads wherever she went.

Clarence Armstrong had absolute trust and total confidence in his team.

"Mornin' Jenny, thanks for comin'," he said with a mouthful of food.

"No problem," she replied as she took a sip of water and swallowed a fat-burner pill. "So what's up?"

"Those things work?" Jesse Ray interrupted her.

"Don't know. I just started takin' 'em," she responded as she put the pack into her purse and then looked at Clarence.

"We met a guy about an easy job in Montgomery," Clarence explained, lowering his voice and leaning forward. "This dude wants us to hide a woman—hold her for a week or so—then make it look like she escaped."

"Hide and hold?" Jenny asked with a furrowed brow.

"Well, she's not exactly gonna be a willin' participant," Clarence explained, choosing his words carefully.

"Officially, we kidnap her," Jesse Ray inserted excitedly.

"Kidnap?" Jenny exclaimed and immediately realized she had said the word a little too loudly.

The group glanced around nervously to see if anyone had heard.

Clarence exhaled and said, "Look, nobody's gonna get hurt, and we'll gross fifty grand!"

"That's the best part," replied Jesse Ray.

Jenny looked apprehensive.

"This dude wants us to make it look like her husband kidnapped her. He wants us to frame him by plantin' evidence so that the police come down on him, hard. And we gotta make *her* think that he's responsible. It's pretty simple, really." Clarence paused for a moment and then continued, "This is easy money, and nobody gets hurt."

"We're burglars, thieves . . . we don't do kidnappings!"

"True. But the money's way too good to pass up."

"It's gonna take some serious plannin' and prep," Jenny stated flatly to the group.

"Yeah . . . here's what I'm thinkin'. Jesse Ray, we need fresh credit cards. I need Jenny in Montgomery to scout things out. She needs to stay at a nice hotel, downtown, for maybe two weeks. Obviously, these cards can't burn her while she's there."

"You got it," Jesse Ray said confidently.

"Jenny, while you're there, tail the Target for a few days and find the right spot to grab her. Go to her husband's office and check it out. We need his e-mail address and anything else you can come up with so that Jesse Ray can put some incriminatin' shit on his computer. We all gotta think about different ways to frame him. We need to find out his personal e-mail account, and we need to check for a Facebook page, if he's got one. "

The waiter returned with their orders, and everyone was silent while he placed their lunches on the giant table.

"Can I get y'all anything else?" he asked, tossing a towel over his shoulder.

"No, man, we're good. Thanks," Clarence replied.

When the waiter walked off, Jenny said, "I don't like it. Kidnappin's some serious shit. It's federal."

"Look, my contact vouched for this fool, and I've seen the color of his money. Y'all help me with the details, and I'll do the snatch. Jenny, I promise, nobody will get hurt. This'll be like a vacation." Clarence smiled as he buttered his potatoes.

Jenny, thinking about the money, said, "All right, but I want plenty of time to study the setup."

Clarence said, "Of course. Go on up there and scope it out . . . the dude says she walks every day at some park. That may be the place to grab her. Pass the cocktail sauce, will ya?"

"Okay. I'm in," Jenny finally said, and then took a small bite of grilled chicken.

"Jesse Ray, get her anything she needs."

They finished their meals, laughing and discussing what they would do with their respective cuts. Jesse Ray wanted a new computer system. Clarence had his eye on a black Hummer, but his two children, Lexus and Mercedes, along with his ex-wife, consumed most of everything that he cleared. Jenny wanted to invest in high-yield mutuals to help achieve her dream of buying a horse farm.

"Girl, you need to live some," Jesse Ray exclaimed as he dipped a hush puppy in ketchup.

"I don't wanna do this forever," Jenny stated, matter-of-factly.

"She's smart, Jesse Ray." Clarence winked at Jenny and then stuffed a huge chunk of meat into his mouth.

As they finished lunch, Clarence held up his glass in a toast, "Here's to diversifyin' our business, stayin' outta jail, and makin' mo money."

"Cheers," they each said in unison as their glasses touched.

CHAPTER 7
1ST MONDAY

Cooper rolled into his office at 7:10 a.m., before any of the office staff had arrived. He treasured his private time each morning. It allowed him to peacefully eat breakfast and read the newspaper. The last few weeks had been extremely stressful, and he often missed lunch. He still preferred to read a real paper instead of an electronic version, and he spent an extra few minutes enjoying the sports section, anticipating college football season.

Tossing the newspaper into the trash can, he could hear several employees arriving, laughing while telling stories about their weekend. Cooper walked out into the hallway to listen. He was so proud of the staff. Several advertising awards had proven their abilities to everyone outside the firm. They were extremely talented and had more work than they could turn out.

Cooper had quickly learned that the real creatives were a bit odd. They certainly had interesting hairstyles, fashion, politics, and coffee, or whatever it was that they called it. The

Tower Agency's reputation was one of creativity and fresh, out-of-the-box ideas.

As Cooper listened to their stories, he thought about Brooke arriving at her work. He felt compelled to call her. He headed toward his office, stopping first to speak to the receptionist, a pleasant matriarch who took great care of him.

"Good morning, Mrs. Riley, you look exceptionally nice today," Cooper sincerely remarked.

She always loved his compliments. He knew it, so he never hesitated in giving her accolades.

"Why, thank you, Cooper," she drawled. "You got some sunshine on your face this weekend."

"Yes, ma'am. I took Ben on a dove shoot in Mississippi."

"I didn't know the season was in?"

"It comes in earlier in Mississippi."

"I hope y'all had some fun?"

"Yes ma'am, we did," he said with a smile and added, "MidState Bank will be here this morning at ten. Please call Gates and remind him to pick up some hot Krispy Kremes on his way in."

"I'm happy to . . . if I can figure out his current cell number," she replied contemptuously. "He's changed it three times this year."

"I know. I've got it if you don't."

"Why does he have to do that so much?"

"I'm guessin' it's related to some woman. Maybe women."

"You're probably right. Okay, I'll try to call him."

"Thank you," he said, and then stepped into his office and uncharacteristically closed the door.

Cooper wondered if it was too early to call. It was 8:30 a.m. She should have had time to drop off her son at school and be in by now. Without thinking of the consequences, he picked up the phone handset and dialed her office number from memory. He drummed on the desktop with a wooden pencil, waiting for an answer.

"Brooke, please," he responded, when the receptionist answered.

Cooper watched the LED display on his phone and counted the seconds until he heard her voice.

"Hello," she answered after glancing at the caller ID screen.

"Brooke?" Cooper asked excitedly, after a deep breath.

"Yeah, hey there . . . how you doin'?" Brooke asked as she got up, walked to her office door, and shut it.

"I'm fine. How was the beach?"

"Great. Grayson caught a bunch of saltwater catfish, and I caught a flounder," she said with a slight laugh.

"No way!"

"Yes way . . . Grayson and I *love* fishin'."

"I'm not a big fan of the beach. After a day in the sand and a couple of good meals, that's 'bout all I need for a year."

"I just *love* eatin' fresh fish, especially fish that *I* caught!" she said, trying to curry favor.

"That's interestin'." He made a mental note to talk to her later about her love of fish and fishing. He said, "I was wonderin' if you could bring me the ad boards later this mornin'?" He was trying to steer the conversation toward business.

"Sure. I was plannin' on it. I just got in, and I have several things I need to do first." She was trying not to sound too eager, but she did blush a little and an eyebrow rose with the hope that Cooper might finally be taking an interest. She had certainly been trying to get his attention.

Brooke looked at the picture of Grayson on her desk and thought about his needing a positive male role model and how she needed help with her life. She believed that Cooper might be open to options since she had heard rumors that his marriage was less than ideal. In fact, Brooke decided weeks ago to slowly bait the trap.

Cooper said, "Sure. I understand. I need to look at the art for the new ads, and we need to talk about the presentation." Cooper was trying to sound earnest about needing to meet.

"Okay, what time?"

"Well, Gates and I have a ten, and then he'll probably want to lunch with 'em."

"Don't you need to be there?" she asked curious.

"Not at all. Plus, I'll be tired of talkin' by then."

"I was under the impression that Gates didn't get that involved in the business anymore?"

"Yeah, I know . . . but, well, he is on this deal." Cooper paused to carefully choose his next words. "Let's just say that he's . . . suddenly gotten interested."

"That's good . . . I guess."

"Maybe. It's complicated . . . look, it's not important. If you can come at twelve, I'll order us some lunch." Cooper knew that most of his staff would be gone, especially the relentlessly inquisitive Mrs. Riley.

"Okay. Sure. That'll be fun," she laughed. "I'll be there . . . but, please, I really can't eat a sandwich." She paused for a brief moment, as though she had never run this scenario before, and then added, "Look, how 'bout I bring *you* a meat and three from Martin's, and I'll get something for me?" Brooke was grinning as she pushed her hair behind her right ear. *The way to a man's heart is through his stomach . . . and this body.*

"Great! That sounds perfect." There was a brief pause in which Cooper could hear someone talking in Brooke's office.

"Look, I gotta run. See you around twelve. Okay?" she quickly said, excited about having some private time with Cooper. It had taken her a little over two months to get to this point with him. She hated to get off the phone, but didn't have a choice due to her unexpected visitor.

"Okay. I can't wait to see the boards. Bye," Cooper replied and then hung up. He leaned back in his chair. *Forget the boards, I just wanna see those tan legs.*

It seemed as though they never got to talk very long— certainly never long enough to really get to know each other. Brooke was very mysterious. Thinking about her was exhilarating. His home life was boring, predictable. His marriage was stagnant, loveless. The imagined concept of Brooke nudged Cooper to the edge.

Glancing at the clock, he realized that in just over three hours she would be there. Right there. Sitting in his office. He was much more excited about seeing her than he was about the guys from MidState Bank. Cooper had to force himself to gather the P&L documents to study in preparation for the bank meeting. *Dammit, I gotta quit thinkin' 'bout those suntanned legs.*

CHAPTER 8

Jenny Johnson arrived in Montgomery with about $2,000 in cash, a recently activated Visa card, and a new cell phone. She knew her way around the city, having grown up in Clanton, just up I-65, about halfway to Birmingham.

With two Louis Vuitton knockoffs packed with everything she could possibly need for a week of scouting and a few weeks holding the hostage, Jenny checked into the chic Renaissance Montgomery Hotel & Spa downtown, looking like a weary business traveler in need of a quiet night's sleep. When asked, Jenny casually explained to the bell captain that she was in town for a computer software conference. The hotel was only a few blocks away from Montgomery's tallest building, the RSA Tower—home of the Tower Agency.

After valeting her nondescript white Honda Accord with bogus tags, she went to her room to unpack and organize her things. Jenny had brought a wide array of clothing. She had everything from business suits to jogging outfits. She made a mental note of the rooftop swimming pool, hoping that she would have a chance to bronze in the sun.

Jenny lay across the king-size bed and pulled an equine magazine from her oversized purse. She loved horses and hoped to spend some time looking at the horse farms on the east side of Montgomery.

After graduating from high school, Jenny had been a cheerleader for the Atlanta Falcons for one season. She tolerated being scantily clad and underpaid, hoping that better opportunities would come her way. It was through the football team that she met Clarence Armstrong and her career was redirected. They were attending an after-game party for the elite when he witnessed Jenny lifting a businessman's wallet while the businessman was busy patting her backside. Jenny didn't think anybody noticed, but Clarence had and was very impressed. With the ease in which she worked, he could tell she had a penchant for crime.

Although Jenny had received plenty of offers for both, she would never be a kept woman, nor would she marry for money. Marriage was sacred to her, based on love founded on shared values, mutual respect, and unreserved trust. It didn't matter that she had yet to find the right guy. She planned to be established before she got married anyway. The young woman had watched others become slaves to credit card debt, car notes, and mortgages, struggling against the bank yet never getting ahead or even catching up. Her ultimate goal was to own, free and clear, a forty-acre horse farm. Ideally, she wanted to do this before turning thirty—just a few years away.

Jenny's life track was determined early when her mother unexpectedly left her and her father. Jenny did her best to take care of him, but he started drinking heavily and gambling. He had worked all his life training racehorses only to have his small farm and everything he owned seized by the IRS. He had quit paying income taxes to satisfy his bookie.

Depression gripped him tighter and tighter until one gloomy Sunday morning Jenny found him hanging by the neck in the barn.

Her past gnawed at her, and her father's death haunted her—driving her need for total independence. The past pain calloused her to the effects of her criminal activities. She really didn't know what she was capable of doing, and she was gradually testing those boundaries. Now, she was in a hotel room planning a kidnapping for her share of a big payday. *Great money for a few weeks of work*, she thought as she put away the magazine and pulled out her surveillance notes.

Once Jenny carefully studied the details, she decided to grab something to eat and then take a drive past the Target's house before dark. A quick Yahoo Maps search produced a diagram of the Wynlakes Golf and Country Club, a first-class private club located within a ritzy residential community. She was careful not to search for the Target's specific address, nor give hers for driving directions. She knew not to trust the Internet with anything that she didn't want broadcast on prime-time network television. She had seen firsthand what Jesse Ray could do through it and with it.

After a few wrong turns within the neighborhood, she finally found the house. The two-story Tudor appeared well maintained, with fresh landscaping. She couldn't tell if anyone was home since there wasn't a car parked in the driveway and the big garage door was closed. Several neighbors waved to her as she drove by them. It was obvious that the house was not a viable location for the grab—too many nosey neighbors.

Jenny needed to confirm the information that the Client provided regarding the Target's daily habits, and she hoped to learn something that would advance their purposes. The Client had stated that the Target regularly walked at a park, not too far from her home, and most often alone. That location sounded much more promising than her home. Driving through the neighborhood, Jenny familiarized herself with every detail. She wrote down exact mileage, noted stop signs, speed bumps, red lights, locations of loose dogs, kids riding bikes or shooting hoops, and any other potential to cause delays or issues. Satisfied that she had observed and recorded everything that she could until making visual contact with the Target later in the evening, Jenny left the subdivision, waving casually to a different guard than the one she had sweet-talked earlier in order to gain access into the gated community.

CHAPTER 9

When Mrs. Riley announced that the MidState Bank executives had arrived, Gates and Cooper had completely different reactions. Gates appeared relieved and jumped up, rushing out of Cooper's office to greet the visitors. Cooper, who was desperately trying to get Gates to explain several new line items on the P&L, could not have been more frustrated. Gates would not clarify several recent major expenses and was very dismissive of Cooper's attempt to understand the basis for their inclusion.

"I'll be in the conference room warming these guys up," Gates excitedly replied as he rushed out.

"I'll be there in just a minute."

Cooper stood and looked around, thinking about Gates, and then headed toward the conference room. As he walked past Mrs. Riley's desk, he said, "Please take messages for me, if anybody calls."

"Okeydoke," Mrs. Riley happily replied. When Cooper was out of sight, she pulled another doughnut from her desk's top drawer.

Just outside the conference room, Cooper paused and glanced around the offices, listening to the sounds of everyone working. Two artists were having a lively discussion about suppressed creativity while an outside sales representative was busy peddling a new time management program. Nobody was aware of what was about to happen on the other side of that door. Cooper was really struggling with selling the business that he had worked so hard to build. It's all he really knew. He swallowed hard and pulled open the solid oak door.

"Hello, gentlemen. Sorry I'm late."

Cooper began shaking the hands of the two well-dressed MidState Bank executives.

The first was Don Daniels. Twenty-five years ago, he had inherited the bank. He was a solid citizen—a widower and a deacon in the First Baptist Church. Cooper didn't personally know him that well but had no reason to not like him. Mr. Daniels had been a local fixture in the community for years, while sitting at the helm of the small, successful bank. He was known to be extremely shrewd and charged the maximum rates for everything from loans to bounced checks. He was reputed to still have every dollar that he had ever made in his life, and he was never satisfied . . . with anything.

The second man, Mark Wright, had been with the bank only a few years. He had cut his teeth in commercial lending for a big brand-name institution and joined MidState Bank after he was offered a chance to be vice president of operations under Don Daniels's tutelage. Mark didn't like it to be known that he was Mr. Daniels's nephew. He preferred for people to think that he had gotten the position based upon his skill set. Mark Wright was all about the dollar, which was a trait his uncle admired, appreciated, and cultivated. Cooper didn't know enough about Mark to have a firm opinion of his character.

"No problem . . . how are you doin'? How's the family?" Don Daniels asked with genuine interest.

"Everybody's fine. Thanks for askin'," Cooper quickly replied, and then offered, "Krispy Kreme? They're still warm."

"No. No, thank you. My blood sugar would shoot through the roof. When you get to be my age, you have to watch it . . . and it's *no* fun."

"That's just great. Somethin' else I've got to look forward to. I've got a colonoscopy later this year, and I'm *really* excited about next year's prostate exam." Cooper shook his head and laughed.

"Aging is no picnic, son."

Since Gates and Mark were in a discussion, Cooper took the opportunity to organize his thoughts. As his mind raced, he placed four Mexican Coca-Colas next to the doughnuts and napkins. He loved introducing friends to his special soft drinks.

"Hello, Mark. How are you doin'?" Cooper asked, noticing that Mark had finally looked at him.

"I'm good," he said, straightening his tie.

"I was just tellin' Mark about us takin' the big boys from Lawler Chemical to the Auburn game this weekend, and he says he might join us." Gates spoke with great enthusiasm as if the business's sale hinged on Mark attending the football game.

"We'd *love* to have you," Cooper said, picking up on Gates's inflection and trying to sound convincing. He actually had little to no desire for Mark to be there.

"I don't wanna impose," Mark said, picking up a Coke with a napkin.

Gates quickly jumped in, "No, no, no. It's not a problem. They're our biggest account, and you need to meet 'em. I can get another ticket easily."

"I don't even know if I'm gonna get to go," Cooper added, somewhat distracted. "I've still got a lot of work to do to get ready for huntin' season."

"Cooper's either fishin' or huntin' something or gettin' ready for huntin' season," Gates interjected with a laugh, and then after a moment added, "He'd never survive in the coat-and-tie world of bankin'!"

"Do you wear jeans every day, at work?" Mark asked Cooper.

"Yeah, pretty much . . . but that's just me," Cooper said smiling, knowing that MidState Bank's corporate culture was the opposite. Cooper did what he could to cultivate a relaxed business atmosphere at the Tower Agency.

"Yeah, ol' Coop wears camo half the year," Gates said, with a slightly veiled snicker.

Mr. Daniels jumped in, saying, "Well, fellows, if this deal goes through, y'all can wear whatever you want, whenever you want." He then turned to Mark and said, "Sorry, Mark, I'll still expect you to be in a tie every day." He winked at Mark as he sat down at the conference table.

Everyone followed Mr. Daniel's lead that the meeting was starting, and they took their places. Mr. Daniels had a thick folder of papers. Mark Wright had an identical stack. Both Gates and Cooper had blank notepads and were uneasy, but for entirely different reasons.

Mr. Daniels led with, "Fellows, we really like what you have done with the Tower Agency. It's very well respected. We believe that it would be a nice fit for MidState Bank as our due diligence indicates. We just have a few items that we need to discuss before we think of fine-tuning an operating agreement—"

"Don," Gates interrupted. "Look, we've opened our books to y'all and have shown you everything. We don't have *any* secrets. We're an open book—me, Coop, the business—so to speak. Just tell us what you need. We'll get you anything else you wanna see." Gates leaned back in his chair.

"Noncompetes . . . we have to make certain—," Don Daniels continued as though Gates hadn't cut in. He put his glasses on and opened the thick folder, obviously having more to say.

"Not a problem—," Gates interrupted, again. It was apparent to all in the room that he would have agreed to anything.

"Whoa! I can't agree to a noncompete without knowing the specific financial terms of this deal. We haven't even set a selling price yet . . . have we?" Cooper quickly stated, glaring at Gates. *That sonofabitch better not have set the price without consulting me. I'll kill him.*

"Okay, fellows, I understand . . . we'll get back to that later," Mr. Daniels replied quickly. He was a skilled negotiator and wouldn't play his most important card until he absolutely must.

Mark jumped in with, "And we need Cooper to stay on to help us transition. We'd want at least a year," but he was looking at Mr. Daniels, who was slightly nodding his agreement as though this hadn't been considered previously.

"What about me?" Gates asked fretfully, looking back and forth between the two bank executives.

Mr. Daniels folded his bifocals and laid them on the table. "Frankly, Gates, we don't need your services. Our research tells us that it's Cooper's day-to-day operating talent that's needed to facilitate the transition."

Gates sat motionless for several long moments before eventually stammering, "Ah . . . well, I see. It's just that's . . . ah . . . that surprises me."

He was clearly stunned. He was counting on a year's salary to help him get back on his feet. His percentage of the sale would get his bookie off his back for a while, but he needed additional income to live on as his trust fund was nearly exhausted.

"Mr. Daniels, let's slow this down a little," Cooper said, letting out an exasperated breath. He found himself feeling sorry for Gates; moreover, he didn't want Don Daniels dictating every aspect of the negotiations. "I think Gates and I need a little time to understand exactly what we want to do, and then for all of us to discuss your requirements. This proposal is very intriguing, but it's also very final, and the advertising and public relations business is just about all we know how to do. Obviously, we need some time to plan our next move. I'm sure you understand."

"I do. But you need to realize that Gates has been insistent on moving this transaction along . . . so, naturally, I thought you *both* were predisposed to the sale. Besides, four times earnings is very fair," Mr. Daniels explained, looking at both Gates and Cooper; then he closed his folder. Gates and Cooper did the math in their heads.

"We just need some time, sir. I'll call you later in the week," Cooper stated, making constant eye contact with Mr. Daniels, and then added, "I promise."

Gates, unable to speak, sat staring with bloodshot eyes at the tabletop.

Mark, head down, busied himself gathering his documents. His sly grin only detectable in his eyes.

While Mr. Daniels calmly picked up his belongings, he said, "I'd like to get this done in no more than two weeks' time. We can talk whenever you need, day or night."

"Yes, sir," Cooper replied, never diverting his eyes. "Thank you. Thank you for your understanding and patience."

Don Daniels smiled and said, "Rumor has it that you're tryin' to buy a piece of land."

"Yes, sir, that's right. It's a little more than I should do, but it's too good of a deal to pass up without at least trying."

"Come see me. I think I can help. I have an idea."

Cooper was surprised to learn that Mr. Daniels knew about the land deal, but was more intrigued by his offer. Borrowing a million dollars was a huge deal that he couldn't do without some very creative financing. He noticed that Mark Wright was staring at him.

Cooper looked over at Gates, whose eyes were glazed over. He then looked back at Don Daniels and, for the first time, felt some hope.

"Great. I'll call you . . . I'd appreciate anything that you can do."

"No problem. Coosa County, right? I like that part of the world, as you may know. Let's get this sale done, and then maybe we can make you a serious landowner."

"I promise, I'll get right back to you," Cooper replied, liking what he was hearing from Mr. Daniels.

Gates finally snapped out of his stupor and babbled frivolous remarks about the football game and eating doughnuts. The other men paid no attention as they walked out of the conference room.

Cooper returned from escorting the bankers to the elevator, shut the door, and said, "We gotta talk."

Gates dropped his head into his hands.

Mark pushed the elevator down button and then turned and smiled at Mr. Daniels. The elevator doors immediately opened, and they walked inside. As the doors shut, Mark spoke, "Something tells me that Gates is extremely motivated to sell. We may can buy the Tower Agency for a bargain price if we play our cards right."

"That would be part of the plan," Mr. Daniels stated, punching the lobby button and smiling. "And it's coming together nicely."

"Did you notice how red Gates's eyes were?"

Mr. Daniels stared at him while the elevator descended. When they walked through the lobby, he finally spoke. "Gates appears unstable and weak. All of which will help me buy his business substantially below book value."

The bankers stood quietly in the lobby for a few moments. Mr. Daniels was in deep thought about the financial aspects of the deal while Mark was mulling Don's use of the word "me."

Don Daniels broke the silence, ordering, "Find out *exactly* how deep into debt Gates is this time. It seems like it may be worse than I thought, and I damn sure don't want to pay a dime more than I have to."

Mark nodded, appearing agreeable, but his concealed hatred for his uncle was growing exponentially.

CHAPTER 10

Cooper and Gates emerged from the conference room thirty minutes after the MidState Bank executives left the building. The discussion had been tense. Cooper was concerned about the whole deal, including the selling price, noncompete clauses, and the future of their staff. Gates was clearly frantic to sell, but he also wanted a twelve-month consulting contract. Cooper couldn't understand and Gates wouldn't explain why he wanted out so badly. The conversation ended in an impasse. Gates had simply quit talking, visibly distraught about something. Cooper eased off a bit, feeling compassion for his old friend, and promised Gates that he would call Mr. Daniels to work out the details. Both guys, mentally exhausted, staggered silently toward their respective offices.

"Cooper?" Mrs. Riley tentatively asked.

"Yes, ma'am?" He stopped at her desk.

"That new plastic surgeon called and wants you to design some ads for him. He asked if you'd trade the work for a boob job," she stated flatly and snickered.

Cooper laughed out loud. It felt good. He smiled and asked, "Well, do you want one?"

"Heavens no! I'm nearly seventy. What would I do with 'em? What about Kelly?" she said, handing him his messages.

"No, ma'am! Don't even *mention* it to her. I'll call the doctor and work out something. We need the billings way more than we need new boobs around here . . . or at home." He walked off, shaking his head, remembering the time that Gates paid for his second ex-wife's tummy tuck with company funds. He categorized the invoice as Repair and Maintenance. The auditors didn't appreciate the humor.

Cooper sat down at his desk and stared at the two fish hovering effortlessly in the large aquarium. He wondered about Gates's desire to sell the agency, *What's drivin' him so hard to make this deal?*

He considered Gates's gambling, but discounted it because of Gates's ready access to family monies and the fact that the company paid practically all of Gates's living expenses. Cooper started running through as many additional scenarios as he could. After quite some time thinking about it, only two reasons for Gates's behavior made any sense to him: either Gates just simply wanted out of the daily grind or he wanted a new challenge. *That's gotta be it. Gates has something else cookin' that doesn't involve me . . . that's why he's bein' so shifty.*

Cooper suddenly noticed the e-mail icon blinking on his computer screen. He clicked on it. The e-mail was from Brooke saying, "I'm leaving to run some errands, but I'll see you at 12!" It had a flashing yellow smiling face at the end of the text. It made him feel like he was in high school again. When he had read it twice, he deleted it. Looking up, he watched Gates walk into his office and plop down in a chair—his exhaustion, both physically and mentally, was obvious.

"Man, I'm sorry . . . I just want to sell this thing and move on with my life," Gates whispered so no one else could hear.

Cooper motioned for him to close the door. Gates got up and eased it shut.

"I can understand that . . . I just don't wanna sell it to some bottom-feeder. I wanna get top dollar," Cooper explained. "You know that I gotta to do whatever you want, but it doesn't make sense to sell it to Daniels . . . or anybody, if we don't get what it's worth."

"I just want out, dude," Gates said as he looked around Cooper's office.

After a long moment, Cooper finally said, "Look, I wish I could afford to buy you out, but you know that I can't come up with that kinda cash, unless, of course you'd finance it yourself?"

Cooper was fishing for Gates's reaction. If Gates would even consider financing the sale, that would shed some light on his economic situation and his true motivation for "just wanting out."

"I can't. I need this to be a cash sale."

"Need or want?" Cooper asked, now realizing that Gates might actually be in serious financial trouble. He also knew that Gates would never readily admit it. Cooper continued, "Just remember, I'm on your team through all this . . . let's communicate and work the sale together. Let's not appear desperate or divided. Okay?"

"Sure. Okay. I swear, if you could just help get the wheels back on this deal . . . I'll make it up to you."

"I'll do what I can. Mr. Daniels has always been nice to me, but I know he's cold-blooded when it comes to money," Cooper replied, staring at Gates.

Gates stood. "Coop, I can't do this without you, buddy. I really need your help. Get 'em back to the table and *please* get me a year's consultin' fee."

"I'll do what I can. I promise."

"Thanks, man. I knew I could count on ya. I've got a freakin' lunch meetin', so I'll be out for a while. Call my cell if you need me," Gates explained as he started for the door. He stopped and turned as though he'd just thought of something, "Hey, can I have one of those south-of-the-border Cokes?"

"Sure."

"You gotta be the only guy in Montgomery with these things. Thanks, man."

Gates walked out of Cooper's office, without opening the bottle. Cooper didn't notice.

CHAPTER 11

After finally finding a parking place, Brooke parked and quickly hurried into the RSA Tower, home to the Tower Agency and many other businesses. The building was a monument to exceptional money management. While the elevator was traveling to the eighth floor, she took out a compact and checked her face. As she put the small mirror back into her purse, she smiled, thinking that this lunch was a significant step in her plans.

The elevator doors opened, and Brooke stepped out, onto the dark brown marble floor of the advertising agency's foyer. She walked through the glass doors to the receptionist area, which was unattended. She looked around but didn't see anyone, so she just walked straight back to Cooper's office. Peeking around the edge of his door facing, she watched him skimming a magazine. Her heart raced a bit.

"Knock, knock. Did you call an escort agency for a lunch date?" she whispered and smiled, holding up lunch with one hand and art boards with the other.

"Hey there! Yes, yes. I definitely need an escort. Come on in. Let me help you with that." Cooper laughed, walked over and took the art from her.

"You're gonna love those boards," she replied confidently.

"Excellent. I can't wait to see 'em, and thank you so for bringin' lunch. This is a real treat," Cooper said eagerly.

"Hamburger steak, black-eyed peas, and mashed potatoes with gravy for you, and a chef's salad for me."

Cooper sat his lunch on the edge of his desk. He then took the ad boards and quickly spread them out on his desk to ensure that their meeting appeared to be all business should anyone walk in.

"This looks *soooo* good," Cooper said as he opened the white Styrofoam tray and stole a quick glance at Brooke's long legs.

"Looks like you got some sun at the beach," Cooper added, casually. "I like your pink toenails." Cooper grinned like a school boy.

Blushing, she replied, "And it looks like you got some sun too?"

"*Waaaay* too much . . . as you can tell," Cooper explained, pulling his hair off his forehead.

"That's gonna peel."

"Yeah, I know. Ben forgot his cap, so I let him borrow mine."

His cellular phone rang and as soon as he saw who was calling, he hit Ignore.

"That reminds me, I lost my cell phone this weekend, and I gotta call my carrier right after lunch—I shoulda done it first thing. Anyway, boy I hate that. I thought I left it in the condo, but I couldn't find it." Brooke shook her head. "I swear, I feel naked without it."

Cooper instantly formed a vivid image of her nude. She had an ideal body. Her waist and chest were in perfect relationship to her hips. She possessed a simple, elegant beauty. All he could manage by way of response was a chuckle and a weak smile.

Brooke sat on the edge of the leather couch. Cooper was at his desk, across from her. They gazed at each other, grinning like love-struck teenagers. They had worked together on several projects over the last year or so, and one day while looking at some illustrations Brooke realized that she was falling for him. She appreciated that he was married, but to her surprise, it didn't *really* bother her too much. She also knew that it was a long shot that their relationship would ever go anywhere.

Brooke was struggling to make it as a single mom, with the added burden of caring for her ailing father. Life's pressure was intense. Compounding it, her ex-husband rarely made child support or alimony payments even though he had a well-paying job. He didn't honor his obligations as a power play and hoped that she would take him to court. But since she was so happy to be out of the marriage, she let it slide, choosing to suffer in silence, for the most part.

She knew that her desire for Cooper was wrong, but she needed a dream, something to anticipate, hope for. She was growing weary of doing everything herself. Right or wrong, she knew that these emotions weren't lust, but she realized they probably were not love either. Tired of being tired, she wanted someone who could help take care of her and Grayson.

"Would you like a Coke?" he asked as he got up and opened his small refrigerator grabbing two glass bottles. Cooper was excited. Being around Brooke made him forget his worries.

"No, thanks. I brought water. Those sure look different, though," she said curiously.

"They're from Mexico . . . they still use real sugar down there, cane sugar actually, and they taste just like the old Cokes used to."

"Whoa, Mexico? Really? That's cool." She was very interested in this newfound idiosyncrasy of the man she wanted.

"It's a weakness. Coke is one of my favorite brands. I love the old Co-Cola taste. Sure you don't want one? They're kinda my thing. I have a buddy that brings 'em to me once a month."

"Nah, you lost me at sugar, *Sugar,*" she said with a wink and then asked, "So where is everybody?" She was beginning to work her plan.

"Probably downstairs at the deli. This place clears out every day at lunchtime. My creative folks worship their free time," Cooper said as he peppered his peas. "If I need to discipline 'em, I make 'em work overtime. Even with the extra pay, they hate it! Particularly the younger ones." Cooper chuckled and shook his head.

They both took bites of their lunches and glanced at each other as they ate.

Finally, Brooke spoke, "I bet this place keeps you busy. You have so many clients."

"It's a challenge to manage."

Brooke tried to think of a good response, but her mind was racing and she didn't want to scare him off, so she just nodded her understanding.

"I gotta leave at 2:30 today to pick up the kids from school," Cooper stated out of the blue and then, without realizing it, sighed. He continued, "Kelly's gone shoppin' in Birmingham."

"Our malls aren't good enough?" she asked sharply, cutting her eyes to watch his reaction as she took a sip of water.

"Don't get me started," he responded with a mouthful of potatoes.

"High maintenance?" she asked, watching his body language.

Cooper swallowed. "Very!" He let out another sigh.

"Excuse me for pryin', but you seem kinda stressed."

"I am."

"Can I help?"

He knew that he should not talk about the business sale, but he realized that he wanted to . . . or maybe needed to talk to someone about it. All of it was weighing heavily on him, and he felt that talking confidentially to Brooke would be safe.

"Well, you gotta keep this secret. Okay?"

"Of course!"

"Okay, nobody outside knows this yet, so you can't share this with anyone."

Brooke nodded and said, "Absolutely! You can trust me with anything."

"Great. Okay, here's the deal: Gates really wants to sell the agency, and we have an interested buyer. They're ready to pull the trigger, but I . . . I don't really want to sell, but I'm trying to buy a piece of property that I *really* can't afford, but I *really* want it. I love it. It's perfect."

"Wow," Brooke said. "I just figured you were stressed about an account or something."

"Yeah, I wish that was it."

"So what does your wife wanna do?"

"She wants the cash from the sale. But she doesn't know about the land."

"Well, I can sure see how all this would definitely be stressin' ya out."

"You can't imagine . . . and please keep all this to yourself. Please. I really shouldn't even be talkin' about it."

"It's no problem. I totally understand. Listen, if you ever need to talk about this stuff . . . or anything, please don't hesitate to call me. I'm a pretty good listener," Brooke said, planting the seed.

Cooper paused, as he thought about her offer, before saying, "Thanks. I may take you up on it. I don't have anybody I can talk to about this stuff. I really don't want to sell. I mean . . . this business is my life . . . but, I hafta do what Gates wants, and he wants to sell *bad*."

He took a swig of Coke, shook his head slightly, and continued, "The last few months have been freakin' crazy 'round here, and I'm concerned about the employees, how they will take it . . . and if the new owner will keep all of 'em on board. It just really sucks!"

"You're right; this is a *huge* deal. You definitely need to talk about it. Have you thought about buying Gates out?"

"Yep. I've thought long and hard about that, but I just can't get my head around the idea of paying so much money for something *I* played the principal role in creating. I just can't do it." Cooper paused for a long moment, and then shook his head while looking out the window and said, "I guess that I'll just start all over . . . if I can figure out a way around the noncompete language—you know, build something new."

He turned to face her and wondered what she was thinking. He was enjoying her rapt attention, so he pressed on, "I'm fairly confident that most of our creative team would follow me . . . and . . . I'll need a good designer. Do you think that you'd be interested?"

"I'm flattered . . . yes, of course, I am." She was thrilled, not so much with the job offer, but with an opportunity to work closely with Cooper. *This is perfect*, she thought.

"Good. Let's keep all this between us. I'll keep you updated as things progress."

"Y'all'll make good money when it sells, won't ya?" she asked timidly.

Cooper didn't hesitate replying, "Yes, especially Gates. He's really pushing to get it done. It's happenin' way too fast for me. I know we could get more . . . but I guess I'll just take my percentage and move on."

"I bet you're gonna miss this awesome view," she said, looking out the window. "The view out my window is of a brick wall."

"Your office is much more practical than this place. The buyer will add another six figures a year to their bottom line by just moving us into their office space. The rent on this place is *extreme* for a business our size."

"I could be *really* creative in this office. The view inspires me." Brooke was looking straight at Cooper, who was staring at the horizon.

"It works just the opposite for me. I catch myself daydreaming." He chuckled.

"So what does Cooper Dixon daydream about?"

"Land with big deer, lots of turkeys, and a lake filled with largemouth bass," he replied with a boyish grin.

She was melting from his smile. "Well . . . that sounds like a dream worth realizing to me. Make it happen."

"Yeah, well . . . I wish it were that easy," Cooper said, taking a swig from his Coke.

"Just build your wife a nice cabin, and she'll love the place too."

"You don't know my wife."

"True, I don't. But you can't give up on *your* dreams just 'cause they aren't *hers*," Brooke said, and then took a small bite of her salad. She looked him in the eyes and continued, "Ya know, it's better to *live* your dreams than it is to just *dream* 'em."

"You're right. You know, you really are easy to talk to."

"Thanks. That's nice to hear."

Not only is she hot, she's wise too, Cooper thought and began cursing his lack of spontaneous wit or wisdom. *Shit, I'll probably think of something really clever after she's gone. Dammit.*

"Wanna look at these drawings?" she asked, with a knowing grin.

"Sure, of course. Let's finish eatin' first. If you've got the time," Cooper responded with a smile. He wanted the maximum amount of time with her. They could leisurely eat and then talk business. He loved her passion as she described her art.

"All. The. Time. You. Need." Brooke let the drawn-out statement hang.

They had just stepped to the razor's edge of the slippery slope.

Cooper tried to rationalize that it had just been an innocent lunch, but he knew better. All he could think about was the way she made him feel.

CHAPTER 12

As Gates drove his BMW through downtown traffic, he became more and more fearful of the wrath of Mitchell Holmes. He had to tell Mitchell something today about his debt. Gates nervously tapped the steering wheel. *Ain't no tellin' what that nut job will do if I don't throw him a bone*, he thought.

He had already liquidated a huge chunk of his portfolio, leaving about $200,000 in stocks. He knew better than to ask his father for assistance. He'd burned that bridge years ago, following the NCAA basketball tournament. His old man sensed that Gates was spiraling out of control. While his father would probably pay for rehab, he wouldn't bail him out of any more legal or financial jams.

The driver behind Gates honked. He looked up to see the light was green. He decided not to call Mitchell, but to see him in person. *Maybe, I can explain this situation and ask for just a little more time . . . and pay higher interest on the whole nut.*

Gates never realized that it was the interest that got him into this tough spot. That and his inability to pick winners or cover the spread.

In the meantime, Gates had another bookie with which he could place smaller bets, just to keep him in the action.

Picking up his cell phone, he hit a speed dial number. "Hey, it's 670, I need to check the early lines. What is it on Alabama? Seven . . . okay, what about Ole Miss and Auburn? Six? Got it . . . and what about LSU? Fourteen! Wow. I'll call back with what I wanna do . . . oh yeah, what about Mississippi State? Good, *good*. Look, just fax me all the lines for this weekend. Thanks, dude."

Gates calmly laid his phone in the tray beside the gear-shift and exhaled. *Man, there are some outstanding matchups this weekend.*

The start of the collegiate football season was the most exciting time of the year for a rabid sports gambler. Gates didn't care who won; he just wanted his team to cover the point spread. Early in his gambling career, he rarely bet on professional sports, but in the last few years he gambled on any sport or anything, anywhere in the world that he could find someone, somewhere to make book on. Gates was desperately trying to catch up. He never appreciated that you couldn't catch up, at least not very often and never for very long.

As Gates pulled into the parking lot of the Johnny Wishbone Sports Bar & Lounge, he scanned the parking lot for any cars he recognized. He couldn't help but see Mitchell's candy apple red Hummer sitting under an awning at the private rear entrance. Its personalized tag read JUICE. He began to sweat.

Gates parked as far away from the other cars as he could. He left the engine and air-conditioning running while he gathered his thoughts. Glancing around, he couldn't see any-one. He quickly opened his glove compartment and pulled out a brown manila envelope. He flipped it upside down. A tiny resealable bag slid out onto his lap. The bag was almost empty. Gates groaned in disappointment. Running his fingers inside the bag, he then placed his thumb and forefinger in his nostrils and sniffed hard.

"Shit! Well, that's gonna hafta do for now," Gates said aloud and then rubbed his nose rapidly while looking at himself in the rearview mirror. He appeared trustworthy and respectable to anyone who didn't really know him. *I can pull this off.*

Gates returned the envelope, pulled off his J.Crew silk tie, threw it onto the backseat, and climbed out. He locked the car over his shoulder as he approached the club.

Johnny Wishbone's was a rough place on the best of days. The smoke-filled bar had more drug deals, stabbings, shoot-ings, and fights than most clubs. Those interested in these activities used the bar as a search engine for whatever they wanted. Mitchell Holmes used it as a money-laundering front for his gambling empire. Once Mitchell figured out how to use credit cards and PayPal accounts for settling his clients' gambling debts, the bar began accepting plastic. That's when his fortunes mushroomed. Taxes and fees were significantly offset by the increased revenue and convenience of account-ing for less physical cash. Now, the majority of cash taken in by the bar and debt payments was easily siphoned off for his personal use and to be personally deposited into his off-shore "asset protection" accounts—which was becoming more difficult lately since the Feds' dogs were now trained to detect large amounts of cash and the TSA either irradiated or molested airline passengers. Gone are the days of easily trav-eling with tens of thousands of dollars in one's underwear.

Gates walked in and headed straight to the bar. The only other patrons were playing video poker. No one paid any attention to the new arrival. Ordering a Jack Black neat, Gates sat down on a stool to look for Mitchell. He realized he was still sweating. When the waitress set down his drink, he tossed her a ten-dollar bill and asked for Mitchell.

The waitress stared him down for a long moment, "Who's askin'?"

"Gates Ballenger," he responded and then took a swig of his whiskey. "He'll wanna see me." *More than I want to see him,* Gates thought.

"Sit tight, sport," she quipped and walked to the back of the bar and out of view.

Gates nervously looked around at all the sports memorabilia. There were dozens of pictures of Auburn and Alabama sports legends. Gates's left foot bounced on the bar-stool rung.

As the waitress sauntered from the back of the building, she motioned for Gates. He got up and walked around the bar. When he turned the corner, he saw a huge muscular black man with a silver metal detecting wand in his hand.

"Spread your arms and legs," the massive man ordered as he walked toward Gates.

Gates assumed the position, holding his drink in one hand. Only an empty money clip caused any suspicion.

"He's clean, Boss," the Muscle hollered down the hall.

"Send him back!"

This was followed by an unintelligible string of words, broken by clearly discernible cursing, making the raspy male voice sound like a drunken sailor. Gates nervously took the final gulp of his drink. He smoothed his shirt and almost hyperventilated before shuffling into Mitchell Holmes's office.

Mitchell never looked away from one of the half-dozen computer monitors and television screens. "Do you think Florida State will cover the spread against Miami?"

"What's the line?"

"Four," Mitchell answered as he swiveled in his chair to look into Gates's eyes.

"Yes . . . absolutely," Gates confidently stated.

"With your luck, I wouldn't bet on it," Mitchell laughed.

Gates nervously laughed along with him.

"In fact, you just convinced me to bet against 'em."

Many people won big betting the opposite of Gates, and it aggravated him to no end. He even tried betting against his gut feelings and still lost.

"Yeah, that one's gonna be interestin'," Gates added with a slight smile.

Leaning back in his chair, Mitchell placed his feet up on his desk and laced his fingers behind his head. "So what's the deal? I'm busy as hell, and I want my money. I notice you ain't carryin' a briefcase filled with cash."

"We met today . . . with the bank . . . and everything is still a go . . . but we didn't set a date . . . just yet. You're gonna get your money . . . I swear . . . I just . . . it's just . . . I wanted to explain the situation to you . . . in person."

Mitchell stared at Gates for a long time and then said, "The problem is I don't like your face. It reminds me that you owe me a hell of a lot of money."

Mitchell lit a cigarette.

"That's a good one," Gates replied anxiously and then slightly laughed.

"Just what's the freakin' holdup?" Mitchell almost yelled.

"These things just take time. MidState Bank has done their due diligence, and we are just tryin' to agree on the final numbers and some minor details. It's gonna happen.

I swear it is. It's just gonna take a little bit longer." Gates cringed while he awaited Mitchell's response.

Mitchell stayed reclined for a moment and then eased down his feet while slowly leaning forward as he took off his reading glasses. Rubbing his eyes, he swiftly stood, and Gates promptly sat down in an involuntary response to Mitchell's predatorily quick movement.

Mitchell Holmes, with a well-deserved reputation for violence, was about fifty years old and physically fit. He had the hard look of significant prison time. Gates had been told that Mitchell always had at least one handgun within easy reach—even when he took a shower. Thinking of that made him more nervous.

"Gates, this gamblin' business, ironically, is based on honesty. You win . . . I pay you. You lose . . . you pay me. Now here's the problem: if you don't pay me and somebody hears about it, then *they* don't pay me and before long I'm just like the freakin' gov'ment—I ain't earnin' money, just handin' it out." Mitchell chuckled. "Understand?"

Gates didn't trust his voice, so he just nodded.

"I never should have let this happen. I shoulda stopped it a long time ago."

Mitchell knew Gates would eventually pay him, and he didn't actually have any cash tied up in Gates's bad run and, most importantly, he stood to profit considerably. He let Gates continue betting just to see how deep a hole he could dig. Gates was jinxed, and Mitchell was capitalizing on it. In fact, Mitchell had a little wager with another bookie on just how much he could milk out of Gates and his wealthy family.

"Look, I'm feelin' generous today 'cause the market's about to set a new record high and I'm gettin' out, so here's what I'm gonna do: I'm gonna give you some more time . . .

but you gotta throw me a bone . . . something serious . . . to prove to me that I should have this kinda faith in you. I got folks in my organization that wanna hurt you . . . or somebody you love . . . to make it as clear as moonshine to you the seriousness of your situation—to get your attention. But I . . . because I like you, I've kept 'em distracted. So I need a real good reason not to break—"

Gates was about to hyperventilate. He was shaking and beginning to sweat through his shirt.

"I own a lake cabin . . . on Lake Martin . . . it's worth maybe four-hundred grand . . . I'll bring you the title. I can execute a quit claim deed," Gates blurted.

The cabin was actually worth about $300,000, but Gates didn't think Mitchell would have it appraised anytime soon, and it would gain him some ground on the debt.

"I like that. I'll have my lawyer draw up the papers. That's good, Gates. That's just what's needed to keep you undamaged . . . for a while anyway."

"I can get the deed tomorrow."

"Do it and call me. This'll buy you thirty days. Not thirty-one. You hear me?"

Gates stood up to leave. "Yes. Thank you. Thank you, Mitchell."

"Sit!" Mitchell yelled.

Gates did.

"Now, I don't wanna hear about you bettin' with anybody else . . . you hear?"

"No, I won't. I've learned my lesson."

"Yeah well . . . we'll see about that. One other thing, I'm workin' on a solution for you to get *all* the proceeds from the sale of your business."

"How would that work?" Gates said, growing numb.

"Don't you worry none 'bout that. Let's just say, I have a man who knows how to get things done. He's . . . *very creative.*"

Gates wanted to run. Every fiber of his being was telling him to get the hell out of there as fast as possible. He began to stand, "I'll call you about the—"

"Sit your ass back down! Let me be clear. You'll wish you were dead if you don't pay in full. Do you understand?"

"Perfectly. Thanks. Can I go?" Gates stood, extending his hand to shake. Mitchell ignored him and turned around to one of his computer screens.

Gates quickly walked out, past the Muscle standing inside, next to the open office door.

Gates didn't look at any of the bar patrons as he hurried out into the bright sunshine of the parking lot, squinting his eyes. He felt a lurch in his stomach. Before he had time to react, he threw up on the gravel parking lot. Wiping his mouth with his shirtsleeve, Gates tried to breathe deep. He looked around to see if anyone was watching.

The investigator across the road sitting in the white surveillance van, painted to look like a telephone company repair vehicle, clicked off a sequence of photographs as the video cameras rolled. He recognized the guy puking in the parking lot.

The other special agent, wearing headphones and making notes, looked over with a sly grin and asked, "Isn't that our buddy, Old Money?"

"Yep."

As Gates approached his car, he clicked the unlock button on his key fob. The BMW's alarm chirped. He climbed in, shut the door, started the engine, and then cranked the AC. Exhausted, he leaned his forehead against the steering wheel.

CHAPTER 13

From birth, Don Daniels was immersed in the ethos of the financial world. It was formalized in college and put into practice upon graduation, with his first job packaging mortgages for a firm in Atlanta. Eight years later, he went to work for his father in the family's title company. A few short years after that, Don began working directly for his father at their bank. When his father died under suspicious circumstances two years later, Don took control of all the family's businesses.

Over the course of the last several years, Don had been left standing at the altar of two mergers—one with a large regional bank and the other a giant Wall Street financial institution. He had wanted both badly. There was something never disclosed to him that made both acquisition teams drop out during their due diligence.

At this stage in his career, Don had hoped to have enough money to burn a wet cow. But things hadn't panned out. The banking business wasn't bad. It just wasn't making him as rich as he wanted. Since his wife died, he had become a bigger risk taker—looking for creative ways to diversify and grow the stale bank. He wanted a way to go out on top. Acquiring the Tower Agency was one small step. Buying it made sense for a variety of reasons. He loved the steady, apparently reliable cash flow, and he had someone in mind to run it. Don had other, much grander, irons in the fire as well.

Don Daniels was sitting in his downtown Montgomery office thinking about Gates. He suspected drug abuse. He knew that Gates had been born into the lucky sperm club and that Gates did not have the strength of character to handle the responsibilities and opportunities afforded by old money. Don didn't want anything to do with Gates after the acquisition.

Don's thoughts drifted to Cooper. He wanted to keep Cooper, since he managed the day-to-day business. The rub was that sellers typically lose their strong connection to their business after they sell, and it was impossible to gauge their future commitment to its success. It was not a matter of if, but when—they all lose their fire.

I can own Cooper if I loan him the money for the property he wants so badly. Hell, in this shitty economy no other bank's gonna mortgage unimproved land for recreational purposes. If I do it, then I'll have even more options.

CHAPTER 14

The sun was about to set when Jenny decided that she had seen enough horse farms for one day and turned around to drive past the Target's house again.

With her digital camera, she had taken a dozen or so photographs of barns, gates, and riding arenas she thought exceptional. She kept a comprehensive folder filled with photos of and magazine articles about the same, hoping that one day she could incorporate the best of what she liked into her own stable. Very few days passed without her either adding something to the folder or daydreaming about her findings.

It was dusk as she approached the entrance to Wynlakes. She noticed that the security station was staffed with a guard she didn't recognize. Calling him a "guard" would be affording him way more status than deserved. This guy was intently listening to a talk radio show, paying little attention to his surroundings. When Jenny slowed to a stop, the old man grudgingly strolled out. When he saw the attractive driver, he perked up.

"Evenin', darlin'. Can I help you?" The old man politely asked with a smile, bending down to her open window.

For the second time, Jenny was going to pour on the charm for one of the development's rent-a-cops.

"Why yes, I know this is going to sound crazy but I . . . I'm just so embarrassed . . . ya see, I'm new in town, and everybody talks about Wynlakes and how nice it is, and I was hopin' I could just drive through and see some of the beautiful houses," she explained as she batted her eyes.

The guard said, "I ain't supposed to let joy riders in. But I'll tell you what: I'll make an exception . . ." as he looked around to make sure no one was watching, "just for you. And be sure you go by the clubhouse. It's *real* nice."

Jenny slowly brushed her hair behind her left ear and said, "Thank you. Thank you so much. You're soooooo sweet," as she drove off with a little wave. Checking her rearview, she noticed that the guard didn't even attempt to look at her car tag. *Thank goodness these guards are all guys.*

As she slowly drove through the neighborhood, she wondered what type of careers these people had in order to afford such nice homes and multiple expensive vehicles.

Turning onto the Target's street, she paid particular attention to the surroundings. The huge door to the garage was up, and she could clearly see a camouflaged golf cart parked very close to the far wall and a red Volvo almost in the center. In the driveway was a dusty, green pickup truck that would have been out of place in any similar neighborhood outside of the South. Lights were on all over the house and through the glass front doors Jenny could see the flickering of a television.

She wrote down the name on a mailbox three houses away from the Target's in case another guard ever challenged her about why she was there. She dialed Clarence's cell number as she pulled out of Wynlakes and onto Vaughn Road.

"Yo, baby," he answered, obviously in a good mood.

"You got a minute?" she asked politely.

"Sure. What's goin' on?"

"I found the house, and I've studied most everything on my list. I still haven't actually seen our *friend* though. But I will tomorrow," Jenny promised, stressing the word "friend" so that Clarence would know she was being careful not to divulge specifics on an unsecured telephone.

"Thoughts?" Clarence asked.

"Nice house, *very* nice neighborhood, but we're gonna have to do this somewhere else."

"Too many eyes?" he asked, seeming to know the setup.

"Way too many. When y'all comin' up?"

"Maybe day after tomorrow, Thursday at the outside. I'll let ya know in plenty of time. When I get there, we need to go over your notes before I check out where we're gonna be . . . *keepin' the merchandise*. That'll give us a few days for . . . J. R. to work his electronic magic."

"Sounds great. Just let me know, and I'll reserve y'all a room."

"Be sure you get two beds," Clarence responded.

"Ahh . . . I thought you and J. R. were tight?"

"Not that tight."

Jenny laughed. "Okay, I understand. When are you thinkin' we'll do this?"

"Don't know yet. I fo show don't wanna rush it. Once all three of us agree that we're buttoned up, we'll get this party started."

"Cool. Just let me know if there's anything else you need me to do."

"Thanks, girl."

"Ciao."

Jenny folded shut the phone and turned on the car's CD player. Sara Evans began singing "New Hometown." Jenny joined in as she thought about her future horse farm and her evening plans—a quick swim in the pool, check e-mails, and then pile into bed for a mini-marathon of *House Hunters International*.

CHAPTER 15

1ST TUESDAY

Cooper arrived at the office at his usual time, carrying a *USA Today* and a Styrofoam to-go box containing his daily dose of cholesterol—cheese grits and smoked sausage.

The previous night had been extremely stressful with Kelly's unrelenting demands relative to getting the house ready for the tea, the kids acting out, and then the remote for the television in the den was missing. He had turned the house upside down unsuccessfully looking for it. Cooper couldn't easily change channels, but he wasn't about to ask Kelly for help nor was he going to watch TV in their bedroom where she was camped out planning her big event. Piper went to a friend's house to study, and Ben was helpless with electronics, although he could hook up the Wii. Cooper finally fell asleep after watching a hunting show about the virtues of food plots.

Leaning back in his office desk chair, he planned the rest of the week—MidState Bank, conference calls, growing piles of paperwork, and a host of client meetings loomed. There wasn't much time for anything else. After a while, Cooper's mind drifted to his marriage. He was miserable and didn't know how much more he could stomach. *I guess I still love her . . . but I've definitely lost that being in love feelin'.*

Kelly was a good mother to their two great kids, but along the way Cooper and Kelly had grown apart. His unrelenting focus on his career had taken a severe toll on their relationship, and Kelly, for inexplicable reasons, decided her life's role was to climb the societal ladder while ignoring their marriage.

Cooper never considered his options until he started thinking and dreaming about Brooke. *I can't think about this shit right now*, he thought as he switched on his computer.

Cooper Dixon had a great number of skills, but operating a computer wasn't one of them. He barely knew the basics, having never taken a class nor having any instruction. Only in the last year or so had personal computers started making a bit more sense to him. The tipping point was when he was told to think of the computer as a big filing cabinet and its desktop as the physical top of his desk, with different files lying on it. Just open a file, work on what's inside, close it; pick up another, do the same thing or move something out of that one and put it in another or make copies and put copies where they need to go; put one file inside another, and so forth and so on. Simple, really.

He leaned forward, clicked on the Internet icon for the Weather Channel to check the central Alabama weekend forecast. No rain, just lots and lots of heat. September, besides being statistically the worst month for the stock market, is the driest month in the Deep South. He smiled at that correlation.

Systematically, he navigated his way to his e-mail icon and opened his in-box. Scanning halfway down, he saw an e-mail from Brooke. His heart skipped a beat. "Hi" was the subject line. The text simply read, "Good morning. How you doing today? Busy?"

Cooper clicked Respond and typed, "I'm fine. Thanks for asking. How are you?" and hit Send.

Leaning back, he waited, wondering if she was at her computer at that very moment. He felt young again, his body stirring.

After only a few moments, Cooper saw her e-mail arrive and anxiously opened it. "I'm good. Lunch?"

Cooper smiled and typed. "Sure. Where?"

"Whatever works for you."

Having never strayed, even mentally, Cooper had to carefully consider where to meet. The more upscale places presented potential problems with one of Kelly's friends seeing him—it would get back to her that he was dining with a beautiful woman, and he didn't need that.

"The Farmers Market Cafe at one?" Cooper smiled as he typed. "They have a great blue-collar lunch and the best fried-green tomatoes." He hit Send and thought, *Although it's usually full of political movers and shakers, it sure ain't on Kelly's list of places to eat. It's as safe as it gets.*

Brooke quickly wrote back, "Sounds GREAT!!! See you there ; -)"

Cooper started sweating. He reread the e-mails before anxiously deleting them. The next e-mail that came in was from Mrs. Riley. He was so tense that he accidentally deleted it too. He smiled at himself as he hit the intercom on his office telephone.

"Mrs. Riley, please resend that e-mail to me," Cooper politely requested, adding, "my computer's actin' up."

"Did you accidentally delete it?"

"Yes, ma'am."

"It's in your Deleted folder."

"No, ma'am. I deleted it."

"Okay, Cooper," she replied. She was too busy to explain. She shook her head and snickered.

As bad as last night was, Cooper's morning was the complete opposite. Energized and with the zest of a fresh college graduate on his first day of a new job, he dove into a stack of paperwork on his desk that he hadn't noticed at the end of business yesterday.

CHAPTER 16

Cooper sat in his favorite chair, awaiting the ten o'clock news. He still couldn't find the remote. He had Piper show him how to change the television channels through the digital receiver. *What a pain in the ass,* he thought.

He closed his eyes and replayed the day's events. Early he had had a productive telephone conversation with Mr. Daniels. It left him feeling pretty good about the business sale for once. Although, he didn't have much hope for Gates getting a consulting contract. It also appeared that he might get the property loan. Soon he'd have to tell Kelly and that was a conversation that he was dreading. When he left for lunch, he had instructed Mrs. Riley that he would return to the office but made it clear that there were to be no calls or text messages unless it was an emergency. He then cracked open Pandora's box.

Cooper had arrived at the restaurant before Brooke. He sat at a small booth in the back and waited uneasily. Surprisingly, he was able to make a few notes on a paper napkin of things he needed to do in preparation for an afternoon meeting. His heart had jumped when he saw Brooke walk into the restaurant. She was wearing black dress pants and a fitted, white sleeveless top. She strode through the restaurant with confidence. She was hot and knew it. Every man in the place watched her and then acted as if they weren't when she got close. Cooper managed to regain his composure in time to stand as she approached.

"Hey you," she said with a smile as she slid into the booth. "How are you today?"

"I'm well. What about you?"

"Me too," she responded. "You look handsome. I like your shirt. That color really looks good on you."

"Thank you, and may I say, you look quite stunning."

"Stunning?" she laughed. "That's a bit much, don't ya think?"

"Not at all. I make my living choosing words that describe a scene or a sense and believe me, 'stunning' is spot-on," he said.

Brooke chuckled and blushed. She held up the menu to read and quietly said, "Spot-on."

A young waitress approached. Brooke ordered water with lemon and asked for a few minutes to decide what she wanted to eat.

Watching Brooke study the menu, Cooper was excited and nervous yet overall at ease. His right leg bounced, betraying his exhilaration and causing tiny round waves to form in their water glasses.

Her leg gently brushed against his. He froze, instantly aware of everything around him and feeling totally exposed in public. Her touch was simple and absolutely electric. Brooke looked up from the menu with a smile. He wondered if she knew what she was doing. Her smile and the sparkle in her eyes said something. To Cooper it meant, "Let's play!" He was flooded with two very clear emotions, fear and lust. Fear of being seen. And lust for her touch. He tried taking deep breaths to relax, but it was impossible. His body was responding. He told himself that no one could see under the table. He tried to act calm and casual, but on the inside he was a bundle of nerves.

"So what are ya havin'?" she asked, sensing his unease.

"The vegetable plate. It's great here," Cooper quickly recommended, excited to have some distracting dialogue. *You're an idiot for even thinkin' about this,* he told himself.

"Sounds delicious. Did you bring your own Mexican Coke?" Brooke asked and folded her menu.

"Not here. There are *some* things I won't do in public," he said with a sly grin.

"Good to know," she replied with an equally devious smile.

When the waitress returned, they ordered and then both leaned back in the seats. Their legs were still touching. Cooper noticed how elegant her hands were. She had thin, tan fingers with long, perfect nails. Slim wrists. She was so feminine. He watched her fold her toned arms across her perfect chest.

"What are you looking at?" she asked, cocking her head to one side, knowing she had his attention. "Do I have something on me?"

"Naw, just you," he dreamily replied.

Cooper knew that he needed to be careful. Montgomery wasn't that big, and he was fairly well known around town. One never knew who was watching.

"Any improvement with the Gates situation?" she asked, squeezing a lemon slice into her water and then dropping the wedge into the glass.

"Not really. He's comin' unraveled and that's puttin' a little more pressure on me."

"Sorry."

"It's just one more thing on my to-do list," Cooper responded casually, trying not to let his frustrations show too much.

"Life, I guess," she smiled and sipped her water.

"So how's Grayson?" he asked as the waitress refilled his glass.

"Good. He loves school so much. Thank goodness," she replied, pleased that Cooper asked about him.

"That's half the battle. Ben likes school okay, but he just doesn't pay attention . . . and his grades show it. When he discovers girls smell different, I'm really gonna be in trouble."

"Like father like son?" she asked with a mischievous smile.

"Uh . . . probably. Hopefully, he'll be smarter than I was."

"Not smart about women?"

"Now, maybe. But I've made some idiotic choices." The words came out before he could stop them.

Brooke moved her leg, just perceptibly, against his. The charge that coursed through him was grounding out what little remained of his rationality. These sensations were new. Years of loveless marriage had numbed him to excitement of this magnitude. Cooper was adrift in a dangerous current.

"Nervous about something?"

"No. Nope. Not at all," he lied.

"Okay." Brooke smiled knowingly and then changed the subject so as not to embarrass him: "Big plans for the weekend?"

"Not really. The agency's takin' some customers to the Auburn game. I'll probably work on the property I was tellin' you about and then meet the guys at the game and spend the night and—"

"I'd like to see it one day," she quickly interjected, sensing an opportunity.

"Auburn?"

"No, silly; I've been there. The land you're talkin' about."

"Really?"

"Really."

Cooper looked deeply into Brooke's eyes. There was an intensity he hadn't seen in a long time, if ever. As he leaned in to say something, the waitress interrupted to serve their food. He waited and then thanked her. When she left, he casually glanced around the room and then leaned forward again, "It's really a special place. I call it my Promised Land."

Brooke smiled. "Sounds like a cheesy name for a Jewish retirement home."

"Really?" Cooper chuckled.

"The pitch needs fine-tunin' before you propose it to your wife." She paused a moment and then asked, "So does she go to the games?" Brooke was skillfully steering the conversation in the direction she wanted it to go.

"No. Never. She *hates* football," Cooper answered, somewhat remorseful.

"That's too bad."

The silence between them was loud. Their eyes meeting excited Cooper to the point that clear thinking was impossible. He had a bad case of Brooke on the brain. He desperately wanted to believe that he glimpsed desire in her eyes too.

"I got an idea," she said in a hushed, sexy voice.

"Yeah?"

"Well . . . I really like you, and I sense . . . well . . ." Brooke seemed to struggle for the right words, but in reality she was playing coy. As if frustrated, she tried to speak and stopped. Smiling, Brooke eagerly leaned closer to Cooper, "Why don't we meet at the game Saturday night?" Her eyes and mannerism implied more than just catching a football game between business colleagues. "It could be fun."

Cooper choked on a piece of corn bread as he tried to act like this sort of thing happened every day.

She stared into his eyes for a few intense moments. She said everything that needed to be said to make her point. The rest was up to him. She wasn't looking for a one-night stand. She wanted him to want her, and playing to his interests and desires was a strategic move.

"Let me think about it," he responded, with a twinkle in his eye and a slight quiver in a voice that betrayed his surprise.

Cooper smiled nervously and took a long drink of water because he had no idea what else to say . . . and was a little afraid to say anything. Her foot touched his leg, jolting his system again. Glancing around the room, he noticed an older lady looking at him with what he interpreted as disgust. *Who the hell is that woman? Does she know me? Could she hear us?*

CHAPTER 17
1ST WEDNESDAY

Clarence and Jesse Ray rode in style and comfort from the Alabama Gulf Coast to Montgomery in Clarence's tricked-out Cadillac Escalade ESV. The only available option not on Mad Dog's ride was an engine block heater. Jesse Ray listened to rap on his iPod. Clarence dialed the satellite radio receiver into a conservative talk channel to listen to the political discussions of the day. The three-hour drive was interrupted by one gas break where Clarence bought cheese, hot pickled sausages, and a grape Nehi drink. Jesse Ray bought a Snickers and a Pepsi.

"We'll eat supper with Jenny," Clarence said as they walked out of the convenience store. "Apparently, there's a really good restaurant close to the hotel."

"I can't believe you're gonna eat that crap," Jesse Ray said, unwrapping his candy bar, looking at Clarence's sausages.

"You need to venture out. Broaden your culinary horizons, ya know? You might like it, and it *will* put some meat on yo skinny ass," Clarence said as he slid the key into the ignition and chuckled.

The pair rolled up I-65 at seventy-four miles an hour and followed the GPS straight to the hotel. After checking in, Clarence watched Jesse Ray set up his computer and assorted gear, marveling at all of the electronic gadgets.

Clarence checked his watch. He had a meeting later that night with the Client to get additional details and the keys to the house where he suggested they hold the woman hostage. Before the meeting, he needed a briefing from Jenny to confirm the accuracy of the Client's claims to date. He dialed her number.

"We're here."

"Good. No problems?" Jenny asked, looking though binoculars, talking on her Bluetooth.

"None. Where are you?" he asked, while flipping through the channels on the muted television.

"Watchin' our *friend*. She's pickin' up her daughter from ridin' lessons," Jenny responded. She never took her eyes off the woman.

"How far away are you?" Clarence asked as he watched a pregnant meteorologist on the Weather Channel gesturing wildly. She looked like she was about to pop.

"Maybe forty-five minutes, depends on traffic," Jenny answered, after thinking about it a moment.

"Are you about done?"

"I'd like to make sure she doesn't make another stop— sticks to her routine. Let's meet for supper in about an hour, and I'll bring you up to speed. I don't want to talk too much on the phone. The place I mentioned is just a few blocks from you. It's called Chris's. They're famous for their small hotdogs with a sauce that's *delicious*."

"Hotdogs? You kiddin' me?"

"I'm tellin' ya, it's your kinda place. Elvis ate there once."

"Perfect. I've been tryin' to get Jesse Ray to stretch

his culinary wings, and this might be the place." Clarence stopped channel surfing when he got to the Home Shopping Network. They were selling flashy jewelry. Clarence liked jewelry because converting it to cash was always easy, everywhere.

"Okay. One hour," Jenny said, laying down the binos on the passenger seat while keeping her eyes on the woman.

"See you there." Clarence broke the connection.

"Hey Jesse Ray, you see this, man?" Clarence was gesturing toward the television as he turned up the volume.

"Yeah, so what? Diamond earrings." Jesse Ray said, when he looked up from his tangle of wires.

"Yes. No. Look how many they're sellin'. Twenty-six-hundred units and countin'. That means they got twice that warehoused. I read about this outfit in the *Wall Street Journal*. They're based in Florida. That's what we need to hit one day . . . could be a huge haul."

"You may be right, Dog. About a month, maybe six weeks before Christmas, they'd be fat with merchandise."

"After this job, we'll check it out." Clarence leaned back on the bed. "All your high-tech know-how would be perfect for that job. But first, we're gonna meet Jenny and *eat!*" Clarence slapped his hands together and rubbed vigorously.

"What time do we meet the Client?" Jesse Ray asked, his attention going back to his efforts to piggyback an Internet connection onto an unsecured wireless signal that he picked up from an adjacent building.

"Ten o'clock, at a car lot on the east side of town," Clarence replied. "MapQuest says it's about fifteen minutes from here."

"I brought my wand so we can make sure he ain't wired, and I got a jammin' device that works for both radio and cell frequencies. We got a trackin' sensor in that cell phone we gave him. I'll also put a trackin' device on his car. We'll be secure at the meet, and we'll know where it is pretty much at all times after that."

"Good. Wake me up in forty-five minutes."

CHAPTER 18

Gates spent almost all of the day hiding in his office. He surfed the Net, reading different football prognosticators' websites trying to gain a modicum of insight into the weekend games. He had locked the door twice, each time doing a liberal line of cocaine off his beautiful antique desk. He tried to think of ways to screw Cooper out of his ownership percentage. He even called an accountant buddy, but that wasn't very helpful because Gates couldn't completely explain exactly what he wanted to do without incriminating himself and the conversation just petered out.

Gates was depressed and disheartened. Both of his ex-wives had called earlier in the day looking for money. Fortunately, his house was paid for and the company made his BMW lease payment. He had the deed to the lake house in a folder on his desk, and he felt nauseated every time he looked at it, thinking about what he was about to do. The Lake Martin house was beautiful, nestled among giant pines on a rocky lot with stunning views. It had been his escape from the daily grind. Gates bought it after the agency enjoyed a particularly successful year. He had been a master at draining every dollar he could out of the business. In fact, although the deed was in his name, the agency had paid for it. He was willing to entertain a few clients there occasionally, but only if they looked good in two-piece swimsuits.

He needed a big score. He was scheming about how to get his hands on a meaningful amount of cash. The Tower Agency was working for the state Republican Party in the upcoming election, which might present him an opportunity to become involved in the campaign finances as an avenue to embezzle funds. He also considered meeting rich women and sweet-talking them into loaning him money. But no immediate candidates came to mind. Finally, he toyed with the idea of robbing his parents' home. He knew where they hid cash and jewelry. The more he thought about it, the more he liked that idea.

Outside his office, he could hear the sounds of everyone working. He stared at the numerous red lights on his phone blinking. He noticed that Cooper's extension had been lit almost all day except for between 12:30 and 2:30 p.m., when he figured Cooper had taken a client to lunch. Cooper worked all the time and was clearly responsible for the business's success. Gates would never admit that to Cooper . . . or anyone, but he knew it.

There was a time when they were best friends and watched each other's backs. The two executives first met in college. They had joined the same fraternity and had helped each other struggle to obtain their degrees. Gates had access to money even back then and gambled consistently. Everyone thought it was funny. No one ever considered that he might have a problem. How could he? He was too young. He appeared to have everything: family connections, good clothes, new cars, and more often than not, the prettiest girlfriends. The reality, however, was much different. Gates's life was a house of cards.

Gates only cared about what could be done for him. If he needed something, he was someone's best friend. Once he got what he wanted, he might not even acknowledge them the next day. The exception was Cooper Dixon, the skinny kid who never had anything that Gates wanted. For inexplicable reasons, they clicked—maybe because they were polar opposites. Whatever the reason, they stuck together and stayed together, even after college when they both moved to different states. Three years later, Gates brought them together again with the promise of owning their own advertising agency. Cooper ended up working sixteen-hour days to develop campaigns that caught the attention of the right people; consequently, the Tower Agency overcame its start-up financial burdens and prospered over the years. Gates pretended to contribute.

Now, Gates had sunk to an all-time low, and he needed something from Cooper, besides hard work. He needed his piece of the agency. Gates leaned back in his chair and closed his eyes, trying to envision another solution. He began to despise himself for what he was considering. *Man, things had really changed,* he thought.

CHAPTER 19

Searching for an empty parking space, Jenny noticed Clarence's SUV as she slowly rolled past Montgomery's oldest eatery. She grabbed her notebook before she locked the doors and headed inside. She was wearing stylish jeans, a tight T-shirt, and big hoop earrings, with her hair pulled into a ponytail. She pushed open the door, walked past the magazines and down the narrow walkway to the back of Chris's Hotdogs where her partners in crime sat already eating—they hadn't waited for her. Clarence had two empty plates stacked up and was working on his third. Jesse Ray was working on his second when Jenny joined them.

"Hey guys. So how's the food?"

"Whoa girl . . . you were right. Sorry, we couldn't wait on ya. This place is righteous!" Clarence exclaimed as he took a bite out of a small hotdog.

With a thumbs-up gesture, Jesse Ray indicated his approval as he devoured another hotdog.

"Glad y'all like it. I'll be right back. Gotta pee," Jenny said, slinging her purse over her shoulder.

"That girl don't eat enough to keep a bird alive," Jesse Ray commented when she had walked off.

"She's worried about her figure . . . you can't fit in those kinda jeans if you eat a lot of these kinda meals," Clarence explained, holding up a hotdog.

Jesse Ray looked around to ensure that no one could hear and asked, "What's on your mind for tomorrow?" He then took a sip of sweet tea.

"Assuming everything goes smooth tonight, I'll go check out where we're gonna hide out with our new friend. Make sure it's secure and defensible."

"Whaddaya want me to do?"

"Create the evidence we'll plant on the guy—nutten instantly obvious, but discoverable without too much effort."

Jenny returned and smiled at Jesse Ray. "How was the drive up?"

"Good. All Dog talked about was eatin'," Jesse Ray said with a burp. "Sorry. Do you know if our guy has a computer?"

"Yeah, for sure at work. The family's got a computer, but I don't know if he has personal e-mail. I spoke with the receptionist at his office, and she suggested I leave him a voice mail instead of an e-mail. Apparently, computers aren't his thing."

"Have you seen his office yet?"

"Not yet. I was plannin' on going there tomorrow. You can see the building when we walk outside. It's the tallest in town," she responded and then continued in an exaggerated formal manner, "The Tower Agency is having a visit from the insurance carrier on the building—to check their smoke alarms, portable fire extinguishers, and fire suppression system. Thank you very much." She smiled proudly.

Jesse Ray nodded his head, "That's a great idea! It'll get you in every room."

"Order some supper, and tell us what you know," Clarence commanded.

Jenny held up two fingers to a waitress, who nodded her understanding.

"Well, the wife's pretty predictable. Give me two more days, and I'll absolutely have her pegged. I'll also have a strong recommendation of where to grab her. She doesn't work and shops at only the most expensive stores. When not shoppin', she's drivin' her teenage daughter all over town. And, the best I can tell, she and her husband are fairly cold to each other, and that's probably puttin' it mildly," Jenny explained, and then stole a french fry from Jesse Ray's plate. She continued, "Their house is very open, and the neighbors are everywhere, all the time. Folks are working in their yards or walkin', walkin' with dogs, and kids are on bikes or skateboards. No way we grab her there. And her husband works long hours during the week—leaves by six thirty and gets home late every night—and he finds things to do away from the house on the weekends, so he's not a consideration."

"What about her exercise habits? Does she, in fact, have a routine?" Clarence asked.

"Yeah. There's a park a few miles from their house. She walks there almost every evening. Occasionally a girlfriend walks with her."

"How big is she?" Jesse Ray asked.

"I don't know . . . one thirty, maybe. She's pretty."

"Think she'll show up here tonight?" Clarence asked sarcastically.

"I doubt it. But here's what's weird: she *loves* drive-thru fast-food."

"Hmm. I might actually end up likin' her then," Clarence commented. "I want ya to go with us tonight to help keep an eye on the Client. We also need your intuition—your gut feelin' about this dude."

"When's the meetin'?"

"At ten, at a car lot on the east side of town."

"Cool. I'm in. Pass the ketchup, please."

CHAPTER 20

Clarence and Jesse Ray followed Jenny to the Eastern Bypass where all the car lots existed. When Clarence suggested it to the Client, he didn't know the specific car dealership; he just knew that all cities the size of Montgomery had acres of car dealerships strung together by flashing lights, giant inflatable gorillas, and sales banners. A wide-open car lot was a relatively safe meeting place. It was difficult to ambush someone because by simply dropping to the ground, you could see the feet or legs of anyone hiding. There was rarely any hassle about being on a car lot at night as dealers welcomed after-hours shoppers since, statistically, most became actual buyers. The key to selecting the ideal lot was to find a midsized lot with no security cameras, which was much tougher today than just a few years ago. Since overall video camera quality had improved drastically and the prices had fallen, security camera systems had effectually eliminated the need for a human on-site. A motion sensor triggered an e-mail to the lot owner or manager, who then with a few clicks or screen touches looked at a live feed on his computer or smartphone and called 911, if necessary.

Jenny's instructions were to approach from the south side and pretend that she was car shopping. Jesse Ray and Clarence would make contact while she observed the Client's behavior from a distance. She would also be on the lookout for police or a security guard.

Jesse Ray brought with him all his electronic gadgets and a very prophetic distrust of outsiders. He always covered the bases, keeping Clarence safe from setups, wiretaps, and eavesdropping. He took his job seriously and was very good at it.

"He's about two miles out, Dog, headed this way," Jesse Ray noted as he watched his laptop screen. "I tell ya, that new cell phone tracker is state of the art."

"J. J., you in position?" Clarence asked Jenny over the radio, not wanting to use actual names on unsecured radios.

"Yep. See him?" she responded from the front seat of her car.

"Not yet, but he's gettin' close—go ahead and start lookin' at cars. We'll alert you when he arrives."

"Ten-four. I've already got my eye on a used Mustang."

Clarence took a deep breath and glanced at his watch. 9:55 p.m. The Client was on time. Clarence and Jesse Ray saw a BMW pull into the lot. "That's him, J. J." Jesse Ray whispered into the radio headset.

"Looks nervous," Clarence commented, watching him through binoculars. "He definitely has a bulge in his right front pocket."

"So do I," Jesse Ray commented.

"Yeah, but his prolly ain't electronic gadgets. I sure hope it's our money and that he's not packin' a piece again. I'd hate to hafta make good on my promise to stick it up his ass," Clarence said.

Both Jenny Johnson and Jesse Ray chuckled quietly over the radio.

"If he's got heat on him or a wire . . . or anything, I'll find it, Dog," Jesse Ray stated confidently.

"I'm countin' on it." Clarence opened his door and headed toward the Client.

Jesse Ray followed with his high-tech gadgetry. He knew Clarence would be using ghetto lingo and that he should play along. Clarence thought it made him more intimidating.

Clarence casually checked out the trucks as he made his way toward the nervous man, all the while studying the Client. The man saw Clarence and began to work his way toward him. For cover, Clarence stopped beside a van. Jesse Ray walked from behind Clarence straight toward the Client, holding out the wand.

Clarence stated, "Yo, dude, I'm allergic to certain insects. My man here's gonna check you for bugs. Cool?"

"Uh . . . sure." The Client held out his arms, away from his waist.

Jesse Ray motioned, "Over here, behind the van."

Jesse Ray waved his wand all over the Client's body while Clarence watched carefully, tightly gripping the pistol inside his jacket pocket. He realized his palms were sweating.

Jesse Ray patted the bulge in the Client's pocket, asking curtly, "What's that?"

"That's your money, a map, and some more information," the Client calmly answered.

"And that?"

"That's a Coke bottle."

"He's clean, Dog."

"Is that what this is about . . . you think I'm a cop?" The Client laughed. "I was thinkin' the same thing about y'all."

"Don't insult me. Show me the cash."

The Client pulled a bundle of bills from his pocket and tossed it to Clarence, who with his thumb flipped though the bills. He pulled out a random one and began closely inspecting it. He then touched it with a counterfeit detector pen.

The Client said, "That's fifteen grand. So, now, with that and what I already gave you, you've got half your fee. You'll get the other twenty-five when the job's done."

"Plus expenses," Clarence shot back, wagging the envelope.

The Client nodded his agreement, saying, "Plus expenses."

Clarence again peeked inside the envelope and again took out one of the hundred dollar bills and examined it. Observing that the Client wasn't bothered by his repeated checking of the bills, Clarence was finally satisfied and stuffed the envelope into his pocket, thinking, *Shit! I wish I'd charged this little turd more.* For Clarence, setting fees was one of the toughest aspects of this business.

"Are you still plannin' to do it as soon as possible?" the Client asked excitedly.

"Yeah, but don't press me!"

"I'm sorry. I just wanna—"

"Look, we got thangs to do, and I gotta check out this place you got for us to use. How long do we keep her? If it's more than ten days, my fee doubles."

"Okay. But I can't tell you the exact day she'll be released. After this douche bag has been splashed all over the news and his reputation ruined, we'll talk. We'll dump her—alive— somewhere remote, and she's gotta believe that her husband's responsible for all of it. Here's more of what I know about him, some of his habits, stuff like that, so you can drop little clues to her."

As the Client handed Clarence another envelope, he had an evil twinkle in his eye.

"Fine. What about this place?"

The Client reached into his front pocket. "Here's a map. The property's three hundred acres in Coosa County—one of the poorest, most isolated counties in the state. It's about an hour northeast of here. Here's the key to the gate and the house. It was the main house of an old plantation. It's got electricity and runnin' water. And it's very remote. Since it belongs to my family, you don't have to worry about anybody botherin' y'all."

Clarence quickly studied the map. Jesse Ray studied Clarence's expressions and watched the Client out of the corner of his eye. Jenny was still observing from a distance and trying to determine if anyone could be eavesdropping.

"We're cool."

"The clues you're plantin' need to be found . . . but not too obvious . . . and they gotta be incriminatin'."

"Shut up! I know what the hell I'm doin'! Do you?" Clarence snapped. "You just keep that phone with you and turned on all the time! Ya feel me?!"

The Client jumped back slightly, "Okay, man. Relax. You don't gotta yell at me."

Clarence almost laughed. A few harsh words reduced this weasel to tears.

Clarence held up the map and said, "I'll check it out and call you Thursday night."

With no small amount of relief, the Client said, a little too excitedly, "Sounds like a plan. Oh, I almost forgot." He pulled from his pocket a small empty Coke bottle inside a Ziploc freezer bag. He handed it to Clarence.

"Plant that someplace obvious wherever you snatch her."

"A Coke bottle?"

"Believe me, it'll point the cops straight to him."

"His prints?"

"Oh yeah, that too."

Clarence studied the unusual markings and then handed it to Jesse Ray. "I'll call," Clarence said, and then he and Jesse Ray backed away from the Client.

In the toughest-sounding voice he could amass, Jesse Ray added, "We call you. You don't call us!"

"Man, you are just like my wife: always gotta get in the last word," Clarence growled in a whisper when they turned to walked away.

"No, I don't," Jesse Ray responded.

CHAPTER 21
1ST THURSDAY

Kelly Dixon's day started just like most. After frantically rushing the kids to get ready, she delivered them to school one minute before the bell. Then she pulled into Starbucks, placing an order at the drive-thru for a cinnamon chip scone and a large caffé latte. It was in the Starbucks parking lot each morning that she planned the balance of her day.

Mrs. Millie Brown, the Dixon's faithful housekeeper came to their house three days a week to vacuum, wash dishes, change sheets, and do whatever else Kelly didn't want to do. She would be coming in this morning, provided her high blood pressure wasn't bothering her too much. Kelly wanted to let her go last year because she had slowed down so much recently, but Cooper wouldn't allow it. He claimed that Millie needed the money more than they needed the house to be spotless. So Kelly made Millie an extensive to-do list and did her best to ensure that she got it all done.

"That'll be six dollars and twelve cents," the drive-thru attendant said.

Kelly opened her huge purse and scrambled to find correct change, removing some of the larger objects during her search.

"Did you know you had your television remote in there?" the attendant inquired. "I've never seen anybody carry one around in her purse."

"Well, I'm doing it just to piss off my husband," she said without even looking up.

The attendant laughed and said, "How long have you had it?"

"Since last Friday night," Kelly replied with a smirk.

"Has he noticed it's missin'?"

"Oh yeah . . . and I *highly* recommend it," Kelly emphasized as she handed the attendant exact change.

"That's hilarious. I hope you have a great day! Here ya go." The attendant laughed again as she handed Kelly her order.

Kelly pulled into a parking space to eat breakfast while she studied her Day Planner. She only had a month before the tea, but she felt confident that if she offered to pay a little more, everyone would find a way to get everything done. Her cell phone rang, and she quickly swallowed a bite. Recognizing the number, Kelly pressed Answer and said, "Hey, Gates," as she placed the phone to her ear.

"Hey, good lookin'! What's cookin'?"

"Not much. What are you up to this mornin'?"

"Tryin' to make your husband some money," he answered with a laugh.

"Make him a bunch. I *need* it." She was dead serious.

"You know he isn't easy to help. Everything has gotta be done a certain way and that really slows down my ideas sometimes," Gates said, trying to act as if he was in control of work and himself.

"When's the sale gonna close? Cooper won't tell me shit. We hardly even speak these days."

"Not soon enough, but I'm pushin' hard. I'm confident I can pull it all together shortly. Go ahead, spend the money."

"Oh, I'm spending it all right," she said laughing.

"Look sweetheart, I need a favor." Gates was turning on the charm.

"What now?"

"I need to borrow fifteen grand real fast. As in today."

"That's a lot of money. I don't know. Why can't you go to the bank or borrow it from the business?"

"My banker's out of town this week, and I don't want to risk messin' up our books because MidState Bank is checkin' everything *very* closely. Baby, I really need it or I wouldn't be askin'. I swear, I'll pay you back in one week, plus five hundred extra for your troubles. Promise."

"Cooper will *freak* if he finds out."

"One week. It's important. Coop will never know."

"Are you gonna tell me what it's for?"

"I'd rather not. I can say this: it'll help me sell the business and get you a big-ass payday." Gates knew that this approach would seal the deal.

"All righty, then. I've got some cash Cooper doesn't know about, nor does he need to know about it."

"Understood. When can I get it?" he anxiously asked.

"And you gotta pay me back in a week!"

"Promise. I will, babe."

"It's in a safety deposit box. I can get it when the bank opens, but I gotta get dressed first."

"Great! Call my cell, and I'll meet ya someplace. Thanks, Kelly. I really appreciate this," Gates said, with noticeable relief in his voice.

"You okay?" Kelly asked, and then took a sip of her latte.

"Never better . . . everythin's fine," he lied, rubbing his irritated nose. "Just dandy."

CHAPTER 22

Jenny applied the finishing touches to her lipstick while looking in the rearview mirror. She was parked in front of the RSA Tower. She checked her briefcase and the business cards that Jesse Ray made with his high-end laser printer. The cards looked and felt like a professional offset print job.

Dropping a quarter into the parking meter, she did a quick scan of the area and then started walking toward the twenty-two-story building. Three construction workers leaned against their shovels to watch her. She wore an expensive black business suit. Her hair fell down onto her shoulders. Her only accessory was a single string of real pearls. She looked like a million dollars.

Jenny took the elevator to the eighth floor. When the door opened, she walked out confidently and turned toward the Tower Agency. Opening the glass doors to the office, she quickly took in the surroundings. The receptionist looked up and smiled.

"May I help you?" the lady asked, spinning her chair around to face Jenny.

"Yes, ma'am. My name's Meagan Massey. I'm with the insurance carrier for RSA Tower. I'm reviewing all the tenants to ensure everything meets the NFPA standards."

Mrs. Riley just stared blankly, not responding.

"Oh, I'm sorry. The National Fire Protection Agency—the fire codes. It's just routine," she explained politely.

"Oh, okay. The fire marshal was just here a few months ago. He didn't see anything wrong."

"Yes, ma'am, we know. For extraordinary properties such as this, we conduct our own inspections," Jenny said as she handed Mrs. Riley her business card. She continued, "All I need to do is look around and ask the tenants a few questions, if that's possible."

The telephone rang before Mrs. Riley could comment. She set down the business card to answer the call. When she realized that her conversation would take a while, she gestured for Jenny to proceed.

Jenny mouthed, "Thank you."

When Mrs. Riley turned her attention to the caller, Jenny surreptitiously retrieved her business card. As she started walking down the hall, she pretended to take notes regarding fire extinguishers, the sprinkler system, and electrical loads. The occupants of the first two offices she came to were not there. She glanced around and then moved on, scribbling on a notepad. The third room was the office of a chatty male art director, who wore his hair in a ponytail. On the wall behind his desk was a framed print of a flying pig. She chuckled to herself. She went through the motions of examining the wiring in the artist's room, acted satisfied and then moved on, trying not to engage the guy more than necessary.

The next office door was closed. She knocked and just as she was about to turn the doorknob, it opened.

"Oh! Excuse me," Jenny said, truly surprised.

"Can I help ya?" Gates Ballenger asked, shocked to see such a beautiful woman standing at his door. The sudden sight of her excited Gates. He had just finished listening to the Phantom, a local radio authority on college football betting, and felt confident that he had the inside track on the weekend's game.

"How do you do? I'm Meagan Massey. I'm with the insurance carrier for the RSA Tower. I'm just doing a routine inspection," Jenny explained as she showed him her card. Gates took it. "Wow, you have a gorgeous office. I see you like antiquities." She extended her hand to shake.

"Thanks, Meagan. I'm Gates. Gates Ballenger," he said, holding her hand a little longer than necessary. "I do love historic pieces. They tend to be very well *built*." Gates stressed the word "built" as he gave her a lascivious appraisal and continued, "Come on in."

Gates sat behind his antique desk, doing his best to look important and ten years younger. "Have a seat."

Jenny gracefully sat down in a leather chair in front of the desk. She slowly crossed her legs, allowing her skirt to slide upward. "This is a very impressive office. And what a view!"

"Thank you, Meagan. So . . . what about you? Where's home?" Gates asked, focusing on her exposed, firm upper thigh.

"I do love that print," she replied, pointing to the far wall. Gates was so enamored with her that he failed to catch the nonanswer.

"Actually, it's an original. Will you be in town for a while?" he asked, noticing that she wasn't wearing any rings on her left hand.

"It'll take two days to inspect all the offices in the building. I must say, yours is the most impressive . . . so far," she replied, playing with the pearls around her neck. Opening her briefcase, she produced a form and then waved it at Gates. "I need to fill out this form. Are you the business owner, Mr. Ballenger? Gates, correct? That's an interesting name."

"Gates is an old family name. Yes, I'm the principal owner. I have a minority partner."

"Impressive," she said as she wrote on the form. "What is your partner's name, please?"

"Cooper Dixon."

"May I get both of your e-mail addresses for our files?"

"Absolutely. Here." He handed her his business card. "It's all there."

"What about Mr. Dixon's?" she asked professionally, writing down everything.

"Um, I think I have one of his cards in here, somewhere." Gates started rummaging through a desk drawer. "Here ya go." He handed it to Jenny. "Can I have yours? Your e-mail, I mean."

"It's on my card," she said with a smile.

"Oh . . . right." Gates looked down at the card and saw the address.

"Do you have a comprehensive policy covering all assets in your offices, including a rider for antiques and art?"

"I'm sure we do, but, you know, I have Cooper handle all the mundane stuff around here."

"Is he here?"

"No, he's out. Mrs. Riley out front should be able to help you, though."

"Okay, great. What about an alarm system?"

"None. The Tower's security is so good I don't see the need."

"From what I've observed that makes sense."

"Since you're here for a couple of days, why don't I take you out for a wonderful meal tonight?"

"I don't go out with strange men," she coyly replied, and then slightly grinned.

"Okay. First off, I'm not strange . . . well, not too strange anyway. And second, you gotta eat while you're in town. It might as well be exceptional food from a great restaurant with a delightful atmosphere . . . and free." Gates was bringing his A game—being slightly self-deprecating, appealing to reason, while proposing a safe, neutral, public place to dine.

Jenny didn't respond immediately, so he took her silence as a positive and pressed forward, "Look. I'm a gentleman; ask anybody. I know a great little local place—it's unbelievable." Gates couldn't get her legs out of his mind and each passing second pushed him closer to dropping to his knees and begging.

Jenny had not listened to the last couple minutes of Gates's pitch. She was trying to decide what value Gates could be to the job. She had less than zero interest in an actual date with him, but she realized that if he had a few drinks, he might tell her everything they needed. She pushed her blonde hair behind her ear and slowly recrossed her legs. She brought the pen in her left hand to her lips and paused a long moment.

Finally, with a sly smile, she drawled out, "I don't know. You seem like trouble."

"Oh, you're good. You pegged me pretty quick. But, look, I promise to behave. Scout's honor." He held up the Boy Scout sign and was grinning like a little kid.

"I'll think about it . . . but first, I need to finish here. May I look at Mr. Dixon's office?"

"Certainly . . . follow me."

Gates allowed her to leave his office first and pointed down the hall toward Cooper's office.

"Let me finish my audit, and I'll come back here in a few minutes; then we can discuss supper."

"Anything you wish. I'll make us reservations. Eight o'clock?"

"I didn't say yes."

"You didn't say no either," he quickly replied.

Giving him a smile, she twisted her pearls and walked off. *This was way too easy,* she thought.

Gates couldn't believe his fortune. *Damn, I'm on a streak today. This is just what I needed,* he thought. He began planning the evening. He would burn up the company credit card trying to impress her.

Jenny slowly studied Cooper's office. She grabbed several business cards and then looked at everything in the office. The large aquarium gave her an odd feeling, like the fish were watching her. She noticed a gold letter opener, engraved with his initials. She quickly glanced around to ensure that Gates or someone else hadn't stopped at the door, and she picked up the opener with a tissue and put it into her purse, careful not to smudge any existing fingerprints or leave any of hers.

She silently closed the office door and then pulled out a digital camera and took pictures of the office. After listening carefully at the door for approaching footsteps and not hearing anything, she began looking inside drawers. Deciding she had pushed her luck far enough, she walked out and back to Gates's office.

"Everything appears in order," she reported.

"Good, I knew it would be. We have dinner reservations at eight. Pick you up around seven thirty? Where you stayin'?"

"I tell you what; I'll go, but I'll meet you there. That's my only condition," she said smiling and added, "so far," for good measure.

Gates didn't have to think. "That's fair. Let me write down the address for ya."

"What should I wear?" she asked, looking around his office again.

Gates wanted to say, "As little as possible." But showing uncharacteristic restraint said, "Casual's fine."

While he was writing, she picked up her business card that was on the edge of his desk. He never noticed.

As he handed her the slip of paper with the name and address of the restaurant, he said, "It's easy to find." After a brief moment, he added, "Don't stand me up."

"I'll be there, unless I get a better offer." Jenny winked, turned, and walked out of his office.

CHAPTER 23

Clarence Armstrong was following every detail of the map as he drove north. He liked that his current plan was coming together nicely. Jesse Ray was meticulously working through ways to plant the evidence that he had created. Tonight, the team would discuss Jesse Ray's ideas over supper. Jenny was at the Tower Agency gathering information, and he was heading to recon their potential hiding place, currently the biggest variable. *The problem is that if this place ain't everything I need, we might hafta abort. Damn it! I hate not havin' a sound backup.*

When Clarence arrived in Rockford, the seat of Coosa County, Alabama, he was pleasantly surprised. He laughed out loud when he saw a sign that read, "Welcome to Rockford, Home of Fred, the Town Dog." Rockford had the only traffic signal in the county. There were no fast-food restaurants or grocery stores, which was a big negative for him, but it was located within an easy hour's drive of abundant food in Montgomery.

At the crossroads, he headed north, and before he passed by Hatchet Creek, he slowed down, looking for his turn. He missed it the first time because kudzu covered the posts and most of the gate. It appeared that no one had been down the drive with any regularity in several years.

Clarence stretched when he stepped out of his Escalade. The small key fit effortlessly into the padlock that secured a large chain wrapped around the gate and a half-rotten wooden post. Pushing the gate open, he listened for any unusual sounds and searched for any prying neighbors. Satisfied he hadn't been seen, Clarence drove onto the property. He noted that the hard gravel drive would not reveal tire tracks. *So far, so good.*

Approximately one half of a mile into the property and out of sight of the county road, Clarence pulled onto the overgrown yard of an obviously abandoned antebellum mansion—the scarred old home, an eerie, silent reminder of grandeur. Huge camellia bushes covered most of the windows. Vines grew up the columns and all over the sides of the once white house. An old oak tree had blown over in the side yard years ago, and no one had bothered to clean it up. The place had once been a majestic estate and, despite decades of neglect, retained an air of Southern aristocracy.

As Clarence circled the house, he noticed an old barn in the back that appeared big enough to hide the team's vehicles.

Slowly climbing the front steps, he studied the door and windows carefully before slipping the larger of the two keys given to him by the Client into the dead bolt. The lock reluctantly released, and Clarence pushed open the door.

The inside of the house was surprisingly clean but unbearably hot. Flipping the first light switch he saw, he was pleased that the electricity worked. Sweat beaded on his forehead.

He noticed a window-mounted air-conditioning unit and walked across the room to it. He twisted a small plastic knob, causing it to turn on with a roar. He stuck his face into the breeze to ensure it was cooling.

Clarence turned away from the AC to take a deeper look into the house. The only furniture was an old couch and chairs in the main room. Lying in the center of the floor was a baby blue rotary dial telephone. Clarence hadn't seen one like it since he was a teenager, staying with his grandmother. Picking up the receiver, he heard a dial tone and then replaced the handset on the cradle. Dozens of black-and-white photos hung at odd angles on all the walls.

The kitchen had an old refrigerator, a table with four chairs, an old stove, and what looked like one of the first microwaves ever made—it was huge. He twisted the sink faucet, and it sputtered before dispensing clear water that had a pungent odor.

Moving out of the kitchen, he found two bedrooms: each had a bed with no sheets and no other furniture or air-conditioning units. The only bathroom downstairs had a claw-foot bathtub and a permanently ring-stained commode.

At the top of the staircase were two large rooms. One was totally empty. The other had a bed and a rocking chair pulled close to one window. A pane of glass was broken. After carefully studying it for several moments, Clarence determined that it had been broken from the inside. For a split second he felt uncomfortable as if someone were watching him. He wheeled around, pistol raised. Nothing. Somewhat spooked, he reholstered his gun inside his waistband and quickly left the room. He went down the stairs nervously whistling. Between the bottom of the stairs and the front door, Clarence turned around for a broad appraisal of the place. *With a TV and satellite dish, box fans for the bedrooms, and some sheets, this place'll do just fine.*

Returning to the kitchen, Clarence noticed an odd padlocked door. He tried the smaller key. The lock sprung open. Carefully opening the door, he saw that the stairs went straight down to a root cellar. A coarse string touched his face when he stuck his head inside to look around. He carefully pulled the string and a bare bulb illuminated directly above his head. *Just like Big Momma's house,* he thought.

Clarence walked down several steep creaking steps into a small, windowless dirt-walled room. The musty air was cool. The walls were lined with crude, handmade wooden shelves. There was only one way in or out. A single army surplus cot was in the center of the space. As Clarence was climbing back up the stairs, he quietly said aloud, "This place is freakin' spooky."

Clarence decided that he should check the refrigerator before leaving. It was marginally cool. The only contents were a box of pharmaceuticals. Clarence opened the box, removed a vial, and read the label, "Succinylcholine Chloride. What the hell's that?"

Clarence pulled his cell phone from his pocket and thumbed in a text message to Jesse Ray, "google succinylcholine chloride call back." When he hit Send, he noticed it didn't immediately send. He looked at the phone's screen. Only one service bar. He shook his head as he put the phone back into his pocket. Overall, Clarence was satisfied with the house.

As he headed for the door, he realized that the air conditioner was not running. *That's weird, I don't remember shuttin' it down.*

He walked over and switched it back on. It again roared to life. He turned it off. Clarence stood quietly, listening and looking around. He didn't hear anything. Nothing seemed out of place. The only disturbing thing was that the people in the old black-and-white photos seemed to stare back. After a moment, he relaxed, shook his head, and walked out of the old mansion, key locking the front door behind him.

He had one thing to check before leaving—the old barn. If there was enough empty space to hide at least two vehicles, maybe three, then Clarence would have a suitable hideout. It exceeded his expectations. *This is gonna be the easiest money I ever made.* He chuckled, thinking about scaring the shit out of the Client for making that very observation.

When he approached his vehicle, he realized that the driver's door was slightly ajar. He didn't remember not shutting it. He quickly felt for the keys and found them. He pulled his weapon and wheeled around, gun at the ready.

"All right, asshole, come on out!"

The big man nervously scanned the area. After what seemed to have been an hour but was only a few minutes, he eased up onto the front porch. He gently tried the doorknob, but it was locked. Under his breath, he said, "Shit, I'm losing my mind. I just musta not shut the door all the way."

With gun still drawn, he hurriedly looked under, around, and inside his vehicle; then reholstering, he climbed in and quickly locked the doors before cranking the engine.

After securing the gate exactly as he had found it, he drove back toward Montgomery. He began listening to a satellite radio news analysis of the global financial effects of the United States' national security concerns resulting from the Chinese government's recent aggressive attempts to further their monopoly of the world's rare earth metals, their mining, and their exportation so that he wouldn't think too much about the odd things in and around the old house.

Fortunately, not too far into the broadcast, his stomach growled and for the rest of the drive his attention was locked onto the idea of mounds of Dreamland's barbecue ribs.

CHAPTER 24

Clarence and Jenny had discussed her supper plans with Gates for ten minutes. He initially didn't want her to go, but she was persistent and persuasive, so he finally relented, "Yeah, okay. I agree. You probably will learn something useful, but you gotta be careful . . . and call me if he gets even remotely outta bounds."

"I will. I'm just gonna eat with the guy and talk. That's all it'll take. There's nutten to worry about," Jenny explained.

"Now you're sure you don't want me or Jesse Ray to tag along?"

"No, no, not at all. I don't figure he'd be relaxed and real chatty if I brought you along," she replied, almost laughing, and then added, "Don't worry about me. I can handle this jerk. Y'all got your own work to do."

"All right. I expect a call as soon as you get back in your car."

"Clarence, I swear, you sound like my daddy," she joked. But she knew that he genuinely cared, more than anyone ever had, and she appreciated it and loved him for it. "Okay. I'll call later . . . I'm here now," she continued. She pulled into a parking space in front of the restaurant and turned off her lights.

"Where's here?" Clarence asked.

"Sinclair's. Not too far from downtown . . . on Fairview Avenue—in the old money side of town. I can't see the street number, but everything's fine. I'll learn something we can use. I can feel it."

"You call me if he gets too friendly or if you feel uncomfortable. Be careful."

"Don't worry. This guy thinks he's a player. I can control him like a hand puppet. Already have. Later." She closed her cell phone, grabbed her purse, shut and locked her door, and then strolled toward the restaurant.

In a parked car across the street sat Gates Ballenger III, watching his date walk. He popped a Viagra, rubbed himself, and thought, *Absolutely the best performance-enhancing drug ever created.*

He chuckled as he ran his fingers through his hair and then drank the last swallow of his imported beer. He quickly got out and hurried to catch up with the hot young blonde.

Opening the restaurant door, he saw Meagan Massey standing, waiting. He immediately apologized for being late, making up a lame excuse about a conference call that he couldn't finish in time.

"You know you're not supposed to keep a lady waiting," Jenny said rather curtly. She could tell by the look in his eyes what he wanted. *Game on*, she thought.

"I'm so sorry. You look fabulous," he added and meant it.

"Thank you," she knew he expected her to compliment him back, but she didn't. "Shall we eat?" She noted his outfit looked new—everything an expensive brand name.

"Certainly," Gates replied and turned to face the maître d'hôtel.

"Good evening, Mr. Ballenger. Your usual table is ready," the headwaiter said, ogling Jenny.

"Thank you, Tony." Gates was certain she was impressed by the way he was being treated. Gates was a big tipper, but only when using the company Amex.

"Tony . . . a bottle of Caymus Cabernet Sauvignon, Special Selection, please. Two thousand seven, if you have it. If not, I'll settle for the two thousand two," Gates said in his most sophisticated voice. Jenny tried to keep a straight face.

"I'm so sorry. I assumed you like wine," Gates said, turning to Jenny to apologize.

"That's fine. You're doing good . . . so far," she replied as the waiter handed her a menu.

"*Wine Spectator*'s review of the two thousand seven vintage is as descriptive of you as it is the wine: 'firm, ripe, and muscular,'" Gates quoted, laying it on thick.

Jenny ignored this comment, held up her menu, and said, "So how's the food?"

"The food here is outstanding! And later, you'll have to try one of their chocolate martinis."

Jenny nodded and then glanced down at the menu. She realized that she was more nervous than hungry. She searched for some words she recognized.

"So tell me, how's a beautiful girl like you single?" Gates asked as he dropped his menu. He knew what he wanted.

"Who said I was single?" Jenny asked, taking a sip of ice water.

"Oh, I . . . uh . . . I just, I assumed. I'm sorry. I didn't know you were married, but it's not a problem with me. I actually prefer married women," Gates said trying to recover.

"Who said I was married?" Jenny asked again.

Gates paused a moment to recover and then said, "Okay. Okay. I'm sorry. I was a bit presumptuous. Let me start over. Tell me about yourself . . . please."

"I'd rather hear about you."

The waiter set the wineglasses on the table. He overheard her words and knew Gates must be in heaven because he certainly loved to talk about himself. He offered the wine bottle for Gates's inspection of the label. Gates nodded his approval. Upon receiving a small sample, Gates made a spectacle of going through the motions of looking at, smelling, and tasting it. He gestured his acceptance and directed the waiter to pour their glasses.

When the waiter left, Gates said, "Well, where do I start? Let's see. I grew up here. My family's been in Montgomery so long people say they helped dig the Alabama River . . . in a supervisory capacity, of course," he added with an air of superiority.

"But of course."

"My parents owned half the county that has now been developed, so money's never been a real concern. After college, I worked for an ad agency here, sort of cut my teeth—learned the ropes, ya know—and then at twenty-five, I established my own firm, the Tower Agency. And now that it's solidly on its feet, I've started backing off some. You know, tryin' to enjoy life more."

"So how does your partner fit into your livin' the life of Riley?" she inquired, hoping he didn't think it odd that she had asked about Cooper.

Perfect, Gates thought. *Thank God she didn't ask about the messy parts, the ex-wives.*

He said, "He's just a minority partner. I call the shots. Cooper is—," he stopped mid-sentence when the waiter approached to refill their wineglasses.

Gates drained his second glass before the waiter left the table. "Just leave the bottle and get another ready," he instructed.

"Where was I? Oh yeah. Cooper's very important to the business. I depend on him to run things. I work him like a dog, but he loves it—a classic workaholic. He's more married to his job than his ole lady. He works; I benefit!" Gates bragged.

It was obvious to Jenny that if she kept Gates drinking and talking, she'd get all the information she needed without really asking many pointed questions or ever raising any suspicions.

Gates continued, "I'm tryin' to decide what my next business move will be. I'm sort of in an enviable position." As soon as he set down his empty glass, the waiter immediately refilled it.

"Are you ready to order, sir?"

The waiter gave Jenny a knowing glance.

"Do you want me to order for you?" Gates asked. "I've tried everything."

Jenny smirked at Gates's arrogance. "No, I prefer to order for myself, thank you. I'll have the Shrimp Athenian." Jenny said and folded her menu, handing it to the waiter. She had no idea what she had just ordered but felt safe with a shrimp dish.

Gates slowly nodded his head. "Bring me the Blue Cajun Filet, cooked very, very rare. It doesn't have to be warm inside. Oh, and bring artichoke dip as an appetizer."

"Yes, sir."

"You were sayin' you're in an enviable position?" Jenny asked, trying to keep Gates on topic.

"That's right. I'm about to sell the agency, relax, and then *really* enjoy life. The whole world's in front of me," Gates made a grand sweeping gesture with outstretched arms, "and I just have to determine what I wanna do. I might develop real estate or just play golf. I haven't decided." Gates was trying to make his story sound as impressive as possible. He followed with a large swallow of wine.

"What about your partner?" she asked, sipping her wine.

"Oh, I imagine he will stay in the business somehow . . . he'll have to, he won't get as much as me. He'll do okay, but his wife's lifestyle is *way* too extravagant for him to stop workin'. She spends every dime the poor, stupid bastard makes."

Gates's mouth was running faster than his mind. After a few seconds it caught up with him. He said, "Please keep all this to yourself. It's not for public consumption yet."

"Of course. Who's gonna buy it, if I may ask?"

Gates took another huge swallow of wine, glanced around the room to make sure no one could overhear, "MidState Bank. Ever heard of 'em?"

"No, I don't think so . . . should I?"

"Probably not, but you will. It's just a local bank, for now. Small by most standards, but they are a steady, dependable financial institution, and I hear there's merger talks in the works . . . with a huge New York City bank."

"You must be so excited. When's your deal happenin'?" she asked nonchalantly.

"Soon. Very soon. We're in the final stages of negotiatin'," he slurred. "I'm so glad you came to dinner with me. You're soooo beautiful."

"Thanks. Me too," she forced a smile.

"I bet all the guys tell you that."

Jenny played along. "Not really. I don't date much."

"Yeah, right. So tell me about you."

"Well, there's not much to tell. I was a dancer at the Moonlight Club in Atlanta before it shut down," she said and watched his mouth literally drop open with excitement and obvious anticipation. She continued, "I made enough money—tax-free—to be comfortable while I decided on another career. My uncle's a bigwig with the insurance group, so that got me in the door. I really don't have to work that hard." Her story just flowed without much thought. She knew he would be distracted, thinking about her being a stripper. She could have said anything after that.

"Wow, I always wanted to date a stripper . . . I mean, dancer." His mind was racing. *I'm havin' supper with a real live stripper. I bet she knows moves . . . I've . . . I've got to get her to do a lap dance for me. This is gonna be the best night of my life!*

She didn't say anything for a while, watching the wheels turn in Gates's head. Then she casually asked, "So . . . how far in the hole are you?"

"Excuse me?"

"I saw the bettin' form on your desk. All gamblers wind up losin', eventually."

"Not me. In fact, I'm up. Actually, I just bet for the hell of it. You know, for entertainment purposes."

"What about your partner? What's his name?"

"Oh shit . . . Cooper? He doesn't gamble . . . he doesn't have any vices. He just works . . . and hunts . . . and fishes." Gates wanted to get the conversation back on track, so he said, "I've heard that most dancers are surgically enhanced. Are they?"

"No. Not all of us. These babies are one hundred percent *nat-u-ralle.*" Jenny pushed out her chest and gave a little laugh.

"Oh. My. God! I like natural. I *love* natural," Gates said enjoying the tête-à-tête. "So what was your stage name?"

"Destiny," Jenny replied without missing a beat and was surprised that the first name she thought of fit so well. She grinned.

Gates's mind was whirling at an incomprehensible speed. He could hardly breathe. He poured himself more wine and topped off her glass.

"So . . . Destiny," Gates winked, "after supper, I'd love to show you my place."

"Maybe. We'll see," she replied with a slight smile. "I just love hearin' about your business. Can I . . ." She stopped when the waiter approached.

Gates was really excited now. *Maybe. That's practically a yes,* he thought.

The waiter carefully delivered their entrées. Jenny caught Gates staring at her Wonderbra-enhanced cleavage and acted as if she enjoyed it, giving him a wink and wily smile. Once everything was in place, the waiter retreated to the kitchen. Jenny was wondering if the Client worked for MidState Bank. *That could be the connection. There's potentially a lot of money at stake if I can believe anything this drunk idiot's sayin'. But why single out Cooper? What's his story?*

"What I was about to say was, can I ask a stupid question—something I've always wondered about?" she continued as she gently skewered a shrimp with her fork.

"Sure . . . anything," he replied, wiping sweat from his brow with his napkin.

"How do you determine how much a business is actually worth?"

"Well, there's a bunch of ways. A good startin' point is three times gross sales or billings or seven times net income. Some fits are strategic, some are for diversification, and some are to get additional market penetration, so what you're willin' to pay really depends on how bad you want it." Gates's slur-filled explanation was intended to impress her with his business acumen.

After taking a small sip of wine, she asked, "Well, how

badly do they want your business?"

"Bad, really bad. We've got positive cash flow—almost as good as the insurance business—and in election years, the amount of cash coming in is staggerin'. They can take our surplus cash and invest it in their other businesses. We're actually a better investment than an insurance company 'cause ad agencies don't have the exposure of massive claims . . . like hurricanes and floods and tornadoes, ya know, that kinda thing. Makes sense for them to buy us."

"Sounds like you're gonna make enough money to be set for life."

"That's right," Gates lied. All he wanted was to impress her for one night. *She didn't need to know the truth,* he thought.

"How exciting," she replied with a slight wiggle, causing her hair to sway. "Good for you. It's so great seein' someone's hard work pay off."

Gates went on a tear, talking nonstop—except to excuse himself once to run into the men's room to do a bump of coke—for another twenty minutes, explaining in greater detail the elements of selling his business and making a case for the bank's acquisition of his business rather than an insurance company, with its commensurate exposure to complex financial instruments such as derivatives.

Jenny basically tuned him out after he came back from the bathroom. She ate most of her meal and had a taste of dessert and a cup of decaf before he finished yammering. Toward the end of his monologue and without Gates noticing, she reached into her purse and grabbed her preplanned distraction, something she knew would buy her some time.

When Gates finally paused long enough to request another bottle of wine, she said, "Excuse me. I need to run to the little girls' room," and stood.

She walked around the table, leaned close to his ear, and whispered seductively, "Here's a little sumpten for ya to think about till I get back." She then pressed into his hand a dark red, lacy thong. She smiled alluringly and then sauntered toward the restroom.

Gates watched her walk away, admiring her skintight black leather skirt. He didn't know what she had placed in his hand. He put it on his lap and then opened his hand. Beads of sweat burst out on his forehead. His palms began sweating too.

Just as Jenny planned, Gates Ballenger III sat stunned for several minutes. He couldn't hear the sounds of the restaurant or see anything other than the panties. He wondered how she could have possibly taken them off at the table. He took a big gulp of wine. *Looks like I still got it,* he thought and smiled.

Jenny rounded the corner and then slipped out the restaurant's front door and into the fresh night air.

CHAPTER 25

Brooke helped Grayson finish his math homework. He then took a quick shower. She saw him pull on his pajamas and collapse onto his bed, with his hair still wet. She went to him and gently rubbed his head and kissed him good night.

"Good night, sweetheart. I love you."

"Night, Mom. Love ya too."

Brooke watched him for a few seconds and then left him to fall asleep. She poured herself a glass of white wine from a box in the refrigerator, armed the alarm system, and then curled up on the couch and clicked on the television. Twice she considered getting up to check her Facebook account but both times decided that she was too exhausted.

She lay back and closed her eyes. She thought of Cooper, and it made her smile. He was mesmerizing to her. She really knew very little about his home life, other than rumors that he wasn't happy in his marriage and what she had surmised from their recent conversations. She had wanted him for some time, but not for a simple affair. She wanted more.

Brooke wanted Cooper to leave Kelly for her and decided that she had to make him think leaving was his idea. She had never done this before, but without remorse Brooke had been building a trap for Cooper. It had taken months for him to display interest, and now he was primed to act on it. Having gotten his attention, she was ready to fast-forward everything. The upcoming football game was the perfect opportunity. In the obscurity of the massive crowd, they could flirt openly. *Maybe I can seduce him. One time with me, and he'll never go back to her.*

Swallowing the last bit of wine, she clicked off the television and walked down the hall to Grayson's room. He was sound asleep. She lightly kissed his warm little cheek and smelled his still damp hair. Her son was priority number one. She kissed her fingers and touched his forehead; then she quietly walked down the hall to her bathroom for a soak.

Once the bathtub filled with hot water, she shed her clothes and quickly climbed into the bubble bath. Within ten minutes she was relaxed, almost comatose. Only her head and toes poked out of the suds.

When the landline rang, she decided to let it go to voice mail. For three weeks, every night at about the same time, someone called from a blocked number and didn't say anything. She was far too comfortable and relaxed to entertain some teenager's prank. What she really wanted to do was write in her journal, it had been well over a month, maybe more since her last entry, but she hadn't been able to find it. *Where the hell did I leave it?* she wondered.

Closing her eyes, she sank beneath the bubbles.

CHAPTER 26

Cooper was walking out the door, heading home, when he noticed the clock read 5:55 p.m. He stopped. Every time he saw clock numbers matching, he thought of his wife and the deal they had made when they were dating. They agreed to think of each other whenever they saw a clock read synchronized single digits from one through five. He was surprised at how often he noticed it.

He decided to call Kelly to see if he needed to get anything on his way. He sat back down at his desk, picked up the phone, and dialed his home number.

"Hello? Dixon residence," said Ben Dixon, answering the phone on the first ring.

"Hey, Ben. How's my little buddy?"

"Fine."

"How was school?"

"Fine. Dad? Can I have an allowance?"

"We'll talk about it when I get home. I'd rather call it a commission. There are no allowances in life."

"What's a commission?"

"We'll talk about it when I get home; I promise, okay? Let me speak to Mom."

"MOM? MOM, IT'S DAD!" Ben screamed as loud as he could.

Cooper looked out the giant windows at the city's skyline. From this vantage, he could see a number of historic old buildings. He focused on a metal adornment atop a law office, which once was a dry goods store. The ornamental piece appeared to be a casket. The local legend is that the owner was terrified of floods, so when he died, his will directed that his body be placed inside the metal vault, high above the city.

"When will you be here?" Kelly quickly asked, out of breath.

"Uh . . . well, I was about to leave, and I thought I'd see if you needed anything," Cooper said, watching a giant military cargo plane bank for a landing at Maxwell Air Force Base. Sensing something was wrong, he exhaled and asked, "What's the matter, now?"

"You forgot that I have a Charity Ball meeting tonight. Didn't ya? I can't find my red dress. I asked you to pick it up at the cleaners before you left!"

"Is Piper there?" Cooper asked, ignoring the issue.

"Dammit, Cooper, I planned on wearin' that dress tonight. I bought it just for that meeting!" Kelly exclaimed, exasperated that Cooper never seemed to value what was important to her.

"I'm sorry. Just wear somethin' else. What about Piper?"

"She's at ridin' lessons. I gotta go pick her up in a few minutes." Kelly paused for a moment and then continued, "I was so excited about wearin' that dress," as she looked at the grandfather clock in the den.

"Well . . ." Cooper rubbed his face and counted to five as

he carefully measured his response and continued, "I can run by the cleaners to see if they have it ready."

Cooper felt no real contrition. It was as though he was merely going through whatever motions these were with Kelly.

"Do it and hurry up. I can't be late," Kelly ordered and hung up on him.

Cooper stared at the phone for a few seconds, listening to the tone, and then he replaced the handset onto the cradle.

Driving home, Cooper wondered what was next in his relationship with Kelly. He was struggling to consider it as a marriage. Aloud, he said, "So much for 'becoming one.' That ship's sailed."

Then the thought of Brooke's body overpowered him, and his mood became as dark and foreboding as the brewing late afternoon thunderstorm.

CHAPTER 27

Jenny jumped into her Honda and was halfway to her hotel before Gates knew that she had left the restaurant. Acting trashy was a part of her job for which she didn't care, although she was really quite good at it. The upside was that they now had vital information that could save their lives or at least help them stay out of jail. She called Clarence at the first traffic light.

"Yo, baby," Clarence answered on the second ring.

"I think I got it figured out. Our Client's trying to devalue a business so it can be bought on the cheap. At least that's what I think."

"Come again?" Clarence then hollered at Jesse Ray to turn down the television. They were watching *Soul Train* reruns.

"There's a chance for us to make a lot more money on this deal. I'll explain when I get there. Give me twenty minutes. I'll come to y'all's room."

"Hurry up. I can't wait to hear this."

Jenny Johnson smelled an opportunity. It would take a collaborative effort to flesh out the details, but she was excited by the prospects. The soundtrack from *Moulin Rouge* began, and she sang "Lady Marmalade" at the top of her lungs.

. . .

Clarence and Jesse Ray were waiting for her when she gave the secret knock. The big guy stooped down to look through the peephole. He smiled as he unlocked the door.

"Let's hear it . . . this must be good."

Jenny walked in and tossed her purse on the first bed.

"Damn you look hot!" Jesse Ray blurted, when he looked up from his computer screen. "That's one fine skirt!"

Jenny ignored him and said, "There's more money in this deal for us, somehow. I can smell it. We just gotta figure out how to get it."

For the next hour Jenny recounted almost verbatim details about Gates, the agency, and the impending sale.

"So, there's obviously a lot of money at stake. Millions, maybe. Apparently, it's a very profitable advertising agency," she concluded.

"Son of a . . ." Clarence exclaimed as he rubbed his chin.

Jesse Ray looked puzzled and commented, "This could be complicated. I'd rather steal IDs and credit card numbers."

"Look, it means this job is worth a lot more to somebody than what we're gettin' paid. We just gotta figure out who that somebody is," Clarence observed, and then took a sip of his drink.

"Right. Exactly," Jenny said. "It's gotta be related to this sale. If we're talking several million dollars . . . well, we've all done a lot more for a whole lot less. We just gotta think of an angle to exploit, but at least we know what's going on."

"Any idea what that angle's gonna be?" Jesse Ray asked.

"Nope, but I bet we can come up with one."

"What'd we learn about our boy Cooper?" Clarence asked.

"Not much. He works all the time."

Jenny was excited about increasing the score. She was getting close to having enough money saved to get out of the game, and this potentially improved gig might be her ticket.

She continued, "And Gates is, like I said, a piece of shit. He's cocky, a womanizer, drinks like a fish; I'm pretty sure he does drugs too. And if I was a bettin' woman, I'd take odds he's up to his eyeballs in gamblin' debt."

"Damn, woman. You learned all this from one dinner?" Jesse Ray asked as he started to laugh. "You psychic?"

"Oh, and he's got a ragin' fantasy about strippers; I mean, if he didn't . . . he does now."

"I don't even wanna know what that means," Clarence commented as he slowly shook his head.

"My whole life I've been around really screwed-up folks, so I've learned to pay attention to what's goin' on around me and to what's said . . . and, most importantly, what's *not* said. And I listen to my gut. If somethin' doesn't feel right, then it ain't right."

Clarence said, "Well, your skills really paid off tonight."

"Before we head too far down the path of workin' this job for hidden money-makin' opportunities, we gotta get the ball rollin' tonight on our primary target. Okay?" Jesse Ray said and then paused, looking the others in the eyes.

Both Clarence and Jenny simply nodded since Jesse Ray didn't talk much, but when he did, they knew that they needed to listen.

"Cool," Jesse Ray continued, "I'm gonna wait till after two in the mornin', so nobody's on their system, and then

I'll worm my way onto the Tower Agency's Internet server. I'll leave a string of postdated e-mails that will be very difficult for him to explain. I'm also gonna make his computer's history show that he's visited several websites on kidnappin' and abduction. I even got a few sites on coverin' up murder, so it'll appear he's been researchin' and plannin' this whole thing for a while. You know, like he's been studyin' what other criminals have done. Learnin' from their mistakes. Maybe I can tie it all together as an insurance payoff. But, to sell it to the cops, we gotta plant some papers in his office."

Jesse Ray paused and stared at Jenny.

"What are you sayin'?" Jenny asked.

"You gotta go back in tomorrow and hide a few file folders in his desk or somewhere," Clarence directed, pointing at a folder on the dresser opposite the beds. "You didn't burn a bridge tonight, did ya?"

"No," she said with a devious smile. "But I'm pretty sure I set it on fire."

Jenny's confident air told the men she could handle it.

CHAPTER 28
2ND FRIDAY

After tailing Cooper from outside of his subdivision to his children's school on the opposite end of town from his office, Jenny parked on the same street and rode the same elevator to the eighth floor of the Tower building as she had done the day before. She had on another new, expensive business suit; this time it was dark green. She carried a black leather briefcase containing several pieces of evidence she was to plant in Cooper's office. Today, however, she was nervous. The prospect of running into Gates wasn't pleasant.

Jesse Ray had been very specific about what she needed to accomplish. He had successfully penetrated the advertising agency's computer system via a hole in its server's firewall. He had planted ten e-mails on Cooper's computer that would certainly point to his guilt. He had also bookmarked over thirty different websites dedicated to specific criminal activity. Any law enforcement agency's computer technician wouldn't have a problem finding the damning data. Cooper could not survive the scrutiny. To cover the bases, Jesse Ray wanted to leave physical evidence of these search results to quickly and convincingly connect the dots.

Stepping through the Tower Agency's outer office door, Jenny once again greeted Mrs. Riley. She held her briefcase with both hands and bowed slightly forward.

"Hello, Mrs. Riley. It's me again, Meagan, with the building's insurance carrier," Jenny said with a sweet smile.

"Yes, of course. How are you today?" Mrs. Riley asked.

"I'm doing just fine, thanks, but . . . I forgot to take some photos yesterday. I'm sorry. It'll only take a minute. Do ya mind?"

"Sure, dear. Make yourself at home."

Jenny walked away just as the telephone rang. She took a deep breath as she headed straight to Cooper's office. The door was open, and the lights were off. She eased inside and set down her briefcase. After Jesse Ray studied the photos that Jenny had actually taken the day before, he pointed out an old antique minnow bucket on a shelf. He had instructed her to hide an envelope of notes inside the old pail. Jenny quickly and carefully raised the lid and inserted a cache of incriminating evidence.

She walked over to a filing cabinet and quickly checked all of the drawers, looking for one that was mostly full. When she settled on the one, about halfway back, she stuffed in a manila folder containing twenty sheets of paper. As she was closing the drawer, she stopped, reached in, and pulled up the file folder so that it was only slightly visible above the rest.

Jenny eased to the office door to listen. The only sound she could hear was the receptionist talking to someone about a *Golden Girls* episode that she had watched last night. Jenny quickly went to Cooper's desk and opened the top drawer on the right side. Quietly rummaging through his belongings, she found a leather-covered checkbook and opened it. Printed on the checks was Cooper's driver's license number. She tore out the last check and slipped it into her jacket pocket. *You gotta be kiddin' me. That was too easy.*

Jenny smoothed her business suit, pushed her hair behind her ears, grabbed her briefcase, and confidently walked out of Cooper's office toward the elevators. Total elapsed time: three minutes—much faster than she expected. She politely thanked the receptionist.

"Bye, dear," Mrs. Riley sang out.

Walking through the Tower Agency's glass doors, Jenny exhaled deeply. Her adrenalin was pumping. She pushed the down button. A moment later, she pushed it again. She unconsciously tapped her right foot as she watched the elevator's digital readout. When the bell sounded, there was a two-second pause before the door opened. There stood Gates Ballenger III with a stupid look on his face that instantly changed to one of welcome surprise.

"It's you!" he said, stepping forward, holding out his arms as if inviting her to hug.

Jenny took a reflexive step backward and then tried to regain her composure.

"Yes! Hey, I came back to find you because I felt *so* bad about havin' to leave like I did." She tried to sound sincere.

"What happened?" Gates asked, willing to believe anything.

"When I was in the restroom, I got a call from my mom; she's not doing so well, and it upset me . . . and I left so I could talk to her. It's a long story. I'm so sorry that I just left you. Please forgive me!" she said, batting her eyes. She even managed a tear.

Gates stared with deep concern. "I do. I do. I understand. I knew it had to be something serious." Gates smiled. After a

moment's pause, he leaned toward her and with a conspirato-
rial tone said, "I've got your panties in my pocket."

"Oh, good. Keep 'em." She had no intention of taking
back her underwear after he'd had a night with them. *No
telling what he did with them.*

"So your mom's okay now?"

"Yes, she's much better." Jenny punched the elevator
button.

"Glad to hear it," Gates said genuinely.

As the elevator door opened, Jenny took a step toward it.

Gates quickly blocked her escape. "Not so fast. You owe
me a complete date."

"Ya think?" Jenny shot back.

"Yes, you do, and it just so happens that I need a date for
the Auburn game Saturday night. We can ride over together.
I'll rent a limo, so we don't hafta worry about drinkin' and
drivin' or parkin'."

"I'm sorry, I can't. I have to be in Atlanta tonight."

"Well then, meet me at the game. Auburn's an easy drive
from Atlanta. We host a big tent to entertain clients before
the game. It'll be fun."

"Do your employees and spouses go?"

"Nope. Just me and Coop. He'll go, but his wife never
comes to the games," Gates explained. "Come on, whaddaya
say? It'll be fun. Good booze, great game . . . besides, you
owe me," he insisted.

Jenny stared at him, thinking. She noticed his cell phone
on his hip. "Give me your cell number, and I'll call you back
after I think about it."

"Don't make me beg," Gates said, literally ready to drop
to his knees.

"I said that I'd think about it . . . I do owe you a date . . . I
suppose."

"Yeah, you do. Here." Gates handed Jenny his business card. "My cell number's on it."

Jenny took the card without saying anything and pushed the down button.

"We'll have a blast at the game, I promise," Gates insisted. He loved her body and knew that all his married frat buddies' eyes would pop out when they saw her.

She looked intently at Gates and said, "I'll call . . . soon."

The elevator door opened. She stepped inside. Before the door closed, she winked at Gates and almost imperceptibly licked her lips.

Jenny now knew when the team should grab the Target.

CHAPTER 29

Cooper parked his truck and checked his watch out of habit as he walked briskly toward the office building. It was half past nine. The meeting at the kids' school ran much longer than he had anticipated. The Booster Club wanted to erect a new scoreboard, and Cooper had been asked to lead the charge. *This is all I need—something else on my list!*

"Good morning," Cooper said to Mrs. Riley as he walked in.

"Mornin'. You doin' okay?" Mrs. Riley asked, concerned.

"Yeah, not bad. Just got hit with something I wasn't expecting. It doesn't matter. How are things round here?"

"Same as always. Busy as a beehive. I have a bunch of messages for you. Oh! That new artist, Crystal, ya know the one with all the piercings," Mrs. Riley whispered while she looked around to make certain no one else could hear, "she thinks she has carpal tunnel syndrome," she rolled her eyes and continued, "and Jamie's computer crashed . . . so you can just imagine her mood."

"Another day in paradise," Cooper said, exhaling audibly.

"Exactly. One other thing: there's a Realtor lookin' for you," she said, glancing through the messages. "Here it is. He says that he *really* needs to talk to you." She placed that message on top of the stack and then handed the pile to Cooper.

"Thank you. That's a beautiful necklace you're wearing."

"Oh this? I've had it for ages," she replied, throwing her right hand forward in a dismissive manner, and then asked, "Are you looking for a new house?"

"No, ma'am. I've got way more than enough house right now." Cooper started toward his office and added, "He's an old buddy. Maybe he needs some advertising."

Cooper's office looked as he had left it, except for a mound of paperwork on his desk. He let out a groan when he saw the six-inch stack of mind-numbing forms and compliance letters. He began unloading everything from his briefcase, making a pile on his desk next to the latest pile. Soon after he began the tedious slog through the governmental bureaucratic crap. "We need an office manager," he mumbled aloud.

Cooper took a break, logging onto his computer to check e-mail. He couldn't believe the volume of spam. Quickly deleting the obvious junk, he searched for any messages from Brooke and was disappointed. There were a dozen business e-mails that needed attention. His mind, however, drifted to the pink message memo from his real estate buddy who specialized in farmland. Cooper stared at the slip, at his computer screen, and then at the still substantial piles of paperwork, and decided to call his friend.

"Mossy Oak Properties," answered the Realtor on the third ring.

"Hey, Will. It's Cooper. How you doin'?" Cooper asked, leaning back in his chair.

"Hey, Coop. I'm good, man. Heard a rumor that you'd found the perfect property and were tryin' to fly under the radar—tryin' to buy it without anybody knowin'."

"Well, yeah, that's true," Cooper confessed. "How'd you hear?"

"It's a small world, dude."

"Obviously, I wasn't flyin' low enough."

"Man, you oughta know you can't fly that low round here. Not for somethin' like this. At any rate, I hate it that I missed the commission . . . but maybe . . . maybe I'll get invited to hunt."

"Of course you will; plus, I'm gonna need an appraisal, so you can have that piece of business."

"A turkey huntin' invite?" Will asked hopefully.

"We're not *that* good of friends," Cooper replied, laughing.

"Man, that hurts! Will you at least tell me about it? Where is it, exactly?"

Cooper sat upright, excitedly explaining the details. He had always dreamed of owning a big piece of land and would much rather talk about it and wildlife management than just about anything else.

"It's in Coosa County. It's got beautiful hardwood timber; in fact, it's got the prettiest stand of giant oaks and hardwood bottoms you've ever seen. There are several Indian mounds on the place, and one side's adjacent to the Wildlife Management Area. I've been huntin' on it for years, and I've fixed up an old house as my camp. It's basic, to say the least . . . but it'll do for a while."

"Sounds perfect. Why's it on the market?"

"It's not. That's the best part. It belongs to a woman who's worked for my family for more than forty years. She practically raised me. She inherited it. The only thing she's done with it is sell a little timber to put some missionary kids through college. She didn't even know 'em. That's the kinda person she is—good as gold. She lost her kids in a car accident when they were babies, so she pretty much thinks of me as her own. I've been leasin' the huntin' rights for several years. A few years back, when I found out she was thinkin' of sellin' it, I got her to give me an option. It's about to expire, so I gotta do somethin', pretty quick."

"Ya stealin' it?"

"No way . . . I've offered her a very fair price," Cooper replied.

"Sounds too good to be true."

"It's a special place to me and to her. All her people are buried on the property. There are several cemeteries, and all the old home places are still there—mostly just some chimneys and concrete steps; some could be fixed up. It used to be part of a big plantation. There was a little community on the place, too, till some disease came through, killin' off everybody. Yellow fever, maybe. Anyway, it means everything to her for somebody to keep it in one big piece—fix up the houses and take care of the cemeteries. I gave her my word I'd do it."

"How much an acre?"

"I'm not sayin' till it's done. I'm scared something's gonna happen, and I'll lose it."

"Well, I can tell you this, Coosa's red-hot right now. Whatever you're payin', you'll do well. Let me know when you want that appraisal. I'll help any way I can."

"Thanks. I'll get you the info in the next few days. I think I finally have the financin' in place. I really don't want to move this fast, but she's startin' to get calls 'bout it, so I need to pull the trigger pretty quick."

After the conversation, Cooper wondered about Coosa County land being "red-hot." He didn't know why. He just assumed close-in hunting property was in high demand. His thoughts drifted to a huge flock of wild turkeys he'd recently seen, and knew that he couldn't let anyone else have his Promised Land.

CHAPTER 30

Jesse Ray had spent several early morning hours manipulating and sabotaging Cooper Dixon's e-mails, his computer's Internet history and its bookmarks. Jesse Ray excitedly woke Clarence at two in the morning to show how this guy was not very computer-savvy. Cooper had 29,348 e-mails in his Deleted folder, a sign that he obviously didn't know to delete its contents or that doing so was even necessary. Jesse Ray howled in laughter. Clarence, conspicuously silent, wondered if he had ever deleted his own.

Several hours later at seven, Clarence who had been pacing the floors thinking a hole in the job, decided to wake up Jesse Ray to get the day rolling.

"Jesse Ray, Jesse Ray get up!" he shouted as he walked into the bathroom to brush his teeth. "Get up, homeboy!"

"Man, what time is it?" Jesse Ray replied, without moving.

"Time to get your ass up. I let you sleep late. We got lots to do," Clarence explained as he squeezed toothpaste onto his brush.

"Yo, Dog . . . won't ya let a brother sleep another hour?" Jesse Ray begged as he peeked out from under the covers.

"Get your narrow ass up, and let's get busy."

"Leave me alone. I need my rest 'cause I got lots to do today, and I gotta be sharp."

"Like what?"

"I gotta hack back into the server and get Cooper's social. Once I've got it, I'll make it appear that's he's in financial trouble, in a large way. Financial Armageddon! When his and his old lady's credit cards quit working, it will hit the fan!"

"Damn, son, I hope you don't ever get pissed off at me."

"So I can go back to sleep?"

"Nope. There's a list of things I need you to go buy for us. Right there by the phone."

Jesse Ray reached over, grabbed the note, and then read aloud from the list: "Duct tape—three; four lightweight sleeping bags, pillows, and cases; DVD player; two cases of beer; four cases of water; food for a week for four; toilet paper; paper towels; paper plates; plastic utensils; big-ass cooler on wheels; three bags of ice; wasp spray; coffeemaker; filters; coffee . . . dude, this'll take me awhile to round up," he said as he continued reading the list to himself.

"We are gonna need all that and more. Get whatever you need to make yourself comfortable."

"I gotta take a shower first and wake up." Jesse Ray swung his feet to the floor, stood, stretched, and scratched his butt cheeks with both hands.

Clarence picked up his keys, stuffed his wallet into his back pocket, and headed for the door, saying, "I'm gonna grab breakfast. I can't think on an empty stomach. I'll be here when you get back from shoppin'."

"Dog, you're actin' strange. You seem . . . I dunno . . . worried. Somethin'. I ain't never seen you worried befo."

"What the hell you talkin' 'bout?"

"Well, for one, you just brushed your teeth with my toothbrush," Jesse Ray pointed out.

"Aww! Man, you serious?!" Clarence started spitting. "I guess . . . well, I ain't worried as much as preoccupied. I woke up tryin' to figure out how to monetize this new information we got from Jenny . . . and I guess I'm kinda anxious for her to get on back. Just got a lot on my mind, that's all. Add a toothbrush to that list."

"Already did, and one for me too . . . now chill, Dog . . . we'll figure it out . . . we always do."

CHAPTER 31

Don Daniels gently slid a vintage Montblanc pen into his pocket when he finished signing the legal papers. He carefully folded the pages and then sealed them inside an envelope before giving them to his secretary to route back to their attorney. Checking the clock on his credenza, he pushed away from the desk and stood. It had been a grueling, monotonous week. He was ready to get the hell out of the office. Leaving early on Fridays was the first step in escaping what he had grown to hate and despise.

"I'll be out the rest of the afternoon," he informed his secretary, "but I'll have my cell phone on, if it's important."

"Yes, sir. What about Cooper Dixon? He's called three times today."

"I'll call him later this afternoon," he said, pulling on his suit coat. "Maybe. If he calls again, tell him I'm in a meeting."

"Yes, sir. A man called a few minutes ago, while you were on the phone," she replied, handing him a note. "He wouldn't leave a name, just a number."

"Thank you."

He looked at the message and then turned and walked purposefully back into his office to return the call. He sat down at his desk and then punched in the number. Staring out the window, he anxiously waited for an answer.

As soon as the call connected, he said, "It's me, what do you have?"

"Things are happenin'. Toyota suddenly ramped up their efforts to get their next plant going, and it's lookin' like Alabama's gonna get it. It's not official . . . yet. Only a handful of folks know, and just like you thought, there are a couple of sites that make the most sense."

"What's the time frame?"

"Within the next few months, they'll announce that they're lookin', but as you know, it'll already be a done deal. They want at least one thousand acres, close to an interstate. The governor will take care of all the tax credits, and the state will be issuing bonds and takin' what property Toyota can't buy by eminent domain. They paid twenty grand an acre for the site near Tupelo, Mississippi, so somebody's gonna get rich when they buy the ground for this plant."

"I know all about how that Mississippi deal was made," Don Daniels said with a sly grin. "And I'm gonna be on the front end of Alabama's opportunity."

"As long as my retainer's paid, the information keeps flowin'." Without another word, the connection was broken.

Don Daniels did a quick mental calculation: 1,200 acres times $25,000 was a cool $30 million, less acquisition costs and retainers. This was "go to the house" money—an opportunity to retire rich. He was willing to do whatever it took to make it happen. For several years, he had been silently piecing together contiguous small land tracts in anticipation of this event. Much to Don's frustration, most of these tracts had been owned by his family many years ago. Since the governor was a close ally, as were several state legislators, Don was confident that enough official incentives and unofficial influence could be placed upon the Japanese automaker to find his site acceptable.

He switched off his office lights and quietly shut the door. As he walked down the hall, smiling broadly, he thought, *I'll do whatever's required to get this deal tied off.*

CHAPTER 32

Jenny punched in Clarence's speed dial number on her cell phone as she hurriedly walked past the water features in front of the huge office building. She knew how crazed the entire state's population was about the two major universities' football teams. The support of one over the other literally divided families and friends. Since the state was not home to any professional sports, watching Auburn and Alabama play football was a high priority for most. With Cooper at the Auburn football game and half of the state watching it on television or listening on the radio, Saturday night would be the perfect time to kidnap his wife. Stores would be empty, roads deserted, and law enforcement would be occupied with either the game, traffic, fights, or drunk drivers. Jenny was certain Clarence would recognize the opportunity. They would have a several-hour window to make the snatch. There was one major obstacle—they only had a day to prepare.

"Talk to me," a gruff voice suddenly answered.

Sitting down on the steps facing the fountain, she looked around to make sure no one could overhear her end of the conversation. "Everything's in place, and listen to this: tomorrow night Auburn plays at home, and our guy's going, without our *friend*. Apparently, she rarely goes to the games."

Clarence knew what she was implying was right. The statewide effect of college football in Alabama was well known around the South. If the University of Alabama happened to be playing at home, that would make the timing even better. He had learned recently that the city of Montgomery usually sent approximately one hundred police officers to Auburn for each home football game, which meant less of a police presence in town when they grabbed the Target.

"Hmm, very interesting. This could be perfect timin'. I just need to figure out where to do it. That's my biggest concern. Come to the Farmers Market Cafe. I'll buy you a late breakfast. I don't wanna talk details on the phone."

"Nah, thanks. I'll meet you at the hotel."

"You don't know what you're missin'. Okay, then, see ya there," he replied and then hung up.

He sopped up the last of several runny eggs with a biscuit and then leaned back in his chair and smiled.

CHAPTER 33

Walking into his home, Cooper was in a foul mood. It started when he saw Kelly's car, as usual, parked in the center of the garage, effectively taking up two spaces. Every light in the house was on. Both the front and back doors were standing wide open. The kitchen, however, was immaculate, so Millie couldn't have been gone for more than a few moments. Piper was likely ensconced in her bedroom Skyping with her friends, although she was supposed to be packing for a trip with her church group. Ben was sweaty, most likely from playing basketball with some neighborhood kids and was stretched out on the leather couch watching TV. There was a high probability that Domino's Pizza would soon arrive. The fact that this was a typical Friday night at the Dixons did nothing to mollify his disposition—it exacerbated it.

"Get off the couch . . . you're all sweaty. You know better than that," Cooper fussed at Ben. "Where's your mother?"

"I dunno," he answered as he slid off the couch and onto the carpet, never taking his eyes off the Nickelodeon program.

"When's the last time you saw her?"

"Uh . . . I don't remember." Ben never looked away from the TV.

"What time do you go to your overnight party tomorrow?"

"After lunch . . . I can't wait!" He replied excitedly, and then turned on his back and watched television upside down.

Cooper walked into the kitchen. He opened the refrigerator to get a cold drink and then, there not being one, slammed the door. He grabbed a glass and filled it halfway with water from the dispenser on front of the refrigerator. Cooper took a big gulp and then looked around at Millie's handiwork. Everything was clean and in place. When he was young, she had cleaned his parents' house. Cleaning really didn't begin to encompass what she did then . . . or now—she managed the household. She was an incredible woman. *Kelly could not begin to survive being a wife and mother without Millie, and yet she resented her. Probably for that reason*, he thought.

Cooper didn't know life without Millie since she had played a substantial role in raising him. The fact that she was selling him her family estate spoke volumes about his connection with her.

Pulling out his shirttail, he returned to the den to attempt a conversation with Ben. "So how was school today?" Cooper bent down to rub the family's Labrador retriever on the head.

"Fine."

"Dixie sure smells good," Cooper said, noting that when clean she was as black as coal.

"I gave her a bath. She loves it. I used y'all's tub, and Mom got *really* mad," Ben said as he looked down, embarrassed.

"Why didn't you use that big tub in the garage?"

"The water's too cold." Ben sat up and turned to look directly at Cooper and asked, "Dad, when does dove season open in Alabama?"

"In two weeks."

"Can we take Dixie?"

"I'd rather not."

"But Dad!"

"She doesn't mind me, and she wants to retrieve everyone's birds. She's a good dog; she's just not a polished retriever, and it drives me crazy."

"She's just a little hardheaded."

"More than a little. We'll hunt, just not with Dixie." Cooper paused, smiling at the thought of Dixie running around out of control. "So you have no idea where Mom is?"

"Nope."

"How 'bout 'No, sir,'" Cooper corrected.

The frustrated father stood for a few moments, watching the cartoon on television. *Wow, they sure have changed since Bugs Bunny.*

A door slamming upstairs got Cooper's attention. Piper raced down the stairs and toward the back of the house.

"Hey, Daddy," Piper called out as she tried to run past him.

"Whoa, girl." Cooper grabbed her by the shirtsleeve, stopping her.

"Where you goin' so fast?"

"My jeans are in the dryer."

"Do you have makeup on?" Cooper inquired as he leaned down to take a closer look.

"Just lipstick." Exasperated, Piper rolled her eyes.

"And some kinda war paint on your eyes," Cooper added, while Ben began laughing.

"All my girlfriends wear it, Dad."

She said, "Dad" as though it was multisyllabic. Piper had always made excellent grades. Both parents had given her some latitude to grow and express herself, but Cooper hated the thought of makeup because the next step was boys and dating.

"You don't have a tattoo . . . do you?" he asked, squinting his eyes.

"Nope, just pierced my tongue though," she said with a straight face.

"What?!" Cooper exploded.

"Just kiddin'," she said with a chuckle.

"Are you tryin' to give me a heart attack?" Cooper said with a smile.

Piper and Ben began laughing. Still chuckling, Piper ran to the laundry room.

"Piper!" Cooper hollered. "Where's your mother?"

"Next door. She went over to talk about Botox." Piper yelled from the laundry room.

"Botox?"

"Yeah. Mom was gettin' a massage today, and all the women were tellin' her that it would keep her young-lookin'," Piper explained as she walked back into the room carrying her jeans.

"Why does she need Botox?"

"It's the 'in' thing, Dad."

Cooper let out a deep sigh. Kelly was driving him crazy. He had to talk to her.

"Dad? Dad!"

"I'm sorry. What is it?"

"I need you to drop me off at Lauren's house tonight."

"I wanna go!" Ben exclaimed.

"We're goin' to the game and then watchin' movies," Piper said as she started up the stairs. "You can't come."

"Stop! Hold up those jeans," Cooper demanded.

Piper held up the pants for inspection and sighed audibly.

"Does your mother know you have those?"

"She bought 'em for me. Relax. They're in style. *Everybody's* wearin' 'em." Piper said, heavily emphasizing "everybody."

Cooper heard Kelly's heels clicking on the hardwood floors behind him at the same time she said, "Those are so cute, and she looks adorable in 'em. Besides, they were well over a hundred dollars."

"Oh. Well, why didn't you say so? If they cost a hundred bucks, then that makes 'em okay," Cooper said sarcastically, watching Piper run up to her room, knowing she intended to wear the low-cut jeans with or without his approval.

"Cooper, I swear, you don't understand jack. Just let me take care of the kids. Will ya?"

"I also don't understand why you want Botox."

"They say it makes you look ten years younger. Don't you think I'd look better without these crow's-feet?"

"I think our bank account would look a *whole lot* better if it actually had some money in it," Cooper contemptuously shot back.

"Well . . . when y'all sell our business, we'll be rich . . . and none of this will matter."

"Whattaya sellin', Dad?" Ben asked.

"Nothing. Don't worry about it," Cooper said, widening his eyes at Kelly.

Cooper was about to lose his cool, but he held it in check. Kelly just walked away. He followed her into the kitchen and watched her open a drawer, pull out the Domino's menu, and begin dialing their telephone number.

"So what are your plans for tomorrow?" he asked, trying to remain calm.

Kelly hung up the phone before it was answered. She turned around to look at him, her arms crossed. She glared and said, "I'm shopping and running errands *all day* tomorrow. But in the mornin', you're gonna need to take Piper to the church at five. I'll take Ben to his party."

"Okay. After I drop off Piper, I'm going to the Auburn game early . . . since we're takin' clients." Thinking about Brooke, Cooper lamely continued, "Ya know, I oughta help set up the tent and grill and stuff. That sorta thing."

"Sure. Whatever. Don't be too late: you've got a *long list* of things to get done around here Sunday, so have your fun tomorrow," she said, dialing the phone. "Want any pizza?"

"No. I'm gonna take a shower . . . I've had a rough day," an exasperated Cooper replied.

CHAPTER 34

The small gang was huddled in room 236 of the hotel trying to make sense out of all the ideas that were being tossed around. So far nothing was sticking.

Jesse Ray wanted to wait; he didn't think they had done enough prep to be able to safely snatch Kelly, hold her, and get away clean. Clarence appreciated the football angle and what a major distraction to the community the game would be, agreeing with Jenny that it was the perfect opportunity. Jenny was now arguing that she should go with Gates to the game in an effort to learn more about their Client's motives.

"You know that what we learn will be ten times more valuable than me driving the getaway car," she explained, directing her comments to Clarence.

"Well, who's gonna drive?" he asked.

Jenny turned to face Jesse Ray. "Do you know somebody you could call to help us?"

"Sure. I got a second cousin that lives in Dothan. He's more muscle than brains, which ain't saying much. He recently did time for stealing manhole covers for scrap."

"Doesn't sound smart," Jenny added.

"Yeah, but it does sound like he's real strong. Those things are heavy," Clarence commented.

"He told me he was gettin' only five bucks each, and he had stole about thirty before he realized it was costin' him more in gas than he was getting from sellin' the covers," Jesse Ray said with a laugh.

"Can we trust him?" Jenny asked sternly.

"With your life," Jesse Ray responded without hesitation.

"No drug problems?" Clarence inquired.

"The only drug problem he's ever had was as a kid when his gran'mama drug his narrow ass with her everywhere she went to keep him outta trouble. He hated that. Still bitches about it."

All the team laughed.

"Okay. Call him. I'll pay a thousand bucks for a week's work," Clarence offered. "But don't give any details over the phone."

Jesse Ray nodded and then began scrolling through his cell phone's address book for the number. At the last family reunion, the two vowed to work together some day. Jesse Ray hoped that he wasn't back in jail.

"Where do you think we should grab her?" Clarence asked Jenny while they waited for Jesse Ray, who had walked into the bathroom to finish his call.

"I still believe that her neighborhood is out. The mall's an option; maybe grab her as she gets outta her car."

"Too risky . . . and it sounds like the only places that she'd shop would have surveillance cameras."

Jenny paused a moment and then said, "We could put a leak in her tire, follow her, and snatch her wherever it goes flat."

"Nah. Too many variables. Keep thinkin'."

After two minutes of silence, Clarence remarked, "We could deliver a pizza and chloroform her when she answers the door."

Jenny said, "I'm tellin' ya, there's way too many eyes in that neighborhood."

Jesse Ray walked back into the room as he disconnected the call. He appeared very pleased. "We have a driver. Maynard will be here tonight."

"Maynard?" Clarence asked. "What's a Maynard?"

"That's his name. My second cousin. He'll be here tonight."

"Okay. That solves one problem. Now we gotta figure out how to get her where we want her, when we want her," Jenny summarized.

"Obviously, easier said than done," Clarence added as he bit into a cold chicken leg that he'd gotten from a KFC takeout bucket.

Everyone was quiet, in deep thought.

Jesse Ray looked back and forth between Clarence and Jenny, who were growing increasingly frustrated, and then he finally said, "Hello? What about me? We've got all this highly sophisticated electronic equipment, not to mention an electronic genius at your disposal, and you never axed me!"

"All right, Albert Afrostein, whaddaya suggest?" Clarence asked, smiling.

"While I was perusin' Cooper's endless supply of e-mails, I noticed a bunch from his wife. Since she's using a cheap ISP, I can easily hack into her account, read her address book, and then send an e-mail from one of her friends, asking her to meet someplace because she has something so secret to tell her that she can't discuss it in an e-mail or over the phone."

Clarence and Jenny looked at each other with eyes wide open. They both started smiling.

"Jesse Ray, you're brilliant. This just might work." Clarence remarked as he stood up.

"Hang on. She's gotta read that specific e-mail and follow the directions, without saying anything to anybody," Jenny cautioned.

"Oh, she'll read it. Give me an hour to worm into her computer. From what we already know about her, I'm willin' to bet significant body parts I'll find someone she e-mails that could motivate her to go *exactly* where we want her . . . at any time we choose."

"But how do you know she'll read it in time?"

"Easy. I'll profile how often she logs on, and if I need to, I'll call, posing as the customer service rep from her Internet service provider. I'll tell her we are havin' issues and that I need her to check her e-mails to make sure that they're bein' delivered. She'll do it."

"And when she types a response?"

"It'll come right back to me," Jesse Ray said, slyly smiling. "I know what I'm doin'."

They were all smiling now, thinking of what they needed to do next.

Clarence reclined on the bed with his back against the headboard, laced his fingers together behind his head, and nodded his consent to Jesse Ray. *Looks like a workable plan's comin' together*, he thought.

Jenny said, "Okay, boys, it looks like I gotta go make a date." She waved her cell phone over her head as she walked toward the door.

Jesse Ray didn't hesitate firing up his laptop. He cracked his knuckles and got busy.

CHAPTER 35
SATURDAY–THE DAY

Cooper hung a pressed shirt on the clip behind the driver's seat of his pickup. He then casually tossed a waxed cotton travel bag on the passenger side floorboard. He looked around, worried that he might be forgetting something or some detail of the story. He realized that he was being paranoid. He took a deep breath, steadied his nerves, and turned to walk inside to say good-bye to Kelly.

Last night's dream was still fresh on his mind—sitting on a sandy beach at night, with a roaring fire, while Brooke, wrapped only in a robe, walks up and sits down on a giant blanket between him and the fire. Her robe falls off one shoulder. Cooper shook his head and stepped through the kitchen door—back into reality.

Kelly was watching the Food Network in the den while she sipped a cup of coffee. When she heard Cooper's approaching footsteps, she slipped the remote control between the couch cushions.

"Do you need me to do anything before I leave?" he asked, afraid of the answer. *It'd be just like her to ask me to clean out the gutters or the garage,* he thought.

"Yeah, but go on. It'll wait till tomorrow," she replied, never taking her eyes off the television.

"Okay, then. Since it's a late game, and we'll be entertaining customers, I'm gonna spend the night rather than risk the drive . . . but I'll be home early in the mornin'," Cooper said, as casually as possible.

"Who all's going?" Kelly asked, leaning forward to set down her mug on the glass-topped coffee table.

"Uh, me, Gates, and the main guys from Lawler Chemical. That's a *big* account for us. And Gates may have invited some others from the office. I'm not sure," Cooper explained and tried to sound like it was no big deal. "Oh yeah, and he invited one of the guys from MidState Bank, but I'm not sure if he's gonna show. We hope he does. It might help us with the sale."

"Who?"

"A guy named Mark Wright," Cooper responded as he checked to make certain that he had his wallet in his back pocket.

"Seems like I've heard that name. Where would I have heard about him?" she asked, making eye contact for the first time. She then reached for her coffee.

"I have *no* idea," Cooper replied, watching someone on television panfry green tomatoes just like Millie did when he was a kid. It instantly flooded him with memories of sitting on the kitchen counter, watching her cook.

"Just curious," Kelly said and then took an obnoxiously loud sip of coffee.

Between that and chomping ice, she's buggin' the ever-lovin' crap out of me these days, he thought. He let out an audible sigh and said, "Anyway . . . I'm sure there'll be some drinkin', and

I don't want any of 'em drivin' home loaded and the agency being held responsible."

"Good ole Cooper. Always lookin' out for everyone. What hotel are y'all stayin' at?" she asked and paused a moment too long before continuing, "In case of an emergency."

Cooper swallowed hard and took an unperceivable deep breath. "Uh . . . you know, I don't know . . . Mrs. Riley made the reservations, and Gates has got all the info. Just call my cell if you need me."

"Why you leavin' so early?" Kelly asked, back to watching her show.

"I wanna go by Millie's farm. I need to get the tractor ready to start plantin' food plots. It's that time of the year, ya know," Cooper responded, hating to say anything to her about the land.

Kelly wheeled around to look Cooper dead in the eye. "It's always that time of the year. You spend more time workin' up there than you do on our house. You know the one. The one that we actually own! How many times do I have to say it? We. Are. Not. Buying. That. Land! We don't need to own any hunting land!"

"It'd be a good investment," Cooper spouted. It was his only comeback.

Kelly spun back to face the television again, indicating her displeasure with him and the topic. "We need things done around here, and this house won't last us forever. We need more room."

"What? Four thousand square feet isn't big enough?"

"Not for entertaining. Besides *I'd* rather have a beach house." She stood and without looking at him, walked to her computer, signaling that the conversation was over.

Cooper started toward the back door, yelling, "I hate sand, and *I'll* never own a beach house!"

"Your job is to supply, not demand!" she yelled in response as the door slammed.

Standing on the porch steps, Cooper realized they had contempt for each other. This was dangerous. Love could be rekindled, angers would calm, fears could be faced, jealousy could be controlled, but contempt—it was the death knell.

Cooper rushed to his truck, jumped in, and slammed the door. He hurriedly backed out of the driveway, avoiding eye contact with his gawking neighbor, who was watering his azaleas. Cooper punched the accelerator in an attempt to put both physical and emotional distance between him, Kelly, and their failing marriage. After a moment, he eased his grip on the steering wheel when he realized that he would be free for twenty-four hours and that Brooke clearly wanted him. *Tonight, my dreams are comin' true!*

CHAPTER 36

Clarence sat in stunned silence, watching Jesse Ray and Maynard interact. He moved into his own room before Maynard arrived, enabling the cousins to bunk together. This was his first time to meet Maynard Scruggs. Maynard was a skinny white guy who dressed and acted liked he was Larry King, the radio and television personality, and he had the whitest teeth that Clarence had ever seen.

Clarence had given Jesse Ray a list of last-minute details that needed to be performed, including stealing several local license plates. Jesse Ray, now with an assistant, delegated the job to Maynard and instructed him how and where to get it done.

Maynard strut out of the room, obviously thrilled to be a part of the team and repeatedly promised to deliver. Clarence really didn't doubt his skills, but he did have a few questions for Jesse Ray.

As soon as the door shut, he fired the first question, "That dude's your cousin?" Clarence looked very confused.

"Second cousin, on my momma's side."

"He's white!"

"No shit?" Jesse Ray replied, without even looking up from his computer. "I never noticed that. Is it a problem?"

"Not a problem. Just a surprise."

"Dog, he's *real good* at following directions. You'll see. His only problem is . . . as you can see . . . he thinks he's Larry King."

"What's up with that?"

"He's obsessed with the guy. Worships the dude. Anyway, Maynard was born to a real young girl. The guy that got her pregnant was some pulpwood hauler that nobody knew. At any rate, growing up, Maynard always wanted to be on the radio. He loves the radio—worked his ass off as a kid to earn enough money to buy a little portable one. You never saw him without it stuck to his head. Early one morning he called the Larry King's radio show—I think he said it was called "Open Phone America" or something like that— anyway they talked for about an hour. Since then, he's been obsessed with the man."

"And you don't think it's a little weird that he wears the same glasses and suspenders?"

"I guess I'm used to it. Like I said, he's obsessed. You should see his trailer—everything's Larry King. Even his livin' room's set up like the studio where Larry King did interviews—when you go to visit him, you don't sit on the couch and talk. You sit on his set, and he interviews you."

"What about his teeth, though? They're so . . . white."

"That's one thing about him that doesn't have anything to do with Larry King. He's just addicted to teeth-whitening strips."

Clarence laughed out loud. "And this dude's a blood relative?"

"It's a trip, ain't it? But we don't have time to get into all that," Jesse Ray said, suddenly growing interested in his computer screen. "Look at this, Dog. I already got an e-mail from our Target, just like I expected."

"No way. What's she say?" Jenny asked.

Clarence moved to look over Jesse Ray's shoulder to read the screen.

"She thinks I'm her sister, and she'll meet me at eight o'clock tonight at Vaughn Road Park." Jesse Ray smiled, gloating in his success.

"You da man! That's perfect," Clarence said and then clapped his hands.

"If you and Jenny are right, the park should be deserted with everybody watching football," Jesse Ray said.

"It will be. But just in case, we need to study these photos Jenny took to make sure we grab the right woman."

"I wanna grab her," Jesse Ray said.

"Do what?"

"Yo, Dog, I've been workin' out. I can do it. I wanna do it. You gotta let me."

For years, Jesse Ray had wanted to break out of his geek role and saw this as a chance to prove his broader value to their missions.

Clarence looked Jesse Ray in the eyes. He had an idea of what was motivating him. *Hell, why not? Kelly Dixon's just some spoiled housewife,* he thought.

"All right, but we gotta get you a wig this afternoon."

"A wig?"

"Yeah, a wig. You gotta look like a woman so you can get close without freaking her out. Ain't no tight-assed white woman's gonna let a wormy-lookin' black dude walk right up to 'em in a dark park. You'd get maced or shot."

Jesse Ray nodded. *I'll do whatever it takes, even if that means I gotta be in drag*, he thought. He smiled big.

"When Larry King gets back, y'all go wig shoppin'."

"My dear sir, I will be acquiring the whole ensemble," Jesse Ray said in his best British accent.

"Easy there, princess. Don't be overdoin' it. You don't need to look like the long-lost black daughter of the Queen of England."

CHAPTER 37

Don Daniels had two weekend-getaway properties, a cabin on Lake Martin and a small deteriorating condominium at Gulf Shores. His late wife inherited the condo, and his bank had repossessed the lake cabin. This weekend Mr. Daniels had intended to escape, alone, to his lake cabin, for quiet reflection and planning. Mark Daniels and his son, however, showed up at the cabin early Saturday morning, unannounced.

Mark's son was sleeping in the car when they arrived at the lake, so Mark roused him, and the boy followed his dad like a trained puppy. They walked down the steps to the deck overlooking the lake where his Uncle Don had been peacefully enjoying a cup of coffee.

"I thought you were going to the game with Gates," Don accused as he peered across the lake, watching a hawk soar.

"I forgot it was my weekend with the kid; plus, I didn't really wanna be around a bunch of drunks. I wouldn't have learned anything valuable from Gates anyway. We can't trust a word he says sober much less after drinkin' all day. Anyway, I thought I'd come for a visit and—"

"And what? Just what were you thinkin'? That we'd act like a normal family?" Don snapped.

"How's the blood sugar today?" Mark asked, quickly changing subjects.

"Good. It's fine. I doubt that I'll need a shot today."

Mark was Don Daniels's heir apparent, and for several years Mark confidently believed his uncle's succession plan was for him to ultimately take over; however, lately he had begun to suspect that Don was positioning the bank to be sold and that he would get completely cut out of the deal. Mark would lose out on the power and prestige that he believed was his birthright. He vowed that wouldn't happen.

Mark nodded and then offered confidently, "Well, that's great to hear. Ya know, I believe we'll hear something about the agency by the end of next week."

Don stood and motioned for Mark to follow. Mark indicated that his son should wait. The men walked out to the end of the long pier.

Don began examining some boards that needed replacing and said, "The auto plant opportunity is definitely happening. My contact confirmed it yesterday."

"You still confident that the property is gonna be exactly what they want?" Mark said, hoping to keep the conversation alive with his aloof uncle.

Don kicked a rotten board into the water with disgust and turned to Mark's son, who had slipped up unnoticed. "The thing about boards is, they never last. As soon as you put a new one down, the clock starts ticking till it's time to replace it. Boards are like people under the right forms of pressure—eventually, they all break down and go bad."

Mark stared at the rotten board in the water and then glanced at his son, who was struggling to understand what was being said. Mark could tell that his uncle was deep in thought. Mark decided to remain quiet, for once.

Don continued, "It's just like money. You can never have enough. You always have to work more, to make more, to replace what you've spent. It's a vicious, tiring cycle."

Mark watched his uncle stare off at the sky, wondering what was really going through his mind.

"They'll want the property. Believe me. Just like we knew Mercedes wanted that land near Tuscaloosa. It's set up. I've been helping and supporting politicians for years, and it's time to collect—to turn it into capital."

Mark decided to test Don and said, "Good. It's finally *our* turn." Mark glanced over to judge his uncle's reaction.

"Why don't you take him for a boat ride?" Don asked, pointing to Mark's son, indicating clearly that he was finished with the discussion. It was time for Mark to give him some space. Don looked at his nephew, handed him a life jacket, and added, "Here, put this on him."

Mark stood still, contemplating his next move. It pissed him off that he never seemed to be able to please Don.

"Take him to see Chimney Rock. Y'all need to spend some time together."

Mark glared at Don and motioned for his son to follow. The two stepped down into a boat tied to the pier. He now knew that Don was making plans that didn't include him, and it infuriated him. Don turned and started walking toward the house.

"Dad, can we go fishin'? Can we, please?" the kid asked excitedly, snapping his life jacket buckles and then hopping onto a seat.

"Just why the hell would I wanna do that?" Mark snapped as he untied the boat.

Although Don Daniels was near the shore, he easily heard the exchange. He kept pace, shaking his head in disgust. *Mark's a rotten board that needs replacin'.*

CHAPTER 38

Arriving at the property around midmorning, Cooper instantly felt invigorated by the sights and sounds of the place. Fall was approaching rapidly, and the woods were on the edge of a change. He paused at a small rocky creek and watched the clear shallow water slowly filter downstream. He loved the sense of peacefulness this place instilled as much as he detested the rushed uncertainty of his everyday existence.

Cooper's camp was an old two-room wooden shack with a dogtrot separating the sleeping area from the cooking/living area in case of fire. The shack had been in near collapse, but Cooper's hand had restored it to a marginally acceptable standard over the years. He had spent many restorative nights there during hunting seasons. It was his refuge. No phones, faxes, e-mails, or arguments. It was heaven. About the only annoyance this place had ever generated for Cooper was once when a guest shot an immature buck. Even then, he told himself it was just a deer, and he didn't allow it to completely ruin his weekend.

Millie Brown was born and raised on this land—being baptized in the creek—and this was precisely why she was willing to take less money to ensure that it remained intact and preserved. Assuring her of this was the only way Cooper would ever be able to afford a property of this caliber.

Cooper had found hundreds of old bricks with rough handprints in them. He called them slave bricks and had carefully stored them to use in a renovation someday.

Millie could not stomach the thought of the property being developed with the old house, barns, and cemetery destroyed. She had fond memories from all over the property. She would make enough money selling the land to Cooper so that she and her husband, Haywood, could retire. They would be able to live comfortably and take care of her church. She always said she personally didn't need much money, but she wanted to create scholarships for every kid in her church who wished to go to college. That's all she really wanted. Cooper often pondered the honest simplicity of her philosophy and worldview.

. . .

Cooper bounced in the seat of his new tractor and contemplated his life. Tractor time was therapy. It was nearly impossible to explain to someone who didn't share the same interests, but plowing, bush hogging, and working the land really helped him unwind. Hard work was also his massage therapy. *This tractor's my midlife crisis . . . without the big-titted, twenty-something-year-old trophy wife.* The thought made him laugh out loud as he plowed.

His desire to own this place reminded him of what Scarlett O'Hara's father said in the movie *Gone with the Wind*, "Why, land is the only thing in the world worth workin' for, worth fightin' for, worth dyin' for because it's the only thing that lasts."

The property and Brooke were both weighing heavily on him. He knew that if Brooke was at the game, she was there for one reason and he was acutely aware that right now he couldn't trust himself. He hadn't been thinking clearly when he invited her. He'd come to the realization that his body wanted more than his conscience would allow.

Cooper knew a few guys who'd had affairs. They all got caught, and most suffered bloody, expensive divorces. It wasn't the money he was thinking about, it was the toll it would take on everyone. He thought about his kids and Kelly. He had made a vow to Kelly and knew that he wasn't an every-other-weekend kind of dad—that would be unbearable.

He tried to block out his idealized image of being with Brooke and the memory of her scent. He had to get his mind off her and on to what was required to get his marriage back on course. That much he knew. The honesty of the work was helping him think straight.

Cooper smiled as he remembered when he and Kelly first married. They decided that whenever they had an argument, they would discuss the issue in the nude. That approach worked great for the first few years, but when the kids got older, it became impractical. The memory made him smile. *Those arguments never lasted long. Maybe that's what we needed to do—fight naked.*

Slowing the tractor to a stop, Cooper wiped sweat from his face. As he stared at the cloudless blue sky, he had a moment of clarity. He would distance himself mentally, physically, and emotionally from all the temptations that Brooke embodied. He briefly thought about surprising Kelly, but the smell of freshly turned dirt made him realize that he had too much work that still needed to be done. He decided that he'd stay at the camp tonight, cook a steak, and watch the game on satellite television. Cooper felt a huge weight lifting from his shoulders, and he knew that he was back on the right track.

He looked at his cell phone. He had just enough bars of service to send a text, but not enough to make a call. He very deliberately, but without going into any details, texted Brooke that he couldn't make it to the game. He considered texting Kelly but was too mentally fried to write something meaningful about their relationship, so he just slipped his phone into his pocket and shifted the tractor into gear.

As the plow bit hard into the earth, Cooper resolved to repair his relationship with Kelly. He wasn't going to let their marriage turn into anymore of a cliché than it already was. If it failed now, it wouldn't be for a lack of trying on his part.

CHAPTER 39

Clarence tried not to laugh as he watched Maynard walk forcefully into the convenience store. Maynard had on his "King specs" and was wearing a pair of too tight, faded gray jeans, held up by black clip-on suspenders. His shirt was a bright long-sleeved deep purple with a spread collar. Maynard had completed his desired look with a black and light purple diagonally striped tie, pulled tight. His natural jet-black hair was a poorly dyed, odd shade of brown.

Clarence slapped his knee and turned to Jesse Ray, who was wearing a wig and a woman's jogging suit, complete with a stuffed bra of Ziploc bags filled with creamy peanut butter. He couldn't suppress the laughter anymore and let roar, "Wow! I wish . . . oh my goodness, I wish Jenny could see y'all!"

"Yeah, well . . . the main thing is that woman ain't gonna have a clue I'm dangerous till I've chloroformed her. She'll never see me as a threat," Jesse Ray said a little too defensively while adjusting his bosom.

"It's a damn good thing it'll be dark. Otherwise, you'd scare the crap outta her."

"Look, you just get your big ass over to me as fast as you can. I won't be able to carry her very far."

"Don't you worry none, Mizz Daisy. I bees only fiddy yards away in them thar trees." Clarence chuckled. He was doing his best to impersonate the Morgan Freeman character in the movie.

When Clarence saw Maynard coming out of the store, he said, "All right, let's get this party started!"

Maynard opened the rear driver's side door of the Escalade and climbed in. He handed Clarence and Jesse Ray each a large canned drink and then fastened his seat belt.

Jesse Ray said, "What the hell's this, Cuz? I wanted Red Bull."

"Neuro Fuel. This stuff's way better than any energy drink. It's loaded with things that accordin' to what the can says, 'may increase the brain's healthy nerve function and structure to enhance coordination, intelligence, and recovery,' and the way I look at it, we need all the help we can get—might as well come in a can."

Jesse Ray and Clarence exchanged glances and opened their drinks as Clarence pulled away from the store.

Clarence said to Jesse Ray, "I wanna go over the list one more time to make sure we got everything we need."

"Whoa, shit, man," Jesse Ray replied, after taking a long pull off his drink and then turning to Maynard. "This stuff's righteous, dude!" Jesse Ray held out his fist to bump with Maynard.

"Told ya." Maynard smiled.

"Let's focus, boys," Clarence interjected and then to Jesse Ray said, "You got the chloroform, radios and earpieces, duct tape and zip ties, keys to the hideout, matching purse and shoes?" Clarence started laughing.

Jesse Ray said angrily, "Come on now, be serious," adjusting his fake boobs with both hands.

Two of the three men broke out laughing.

After regaining his composure, Clarence said, "Okay. You're right. Sorry. Tonight when you're done with those things, I wanna make a sandwich." He started laughing again. After a moment, he added, "J-Ray you've single-handedly given new meaning to PB and J!"

He then reached over to turn up the music on the car's stereo. He was feeling the rush from his plan coming together, or maybe it was the Neuro Fuel kicking in.

CHAPTER 40

Not long after Cooper had left, Kelly Dixon went to the spa, enjoying a mud bath and a facial. She returned home just in time to relieve the sitter, pick up Ben, and take him to the birthday party. Afterward, she looked at a new Suburban, loaded with every available accessory including a DVD player. Her Volvo was out of vogue. She needed something new. She envied the other soccer moms' big comfortable SUVs. Kelly promised to call the salesman next week and then headed to East Chase Mall for some power shopping.

She had $1,300 worth of clothes on the counter when she was informed that her credit card had been declined. Incredulous, she gave them another card, which was also promptly declined. Kelly Dixon was coming unglued. Several store clerks walked off to avoid laughing in her face. She demanded that they retry all the cards. Again, all were declined. Growing increasingly furious, she called Cooper.

"Kelly, what can I do? I paid the bill last week," a confused Cooper replied, wishing he hadn't answered and was surprised that he had strong enough service to talk. *Just my luck.*

Kelly walked away from the sales counter in an attempt at privacy, but the clerks could clearly hear everything she said.

"Well, obviously your sorry ass didn't. You're always forgettin' things, important things! You're gonna destroy our credit." There was venom in her tone. The clerks rolled their eyes at each other and did their best to maintain a modicum of composure.

"Kelly, I promise to you, I made payments. I didn't pay them off, but I made the minimum payments. It's gotta be some kinda computer error."

"I think you did this on purpose. You're always complainin' about me using my cards. If I find out that you canceled them, I swear to God, I will make your life a livin' hell," she whispered into the phone.

"So tell me, how would I know the difference?" Cooper passively asked, standing next to his pickup in the serene woods.

He immediately remembered his pledge to fix their relationship, regretted the words, and said, "I'm sorry, Kelly. Look, I'm sorry. I need to tell you somethin'."

"Oh, I'll tell you somethin' when I see you again. I'm just gettin' started, buddy boy. Get this card situation fixed. NOW!" Kelly punched the End button as hard as she could, jammed the phone into her purse and marched back to the counter.

Kelly forced a smile and said, "My husband thinks it must be a computer error. He's talking with them now. I'll tell you what. I'll just get the shoes and that blouse and write y'all a check." She pulled her matching wallet from her purse.

"Yes, ma'am. Don't worry, this kinda thing happens all the time," the assistant store manager replied reassuringly.

"Thank you. You've been so nice. Please hold that merchandise for me. I'll be back for it on Monday."

"Yes, ma'am," she answered and began to carefully fold the expensive clothes and label the bundle with Kelly Dixon's name.

As Kelly walked to her car, her anger with Cooper grew to epic proportions. She vowed to make him pay. When she got into the car, she slung her purchase into the backseat, cranked the engine, and sat there fuming. After several minutes of a profanity-laced, stream-of-consciousness rant about Cooper, she began to focus again. The first thing that she saw was the car salesman's business card, and a smile started to form at the corners of her mouth. She dialed the number and asked for the salesman.

With the calm that comes from great clarity, Kelly casually said, "Hey, Robert, this is Kelly Dixon. Yep, that's me—lookin' at the silver Suburban. I want it. Yep, that's right. This afternoon, if possible. Can you do that? Please check with your sales manager—he and my husband are good friends. All you gotta do is tell him that Cooper Dixon's wife wants that vehicle and that Cooper will come down Monday for y'all to work out the details."

Kelly listened patiently as the excited salesman jotted down all the pertinent information, including her cell phone number. *This'll teach him,* she thought.

"Okay, great! Just give me a call when you have it ready, and I'll bring you my car for the trade-in." Kelly smiled as she started her Volvo. "Thank you. Thank you so much. You have been very helpful. I'll be sure to tell your boss."

Kelly's spirits were lifted in less than two minutes. Revenge was so sweet, and to put the proverbial icing on the cake while she waited for her new SUV, she took a left out of the mall parking lot, heading to a high-end home furnishings store where she had a charge account. Besides a bit more shopping and picking up her new vehicle, the only thing left on her day's itinerary was a walk in the park with her sister at eight. *I can't wait to show off my new SUV . . . and to tell her another story of Cooper being a total ass.*

CHAPTER 41

S moke from hundreds, if not thousands, of barbecue
grills hung in the afternoon air around Jordan-Hare
Stadium, creating a blue-gray haze. Jenny had never
seen so many people so anxious and excited about anything,
particularly a football game. Now she appreciated Gates's
remark yesterday about why the fans and stadium regularly
make published lists of Best Game Day Atmosphere. It was
a zoo.

Jenny might have enjoyed the festivities were it not for
having to endure Gates's nonstop, totally lame jokes and stories. She took careful mental notes of everyone in and around
the Tower Agency's tent, trying to understand his or her particular role in this drama. It didn't take her too long to focus
on Brooke. They talked more or less privately for almost an
hour until she couldn't avoid dealing with Gates any longer.

Gates's hands had been all over her. She almost slapped
him once, but she decided to suffer through it. He had been
drinking for hours and was quite intoxicated. From the staring and snickering of the male guests, she knew Gates had

made up stories—bragging—about her to them. That was clearly his style. Throughout the entire ordeal, she had gathered a few facts but nothing substantive. Twice she excused herself to call Clarence. *At least everything was on track there,* she thought.

Jenny watched Gates finish another story, laugh too hard at his perceived wit, and then leave the huddle of men to go refill his drink. She glided to his side, "Y'all really know how to throw a party."

"It's always fun, especially when we play another SEC team," Gates replied, glancing down at his cell phone to check scores. "Damn it!"

"Won anything yet?"

"I'm one for three . . . so far," he answered, jamming the phone into his pants pocket.

"This is just sooo exciting. Are your buyers here?" she whispered.

"I don't think so. Not yet. I haven't seen 'em," Gates slurred, spilling his drink on his shoes. "Damn it."

Jenny was disappointed but didn't show it. She decided it was a good time to wake him up. "So, how long have Brooke and Cooper been havin' a fling?"

"What!?"

"Shh. Don't say anything." Jenny placed a finger to his lips.

"Cooper? Nah. Ya think?" Gates asked with a smirk. "No . . . not Cooper; 'sides his wife would gut him, and he knows it."

"Well, sumthin's goin' on because she and I are bein' watched. Don't turn to look. There's a man three tents down that hasn't stopped watchin' Brooke and me. He might be a cop, but I doubt it. His shoes aren't right. They're too nice. My guess is he's a private investigator."

Ignoring Jenny's request, Gates wobbled as he turned to look for the man. Turning back to face Jenny, he said, "You're crazy. Y'all two are the hottest women round here . . . hell, probably in the whole stadium area. He's just enjoyin' the view."

"I know when I'm being watched and when someone's just checkin' me out," she replied with raised eyebrows and folded arms.

Suddenly, Gates got a serious look on his face. "Okay, I'll tell you a secret."

Jenny leaned forward in anticipation.

Gates, holding his drink in his left hand, slowly moved his right outstretched arm and hand, palm up, in a broad sweeping motion, indicating everything in view, whispered, "Just so you know . . . every man here . . . no exceptions . . . wishes that they were me." Gates winked, and then after a brief moment's pause, continued, "Now . . . that's not *that* unusual . . . but 'cause you're so damn fine, you clearly up my game!"

Gates then reached over and gave Jenny's butt a squeeze. She whirled around, grabbed him by the shirt collar, pulled him close and hissed, "Look, you obnoxious asshole, in the *real world*, being a drunk ain't like Otis on the *Andy Griffith Show*. You're not cute or endearing. You're a piece of shit. And if you ever touch me again, I'll hurt you in ways you can't possibly comprehend. Am I clear?"

All that Gates could do was nod, with wide, unblinking eyes.

• • •

A few hours later, while eating a piece of grilled deer sausage, Brooke's cell phone vibrated in her pocket, indicating the arrival of a text message. When she read Cooper's note saying he wasn't coming to the game, she was crushed. She quickly typed a courteous but regretful reply and then returned the phone to her pocket. But as she gathered her purse to leave the tent, she became furious. For several days she had been excited about spending time with Cooper, and now she was near tears and livid. She was pissed off at Cooper and disappointed at the missed opportunity to further put him under her spell. Eighty-nine thousand crazed football fans were beginning to make their way into the stadium, anticipating victory. As she started walking away from the game, she began feeling a painful loss.

Jenny's plan had been to furtively slip away at halftime if she didn't get a significant amount of actionable information. The only thing of value so far was not anything factual but a strong intuitive sense that Brooke was somehow part of the conspiracy. When she overheard Brooke explaining to Gates that Cooper wasn't going to make it for the game, she could see the disappointment in Brooke's eyes and body language—Brooke's facial expression later turning to one of scorn spoke volumes. *Well then*, Jenny thought, *looks like little Miss Brooke is far more complex than I gave her credit for.*

Jenny noticed Gates start telling another joke as Brooke was hurriedly walking away, never saying good-bye to anyone. She also observed that the mystery man from three tents south had vanished. Jenny knew that this was her cue to get out of there.

CHAPTER 42

Darkness was approaching as Clarence, Jesse Ray, and Maynard arrived at Vaughn Road Park, which was basically deserted, except for an older lady walking her dog on a leash. The poor pooch didn't look like it would be able to make another lap around the mile-long path. The only vehicle in the parking area was a dark blue Honda mini-van, presumably owned by the dog-walking woman.

Clarence really liked the park's setup for this job. The trees offered adequate concealment, and I-85 was only about a half mile away. His plan to grab the Target and then hop on the interstate to quickly and easily leave the area made tactical sense.

Jesse Ray helped fit Clarence and Maynard with their radio earpieces and microphones. Clarence poked fun at Jesse Ray and pretended to flirt with him. Jesse Ray did his best to ignore him and concentrate on the tasks at hand.

"Okay, boys and girls, let's do radio checks," Clarence said not quite transitioning into the seriousness of the mission.

Jesse Ray said, "Clarence's radio name will be Big Dog; I'll be Chase Dog; and Maynard you can be—"

"Hound Dog!" Clarence interrupted.

"I like that. That's fittin'. You know, Larry's been married seven times," Maynard chimed in, pleased with his radio name.

Jesse Ray said, "Whatever." Then into his headset, he said, "Chase Dog to Big Dog, you copy?"

"Copy that." Clarence replied into his headset.

"Chase Dog to Hound Dog, you copy?"

Maynard said, "Yep, I can hear ya."

"Good. Is the volume okay?" Jesse Ray asked and watched both men nod their heads. "Could you hear each other?"

Both men said, "Yes," into their headsets and nodded again when they heard each other's voices.

"Okay. No real names, and be careful what you say. This is not a secure system. You never know who's listenin'. The system's voice-activated, so just talk low and keep everybody informed. Big Dog, here's a night-vision monocular in case you need it. Pleeezze don't leave it behind. It's expensive. Let's take off these radios for now—we don't wanna be broadcasting yet."

All of the men removed their headsets for the moment.

Maynard started opening the wrapper of a Crest whitening strip and asked, "What will we call our girl?" He pointed to the photos that Jenny had given them.

"We've been callin' her *friend* or Target, but tonight we're gonna call her the Rabbit," Jesse Ray replied, proud of his wit.

Clarence reached around into the backseat and grabbed a small black bag filled with assorted medical supplies, including premeasured syringes of Lorazepam to keep Rabbit knocked out until they were completely secure in the hideout. And if she got out of control, he would give her an IV cocktail of Lorazepam, Lidocaine, and Milk of Amnesia.

"Big Dog, how fast does chloroform work?" Jesse Ray asked, fingering a quart-sized Ziploc that contained a shop rag soaking in it.

"Almost immediate since she'll be takin' deep breaths," Clarence replied after he stowed the night-vision gear inside his black gear bag. "You sure you can handle grabbin' her?"

"Don't worry about me," Jesse Ray replied confidently.

"You sure don't look like it," Clarence said with a chuckle while looking at Jesse Ray's more than ample bosom. "Okay, listen up. Don't let her scream, and after she's out, you gotta be careful that she doesn't fall and hit her head. I don't want her to get hurt. We can't be goin' to the hospital."

"I know, I know."

"I'll be just a few yards from you, ready to carry her. Hound Dog will meet us with the truck. You'll need to make sure the back doors are open. This whole thing should take less than two minutes from start to finish. Perfect timing's required," Clarence explained, looking at each of them in the eyes. They were nodding their heads. He continued, "We have a plan, and all we gotta do is work it and to communicate. If anybody gets close and sees us, we abort, and that's okay. Am I clear? Abortin' the job is better than gettin' busted. We can regroup and reload later."

"Rabbit should be here in thirty minutes," Jesse Ray announced after checking his watch.

"All right, let's get into position. Remember, she drives a red Volvo," Clarence said.

Deadly serious, he turned to face Maynard in the back-seat. "Hound Dog, if you leave us, I'll hunt you down and hang you with those suspenders."

"Ten-fo. Stay tuned. We've gotta *great* show tonight!" Maynard replied, upbeat and in his best Larry King voice. He was thrilled to be a part of the team.

CHAPTER 43

Maynard was sitting patiently when a silver Suburban pulled in a few parking spaces away. Tapping a tune on the steering wheel, he paid little attention to the vehicle. He considered for a moment that they didn't need any witness to what was about to happen, but he didn't know what to do as he was specifically instructed not to work off script. He just sucked harder on a fresh whitening strip, which soothed him somewhat.

Kelly's plan to aggravate Cooper was executed to perfection. She left her car at the Chevrolet dealership, promising faithfully that Cooper would be down first thing Monday morning to sign all the papers. She loved her brand-new vehicle. The new car smell was intoxicating, but the smooth, tight leather seats made her back sweat until she finally figured out how to adjust the thermostat. On the way she had tried unsuccessfully to reach her sister, realizing that she would be looking for her Volvo. Kelly was certain that Cooper would blow a gasket when he arrived home tomorrow and saw the

$56,000 vehicle parked in the driveway. *Thank goodness for connections.* She chuckled as she slid out of the vehicle.

"Big Dog to Hound Dog, you see anything?" Clarence asked.

"Nope."

"Who just pulled up there?"

"Dunno. It's a silver Suburban. I can't see who it is yet."

When Kelly closed the Suburban's door, she pressed the lock button on her key chain. The lights flashed, and the horn chirped. She smiled, paid no attention to the only other vehicle in the parking lot, and began stretching her arms and back as she walked toward the path. She had decided to walk a lap or two until her sister arrived.

"The skeeters are eatin' my ass alive," Jesse Ray responded.

"It's that perfume you're wearin'," Clarence said.

"I ain't wearin' no perfume," Jesse Ray replied. He was sitting on a wooden park bench and had his legs crossed in a very unladylike fashion.

"Well, they ain't botherin' me," Clarence replied from his vantage point in the trees at the edge of the walking track, approximately fifty yards from Jesse Ray.

"That's cuz you stink," Jesse Ray whispered.

"Has anybody ever told you that you look just like Oprah? I swear, y'all could be twins," Clarence said with a chuckle.

Jesse Ray said snidely, "Well, thank you, Gayle."

"What?"

"Never mind. It's a complicated relationship."

Clarence took a deep breath trying to refocus on the job, but when he glanced again at Jesse Ray, he couldn't help but grin.

Sitting low in the driver's seat of Clarence's Escalade, Maynard stared at the blonde who was about to walk by his position. *Damn, she looks like the Rabbit,* he thought. *But there's no red Volvo?*

"Yo, dogs . . . I uh . . . I think the Rabbit's here, but she ain't in no red Volvo."

"What?"

"She drove up in a brand-spankin'-new Suburban," Maynard answered. "She just walked by me, and I swear it's her."

"We gotta be sure . . . are you sure?" Clarence asked excitedly.

"I know. She looks just like the woman in these pictures. She's walkin' toward y'all right now," Maynard said as he looked at the woman and back at the photos.

"I see her, but I can't tell shit with this monocular. You see her, Jesse Ray?"

Jesse Ray cringed that radio protocols were immediately breaking down under pressure. "Big Dog, I got her, but I can't tell for sure."

"Chase Dog, we gotta be sure," Clarence cautioned Jesse Ray.

"I know. I know. I got an idea. Hold tight," Jesse Ray responded.

"Whattaya gonna do?"

"When she gets close, I'm gonna make sure she identifies herself," Jesse Ray was confident that even if he gave her a three-second head start, he could chase her down. "Y'all just make sure the coast is clear."

"All clear in the parking lot," Maynard quickly responded.

Clarence didn't have any faith in Jesse Ray's athletic abilities but was counting on the element of surprise. He hoped that Jesse Ray wasn't going to blow this one thing that he had in his favor.

"Chase Dog . . . talk to me: what are you thinkin'? Chase?" he said in a loud whisper. "Damn it, don't do anything stupid."

"Let me think."

"Don't think. We have a plan, and we execute it. Is it the Rabbit?"

The woman was a couple hundred yards away, slowly walking toward them. Jesse Ray had decided to ask her if she was Kelly Dixon. He could say that her sister left a message. He knew it would work. *I've always been brilliant under pressure*, he thought.

"Chase Dog, I want to abort. I can't tell. It looks like her, but shit, man, I can't be certain. I can only see the side of her face," Clarence said as he studied her through the night vision. "Jesse Ray, you listenin'?"

The walking trail would bring the woman to within fifteen yards of Clarence's position. Clarence, on his knees in the dark shadows, watched her approach. It looked like her, but it was impossible to be certain. Clarence watched her punch numbers into her cell phone as she continued walking toward him.

"Hey, it's Kelly, where are you? Call me," the woman said and then ended the call.

Clarence clearly heard what she said and smiled with satisfaction. "It's her. It's her, Chase Dog. She's all yours," he whispered into his mic.

"Got it," Jesse Ray replied nervously.

Through the trees, Clarence glimpsed Maynard begin moving into the extract position just as planned. Clarence slowly rose to his feet and realized that one leg had gone to sleep. He quietly shook and then rubbed his leg, desperately trying to regain feeling.

"Coast is clear," Maynard reported.

Clarence watched Jesse Ray stretch and act as if he was just getting up from resting to continue his walk. Jesse Ray was also pretending to check his pulse on his neck while looking at his wristwatch. *Hell of an actor,* Clarence thought. The Rabbit was quickly approaching Chase Dog's position.

Kelly glanced toward the black woman but didn't pay her much attention. She would not have purposely engaged her in conversation. The woman's jogging outfit was hideous, almost causing Kelly to laugh aloud. Glancing around as she walked, Kelly looked for her sister. Kelly was the one who intentionally made people wait on her—she wasn't accustomed to the tables being turned. *Where the hell is she!?* Kelly wondered.

Jesse Ray took a deep breath as he reached into his pocket for the chloroform-soaked rag. His muscles tensed, anticipating his next move. He purposely bent over to act as if he was stretching, forgetting the wig. His left hand caught it a moment before it fell off his head. His heart raced.

Kelly walked past Jesse Ray, who was careful not to make eye contact. The moment she was a step past him, he was moving toward her, prepared to cover her face with the damp rag.

"Move!" Clarence whispered into his ear, and Maynard stepped on the gas at the same time. Clarence slowly and painfully worked himself into a position that would allow him to sprint.

Jesse Ray ran forward, and his third step crunched a piece of gravel on the concrete, causing Kelly to spin around and see him approaching. She started screaming and running. Jesse Ray leaped to tackle her. He caught only her left leg. Holding her cell phone in her right hand, she screamed and then hit Jesse Ray in the face as hard as she could. Jesse

Ray, dazed, lost his grip and screamed in agony. Kelly took off running, straight for her vehicle.

Jesse Ray's nose was on fire with pain, but he struggled to his feet and gave chase. He glanced toward Clarence who was running to assist but lost his balance and veered off course slightly. The Rabbit was now ten yards ahead of Jesse Ray, but Clarence was approaching rapidly as he adjusted his angle of pursuit to cut off the panicked woman.

For Clarence, the chase was just like running down the ball carrier when he was in college. The only attack angle, however, would force him to jump a forty-four-inch-tall park bench set in concrete. His football form instantly came back to him as he hit full speed. Upon reaching the bench, like a high-hurdler, he stretched to jump.

Maynard slid the vehicle to a stop exactly where he was supposed to be. In the darkness he could see Jesse Ray holding his wig in one hand and chasing the woman. Suddenly, he saw Clarence's jumbo frame fly through the air, crash, and skid across the dirt as if he were stealing home in the World Series. Only managing a vertical height of forty-three-and-one-half inches, Clarence's trailing foot had caught the seat back, causing him to plow face-first into the gravel.

Blocking out the pain, Clarence stood and looked to see if Jesse Ray was going to catch the Rabbit. He then quickly glanced to see if Maynard was in position.

"Maynard, come get me, we'll have to cut her off with the car!" he screamed into his microphone, unsure if it was even working after his crash. "Damn it! Jesse Ray forget her!" he said as he struggled to run toward Maynard and the waiting vehicle. Jesse Ray pulled off the Rabbit and ran to their SUV.

Maynard backed up and turned around. The tires didn't stop screeching and smoking. Maynard stopped as Jesse Ray jumped into the backseat and Clarence jumped into the passenger seat.

In a crazed voice, Clarence yelled, "Follow her, damn it!" Clarence turned around to face Jesse Ray, screaming, "I knew I shouldn't let you grab her!"

The engine roared as they raced to the parking lot.

"Go! Go! Go!" Clarence screamed at Maynard, who slid the Escalade around the corner.

"That bitch hit me with her cell phone!" Jesse Ray screamed. "She broke it on my face!"

"Shut up!" Clarence screamed, "Go faster!"

They watched the Rabbit fly out of the park from the opposite side.

· · ·

Kelly, in a state of panic, turned into the residential neighborhood instead of toward a major road. She was freaking out, thinking that she had almost gotten mugged. Not until she noticed they were following her did she comprehend fully what was happening. Her heart raced, and she tried to think of where she should go. She didn't have her cell phone anymore, and her overriding instinct was to put as much distance between her and her attackers as possible. She stomped on the accelerator.

Clarence did a quick 360-degree survey of the area. There were no cars or people outside. This made him feel a little better about what they were doing. He was hurting from the fall. Jesse Ray was bleeding from his nose and trying to reattach his wig. Maynard drove like a NASCAR champ and, in short order, they were right on the Rabbit's tail, following her through the neighborhood.

Kelly let out a blood-curdling scream when she looked into her rearview mirror at the big Cadillac SUV with three odd-looking people inside. Everything was happening so fast that she couldn't think straight. The Suburban handled much differently than her sporty Volvo. She was having trouble steering around corners and was sliding in the slick leather seats because she hadn't fastened her seat belt and didn't have time to do it now. Rounding the next curve, Kelly had to slam on the brakes to avoid broadsiding a car backing out of a driveway. The Suburban slid to a stop inches away, the headlights brightly illuminating an old couple paralyzed by fear.

Maynard slid the Escalade to a stop. Wearing a Sammy Davis Jr. mask, Clarence jumped out of the SUV with a Coke bottle of chloroform in one hand. As soon as he ran around the front of his vehicle, Kelly reversed violently, knocking Clarence into his vehicle. Shaken, but not broken, he hurriedly approached the Suburban.

Kelly opened her door to run and then saw Clarence. Immediately, she pulled her door shut. She was pinned between the old couple's car and the black SUV behind her. She frantically began pushing buttons, trying to lock the doors. Suddenly, the driver's side door was snatched open and a wet hand went over her face. She screamed and clawed until she quickly succumbed to the fumes. Her body went limp.

"Come up and help me!" Clarence screamed.

Maynard backed up and then pulled the Escalade forward until it was even with Clarence. He jumped out to open the rear hatch. Clarence carried the Rabbit like a rolled-up rug and laid her in the back of his vehicle.

Barking like a marine drill sergeant, Clarence ordered Jesse Ray to drive the woman's car. "Follow us!" he yelled, climbing into the front passenger seat. He then threw his earpiece and radio down on the floorboard and screamed, "Shit! Shit! Shit!"

Maynard jumped into the front seat and punched the gas before he even shut his door. Clarence glanced over at the old couple, frozen from the terror they were witnessing. Jesse Ray tossed the Coke bottle the Client had given them out the window and immediately followed close behind Maynard.

"Slow down. Let's not attract any more attention," Clarence said after they had gone about a mile. He yanked off the mask and threw it onto the backseat. "We gotta get on the interstate. Damn that Jesse Ray! We gotta ditch her car. Keep driving, I'll tell you where, and turn that damn radio off." Clarence was pissed. He looked behind him and saw Jesse Ray, still wearing the wig, following close in the victim's car.

"Are you okay?" Maynard nervously asked—his eyes wide as half dollars.

"Yeah," Clarence said as he shook his shirt, gravel falling onto the car seat. "I guess. Oh, man . . . I'm bettin' I knocked a kidney stone loose, though."

CHAPTER 44

Jenny set the cruise control on her Honda at precisely seventy-three miles per hour as she traveled I-85 back to Montgomery. She desperately wanted to take a shower and wash off Gates's smell and slimy paw prints. Attending the game had not been as productive or informative as she had hoped since neither Cooper nor the buyer showed. She knew Clarence would be disappointed. Her only takeaway was her conviction that Brooke was somehow involved in the job. Plugging her cell phone into the cigarette lighter port to charge, she waited for Clarence's call. As she drove, she thought through multiple scenarios of how Gates and the Client, whoever he . . . or she was, could be scheming to take advantage of Cooper. The Tower Agency was selling. That was a fact she knew.

She began running though potential setups that would net her crew more scratch for the job. Tapping her foot to the Hollies singing, "Long Cool Woman," she found her lighter and lit her first cigarette in two months. When her phone rang, she quickly turned off the radio and hit Answer. "Hey there."

"Yo, girl, where are you?" Clarence said loudly.

"Let's see. I'm, um, twenty-five miles to Montgomery, according to that sign. What's up? Is our *friend* with you?" She could tell by his voice that something wasn't right.

"Yeah, she's with us, but it wasn't pretty—not our style," Clarence said, letting out a deep sigh.

"What happened?" she asked, nervously blowing smoke out the crack in her window.

"Too long of a story and too risky to discuss on the phone. Let's just say, I broke a long-standing rule and improvised—we chased her down and snatched her out of her car, just like a bunch of lowlife hoods."

"Were there any witnesses?" Jenny asked, shocked by what she was hearing.

"A really old couple . . . but I was wearin' my Sammy Davis mask, and Jesse Ray was looking like Oprah in a cheap joggin' suit. They didn't see Larry King here . . . I don't think. I'm so pissed off I could chew nails."

"Is our *friend* restin' comfortably?"

"Yeah, and I have some shootin' muffs on her. I'm lookin' for a place to ditch her car, which, by the way, is a *brand-new* silver Suburban," Clarence said, slowly emphasizing the difference between it and what Jenny had told them.

"What? Are you positive you got the right woman?" she asked incredulously.

"Absolutely. I heard her say her name before things went to hell." Clarence added, "She's the woman you photographed."

"I haven't seen a silver Suburban, and she hasn't gone by any dealerships since I've been watchin' her," Jenny commented. "Damn! I shoulda stayed and helped y'all. I didn't get anything . . . worthwhile."

"I'm ninety-nine point nine-nine percent sure it's her. But I'll check her purse when I can."

"Good idea. Y'all be careful of surveillance cameras in all the high-traffic areas. Montgomery's full of cameras. Put down the visors, at least. What's next?"

"Go to the hotel, and wait on my call. We're going straight to our spot to get our *friend* comfortable, if you know what I mean."

"Okay. You sure I don't need to go and clean anything up?"

"I don't think so. I'll think about it and call you back," Clarence said with a sigh and a groan.

"Don't leave any trace in her car," Jenny reminded him. "Use the Clorox wipes, and wipe down every surface inside and out that y'all may have touched."

"Yeah, you're right," Clarence replied, trying to slow down mentally and focus on the details. "We will."

"I'll monitor the scanner for any chatter."

"Good. All right. I'll call," Clarence mumbled. He was barely audible.

"Are you okay? You sound terrible."

"Yeah, I'm fine. Just pulled some muscles in my back. Bye," he answered and then ended the call.

Maynard nervously sucked on a whitening strip, glancing over periodically at Clarence.

"Just drive, Larry, and let me think . . . and whatever you do, don't get us pulled over," Clarence groaned in disgust as he stared out the window.

The conversation with Jenny had made him anxious to look through the woman's purse for her identification.

It's gotta be Kelly Dixon, he thought. He knew it was. He had studied the photos. He heard her say her name. Still, a brand-new, expensive SUV created some doubt. What was really upsetting to him was that he had deviated from his plan. Clarence strongly believed that the world belonged to those with strategies, and he felt as though he had betrayed one of his core values while placing the group in danger. Clarence Armstrong feared incarceration more than anything else. He had kids to provide for, and he couldn't do that behind bars.

"Okay Maynard, turn left at that light, and go straight . . . there are some softball fields up ahead at Lagoon Park. We'll ditch her car there. There shouldn't be any cameras in the parking lot. If there are, just keep drivin'."

Clarence moved his seat back as far as it would go and then tried to straighten his legs. His back was hurting, and he had a throbbing pain in his groin. He knew he was going to be extremely sore in the morning and feel even worse the next day.

Maynard pulled into the parking lot and drove to the far end. The lot was only at about 25 percent capacity. Jesse Ray pulled in beside them.

Clarence got out with the Clorox wipes and began instructing Jesse Ray to wipe down the steering wheel and anything else he even thought about touching. "Hit the radio controls, seat controls, ignition, the door handles inside and out, rearview mirror."

Jesse Ray didn't say much. The drying blood on his face spoke for him.

"And make certain you didn't drip any blood on the seats or carpet," Clarence instructed as he rummaged through the woman's purse. He looked at her driver's license.

"It's her. I already checked."

Clarence read aloud, "Kelly Martin Dixon." He clapped his hands together, "That's good, real good. Come on, Jesse Ray, hurry up, man; let's go."

"I'm ready," Jesse Ray said as he shut the door of Kelly's new vehicle and then wiped off the handle.

"Let's roll," Clarence shouted, slamming the door to his SUV.

After everyone was back inside the vehicle, Maynard stomped on the gas, causing the tires to lightly squeal. Their passenger was still out cold.

"Slow down," Clarence barked.

"Relax, Big Dog. We had a great show tonight," Maynard said with confidence and then turned up the radio volume.

Clarence reached over and turned off the radio. He glared at Maynard and then directed his attention to the backseat. "Jesse Ray, what the hell happened? We're lucky as hell that we ain't in handcuffs right now."

"She heard me step on something and then turned to run. I think she broke my nose."

"I oughta break your freakin' neck is what I oughta do," Clarence said angrily.

"Dog, it wasn't my fault, and it wasn't my idea to chase her down."

"You're right. You're right. That was my bad. I just lost it when I saw her runnin' and thought we only had one chance to save the operation," Clarence said, shaking his head as he turned around to face forward. "I probably won't be able to walk in the mornin'," he said with a groan as he readjusted his position. "I pulled muscles that I ain't used in years." Clarence stretched, pulling his shirt out of his pants. More gravel fell onto the seat.

Maynard started laughing. "Man, you slid like a major leaguer!"

"I didn't slide on purpose, dumbass!" Clarence exclaimed, tossing the gravel out of the window. "Just get me to the hideout so that I can take some painkillers."

"Yes, sir, boss."

"Jesse Ray, keep an eye on our girl and let me know if she starts to wake up . . . and don't *ever* ask to do anything but tech stuff again. You ain't cut out for the physical side of this business."

Jesse Ray didn't respond. He knew he blew it.

A moment later when Clarence realized that he had hurt Jesse Ray's feelings, Clarence added, "You're way too smart." Even though Clarence was pissed off, he needed Jesse Ray to know that he was invaluable to the team. He continued, "We can hire muscle anywhere, but there's no way I can replace you. We need you to concentrate on what you do best. Okay? Are you sure you're all right?"

"Yeah, I'm fine. It only hurts when I breathe."

Clarence glanced at the clock and calculated how long they had been driving, and then he said to Jesse Ray, "Hand me my bag from back there."

To Maynard, Clarence said, "In a few miles, after we cross the Tallapoosa River, there's a rest stop on the top of this big hill. Pull in there, and park away from anyone. I need to give her a shot."

Clarence pulled from the bag one of the prepared syringes, rocked the liquid in the syringe, and said, "I may need some of this 'fore the night's over myself."

"Me and you both," Jesse Ray said as he felt his nose.

"We can't all be knocked out. That would only leave Larry King, here," Clarence said as he turned, looked over at Maynard, and laughed. He continued, "By the way, you did real good back there. That was some fine driving. I'm impressed."

Seeing the Rest Stop sign, Clarence slightly pressed the syringe's plunger. The small squirt of fluid ensured that there was no air inside. "Make a list of anything you need from the drugstore, and we'll call Jenny and get her to bring it to us."

"I need some teeth whitener," Maynard exclaimed, with a glowing, toothy grin as he turned into the Rest Area.

Clarence ignored the request as he steadied the syringe in his left hand and grabbed the door handle with his right. When the Escalade came to a stop, Clarence groaned, straining to climb out.

CHAPTER 45

Jenny spent the past two hours shopping for last-minute supplies before driving to the hideout. Evidently, both Jesse Ray and Clarence were in serious pain from their injuries. She was concerned about them and was anxious to hear all of the details of the night's activities. She touched her brakes after checking her rearview mirror to make sure that she wasn't being followed. The darkness reassured her, and she pressed her brakes harder turning left onto the gloomy gravel road that led to the hideout.

The gate was closed and locked, but the key was hidden right where Clarence promised. It made a low, steady creak as she pushed it open. An owl hooted, scaring the crap out of her. She quickly jumped back into her car, slammed the door, and locked it.

Gravel crunched under her car tires as she drove up to the old mansion. When she saw the house, she couldn't help but think how beautiful it would be restored, with horses grazing under the canopy of huge live oaks that nearly surrounded the home. She parked next to Clarence's SUV.

Entering the house, Jenny was immediately struck by the sight of Maynard. She had never seen anyone impersonate Larry King. His hair color was a bit off and there was more of it, but other than that, he was a dead ringer. Maynard smiled and introduced himself politely using his best King voice, teeth glowing brightly.

Through the greatest of effort, Jenny hid her surprise, saying, "Hello," and then slowly turning to make wide-eyed contact with Clarence.

"This is Jesse Ray's second cousin," Clarence explained, anxious to watch Jenny's reaction, "on his momma's side."

"Oh . . . yeah. Oh . . . huh, I guess I . . . you're not at all what I expected," she finally just came out and said it.

Clarence laughed deeply and patted Maynard on the back. "He's all right. He's a hell of a fine driver."

"Where is she? Has she woke up yet?" Jenny turned the conversation to business.

"She's in the cellar. Sedated. Jesse Ray's down there with her. I don't expect her to wake up for another couple hours."

"If you go downstairs, put on your mask. It's on the counter. I'm Sammy Davis Junior; Jesse Ray's Dean Martin, when he's not Oprah; and we got you Marilyn Monroe," Clarence replied.

"What about me?" Maynard asked.

"You're Larry King, remember?" Clarence said. "You probably shouldn't go down there just yet."

"Whatever you say, Big Dog," he answered, reaching into his pocket for a whitening strip.

"It's Mad Dog," Clarence rolled his eyes at Jenny who had to bite her lip.

Clarence turned serious and then swallowed two pain-killers. "I think everything's in order, Jenny. We just wait to see how long it takes for her to be missed and the police to get rollin'."

"I wanna hear how Jesse Ray got punched."

"He wanted to be the one to grab her, and I made the stupid decision to let him. I guess I wasn't thinking clearly," Clarence said with a sigh.

"And she wasn't in her Volvo?"

"Nope. She was drivin' a brand-new Suburban. It only had twenty-three miles on it."

"That's really odd. You're sure you got the right woman?"

"Absolutely."

"Good thing you guys were so observant."

"Larry King there recognized her from your recon photos, and if I hadn't heard her say her name on her cell phone, I'da called it off."

"I bet Jesse Ray was gung ho," Jenny cut her eyes over at Maynard. She didn't want to say anything bad about Jesse Ray in front of his cousin.

"Maynard, take a flashlight and this pistol, and go patrol the yard. Make sure the gate's locked too. You know how to handle a gun?"

"Yeah, I left it open," Jenny explained.

Maynard walked over to Clarence holding out his hand, palm up, for the gun. Clarence put the Smith & Wesson M&P compact .45-caliber semiautomatic pistol into Maynard's outstretched hand.

Maynard pointed the muzzle in a safe direction, checked the visual port for a chambered round, dropped the loaded magazine, and quickly racked the slide several times to ensure there wasn't a round in the chamber. He replaced the magazine, racked it once, chambering a round, and then slid the pistol inside his waistband at the small of his back.

"So . . . I guess that answered that question," Jenny remarked admiringly.

"You expectin' trouble, Big Dog?" Maynard inquired as he picked up the flashlight from the table.

"Well . . . let's see, we just kidnapped a woman, that's a felony, and we have her sedated in the basement, which is probably another felony as well, so yes and no. I'm not expectin' trouble, but you can bet your ass it's out there looking for us. So go lock the gate, and keep your eyes peeled. Make sure you got your phone with ya. When Jesse Ray gets back up here, he'll get us all set up with walkie-talkies. Until then, you'll have to use your cell. And my name's not Big Dog!"

"Gotcha," Maynard said as he walked toward the kitchen door.

CHAPTER 46
SUNDAY—DAY 1

Maynard was carefully leveling the fourth cinder block when Jenny's curiosity finally got the best of her. She had tried to get a catnap on the couch, but Maynard kept shuffling in and out, disturbing her.

"Just what in the hell are you doin'?" she finally asked, smiling at Maynard's enthusiasm.

Maynard was startled. He had thought she was asleep. "Uh . . . well . . . uh—"

"Maynard, what's with the cinder blocks?"

"Oh, I'm just buildin' us an entertainment center. All I got left to do is bring in the boards. I'm just tryin' to make it more comfortable in here."

"Good thinkin'." Now wide-awake, Jenny really wanted to hear this guy's story. "So, tell me about yourself."

Maynard was thrilled that Jenny was talking to him. She was the most beautiful woman who he had been with in the same room. He was more than a little nervous. "I'm Jesse Ray's cousin, by marriage . . . on his momma's side. And, well, I do a little business back home, but I'm pretty much a low-key operator."

"Whatcha got goin'?" she asked.

"Well, I just got off house arrest; it's a long story, and it wasn't my fault. Anyway, I've been workin' a project from home. I managed to acquire a case of Subway frequent-buyer cards and matching stamps. I've been sellin' the cards . . . you know, the ones where eight stamps get you a free sandwich? At any rate, I'm sellin' the cards on eBay, five for five dollars."

"You gotta be kiddin' me?"

"Nope. It's a sweet deal. Five cards are worth like at least twenty bucks. It's *real* easy money, especially when I couldn't leave the house."

"That's amazing," Jenny said. She didn't know if she was more surprised that someone would steal Subway coupons or that someone else would actually buy them.

"And Jesse Ray's got some really sweet e-mail scams goin' that are generatin' good money. I just don't know how to do all that computer crap."

"Me neither." She paused for a moment and then said, "It appears that you're a fan of Larry King."

"Are you kiddin'? He was the king of talk. I love him," Maynard said. "I'd straddle a mile of barbwire naked to listen to one of his radio shows over a pay phone."

Jenny smiled big, thinking, *He may not be the brightest bulb in the box, but he knows how to handle a weapon, he's got heart, and he sure tries hard at everythang else.* She said, "I'm not really a fan, but I use to watch some nights when I couldn't sleep."

"Wow, so you *did* watch him?" Maynard glowed as he felt around inside his pocket, eventually finding a whitening strip.

"Yep, I watched him a lot when Michael Jackson died. So, what's next after this job?" she asked and then her attention shifted to Clarence limping into the den, holding his back. "You all right?" she asked, standing up.

"I don't know . . . my lower back's killin' me, and my groin's throbbin' like a sumbitch," Clarence groaned and leaned against the wall. "I know that's more information than you wanted . . . but you asked."

Jenny raised her eyebrows and scrunched her nose.

Maynard shivered and then headed outside, presumably to finish construction of his entertainment center.

"If I could just get comfortable, I'd feel a lot better," Clarence winced as he stretched. "You heard anything from her?" Clarence motioned at the door in the kitchen.

"No, not a peep," Jenny said, looking at her watch. "When we sedate her again in a coupla hours, I want to go down."

"Fine. When Jesse Ray wakes up, let's have a meetin' and make sure we got all our shit in one sock. What's Larry doin', anyway?" Clarence asked, stretching his back again.

"Some interior decoratin'. I think he's goin' for some kind of a redneck low-budget effect."

Clarence groaned.

Jenny tried to take his mind off the pain by asking, "So whaddaya think of Maynard, anyway?"

"He's okay. He's just got planet issues."

"Meaning?"

"He ain't been on this planet long enough to understand some things."

"I can see that," she responded. *I think Maynard's kinda cute, but I'd never be able to tell Clarence that.*

"I tell you what, though, that guy would stack greasy BBs if I asked him to."

"You do gotta love his attitude . . . and his teeth," Jenny commented.

"Yeah, he's addicted to teeth whitener. It beats anythin' I've ever seen; they freakin' glow in the dark."

"You hungry?" she asked, wanting to keep the conversation moving.

"Not at all . . . I don't think I could keep it down."

"Wow, you must be really hurtin' bad," Jenny remarked, now deeply concerned.

CHAPTER 47

Ben did not realize that his mother wasn't home. He and his buddy's mom, who was dropping him off after the overnight party, assumed that her car was inside the closed garage. He had his sleeping bag in one hand and a small duffle in the other as he walked up the side steps to the house. He waved, and she started to back up. After ringing the bell twice with no one answering the door, he impatiently grabbed the key from under the secret rock and let himself in. His ride home took off out of the driveway upon seeing Ben open the door.

Tossing his bag on the den floor, he switched on the television and manually tuned into the Discovery Channel.

"Mom?! Dad?! I'm home!" he screamed, plopping down on the couch. Ben hadn't gotten much sleep at the party, and his tired little body welcomed the solitude. It wasn't long before he was sound asleep.

• • •

Cooper left the Promised Land refreshed. With each passing mile, however, an uneasy feeling began creeping in, and then it hit him full throttle as he was filled with more thoughts and conflicting emotions than he could process. He had willingly and eagerly walked right to the edge of an abyss with Brooke. He now knew how easy it would have been to cheat. If he had gone to the game and Brooke was there, it would have happened. He felt it in his bones.

Cooper's thoughts jumped to his parents. *No way was there even the hint of infidelity in their relationship.* They sometimes joked that they stayed together to make each other miserable, but the truth was they had been very happily married for forty-five years. *How'd they do it?*

Knowing that when he left Kelly yesterday he had actually planned to break his marriage vows was haunting him. But for that moment of clarity while riding his tractor, he would have destroyed not only himself but also his family and his relationship with his children, if not their own value systems. *I'm such an idiot! Lord, please, please forgive me. If my marriage is over, then I need to make it real. I gotta man up about this. No more dancin' around it!*

Sundays were usually peaceful and easy for Cooper, but not today. His stomach was in a knot. He plugged in his cell phone charger and dialed home. No one answered. That really didn't surprise him. He knew the kids were out and that Kelly could be walking or in the shower getting ready for church.

Setting the cruise control on seventy, he then dialed Gates, hoping that he had made it back to his hotel without any problems. He listened to it ring five times and then someone picked up but didn't say anything right away.

"Gates?"

"Umm hmmm," an unsteady voice replied. "Yeah? Hello?"

"Gates, it's Cooper. You okay?"

"Yeah, man. My head's killin' me though. Whew. What a night, what a game. Where the hell are you?"

"I'm headed back to Montgomery. Do you need me?"

"No, dude, I'm okay . . . I just haven't gotten up yet."

"Everything go smoothly last night?"

"Naw. My date ditched me before the game even started, that bitch . . . so did Brooke, but the Lawler boys had a big time anyway."

"Brooke left early?"

"Yep, and she was smokin' hot too. Shoulda seen her! Damn. Man, she was *extremely* disappointed when she found out that you couldn't make it."

"Thanks for takin' care of her, and I appreciate ya entertainin' the guys."

"No problemo. So you and Brooke got a little sumpten goin' on?"

"No."

"You sure?"

"Of course, I'm sure. Why you askin'?"

"Well, it was kinda awkward when Kelly called lookin' for you last night, right before kickoff."

"Really!?" Cooper asked, surprised she hadn't tried calling his cell phone.

"It kinda felt like she was checkin' up on you. I told her that you weren't here yet but that you were on the way."

Cooper didn't want to explain his mess to Gates, so he simply said, "Okay. Thanks buddy. That's fine."

"Then, get this, she asked if Brooke was there. By name."

"What?! Shit! Really? What did ya say?"

"I said she was there but had just gone to pee. Dude, look, if I need to be coverin' for ya . . . you gotta give me a heads-up."

"No, it's nothin' like that. Thanks. I'll see ya in the mornin'."

Cooper ended the call. His stomach was suddenly in a painful knot. He was now dreading two conversations with Kelly that he had to have very soon. He tried again unsuccessfully to reach Kelly. *This sucks!*

CHAPTER 48

The Client snuffed out his cigarette and grabbed the television remote control. He waved it around, bouncing the beam off a wall behind him as he impatiently flipped through the news channels. He didn't really believe her disappearance would be on TV so soon. Maybe tonight the story would start to get some local traction. By tomorrow, it could be statewide, front page, above the fold, lead television news story, news. With a little luck it would be a slow national news day and the networks or national cable news outlets might pick up the story; he craved CNN or Fox News coverage. *Oh, the damage they'll do,* he thought and laughed aloud.

Lighting another cigarette, he strolled down the hall to his secret room. He unlocked the door and then walked inside. For a moment, he stood in the dark, the only illumination coming from down the hall, staring at the flat-screen monitors hanging on three walls. He clicked on the master remote, and each screen popped to life and thus began the synchronized electronic shrine built for his obsession. He

shut the door. Thousands of high-resolution, digital photographs and video clips looped continuously. Each photo
or clip materialized, shone vividly for eight to fifteen seconds before fading and being randomly replaced. Neatly surrounding all sides of the monitors was a vast collection of
necklaces, earrings, panties, and even a few tufts of human
hair. Very little of the walls were visible.

The Client would sit for hours in the center of the room,
watching the screens and staring at his treasures. Doing so
gave his life purpose. Focus.

He sat down in the vinyl-covered chair, soaking into his
demented brain all the sights, smells, and textures. *My plan
can't fail. I'm so much smarter than all those idiots out there*, he
thought.

The Client leaned back his head and closed his eyes. He
knew he should rest, but he was far too jacked up on crank.
He hadn't slept in days. He switched the monitor directly in
front of the chair to television mode. To the right side of the
main image, which was tuned to CNN, a picture-in-picture
column of eight other of his favorite news stations played.
The monitors to his left and right were devoted to the slide
and video show.

Sitting inside the room, he monitored a state-of-the-art,
handheld digitally trunked police scanner that was connected
to an external antenna. So far, there had been no interesting
chatter. He had received one phone call from his hired man
who reported everything was in play but provided no details.
After hanging up and having a bump of coke, he became
eager for details of the mission.

To satisfy himself, he sprayed a mist of her perfume into
the air and inhaled deeply. After placing stereo headphones
on his ears and cranking up the volume to "their song," he
leaned back and stared deliriously around the shrine. *Not*

much longer, and she'll be mine, he thought and believed it to be true a few minutes later.

CHAPTER 49

Obviously, Clarence was in excruciating pain. He grimaced and groaned almost every time he moved, but he could not be still. His forehead was covered in sweat. He tried sitting at the table but couldn't get comfortable, so he paced the floor.

"Dog, you look like shit," Jesse Ray offered as he sat down on a cheap folding chair.

"You don't look so great yourself," he said with a grunt.

Maynard was eating Fruit Loops from a Cool Whip bowl. He had just finished an hour of jail cell exercises. Jenny had stolen a few glances at him doing push-ups shirtless, but at the moment she was worrying about Clarence.

"Let me take you to the ER. Clarence, you gotta get checked out," Jenny insisted. "It could be serious."

"I'm okay."

"Are you sure?"

"Yeah. I'll be fine." Looking at the group, Clarence said, "Okay gang, pay attention. Here are the rules. The basement door lock *never* comes off unless we're goin' down. We always wear our masks. Always. We re-dose her before she regains consciousness. She won't remember much, if anything, if we do it that way. Two hours a day we will let her come to just enough to eat, drink, and use the toilet. We'll keep her in fresh Depends, to be safe. We gotta check her diaper every time we dose her. Change her and clean her up, if necessary. It ain't fun, but it's important to keep her from gettin' an infection. The supplies are all laid out. Put dirty diapers inside the five-gallon bucket. It's got odor-killin' plastic bags inside, and the lid's airtight. Whenever she's awake, even a little bit, we make her think her husband's behind all this. Jesse Ray's got scripts for everybody. Got all that?"

Everyone nodded their agreement or said, "Yep."

Clarence went on, "Cool. She'll stay very groggy when she's awake, but it's vital that we feed her and make sure she keeps peein'."

Clarence turned to look directly at Maynard to emphasize to him his next point, "She is not, for any reason, to be allowed up here. If somethin' happens and she tries to get away, do whatever's necessary to stop her from comin' through that door . . . short of killin' her. Shoot her if you gotta, but don't kill her."

Maynard nodded and said, "Got it."

"Jenny, at least twice a day check her vital signs and keep records. We can't let her crash," Clarence explained.

"I can handle that. But I can't take care of all her personal needs by myself. Y'all don't skip doin' any of it, waitin' on my shift," Jenny said, looking at Jesse Ray and Maynard.

"They better not skip any part of this," Clarence stated firmly. "I got the drugs premeasured. The syringes are in the mini-fridge. Each dose should work every four hours."

"Just tell me how to do it," Maynard responded as he inserted a whitening strip.

"As long as I don't have to wrestle her . . . I'm cool," Jesse Ray said as he touched his nose and grimaced.

"Good. We'll keep one room at the hotel as a base. It'll be nice to have hot showers that don't smell like egg and beer farts. This place ain't exactly up to my standards. It gives me the creeps, and I'm pretty sure if we look around, we'll find white hoods somewhere."

"I agree," Jesse Ray added. "I think this place is haunted."

Clarence continued, "Let's keep Jenny's room. She has the better excuse for an extended stay. We'll work shifts to monitor the news, scanners, and take care of our girl. We keep all the vehicles in the barn, and Jenny you gotta shut the gate when you come in. Okay? No excuses. The gate stays closed. Jesse Ray's gonna set up wireless surveillance cameras at the gate. And Jesse Ray, I want you to devise a couple of alternative evacuation routes and plans."

Everyone nodded.

"Maynard, I'm gonna let you stay on at a grand a week. But you gotta do whatever we ask, me or Jesse Ray or Jenny . . . immediately with no questions asked."

Maynard looked at Jenny with hope in his eyes. "You got it."

"Don't be holdin' your breath there, Larry King," Jenny said.

"The kidnappin' should start gettin' some airtime in the next coupla days," Clarence explained, with a grimace. "Oh yeah, if somethin' goes wrong and we gotta blow outta here, everybody's on their own. We'll meet back up at the Pink Pony four days later, at noon. No communications between us until then. And while we're here, be very, very careful what you say on your cell phones."

CHAPTER 50

Cooper stood in the doorway of his bedroom, frozen, looking at the perfectly made bed. After a moment he swallowed hard. The condition of the bed was a dead giveaway that she had not been at home last night. In twelve years of marriage she had never made up the bed. A knot began to grow in his stomach, and his head began to spin. *Maybe she jumped to conclusions about me and Brooke.*

He went downstairs to talk to Ben. "Mom wasn't here when you got home this morning?"

"No, sir," he answered. "Well, I don't think so. I yelled for her when I came in."

"What time was that?" he asked, staring at the clock.

"I dunno . . . I've watched two cartoons, so an hour? I'm hungry."

"Okay . . ." Cooper said trying to think. "Uh . . . how about a waffle?" He was basically on automatic pilot.

"Can you put 'em in the toaster?"

"Sure," Cooper answered as he began pacing the floor. He didn't have any idea where Kelly could be. *Church, maybe.*

Maybe something had happened to Piper. That thought compounded his worry. He raced to the kitchen portable phone and hurriedly dialed Kelly's cell phone number. He placed the receiver to his ear and listened to it ring. The announcement stated that she had either turned off her phone or traveled outside of the service area.

Cooper sat down, telling himself to remain calm, to think through potential scenarios. After a few moments of staring at the floor, he decided to call her sister. Maybe she would know Kelly's whereabouts.

Cooper reached for the phone book to look up the number. Donna was four years older than Kelly, and they were very close. She would know if Kelly had done anything crazy or if anything had happened to Piper. Cooper liked Donna, but she was in her third marriage and resented Cooper and Kelly's affluence.

"Hello?"

"Donna, it's Cooper," he said, trying to stay calm.

"Hey, Cooper," she responded as she turned down the volume on the TV.

"Do you happen to know where Kelly is?"

"Nope. I haven't talked to her in a couple of days. Last night, though, she left me a strange message saying that she was at the park waitin' on me. Like we had plans or something. We didn't make any plans," she explained. "I tried to call her back but never got her."

"What park?"

"I assume Vaughn Road; we walk there sometimes. What's goin' on? Is everythin' all right?"

"I don't know. I spent the night at the huntin' camp, and when I got home she wasn't here. And I don't think she slept in our bed last night."

"She hasn't told me of a boyfriend, if that's what's going

through your mind," she said with a trace of sarcasm.

"No, not at all. Why did you say that?"

Ignoring the question, Donna asked, "What about Ben?" She furrowed her brow at the thought of Kelly not being at home last night. Sitting up, she clicked off the television.

"He's here; he spent the night at a friend's house, and they just brought him home. Piper's on a church trip, maybe something happened to her, and Kelly went to get her?"

"She would've called you if something had happened to Piper . . . wouldn't she?"

"I'd hope so, I mean yeah, I'm sure she would have."

"Obviously, you've tried her cell phone?"

"Yeah, no answer," he replied, hanging his head.

"What time's Piper due back?"

"I don't know for sure . . . I could call the church or some of her friends' parents," he said, exhaling deeply. His lack of knowledge of his daughter's activities was inexcusable. It hit him like a train. He had been so preoccupied thinking of Brooke, he hadn't bothered to ask. He said, "Oh, God!"

"Find out, and call me back." Donna wrapped her robe around herself and headed to the bathroom. She continued, "I'm gonna get dressed in case you need me."

Cooper sat down at the kitchen table and with shaking hands flipped through the phone book, looking for their church's number. He didn't have a good feeling, and he certainly didn't like the possibility of Kelly thinking he was cheating last night. *How the hell did she even know about Brooke,* he wondered and worried.

CHAPTER 51

Donna pulled into the Dixon driveway and sat in her car, trying to remember if she had ever been to their house when Kelly wasn't home. She couldn't recall one time. She left her keys in her car, walked to the front door, and without bothering to knock, walked inside. Cooper met her in the foyer.

Ben ran up and hugged her, "Hey, Aunt Donna. Whaddaya doin' here?"

Before she could answer, Ben looked past her, through the open door, to see several of his buddies waiting on him outside, tossing a football around. The enticement was more than he could bear. He pulled away and dashed outside without another word.

Donna could tell that Cooper was distraught. She hugged him out of genuine concern. Even though Donna harbored a misdirected resentment, she and Cooper had gotten along fairly well. She was the black sheep of her family and constantly at odds with them. Cooper considered her an adventurous free spirit. She perceived him to be the only man who could tolerate her sister. There was an unspoken mutual respect, at some level, for each other.

"Thanks for comin'," Cooper said in a low voice as he nervously ran his fingers through his hair.

"Sure. So tell me what's goin' on."

Cooper leaned against the end of the couch and said, "She won't answer her cell phone. She hasn't been home since she dropped Ben off at the party . . . I did talk to her sometime yesterday afternoon, I don't remember exactly when, but she was really pissed at me because her credit card was denied and she blamed me."

"Piper's okay, right?"

"Yeah, she'll be here about four," Cooper added, noting the time was 1:11 p.m. The last several times he had looked at a clock, the numbers had been all the same. "I can't imagine where Kelly could be," he continued. "I'm so relieved that Piper's all right. But I can't imagine what's goin' on with Kelly. Where she could be or that she's still so pissed off at me that she won't answer her phone?"

"She coulda dropped Ben off, headed to Birmingham to do some shoppin', spent the night at the Wynfrey, and is headed home now," Donna said confidently.

"But why won't she answer her cell?"

"Maybe her phone died . . . you know, the battery's fried . . . or the service has been cut off. Did you pay the bill?"

"She pays that bill, and that's not it." Cooper shook his head slowly, turning over the facts he knew, with what Donna was suggesting.

"Okay. Let me try callin' her again on my cell," Donna suggested, reaching for her phone. As she dialed, she smiled at Cooper. "Maybe this'll teach you to pay your credit card bill on time," she said as she shook all her hair to the right side exposing her left ear. "It's ringin'."

Watching his sister-in-law's face, Cooper finally asked, "Is it still ringin'?" He had a hopeful tone to his voice.

"No, it says she either has it turned off or has traveled outside the service area," Donna said slowly, folding her phone and staring at Cooper.

"My credit card was also denied yesterday when I tried to buy gas. I had to use my business card," Cooper explained. Letting out a deep sigh, he rubbed his face with his hands. "She was *pissed* . . . I mean *really pissed* when she called me yesterday."

"It seems that lately she's always angry at you for somethin'."

Deep in his own thoughts, Cooper didn't hear Donna's remark. He stated, "If we haven't heard from her by the time Piper gets here, I'm callin' the police."

"Have y'all been fightin'?"

"What? No. Not really. Not any more than usual."

"Are you tellin' me everything? I know something's up. Are you tellin' me all you know?" she asked, squinting her eyes.

"What are you talkin' about?"

"I talked to Kelly the other day, and she was pretty upset."

"Upset about what?"

"This is really between y'all, and I don't want to get in the middle of it."

"Well, you are now, so just tell me!" Cooper pleaded.

"You've been talkin' in your sleep. Enough to wake Kelly up."

"Talkin' in my sleep?"

"Yep, and you were talkin' about another woman," she answered with a disgusted look.

Cooper was shocked and didn't know what to say. "This isn't what you're thinkin'."

"Believe me, I know how it can be. But like I said, this is between y'all. You need to work it out with her."

"Good grief," Cooper responded, burying his face in his hands.

"So for the last week or so, if you've done anything stupid, she probably knows. I bet she hired a private detective. She was thinkin' about it."

"Well, I haven't done anything wrong, that I can think of," Cooper instantly replied, thinking about his lunch with Brooke.

"Well, I'm glad to hear it. You're good for each other. I want y'all to work this out."

"Thanks."

"I'll ride around and check on a few places she could be. I'll be back shortly. It won't take me an hour."

"Yeah, that's a good idea."

"I'll write my cell phone number down and stick it on the refrigerator. Call me if she shows up," Donna explained as she headed toward the kitchen.

"You okay, Coop?" she asked, stopping to look closely at him.

Cooper paused for a second before answering, "Yeah, I just don't know what to do."

"You kinda got that deer-in-the-headlights look."

"I feel like it."

"Just stay here; she'll call or just show up. Please call me if anything changes."

"I will. Thank you so much for everything. I'll call as soon as I know anything."

Donna left, and Cooper tried to imagine what he could have said in his sleep and then remembered the dreams he'd been having at work. "Shit!"

He had to talk to Kelly. The edges of guilt were beginning to creep in. *How in the world could she have known what I planned last night? Though, she did ask a lot of questions before I left, which was a first. Was she just fishin'? Would she have just run off?*

Cooper needed to know. He had been the good guy all his life, never even thinking of straying. His stomach lurched as the gamut of emotions and images coursed through him. This was a new, very unpleasant experience. He ran into the half bath under the staircase and vomited.

CHAPTER 52

Jesse Ray finished putting the last of his electronic fortress into place and then spun his hat around backward as he sat down to synchronize everything from his command center. His laptop glowed, awaiting action. He methodically clicked a few buttons and adjusted the contrast on the LED monitors. A state-of-the-art surveillance camera was trained on the sleeping woman. He had wireless, unattended ground sensors strategically placed around the house that would cue a camera to take a wide field-of-view image of intruders in all light conditions and immediately transmit the image to him. He also had constant-on video cameras covering the obvious entry points onto the property and into the house. Jesse Ray felt confident of his work and leaned back in his chair with his arms folded across his chest.

"Hey, Cuz . . . uh . . . can I ask a question?" Maynard asked, popping the top on a cold beer.

"Sure," Jesse Ray replied as he carefully attached the phone line into his laptop.

"What happens if the electricity goes out?" Maynard asked, scratching his head.

Jesse Ray touched his chin with his index finger as if he were pondering the question. "We are screwed. We only got battery backup for about fifteen minutes."

"That's what I thought, so I've been workin' on some protections myself. They ain't as high-tech as yours, but they work."

"No shit? So whatcha got, some strings with cans tied on the ends?"

Maynard set his beer on the counter. He needed his hands to talk. In that respect, he was like a Southern preacher, hand-cuffing him would be the same as putting a gag in his mouth. "Well . . . I found some boards in the barn, and I drove a bunch of rusty nails through 'em, so they all stick out on one side, and I placed 'em under all the windows. Sharp side up."

"You thought of that?"

"Seen it in a movie. Somebody sneaks up on us and tries to look in the windows . . . we'll hear 'em scream . . . and we'll find 'em stuck to a board."

"I hope we ain't gotta jump out the windows."

"Iffin you gotta, jump as far as you can," Maynard said flatly, after taking a big swallow of beer.

"You better tell everyone about them boards, 'cause I don't think Mad Dog has any tetanus shots in his medical kit," Jesse Ray suggested as he watched Jenny bound through the back door. "Where you been, girl?"

"I was lookin' around in the barn. Somebody is visiting the place pretty regularly."

"Shit, I can't imagine why? This freakin' place is spooky."

"Well, there are fresh footprints around the barn, and they're too small to be Maynard's."

"I don't like this place . . . I got bad vibes." Jesse Ray shook his head.

"Well, this gig will go to hell if somebody shows up. They might be making meth and that *really* ain't good." Jenny continued explaining, "Meth heads are bat-shit crazy. You can't predict a thing about their behavior."

"I feel ya. I'll go put up some cameras and ground sensors. Come on, Maynard. Grab my toolbox and that extension cord."

Maynard did as directed, and the two men started out the back door.

As their voices slowly drifted away, the door to Clarence's room eased opened. A moment later, he hobbled out wearing black boxers and a white T-shirt.

"You look like hell," Jenny said, reaching into the refrigerator for a bottle of water.

Clarence strained to reply, "I feel like it." He grimaced in pain and stretched to sit down in a chair in front of Maynard's entertainment center. Jesse Ray had set up a satellite television dish that picked up every station except local channels. Maynard had found a black-and-white television in a closet upstairs and added aluminum foil to the rabbit ears, allowing the NBC and Fox affiliates from Montgomery to come in, albeit fuzzy.

Jenny held the cold bottle to her forehead. The old plantation house was hot inside despite fans running in every room. The AC window unit in the den had not stopped running since they arrived—only suggesting the air was conditioned.

Clarence groaned again and then said, "Jenny?"

She knew he was serious about something. He rarely called her just plain Jenny. "Yeah?"

"I think you need to take me to the hospital. I got a kidney stone."

"Oh shit. Are you serious?"

"Yeah . . . I'm hurtin' . . . and I've been pukin'."

"Okay. There's a hospital just two exits down from
Vaughn Road Park."

"I hate it . . . but I'm really hurtin'. Tell the boys. We'll
sedate the girl again, and then you and I can go."

"You got insurance?" Jenny asked trying to think ahead.

"Yeah, but I don't wanna use it. I don't want any record
of me being up here. I got cash," he answered in a strained
voice, "and even if I didn't, they gotta help."

CHAPTER 53

Piper came dancing into the house, white wires hanging from her ears. She had her iPod in one hand and a
travel bag in the other. Cooper and Donna met her in
the foyer. Cooper and Piper hugged briefly, and before Piper
had a chance to say anything to her aunt, Cooper asked if she
knew where her mother might be.

Piper looked at him in a strange way, and then at Donna
and shook her head. "What's wrong?" she asked, dropping
her designer bag.

"We don't know, babe. Nobody has seen her today. She
wasn't here when we got home."

Cooper and Donna glanced quickly at each other. A
wave of fear shot through his body. He uncrossed his arms
to rub his unshaven face. He needed to call the police. He
dreaded it. It was acknowledgment of what was going on and
what it might mean.

"Go unpack your bags, and put away your clothes,"
Cooper gently instructed. He needed to keep her busy while
he called the police.

"Yes, sir," she replied, recognizing the serious tone of his voice.

Cooper watched her run up the stairs. He turned and made eye contact with Donna. He let out a deep breath.

"You need to call, Coop. She may have been in an accident. Do you know anybody on the force?"

"I met a policeman at the Lions Club a year ago . . . what was his name?" he replied, rubbing his forehead. "I don't know. I'll just call."

"Tell them what's going on. They'll know what to do."

Cooper nervously walked into the kitchen and picked up the telephone. He hesitated, almost dialing 911 before he realized what he was doing. He had never called the police before. Searching the phone book, he found the number.

Donna sat down at the kitchen table, watching Cooper dial the number and wait for an answer.

"Yes, ma'am. My name's Cooper Dixon. I . . . uh . . . I live here in Montgomery, and my wife is missing."

"How long has she been missing, sir?"

"Well, I don't really know . . . I just realized it this morning, but something could of happened last night."

"Sir, normally we can't do anything until twenty-four hours has passed. Would it be safe to say that she has been missing that long?" the officer asked.

"I really don't know . . . I was also wondering if maybe there was a way to check with the hospitals and see . . . if maybe . . . you know, she was in an accident."

"Yes, sir, we can do that. Let me get some information from you, and I will dispatch a unit to your house to gather additional details."

"Thank you, ma'am."

"No problem, sir," she responded professionally. "Now, let me ask you a few questions."

Cooper sat down at the table across from Donna and answered the police officer's questions.

CHAPTER 54

Clarence rode in the front passenger's seat of his Escalade, with the seat fully reclined. In his hands was a plastic trash bag in case he needed to throw up again. The big man writhed in pain and grunted in agony each time Jenny hit a bump.

Jenny asked, "So how many of these stone things have you had?"

As she drove, she blindly searched her purse for a cigarette.

"Too many . . . three for sure. My pops had 'em too. It runs in the family. Damn girl! Are you trying to hit *every* pothole in the road? 'Cause I think you missed one back there."

Jenny ignored his sarcasm. "Are you worried about giving the hospital your name? Establishing that we were here?"

"I'm not. I'm gonna give 'em a fake name and address and say that I don't have any ID because I lost my wallet at the Auburn game. I'll pay with cash."

"I dunno."

Jenny cracked her window and then lit a cigarette.

"Everythin' gonna be fine. I'm positive. When did ya start smokin'?"

"I only do it when I get nervous," she said through tight lips, taking a drag. "Do you think you'll have to spend the night?" She blew smoke out the window and then reached over to adjust the radio to find a local news broadcast.

"Did you hear if State won yesterday?" Clarence asked.

"Yep, they did. Gates was pissed 'cause he bet against 'em."

"That's my boys."

Clarence tried to vomit but couldn't. Jenny lowered the air-conditioning thermostat and turned the blower to high. She sped up just perceptibly and blew another stream of smoke toward the cracked window.

"I shouldn't have to spend the night. I just need some heavy-duty-no-shit painkillers, and I'll be okay. Don't worry, everything's gonna be fine . . . once they drug my big ass," he groaned. "I just gotta get some relief . . . quick."

Jenny didn't believe that a simple prescription was going to solve his problems. He looked horrible and was obviously in a great deal of pain. Jesse Ray and Maynard being left unsupervised added to her stress level. *Nothin' about this job's goin' smoothly*, she thought.

They drove in silence the rest of the way to Jackson Hospital's Emergency Room, right off I-85 at the second exit. A wiry black orderly spotted Jenny trying to get Clarence to his feet and rushed a wheelchair out to them.

"Thanks, man," Clarence mumbled as he placed his feet on the footrests.

As the electric doors opened, a heavyset, older black nurse, who appeared to be in charge, glanced up to assess the new arrival. There were dozens of patients awaiting treatment.

"Well, shugga, either you're having a heart attack or a kidney stone . . . which is it?"

"Stones, he thinks," Jenny replied politely.

The nurse looked at Jenny for a long moment. "Let me get you some forms to fill out . . . your wife can do it while I take you on back."

Jenny almost shot back that she wasn't his wife but realized things might go smoother if she played along. She had to get Clarence in and out with as little commotion as possible. "Yes, ma'am. Just tell me what I need to do," she offered.

The nurse handed Jenny a clipboard thick with papers. Pointing at another nurse behind the desk, she instructed Jenny to ask her for any help if she needed it.

A buzzer sounded, and the orderly rolled Clarence through a door. Jenny knew she could not completely fill out all the information, so she took an open seat and then looked around the waiting room. There was a kid with a fresh cast on his arm; his parents and a doctor were talking. An older man read a newspaper. There were several sick kids with parents. A shirtless guy had a hand wrapped in a blood-soaked T-shirt, trying to fill out paperwork. An ambulance slowly backed into the unloading area, its red lights flashing. A white female orderly anxiously waited. *I hate hospitals,* thought Jenny. *I wonder how long we'll be here.* She felt exposed and trapped.

When the patient from the ambulance distracted everyone, Jenny slipped through the previously locked internal door to search for Clarence. The only treatment room she couldn't see in was divided into two areas, separated by a curtain. "Clarence? Where are you? Are you decent?"

"Yeah . . . come on in. I can't get comfortable," he groaned.

"I need to ask you some questions to get these forms filled out," she said quietly as she pushed back the curtain. "That gown looks . . . well, let's just say there's more you than there's gown."

"I don't care. I'm hurtin'," he said, rolling onto his side, trying to get comfortable.

Jenny spent the next few minutes asking Clarence questions and filling in his responses. When she finally had as much completed as she could, she left to turn in the paperwork.

"He's really hurtin'," she said, handing the paperwork to the head nurse.

"We'll get to him shortly. A gunshot victim just arrived."

Nodding as if she totally understood, Jenny left the forms and walked outside to have a smoke. *I guess a gunshot wound did trump a kidney stone,* she thought.

Her lighter glowed briefly as she took a long, deep drag, lighting her cigarette. *I sure as hell hope this doesn't get us caught!*

They were way off script. She thought about everything from Gates to Maynard to how bad she needed the money from this job. Between drags she unconsciously folded her arms tightly across her chest. A few minutes later, invigorated by the nicotine, she snuffed out the cigarette in the grass and walked back inside.

She slipped into the exam room area again, and as she turned the corner heading for Clarence's room, she saw him leaning against the nurses' station counter, his gown hanging at an oblique angle from around his *neck,* the only part of his body actually covered by the gown. The nurses didn't seem to notice that he was bare-ass naked. When the waiting room door opened, the people there could clearly see Clarence's entire backside. For those who hadn't just witnessed a head-on collision, their facial expressions looked as though they had.

"Clarence! Clarence!" Jenny called under her breath as she scrambled to cover him.

"I ain't movin', and I don't care what anybody sees," he mumbled. "This is the first time in days that I ain't been hurtin'."

"Honey, if he's comfortable, let him stay, we've seen it all. We don't care," an older nurse said absently.

Jenny looked at Clarence's big butt sticking out in the hallway, aimed straight at the waiting room and sheepishly asked, "Well, can we at least get a bedsheet to cover him?"

The nurse looked up over her bifocals at Jenny and then past her out into the waiting room, where she saw several people staring straight at Clarence's ass. She chuckled and then said, "Yeah . . . sure thing, sweetie."

CHAPTER 55
MONDAY—DAY 2

Cooper didn't sleep a wink all Sunday night. He paced the house and watched the driveway, hoping Kelly would pull up. By six on Monday morning he was a total wreck. As seven approached, he realized that he had to put on a brave face for the kids. The police promised to have an officer over first thing that morning to open up a full-scale investigation. He welcomed the idea of the kids being at school instead of having them listen to his conversation with the police. At least at this point the kids didn't know enough to be upset.

He wondered what he needed to do to get Piper and Ben ready. Kelly always took care of the school details. When they came downstairs, each bombarded him with questions that he tried to answer, but really couldn't. However it happened, they seemed satisfied with his explanations. The carpool had them out of the house by 7:40 a.m. He hoped they had everything they were supposed to have. He had given them each a wad of cash with instructions to buy whatever they needed.

At eight, Cooper called the office to inform them that he wouldn't be in today. As expected, that opened up a round of questions that he diverted. He tried to end his conversation with Mrs. Riley by saying, "I'll check in periodically, and please tell Gates to call me when he gets in."

Mrs. Riley shocked him with the news that Gates was already locked in his office, presumably working since he was on the phone. Cooper told her to give him a message to call.

Cooper was on the phone, glancing out the window when he saw an unmarked police car park in front of his house. A plainclothes officer got out and walked to the front door. Cooper didn't wait for him to ring the bell and quickly opened the door.

There stood Henry Obermeyer, a detective who at six foot two and 225 pounds was a big man—except he wasn't muscular, he was just big. He had been on the force for fifteen years and was fixated with doing everything exactly, painstakingly, by the book. No deviations and no exceptions. The other officers loved making fun of him; consequently, he was the butt of countless jokes. He suffered from a spastic colon, was lactose-intolerant, and whenever he got too nervous or excited, he always had to run to the nearest restroom. Because of his condition, he had missed participating in several key dynamic entry arrests, and this was very troubling to him.

His colleagues jokingly called him Dirty Henry because he idolized the fictional detective Harry Callahan of the *Dirty Harry* movie series. Ironically, in fifteen years of service, Detective Obermeyer had never discharged his firearm in the line of duty, but he practiced shooting religiously, at least once a week. No one could beat his range scores or his command of shoot/don't shoot scenarios. No one was more prepared.

Obermeyer's peculiar behavior and odd mannerisms created a major problem on the police force in that he could not keep a partner. The big detective's odd ways drove several to tender resignations if they were not reassigned another partner. Detective Obermeyer was so successful at solving crimes, however, that the top brass gave up, allowing him to work solo.

Obermeyer, a major case investigator, had been assigned this mundane "missing wife" incident because things were slow and the officer responsible for case assignments didn't like him or *Dirty Harry* movies. Obermeyer had lost the argument with his immediate superior officer that this case was a waste of his skills and abilities.

Detective Obermeyer, without introducing himself, calmly shook Cooper's hand as he quickly scanned the surrounding area. His first words to Cooper were, "Stand by, please." He then slowly stared around the entry hall, but mostly at Cooper.

"Excuse me?"

"Stand by. I'm absorbing, it's part of what I do." After a moment he said, "I'm Detective Obermeyer."

At Cooper's offering, they walked into the kitchen and sat at the table. Cooper figured this guy to be some kind of nut job but went ahead and explained all he could while he watched the officer make notes on his BlackBerry. He paused to allow the policeman to catch up.

"I e-mail these notes to myself and make folders at night with all the documents," the detective explained, knowing the question was coming.

"Kinda like Jim Rockford on the *Rockford Files*," Cooper responded.

Obermeyer was surprised and felt an instant connection

with Cooper. Nobody had ever understood what he did.

"Exactly . . . only he mailed his notes . . . this, of course, is much more efficient," the detective proudly proclaimed. "So the last time you or anyone actually talked to your wife was Saturday afternoon sometime?" the detective asked.

"Yes, about two o'clock I think; it coulda been later though—I really wasn't checking my watch."

"Surely you have a point of reference in which to relate the time."

Cooper tried to think back. "I'm sorry, but I don't. Maybe two o'clock." Cooper hesitated, adding, "I kinda mentally checked out Saturday."

Obermeyer noted Cooper's pause. "Checked out?"

"I needed to get away and do some thinkin'." Cooper then explained where he was and what he was doing. He watched the detective's thumbs type the details.

"I see. An exact time would be helpful," he explained, thinking they were probably in the middle of an argument. Obermeyer quickly typed in the information on the tiny keypad.

When Cooper didn't say anything, the detective asked, "And to your knowledge, she hadn't planned to visit any relatives . . . or anything that would take her out of town for a few days?"

Most disappearances like this were the results of a marital spat or an affair. Affairs were universal, and it wasn't uncommon, just less obvious with the upper class. A few cases were simple communication breakdowns—where one spouse fails to tell the other where they are going, or most often, the other fails to listen. These cases bored Detective Obermeyer.

"No," Cooper responded nervously.

"Had any recent issues?"

"No. Well. Not really . . . maybe," Cooper said as he dropped his face into his hands. "We argue all the time lately."

"And you had a confrontation Saturday?" Detective Obermeyer asked without looking up.

"Yeah, but confrontation doesn't, well yeah, I guess it does. Evidently her credit card didn't work, I mean it was declined while she was shopping, and she blamed me," he explained and then drew a deep breath.

"Do you know the exact location the transaction was being attempted?" Detective Obermeyer asked, knowing that he had just gotten a good lead.

"No, I don't."

"Stand by."

Cooper watched him stare off into space and wondered what this odd guy was thinking.

"Do you have a list of her credit cards? I need to run it, and then we can piece together where she was Saturday and begin putting together a historical trail. We might find something simple like a plane ticket to Cozumel," the officer stated flatly, in a tone that conveyed situations like this happened every day.

"No, she wouldn't have done that, but I'll get you a list of cards," Cooper said as he opened a drawer that was home to all of their bills.

Detective Obermeyer silently seethed that his task for the day was chasing down a pissed-off housewife who probably escaped for a day from her boring life. He checked his cell phone to make certain he hadn't missed any calls.

"Look, is there any way you can check the hospitals around Birmingham? She loves to shop there. I called the ones here already," Cooper asked as he stood and began pacing. He couldn't sit still any longer.

"Yes, sir, that's already been done. It's standard procedure. I need to gather some additional information. This
won't take too long. What kind of vehicle does she drive?"

"A red Volvo sedan . . . it's two years old."

The questions continued for a full fifteen minutes as
Obermeyer followed the official script. The process exhausted
Cooper and made him more anxious. His mind raced with
thoughts of Kelly, the office, the kids, and what needed to be
done. *All this is my fault. All of it,* he thought.

Obermeyer spotted the coffeepot. He stared at it until
Cooper offered him a cup. While he stirred cream into
his coffee, he asked if there were any signs of a break-in or
anything missing or out of place in the house or garage.
Not expecting a positive answer, he glanced around the
kitchen, noticing nothing out of the ordinary, except some
strange-looking Coke bottles.

"No, everything's here, including her suitcases. I
checked."

"Does she have an attorney?"

"An attorney? What do you mean?"

"A lawyer. Worst case . . . just thinking worst case: she
could be planning a divorce. I see it a lot."

"Your worst case and my worst case are worlds apart. I'm
thinking she's been in an accident. Sure we argue or have
confrontations, as you put it, but I don't think she wants a
divorce," Cooper explained. As the words hung in the air he
wondered about her calling Gates and asking about Brooke.
That could have made her leave. He needed to talk to her to
explain.

"You okay, sir?" the detective asked, noting Cooper's
sudden disengagement.

"Yeah, I was just thinking about what you said. It kind of
shocked me, I guess."

"Okay. This should get me started."

Cooper nodded his agreement, somewhat in a trance, running his fingers through his hair. He managed to ask, "So whadda I do?"

"Call any of her friends you can think of. If you find her, please call me. Here's my card, it's got all my numbers on it." The detective slowly rose from the table. "I need to get this info into our system. I'll be in touch. If you think of anything or hear something, please call me."

Cooper nodded his understanding and buried his face in his hands.

Walking toward the door the hulking detective stopped, stared a second, and walked back into the kitchen. "I'll ask your neighbors if they've noticed anything unusual. Something may turn up."

Cooper sighed deeply and answered, "Please, whatever you need to do, just find my wife."

CHAPTER 56

Jenny had decided that Clarence would be more comfortable recovering at the hotel rather than at the hideout. The hospital had gladly accepted cash for the services, without asking any potentially compromising questions. Any other time, the gang's protocols would dictate that they abandon the job and vanish without a trace. Clarence's medical condition, however, necessitated that they not travel.

Once Clarence was settled into the room and heavily medicated, Jenny headed back to the hideout to check on the boys. Jesse Ray and Maynard alone with their captive made her nervous. While she drove the hour to the old house, she thought long and hard about everything surrounding this job and was beginning to regret her participation. The cost-benefit analysis had changed over the last day—there was beginning to be too much risk for too little reward. The stress had also caused her to start smoking again.

Parking her car near the barn, she studied the old house for a long moment. She was surprised and concerned that there was no visible movement in the main room or at any of the other windows. Unlocking the kitchen door, she startled Maynard who had fallen asleep on the couch, reading one of her horse magazines. She noticed a nearby pile of teeth-whitener wrappers.

"Just what the hell are you doin'?" she bluntly asked.

"I fell asleep. Sorry." He responded sheepishly, checking his watch. Motioning downstairs, he quickly added, "Don't worry. She's out. We just gave her some more drugs . . . about an hour ago."

"What worries me is that you didn't hear me drive up. That's the first problem, and the second is that you're readin' my magazine, which means *you* went into *my* room," Jenny stated, pointing an accusatory finger at Maynard.

"I'm sorry. It's just . . . I'm really sorry . . . it's just that I really like horses."

Jenny was taken aback by his response to her anger. "What? You do?" she asked suspiciously.

"Yeah. Several years ago, when I lived in Hot Springs, I used to walk and warm up horses at Oaklawn Park during racin' season."

Jenny shook her head in disbelief. "What?"

"Yep, I met this really cool jockey, Otto Thorwarth, who got me the job."

Jenny was clearly intrigued and was suddenly curious. "I never figured you for a horse guy."

"I really love 'em. I even wanted to be a jockey . . . but really . . . I didn't like going that fast on something that big that didn't have brakes."

"I'll bet it's intense."

"Oh yeah, but it's not really for me . . . so I was happy to just walk and warm up the horses after that. I can talk Thoroughbreds all day—you know, like how they're pretty much clueless about traditional rein aids and commands. They've kinda learned a different language than offtrack horses, ya know." Maynard was starting to get animated.

Jenny was surprised by how much Maynard really did sound like Larry King and impressed that he appeared much deeper than she first thought. She wanted to learn more, and she knew that she'd have time over the next several days, but right now she had to make certain that she set clear parameters regarding her privacy.

Jenny said, "Look, just don't go in my room. Okay?"

"I'm sorry. The door was cracked, and I saw the magazine lying on the bed. I needed somethin' to read. The dial-up Internet connection is molasses slow, and all Jesse Ray's got to read are geek magazines," he said, pointing to the kitchen table.

"You can read my magazines, but my room's off-limits. Just respect my privacy, and we won't have any problems. Clear?"

"Perfectly. No sweat. I'm sorry. I won't do it again. I swear."

"Okay, where's Jesse Ray?"

"He's in the other room . . . nursin' a headache. He said he couldn't concentrate."

"Jeez, this crew's the walkin' wounded. I can't believe this," she replied, kicking off her shoes.

"It wasn't just his head hurtin', he said he feels like somebody's watchin' him. He got a little spooked," Maynard said with a smile.

"Watchin'?"

"Yeah, like a haint."

"A haint?"

"You know, a ghost. They don't bother me though. I've lived in old houses all my life."

"This place is haunted?" Jenny asked, looking around carefully. "Clarence will love this."

"There's some weird shit that goes on for sure—lights going off and on, and what sounds like footsteps. What about Clarence? Is he okay?" he asked.

"Yeah, but he's all doped up on some powerful painkillers. He's got a herniated disk and a huge kidney stone, and when they started talking surgery to install a stint, he started hyperventilatin'. He finally told them to just give him some drugs, and he'd deal with it when he got home. I left him at the hotel to rest."

"That don't sound good."

"It's not. Every one of us needs to be concentratin' on this job, and he can't. The pain's pretty bad."

"So . . . he's got a stint comin' out his . . ." Maynard's words trailed off with a shutter.

"No. No. They didn't do the procedure. It woulda required an overnight stay and about ten grand. Clarence wasn't gonna pay cash for it here when his insurance will cover it at home. He said all he wanted was pain meds and a case of beer. The doctor laughed and said, 'Okay on the drugs, but no drinkin' too.'"

Jenny tossed her purse on the kitchen table. The toll of her concern for Clarence, their hostage, her cut of the money, Jesse Ray's busted face and bruised ego, Maynard sleeping instead of pulling guard duty, and now a ghost hit hard and at once. *I gotta tighten up this group, but first I gotta get some sleep. I can't think.*

She paused at her bedroom door and looked back at Maynard, "I gotta get some sleep." Then she added, "I like Thoroughbreds."

Maynard smiled big, showing his white teeth.

She added, "Keep an eye out for ghosts and don't screw up or I'll personally make you a geldin'."

"Don't you worry."

He leaned forward just like the real Larry King and said, "Stay tuned: we have a great show tonight!"

Jenny went into her room and picked up a bundle of blooming honeysuckle and red spider lilies wrapped in bailing twine that were lying on the bedside table. She stuck her head out of the room and said, "Hey, Maynard, who put these wildflowers in my room?"

"Don't know," replied Maynard, clearly smitten. "Musta been the haint."

CHAPTER 57

The Client couldn't wait to get to work Monday morning—not from a genuine desire to be a contributing member of society, but to keep up appearances. He'd been awake since five and when his newspaper hadn't yet been delivered, he went to a nearby gas station to buy one. Frustrated with the lack of breaking news about the abduction, he tried to convince himself it was still early in the game.

He went to his office, hardly able to control his thoughts or his actions. He was a wreck and had begun talking to himself. His coworkers noticed, but no one cared enough to say anything. As was typical, they stayed out of his way and now tried to avoid having any dealings with him at all, if possible.

Sitting at his desk, he held the small cell phone his hired gun had given him and stared at a small photograph of his obsession. He desperately wanted an update, but fear of the huge man outweighed his curiosity—his last scrap of discretion. *I can wait. Just makes it all the more sweeter,* he thought, opening his desk drawer to stash the phone and photo. Inside, he saw his prescribed pharmaceuticals and smiled. *Don't need 'em anymore.*

Two weeks off the meds and he felt better than ever, but suddenly everybody was out to get him. Paranoia was his newest companion.

CHAPTER 58

It had been a torturous day for Cooper. By the time the kids got home from school, he had convinced himself that Kelly knew everything about Brooke. Donna had called all of Kelly's friends but to no avail. Cooper had reduced himself to driving around looking for her like she was a lost puppy. He didn't know what else to do.

Earlier in the day when Millie arrived to clean house, Cooper avoided telling her about Kelly. He struggled for words to explain his situation—he wanted to tell her everything, to ask her advice, but the words wouldn't come. She didn't press him and with quiet resignation, the elderly woman went about her daily duties, worrying about Cooper as she eavesdropped on several conversations. Millie didn't believe Kelly would leave Cooper because she was too selfish—she had everything to lose in a divorce. Millie worked at a snail's pace while within hearing distance of Cooper and fast as a squirrel getting ready for winter when she had to catch up to him.

Brooke called Cooper midmorning on his cell phone.

She seemed stunned and desperate to be helpful, volunteering to do whatever he needed. He hung his head in despair and could only respond by telling her that he was to blame. Brooke didn't seem to understand and offered empty words of comfort. Feeling awkward and uncomfortable, Cooper told her he was really busy and needed to go. He felt guilty for even having a simple conversation with her, and he suddenly didn't want her number in his cell phone call history.

Around five thirty in the afternoon—Millie was preparing to leave, Donna was talking to Piper upstairs, and Cooper was sitting in a trance—the phone rang. Cooper jumped to answer it. As he picked up the receiver, he could see that the caller ID displayed Kelly's cell phone number.

"Kelly! Kelly!" he exclaimed. Footsteps raced all over the house.

"Um, no, this ain't Kelly. My grandmother found this phone while walking at the park, and I saw this number in the memory so—," a young girl's voice explained.

"You said you found it?" Cooper interrupted. He knew Kelly never went anywhere without her cell phone.

"No, sir, my grandmother found it this afternoon, and it's pretty smashed up. The battery was out of it, so I put my battery in, and it worked. I know it's expensive, so I thought you'd want it back."

"Yes, I do, it's my wife's phone," Cooper answered, watching every face around him fill with anticipation. "Which park did she find it in?"

"Vaughn Road. She found it in the grass," she answered. "She probably dropped it while she was joggin'."

"Can I come and get it right now?" he asked.

Cooper scribbled down the address, hung up the phone, and stood, looking at the faces of the kids he'd disappointed, the sister of the woman he'd betrayed, and a lifelong dear friend, whom he also felt he had let down. Searching a moment for what to say, he finally explained the few new facts but that he didn't really know what any of it meant.

"I'll be right back."

"Cooper, you should call that detective," Donna said as he grabbed his keys.

Retrieving the detective's card from the counter, he dropped it into his shirt pocket and promised to call him. As an afterthought, he asked, "Do you mind staying with the kids?"

"No. Go, I'll take care of 'em," she replied.

As Cooper backed out of the driveway, he saw Haywood Brown, Millie's devoted husband of sixty years slowly pull to the curb at the front of the house. He grabbed his BlackBerry to call the detective but hesitated a moment as he reflected on the difference between his life and Mr. Brown's. Cooper was mortgaged up to his eyeballs and had the façade of a perfect life and marriage. Mr. Brown had married Millie at eighteen, worked in a steel factory most of his adult life, enduring backbreaking labor, and devoted his whole life and being to his wife. They had a small, warm home and didn't owe a dime or anything to anyone. They didn't have much in terms of material possessions, but they had an overwhelming love and respect for each other. Neither one ever uttered a complaining word . . . about anything, ever. They both worked hard, long days. Millie had often commented that a hard day's work was the best birth control ever invented. He smiled briefly, thinking of the simplicity of their life and love, momentarily forgetting his worries. The Browns had endured their own tragedy, losing their only two children as babies in a car accident. The loss, however, drew them closer to each other.

Snapping back to reality, Cooper waved at Mr. Brown, dialed the detective's number, and hit the gas.

"Detective Obermeyer," the officer answered with absolute professionalism.

"Detective, Cooper Dixon. I just got a call from a lady who found Kelly's cell phone at Vaughn Road Park. I'm on my way to pick it up and thought you'd wanna know."

"Vaughn Road Park? That's interesting."

"Yeah well . . . she walks there most days."

"Stand by!"

"What?"

"Stand by!"

"Detective, I'm on my way to pick up the phone."

"Two nights ago we received a report of a woman being kidnapped near the park."

"What? And you're just now telling me?!"

"The facts did not fit your case. The woman was allegedly kidnapped from a gray Chevy Suburban. Moreover, we believed it to be some kind of college prank. The elderly couple that called it in said the alleged perps were Larry King, Sammy Davis Junior, and Oprah. We wrote it off as a joke."

"Kelly doesn't drive a Suburban."

"I confirmed that first thing this morning with the DMV. What's the address of the person who found the phone? I'll meet you there."

Cooper gave him the address.

CHAPTER 59

Kelly groggily opened her eyes for the third time since she had been held captive in the cellar. She still didn't know where she was or how long she'd been unconscious. She became more alert than she'd been allowed the other times she'd regained consciousness. The space was cool. The air musty.

Struggling to lift her head to read her small watch, she finally determined that it was six o'clock. *Is it morning or night,* she wondered. By the faint glow of light coming from the top of the stairs, she could make out an old armoire and a bucket with a toilet seat on one side of her. The walls looked to be red dirt. On her other side, she could see a small table near the stairs. On its top were what appeared to be stacks of bedsheets and towels. There were also several brown prescription bottles, small clear glass vials, syringes, full IV bags, and bottles of water and Ensure.

Her arms and legs felt heavy. She lay still, trying to acclimatize. She wanted to stand but didn't have the strength. Then she realized that she was bound to a bed. That confused her. Her mind was foggy. She kept staring at the red dirt walls, trying to determine where she was. The IV catheter in her left arm itched, but there was nothing she could do about it. She couldn't figure out who was doing this or why, especially why. She vaguely recalled her captors telling her that Cooper hired them. *Why would he do this to me?*

She could recall that at all times they were careful not to show their faces. Her blood pressure and heart rate were being checked regularly, and when needed, she would be cleaned and refitted with a new pair of Depends. The best that she could determine, about every six hours, they would try to feed her or force her to drink a warm bottle of Ensure.

The last time Kelly was lucid, she stared at her IV catheter and the surrounding tape. She tried to think through a plan, but the drugs clouded her judgment. *What if I can pull it out enough to . . . but I'll bleed, and they'll catch me, then what will they do to me?*

CHAPTER 60

At eight o'clock Detective Obermeyer was sitting alone in a diner, drinking coffee, working. Being unattached allowed him to work nearly nonstop, which he did and loved. He had retrieved the missing phone, forced Cooper to go home, interviewed the witnesses to the alleged kidnapping, and searched all of the area around the asphalt walking path at the park where the phone was found and the parking lot. He sipped coffee as he read his notes for the third time. He then prepared a new electronic folder.

This missing person case had become intriguing. Earlier, he had assumed that Kelly Dixon was a bored housewife looking to get out of the marriage or just have a fling. He knew either might be the case, but as the facts were developing, they started to captivate him. Maybe his excitement was stemming from his own boredom—that he wanted to believe there might be more in play.

Kelly's cell phone was expensive, and based on what he had learned about her, it would be out of character—maybe not even in the realm of possibility—to simply leave it somewhere, whether intentionally or not. That phone would have been her lifeline—to constantly keep in touch with her kids, their school, their friends and hers, parents, and even her husband or a significant other. Busy housewives tend not to lose cell phones. The fact that the victim was taken from a Suburban was also puzzling. It would be difficult if not impossible to confuse a sleek red Volvo and a barge-sized silver Suburban . . . unless the Suburban was her lover's. *Cooper could have paid someone to snatch his wife. It's been done before.* The detective made a note to explore that thought.

Tomorrow, if she hadn't shown up, Detective Obermeyer planned to go down to Cooper's office to question his staff. He didn't suspect Cooper of any wrongdoing, but things were rarely as they appeared. And the Montgomery Police Department paid him to be suspicious. Random violent acts between strangers are rare. Spouses and live-in partners, however, are capable of almost anything. *In a case like this, you gotta start with the spouse. Always,* he thought.

While he typed on his laptop, he noticed several teenage punks in a corner booth laughing at him. He was used to it. He had been picked on and made fun of for as long as he could remember. He opened his suit jacket slightly, revealing his service weapon held securely under his left arm by a Galco Miami Classic shoulder holster. The kids left, so he continued his note taking. His cell phone rang.

"Detective Obermeyer," he answered, after first clearing his throat.

"Detective, this is Cooper Dixon. I think we need to go to the media, get Kelly's picture on the news and see if anyone has seen her or knows anything."

"Are you ready for the scrutiny?"

"I can handle that. What I can't handle is the not knowin'. This is so unlike her. Finding her phone really concerns

me . . . she never goes *anywhere* without it. She practically
sleeps with the damn thing. There's no way she'd just lose it.
Somethin' bad's happened, I know it."

"Stand by," the detective responded and went into a deep
thought. *If Cooper were guilty, what would he be trying to do right
now? Divert attention and scream innocence. If he were innocent,
what would he be trying to do?*

Obermeyer recognized that he could get the media to
help, and it might force something or someone out into the
open sooner, which could be either good or bad for Cooper.
He said, "Okay, I'll reach out to the TV stations and the
newspaper too."

"Look, I know people at the television stations, and
the editor of the paper is a good friend," Cooper added
enthusiastically.

"You do realize that your life will turn upside down
when this hits? Regardless of your personal relationships, the
media is relentless. If you have any skeletons in your closet,
they will get dragged out," the detective advised and then
added, "I'm not a fan of the media, but this could help get
us leads."

"I just wanna find my wife. You should see my kids;
they're pitiful. I don't know what to tell 'em."

"Speakin' of children. Is there any chance your wife is
pregnant?"

"No . . . no chance . . . why do you ask?" Cooper realized
that he couldn't remember the last time they slept together.

"You're sure?"

"Yes! Absolutely, why?" Cooper asked almost frantic.

"Is it possible that she could have been having an affair?"

Cooper was stunned. He'd never thought about that.
Thoughts of Kelly and her daily activities went through his

mind. He realized that he didn't truly know what she did during the day.

"Cooper, it happens."

"She's not havin' an affair . . . at least I don't think she is. I don't know how I'd know if she was," he answered. "And why are you askin' if she's pregnant?"

"Well, if she was pregnant and didn't want the baby, she may have slipped off to Atlanta for an abortion."

"No! No way in hell she'd ever have an abortion!" Cooper stated emphatically.

"These are questions I have to ask and you have to consider," the detective responded, sipping his coffee.

"I'm sure."

"Okay then. I'll prepare a statement for the press. I'll start working on it right now. Can you e-mail me a current photo of Kelly?"

"Sure. Absolutely. I'll hafta get somebody to help me, though," Cooper responded enthusiastically and added, "Detective, you need to know that I haven't done anything to harm my wife. The only thing I'm guilty of is being a shitty husband."

Obermeyer nodded, thinking for a moment, and then said, "Yeah, sure. Stand by."

CHAPTER 61

Gates Ballenger learned of the messy situation from Cooper by phone. He had never heard Cooper sound so depressed and disoriented. He did his best to comfort his partner, insisting that he stay away from the office and take care of his family. Gates said all the right things. He promised Cooper that he would take care of the day-to-day business and told him not to worry.

Exhaling deeply, Gates stared out the window of his office at the view of downtown Montgomery. Gates was living on borrowed time, and every day, every hour, the noose was slowly getting tighter. He needed drugs, he needed cash, and he needed this business to support him, either through milking it as he had since day one or from the sale to MidState Bank, which wasn't going to close as quickly as he had hoped.

Leaning back in his chair and putting his feet on the desk, Gates smiled at the thought of a legal point that he had written into the operating agreement when he and Cooper formed their company. The language creates a chance for

Gates to own 100 percent of the Tower Agency. It was actually Gates's father who insisted on a contractual clause providing that in the event Cooper was ever convicted of a crime and served any jail or prison time, even one day, as a result, his ownership percentage in the agency reverted wholly back to Gates on the date of his incarceration.

Years ago, Gates's father had owned a roofing business with another man who later had been convicted of bribing a federal judge. The senior Ballenger always despised having to share profits with a man in prison. He would say, "Always have control of your business and always have a way to keep control."

Gates smiled as he remembered Cooper laughing at the clause and naively dismissing it, saying that the clause was the absolute least of his worries. He stared at one of Cooper's Mexican Coke bottles and wondered about his next move now that he had options.

CHAPTER 62

By the end of the day, all of the local television stations had aired stories based on the prepared release during their news broadcasts. The Client was ecstatic. The story was finally taking shape, and it was certain to grow. It was tailor made for today's media interests. It was hard to predict what the major cable news outlets would pick up, but this story would eventually have all the elements they craved—an attractive upper-middle-class family, the mysterious disappearance of the mother, and most important, unlimited unanswerable questions for their panels of so-called experts.

It wouldn't be long before Cooper Dixon would be dragged through the mud and ruined.

The Client was feeling bulletproof and euphoric. For the fourth time in eleven months he decided to reward himself. He felt that he deserved it.

. . .

Detective Obermeyer's thumbs were tired from e-mailing himself information from his tiny BlackBerry keyboard. So while he waited for the Chevrolet dealership to trace Kelly's new Suburban through OnStar, he called his commander to bring her up to speed: "I was at the Tower Agency waitin' to interview Mr. Gates Ballenger, when I overheard the office receptionist's conversation with a car salesman who was sorta frantically lookin' for Cooper."

Obermeyer took a sip of coffee and then continued, "Kelly Dixon traded her Volvo for a brand-new silver Suburban and told the salesman to contact her husband on Monday to sort out the details. She drove it off the lot Saturday afternoon. Her Volvo's at the dealership."

Obermeyer's superiors had given him a long rope several years back, and the detective had never disappointed them. Obermeyer was quirky and odd in both looks and personality, but he was capable of understanding complex fact patterns and situations. To everyone's frustration, he would not make a quick analysis, but given a few minutes to think it through, he was spooky with accuracy in his conclusions. That's how and why he developed the habit of saying, "stand by," whenever he needed time to think.

"Keep me in the loop," the commander demanded and then, without another word, hung up the phone.

"Yes, ma'am," he replied into dead air. He looked intently across the car lot at nothing in particular as he slid the phone into his pocket.

Obermeyer was in deep thought when the dealership's general manager rushed up to him saying, "Detective? Detective! It's at Lagoon Park Softball Complex. It hasn't moved since Saturday night!"

CHAPTER 63
TUESDAY—DAY 3

When Clarence finally awoke, he felt as though he hadn't urinated in days. He hurried to the toilet holding onto himself. After voiding his bladder and being horrified at seeing traces of blood in his urine, he dialed Jesse Ray's cell number.

"Yo, Dog. You feelin' better?" Jesse Ray answered on the second ring.

"Yeah, for the time being. Give me an update," Clarence demanded.

"Pretty smooth on this end: the package is fine, vitals good, the story broke last night on the local stations . . . I'm expectin' more on tonight's news. It should start gettin' some serious traction."

"Good."

"It gets better. Listenin' to scanner chatter, it seems MPD put their best detective on it."

"Figures. She's rich and white. Well, this is good. It's what the Client wanted. So how's the crew?"

"Everybody's good. I got two black eyes and a swollen face. J. J.'s taken over and has Mr. King jumpin' through hoops."

"She has a tendency to do that."

"Yo, Dog, this place is spookin' the shit outta me. I haven't slept since I got here."

"Whaddaya talkin' 'bout?"

"It's haunted, bro. I hear shit goin' on all night. Sounds like somebody walkin', marbles rollin' around, doors openin'; it's crazy. I'm just waitin' on my security cameras to pick up something so I can sell it to the Discovery Channel."

"You serious?"

"Damn straight. I feel like somebody's watchin' me all the damn time. It's okay during the day, but at night, I'm tellin' you . . . this place gives me the creeps. I'm ready to get the hell outta here, Dog."

"I'll be there directly, and we'll figure it out," Clarence said and then ended the call.

Clarence's back was hurting. He reached to the nightstand for his pain meds. He was thankful to be under cool sheets in the clean hotel room rather than suffering in a hot, haunted house.

CHAPTER 64

Cooper sat nervously in a private conference room at the police headquarters. He was relieved to be away from the constant ringing of his home telephone and the endless questioning, all thanks to the television reports. He tightly held his BlackBerry in case Kelly called. Donna and his mother were keeping the kids, trying to hold together his family.

Detective Obermeyer had informed Cooper about the vehicles—that they located Kelly's Volvo and the Suburban. Cooper also knew that the police now considered Kelly to be the victim of a kidnapping, which was blowing Cooper's mind. He sat there, head in his hands, trying to make sense of things. A day earlier he was convinced that she had run off and left him because she believed he had cheated on her; then he learns that she's been kidnapped. He was worried sick about Kelly but oddly relieved that she hadn't left him. The spectrum of emotions coursed though him. *Kidnapped!?* *This is insane,* he thought and buried his head in his arms, mentally and physically exhausted.

Detective Obermeyer walked in and slowly shut the door. "Okay, Cooper, what aren't you tellin' me?" The detective sat down and then took a sip from a bottle of Pepto-Bismol.

Cooper just shook his head. After a long moment, he said, "I . . . I can't think of anything."

"Kelly intended for you to buy that Suburban. It just took a while for the salesman to get up with you. And you had no idea?"

"He called me a couple times Monday, but he always calls me when he's tight on his monthly sales quota. That's why I didn't return his call."

"And your wife *never* mentioned that she was lookin' for a new vehicle?"

"She's always wantin' somethin', you know? But we hadn't discussed a Suburban," Cooper explained, restlessly running his hands through his hair.

"Okay, stand by."

"What about a ransom note? Was there one in the Suburban?" Cooper asked immediately. He was clearly not "standing by." He wanted answers.

"No. That's what I'm tryin' to think through. If this is a kidnapping, you should have heard something by now. If and when you do, then we have to bring in the FBI."

"Shit!"

Detective Obermeyer was concentrating intently. "Unless they're trying to let you get really worked up, panicked, and then they'll hit you with the demand . . . but the longer this goes on, the more likely law enforcement would become involved, and they wouldn't want that if it was a straightforward abduction for money." The detective paused and then asked, "Do you know why your wife went to the bank and took something out of your safety deposit box on Friday?"

"I have no idea."

"None?"

"Hell, I didn't even know we had a safety deposit box!" Cooper snapped back in frustration.

"This is confusing, perplexing, and not just the least bit mystifying, to say the least."

"Well, do your stand by thing, 'cause right now, you're all I got."

"How liquid are you? Help me understand that . . . if they called with a big ransom, could you handle it?"

"I could get my hands on about a hundred thousand, but I would have to sell some investments. I'm not flush by any means."

"Y'all look like you're doin' well, financially," the detective remarked, wanting to hear the inflection in Cooper's reply.

"Appearances can be deceivin'. I'm just like everybody else, mortgaged up to my eyeballs, and I don't draw a big salary. I'm tryin' to build up equity in the business."

"Mr. Dixon, does your wife have a life insurance policy?" the detective asked, taking another hit of Pepto-Bismol and watching Cooper's expression.

Cooper immediately looked up and made eye contact. Nothing was said for several long moments. Cooper finally said, "Look, I'm gonna say one more time: I. Haven't. Done. Anything. To. My. Wife!"

"That doesn't answer my question. What about it? Do you?"

"Yes. Yes, there is. There's a million-dollar policy on her; we did it a few years ago . . . that's to make sure I have some way to help take care of the kids. I didn't really want it; our neighbor's an insurance agent, and he talked us into it."

"That's a lot of money."

"Well, there's two million dollars on me! This agent . . . you can talk to him . . . he said we needed a multiple of my salary and our debts. I did what he recommended . . . just in case. If something happened to Kelly, I'd need help with the kids for sure. My business takes a lot of my time. I'd probably have to have live-in help. We were just tryin' to be responsible. That's pretty normal, I think." Cooper paused and added, "Look, I'm not rich, but we're not in too bad of shape either. Nobody knows this, but MidState Bank is about to purchase the Tower Agency, and I stand to make some good money."

"I hadn't heard that," the detective said, looking at Cooper, trying to read his body language. He continued, "All right Cooper . . . go home, but be careful. I got a tip that CNN is sendin' a crew down here."

"Should I talk to 'em?"

"Honestly, at this point, I don't know. They could fry you and the Montgomery Police Department, or they could shake something loose."

"I just want my wife back," Cooper said, almost losing control of his emotions.

A female officer walked into the room and handed Obermeyer a note, which he slowly read.

"What is it?" Cooper asked nervously.

"Are you sure there's nothing else you wanna tell me?" the detective asked as he reread the note from a well-known private investigator, claiming to have information about Cooper Dixon and his marriage. Obermeyer smiled as a piece of the puzzle quietly dropped into place.

"I swear to you . . . I don't know what's goin' on," Cooper pleaded.

"Fine. If that's how you wanna play it. Read this." Obermeyer slid the note across the table.

Cooper's eyes quickly scanned the note and recognized the private investigator's name from his obnoxious advertising on late-night cable television.

"I can explain. I swear; this is all just a big misunderstandin'."

CHAPTER 65

Brooke was struggling to be creative at work and also having difficulties focusing on her private life. She desperately wanted to talk to Cooper. She decided that this was her time to show him how much she really cared about him and his well-being. This was her chance to be there for him, however and whenever he needed.

When the phone rang, Cooper didn't immediately recognize the number, so he anxiously answered it on the first ring.

"Hello?"

"Cooper, this is Brooke. Are you okay?"

Cooper's heart jumped. "I've been better. I've had a rough few days."

"Is there *anything* I can do?"

"No. I appreciate it though."

"Promise me, if there is, that you'll call me. Please," she asked, wanting to help. "It's just so weird . . . I saw her Saturday mornin' at the spa. We talked."

"You did? Whatja say?" Cooper asked, shocked.

"Oh, it was harmless. Don't worry."

"Did she say anything that might help us understand what's happenin'?"

"No, not at all. We just basically said hey and talked about the spa."

"Brooke, I don't know what to say. I'm really confused. I've led you on, and now I'm payin' the price."

"No, you didn't lead me on." She paused for a moment and then said, "I know what you're thinkin'. Look, we're at two different places in our lives. We both felt the sparks. That was my fault."

Her words were making Cooper ill, and he wanted off the phone as fast as possible, so he said, "Look, I gotta run. I promise I'll call if I need anything. Bye."

Immediately after hanging up, he began to dry heave. A short few days ago her voice made him as giddy as a schoolboy. Today, she scared the hell out of him and made him physically sick. *Kelly knows. What have I done?*

CHAPTER 66

Detective Obermeyer sat on his couch halfheartedly watching *The Enforcer* on DVD. Wearing plaid boxers, a tight white T-shirt and his shoulder holster rig, the big man reread his daily notes. A warm, untouched beer was on the table next to his Pepto. It was slightly past eight. He was turning over the details of the case, which he sensed was going to quickly turn high-profile.

The last time CNN was in town for a major crime was during the DC sniper case that gripped the country. Some fine police work by the MPD, following a video store holdup, linked fingerprints and weapons that helped to break open that case. Obermeyer had watched the police chief explain to a national television audience Obermeyer's unit's role in gathering crucial evidence. It had been one of his proudest moments and with the current trajectory of the Dixon case, it might make second place.

None of the Tower Agency employees had anything negative to say about Cooper. In fact, they all seemed to genuinely adore him, especially the receptionist. Gates Ballenger had been the lone exception; although, he didn't actually say anything bad about Cooper. He just thought too long before each answer. And the answers didn't come across naturally, which bothered Obermeyer. Gates obviously was hiding something. He had also insisted that Cooper was at the game Saturday night, which the detective knew specifically from Cooper to be a lie. Obermeyer sensed that he should not trust anything Gates said since he also denied having talked to Kelly two days before she disappeared. Obermeyer had her phone records to establish those facts. He made a note to set up Gates. *Gates is culpable of somethin', or he's just plain stupid. Maybe a little of both.*

When his cell phone rang, he cleared his mind quickly and answered. He was shocked to learn of another local rape. It had occurred several hours earlier, but the victim had just been admitted to the hospital. He listened to the details and now knew that in this case they were dealing with a serial rapist. This was the fifth rape in about a year following a very similar pattern. All the victims had dark hair, olive complexions, athletic builds, and were roughly the same ages. A particularly troubling element of these crimes was that they were spread over several months, suggesting the rapist may have carefully planned the attacks, unless, of course, there were unreported rapes.

Obermeyer typed a note to map where each victim lived and the locations of the attacks, if in the unlikely event it was not in their homes. *Ten dollars to a doughnut says all the attacks happened within a five-mile radius and that the perp lives within that seventy-nine-square-mile area.*

The latest victim, a cattleman's daughter, had just left the local farmers' co-op with a new bottle of screwworm ointment. She had the presence of mind to squirt her attacker in the face with the purple staining medication. The officer explained to Obermeyer that the staining effects were instant and almost permanent—typically only vanishing with time. Detective Obermeyer, excited to learn that they finally had a lead to pursue, said that he would come to the precinct as quickly as possible.

Obermeyer was probably the only detective in the state with firsthand experience with these conditions. During spring break his freshman year of college, a group of farm-raised frat boys held him down on the beach and painted him from his toes to his neck with it. He was humiliated. It took weeks to wear off, but it was on the first day of his purple period that he decided on a career in law enforcement. He would help the helpless, fight for the underdogs. Hiding in his motel room, he glimpsed his life's calling.

Now, I just gotta find the purple perp. The thought made him chuckle, while the youthful memory made him cringe a little.

CHAPTER 67

It had been a tough night for Detective Obermeyer. The rape was almost exactly like the others. The perp took his usual trophy. A fact the police did not release. The chief of police called in the FBI to help profile the attacker. The perp meticulously cleaned up and had yet to leave a solid clue, which frustrated the detective beyond measure. Conferring with several investigators on how to pursue the purple angle, they all agreed to leak that piece of information to the media, hoping that someone would recognize him.

Obermeyer had been "standing by," carefully studying crime scene photographs when he noticed Cooper on CNN telling his story. "Turn it up!" the detective hollered across the room to no one in particular, and no one raised a finger to assist. Frustrated, he walked across the room and turned up the volume himself. It was a basic interview and, of course, CNN didn't have all the facts yet, but the detective sensed that this story was cherry-picked to be sensationalized. *Cooper's got no idea what's in store for him now.*

"I just want my wife back . . . and I'll do whatever I need to do . . . if anyone knows anything, please come forward," Cooper pleaded sincerely. "Right now the police think she's been kidnapped, but I haven't heard from anyone, so I really don't know what to think. My family's devastated—absolutely falling apart—and I'd like to add that if somebody watchin' does have my wife, please don't hurt her. I'll pay whatever you want, someway, somehow, to get her back. Please call. Call, please!" Cooper spoke rapidly and was obviously nervous.

The CNN reporter added some generic comments, and then they were off to another story.

"Hey, O, come in here," Obermeyer's commander called. Everyone in the War Room turned to watch.

"Yes, ma'am," Obermeyer said respectfully.

"I guess you saw that?"

"Yes, ma'am, I caught the tail end of it."

"I'm sure the national media picked this up for the ratings more than the story itself." The commander slammed down a folder on her desk, punctuating her disdain for the press and said, "We don't need this shit!"

"No, ma'am. And on top of things, looks like we've got a serial rapist huntin' in our backyard," he said as he felt for his bottle of Pepto.

"I've been on the losin' end of these national reporters' investigations into our cases, and I'm not gonna let that happen with the Dixons. Before this goes any further, dig into all of the Dixons' lives. Make sure we aren't missing anything. I particularly wanna know about the husband. I think he's hidin' something. So dig deep. If you need help, I'll approve the expenses. Just don't miss anything. If he got detention in high school for shootin' spitballs, I wanna know. If you don't already have it, make him account for every second of the last five days, look into his financials, have the techs look at his cell phone, computers at home and at work, tablets, e-readers, any and every communication device he might have . . . you know the drill. If he's as pure and innocent as he's sayin', you won't need a warrant."

"I've already got it started."

"Good," the commander exhaled.

"Has he lawyered up?"

"No, ma'am. Not to my knowledge."

"Well, keep me posted. I know that old couple thinks they witnessed a kidnappin', but why hasn't Dixon heard anything yet? Nothing about this makes sense. I wanna know what's happenin' before the networks do! I do *not* wanna learn about our case by watchin' the news. Am I clear?"

"Crystal. I understand."

"Be careful what you say if a camera finds its way into your face."

Obermeyer nodded.

"And remember this when it gets crazy: *nothing* is ever as it seems." The commander then stood, indicating that the meeting was over.

"I'm on it, Commander."

The detective saluted and then turned to leave but was stopped by the commander, who said, "And while you're tearing apart Dixon's life, see if you can catch that rapist . . . and . . . unofficially, if the opportunity arises, shoot him."

CHAPTER 68

Kelly lay in a deep fog of drugs for far more hours than she was awake. Several times, she had been able to work loose the IV, and on each occasion it had been noticed and reinserted.

Today, her captors were late sedating her and with each passing minute she gathered strength. Straining to hold up her head, the only thing she could see clearly in the pitch black were old stairs, illuminated from the light filtering down from under the door at the top. Occasionally a shadow would move past. She tried desperately to hear the conversations occurring overhead. Heavy footsteps on the floors made her flinch.

Suddenly, all movement and conversation upstairs stopped. It was silent except for the sound of a newscast on a television. Periodic cheers rang out.

She tried not to think too much about what was happening to her, but it was no use. The last time she was conscious, the kidnappers told her that Cooper was responsible. Scared and angry, she believed them because they said that he was going to use her life insurance proceeds to buy hunting land and go on an African safari. Both of which were Cooper's lifelong goals. *Why, Cooper? Why do this to me? How can you hate me that much? What about the kids?*

Kelly began to cry. She desperately wanted to see her children, to hear them, to smell their unique scents. She knew that her marriage was frazzled, but she couldn't make sense of Cooper wanting her dead.

This can't be coming from Cooper. He doesn't have the skills. If he can't even successfully plan a dinner party, how in the world did he organize this? Plus, he would never do this to me because no matter how thickheaded or self-centered he is or how much he may hate my guts, he would have to know that it would destroy the kids.

Something Kelly couldn't name kept her from believing that Cooper was capable of such evil. At that moment she knew, with absolute certainty, at the deepest levels of her being, that he wouldn't be involved, if for no other reason than the horrendous and devastating effect it would have on the children. Thinking about that began to calm her, and holding fast to the love she knew Cooper had always had for the children was enabling her to stay sane.

Fond memories of Cooper then began to bathe her mind. And then the realization that she had taken Cooper and their marriage for granted started creeping into the corners of her consciousness until she had to acknowledge that she truly had everything she needed in life, except for a strong marriage.

With remarkable clarity, Kelly knew that a solid marriage with Cooper was what she wanted and needed. That is what had been missing from her life—the void she desperately tried filling with societal position and material possessions—and it was her fault.

Tears again welled in her eyes, and then she sobbed uncontrollably for a long while. When she had regained

her composure somewhat, she silently prayed for another
chance—an opportunity to get her relationship with Cooper
back on track.

CHAPTER 69

"Don't you need a warrant to look through his office like this?" Mrs. Riley asked and then said, "They do on television."

"This isn't television. This is real life, ma'am."

"Well, I just thought you needed somethin', a warrant or permission."

"Mr. Dixon gave us permission to search his office," the detective answered as he closed a filing cabinet drawer. On the other side of the room, a female detective was enthusiastically searching through Cooper's computer.

"Okay. I pray that you find Kelly safe and sound. We're all so upset that people think he's involved somehow."

"The police have not stated that Mr. Dixon is a person of interest."

"I know, but you know how people talk."

The detective looked intently around the office. *Lots of places to hide stuff*, he noted as he opened the mini refrigerator. The only things inside were a dozen small bottles of

Coca-Cola. Moving on, he looked behind, under, and inside the couch, eliminating the obvious places first.

"He knows so many people. The phone's been ringing off the hook with friends checkin' on him. I can't believe he was on Nancy Grace's show. This whole thing is just so hard to believe."

Looking inside an antique metal minnow bucket, the detective impatiently said, "Stand by."

"Huh? Look, he's a good guy. You just wouldn't think anything like this could happen to him." Mrs. Riley shook her head. When nervous or upset she tended to chatter continuously.

"That's interesting," he said aloud but mostly to himself as he pulled a folded manila envelope out of the bucket.

"Yeah, it's ironic, 'cause some of the folks Gates deals with seem pretty rough, but not Cooper's acquaintances. His friends are—"

"Not that. This," the detective said, opening the envelope.

"What is it?"

"I can't discuss the case. Stand by."

"Do what?" she asked, clearly confused.

"Ma'am, could you give us some privacy, please."

"Sure, of course. Just call if I can help," she replied perturbed and slowly backed out of the office.

Detective Obermeyer was shocked to see sheaves of printed Internet articles about various anesthetics and other pharmaceuticals, restraint techniques, and articles about kidnappings. Each page cast additional doubt on Cooper's innocence.

"O, you're gonna want to see all this," the female detective said excitedly.

Shaking his head and closing the folder, he walked over.

"Whatcha got?"

"Either Cooper Dixon is the most computer-illiterate person I've come across or he wants us to catch him. Check this out," she said in an energized whisper.

"Go on," he said, bending over to better see the screen.

"Evidently he doesn't know how to delete the Deleted folder. There are tens of thousands of e-mails in that folder. They go back years."

"Being an idiot with respect to computers isn't a crime."

"No, but check out his Internet history. Totally incriminating. Look at these websites. They're a blueprint for kidnappin', druggin' somebody, even murder. I mean there are *dozens* of sites," she said as she pointed to the screen showing his recent web travels.

"Stand by."

"And look at these e-mails . . . there are at least six of them to a Hotmail account. They clearly establish how he found and hired someone to kidnap his ole lady. It's all here."

"Please, stand by," he said, reaching for his Pepto-Bismol to calm his rumbling stomach. The detective was trying to digest the large volume of apparently incriminating information. He walked over to shut the office door. He needed quiet to think. He finally said, "Forward those e-mails to me. We need to get this room locked down. Let's take that computer and what I found and get out of here—exigent circumstances will cover us. Based on what I'm seein', Cooper's capable of anything. I sure hope Mrs. Dixon's still alive."

The female detective pointed the mouse, clicked, and rapidly typed. After a moment she said, "Done. The agency's server capacity is huge, allowing all of these e-mails to be saved. Give me a little time, and there's no telling what I'll uncover. Our boy's been bad."

Detective Obermeyer said, "This is almost too easy. We gotta be careful. I'll get a warrant to seize the company's . . . whaddaya call it? Server?"

"Yep. It's the main computer for the business. You'll also need to include in the warrant application this desktop computer. It appears that each office's computer is networked with the server, so we need both." She looked up, noticing the envelope in Obermeyer's hand and asked, "What's that?"

"I gotta tell the commander that we need to arrest him ASAP. We've got enough now, and you're right, there's no telling what else we'll find."

Obermeyer stood looking around Cooper's office. Some criminals tried to hide their guilt by complete cooperation with the authorities. He had seen it before. But he had never seen incriminating evidence so easily found. *The minnow bucket was a pretty good hiding spot, but not deleting his e-mails— that's just stupid. Oh, well, it's almost always the spouse anyhow.*

CHAPTER 70

CNN and Fox News wanted to set up camp in front of the Dixon home, but since it was a private gated community, the guards stopped them. Network lawyers quickly determined that the city owned the streets and the guards were bluffing. It was game on at that point, to the horror of the other residents. They never dreamed the outside world could just waltz into their exclusive neighborhood. News trucks poured through what everyone had assumed was their protection from "those people." The guards had to just watch them drive by.

So the national media, along with its satellite dishes and noisy generators, decided to set up at two locations: the Dixons' home and the Montgomery police headquarters.

The Client had driven by the police station three times during the day and was ecstatic at all the attention he had created. He was so totally focused on destroying Cooper that he couldn't see or think about anything else now. He was close to his goal, and he was a much better man since he quit taking all those prescription drugs. The world would soon see.

He turned up the volume to the Bon Jovi tune "Wanted . . ." and sang the words "dead or alive" in an ominous voice.

Detective Obermeyer drove to the rear of the police station in an effort to avoid the press, hoping not to see the *Montgomery Advertiser* newspaper reporter waiting—she had the scary ability to make him talk. More than once he had inadvertently leaked information to her under the spell of her sultry brown eyes. He had to keep a level head to concentrate on finding Kelly Dixon. He was assuming and hoping she was still alive, but each passing day worked against the statistics.

CHAPTER 71

Clarence had planned the final payment drop for tonight and was busy preparing his team for any eventuality. He had Jesse Ray ready the area with a wireless security camera, and Jenny would be watching from a vantage point ready to alert them at any sign of danger. Clarence liked the rest area that was just across the Tallapoosa River, north of Montgomery. It was semiprivate and perfect for a drive-in and drive-out scenario. It also allowed them a certain element of control. The Client didn't know where the meeting was, he just knew to expect a call tonight and to be ready to move.

Confident they had a workable plan, Clarence checked his watch: 8:30 p.m. Nodding his head at Jesse Ray, he used his cell phone to call the disposable cell that he had given to the Client. If he hadn't been dealing with the kidney stones and a herniated disk, he would have tried to work the Client for more money. He and Jenny had decided after a long discussion to simply finish the job, take the money, and run.

"The sumbitch ain't answerin'!" Clarence said to Jenny and Jesse Ray.

"Let it keep ringing, he could be in a crowd," Jenny answered. "You never know . . . he could be trying to get somewhere private and answer it."

"Or he could be standin' us up!" Clarence said with distrust in his voice.

"Want me to track him?" Jesse Ray asked.

"Yeah, go ahead. If he don't answer in ten minutes, we'll go find him."

"Could be a simple reason," Jenny offered optimistically.

"It had better be; we've done everything he wanted. He's gonna pay up."

Jesse Ray launched the computer program to track the GPS coordinates of the cell phone they gave to the Client. "It'll take a few minutes."

"Y'all hungry?" Clarence asked. "There's a Mexican joint back up the road."

"I could eat something; I can always eat somethin'," Jesse Ray added.

"Let's go . . . I'm cravin' some chicken fajitas," Clarence explained.

CHAPTER 72

Detective Obermeyer walked with purpose up the stairs to his perfectly organized desk. When his phone rang it surprised him, but palming it out of his pocket he immediately recognized the number. He quickly set down his briefcase and watched it ring twice more. Taking a deep breath, he thought how he'd handle the call, finally deciding to just follow his instincts.

On the third ring, he answered, "Detective Obermeyer."

"Detective, I don't know what the hell's going on, but I was checkin' my BlackBerry about twenty minutes ago, and it looks like someone sent you some really crazy shit from my computer!" Cooper yelled.

The detective quickly realized that Cooper's PDA was synchronized with his desktop and when the detective caused the e-mails to be forwarded to him, they showed as sent mail on his handheld unit. *Damn it! I shoulda been more thorough.*

Cooper continued, "And they were sent to you! What the hell's goin' on?"

"I really need you to come downtown . . . or tell me where you are, and I'll come to you. We need to talk," the detective said. He thought, *I need to get a rope around Cooper quick.*

"I don't think so . . . you think I did it. Don't you?"

"Did what?"

"You know damn well what—that I had somethin' to do with my wife's disappearance!"

"I just want you to explain the e—"

"I can't explain 'em. I've never seen those e-mails in my life!" Cooper interrupted.

"Okay, that's fine. I understand, but we really do need to talk in person. Where are you?"

"I should call a lawyer first."

"Do you need one?"

"Yeah, apparently I do since you've decided that I'm guilty. I don't *need* one, but I sure as hell *want* one!"

"Just let me come get you."

"Free ride downtown right? You gonna arrest me?"

"I'll be honest, Cooper. It's all pointin' at you," Obermeyer stated and suddenly wished he hadn't.

"This is bullshit! I haven't slept in days, my kids are freakin' out, my phone's not stopped ringin', TV crews are camped outside our house . . . I just want my wife and my life back," Cooper said, sweating and panicked.

"Where's Kelly now? I can help you."

"I don't know."

"Where's she hidden?"

"I. Don't. Know! Aren't you listening? How can you say it's pointin' at me?!"

"The e-mails for one."

"They aren't mine! I swear to you. I've never seen them before. Besides, what's my motive?"

"I haven't got that figured out yet. I have a lot of other unanswered questions, for example, I can't account for where you were Saturday night."

"I told you. I was at my huntin' camp."

"Can anyone confirm your alibi?"

"Not exactly, but I was there." Cooper wished now that he had gone to the football game so that someone could vouch for him.

"Gates stated that you were at the game."

Cooper was stunned for a moment. "Gates is lying. He thinks I'm havin' an affair and is tryin' to cover for me."

"So are you?"

Cooper was silent. The detective tried to allow the silence to force a comment. After a few seconds, he decided to shock a response.

"I talked to the private investigator Kelly hired to follow you."

"I expected you would," Cooper replied.

"He said there was such a big crowd at the game, you gave him the slip. He said he could feel it in his bones that something was about to happen, and then it just vaporized. Like you got tipped off."

The detective was surprised by Cooper's silence. He then added, "Evidently, you're pretty slick, or the PI got started late."

"Obviously, they aren't any good, or they'd know that I was at my camp Saturday night, alone, and not at the ball game. Look, I don't know what's happenin'!"

"It may come as a surprise to you, but kidnappings are rare in the United States. They occur in Central America and along the Mexican US border but not around here. So what's going on, Cooper? Why did you kidnap your wife? Help me help you."

"I'm trying to help. Somebody's settin' me up."

"That's why you need to come in and explain some things to us."

"No, I need to think. I'll get back in touch later."

"If you don't come in now, I'm goin' to the media. And when I do, they will unleash a world of shit on you. Do you understand me?"

"I understand that you aren't doin' your freakin' job or you'd *know* it's *not me.*"

"Oh, I believe we've found who's responsible."

"You're wrong. I'm not comin' in."

"Officers are on their way to your house right now. They'll be there in five minutes. If you're not there, I'll ping your cell. I'll find you. When the media gets ahold of this, you won't be able to hide under a rock. Wise up; it's over, buddy boy."

Cooper had been driving home on the interstate when the e-mails caught his attention. As he talked to the detective, two black-and-white units raced past on the service road, lights flashing but no sirens. He knew that he couldn't go home and that he needed to turn off his cell phone. Panic gripped him. Common sense was telling him to go "downtown," but some deeper portion of his brain drove him to run, stay free, and do what he could on his own to find Kelly. He didn't know where to start or how to look, but he knew that if he were locked in a cell, it wouldn't help anyone. *I gotta find Kelly and figure out why I'm bein' set up.*

"I'll be in touch." Cooper broke the connection and then removed the cell phone's battery.

"Cooper! Cooper! Damn it!"

The detective grabbed his briefcase and charged up the stairs to talk to his waiting commander and the Montgomery County district attorney.

CHAPTER 73

The Client finally answered the disposable phone, giving a ridiculous excuse for his delay that provoked screams of anger from Clarence. The Client simply hung up in the middle of Clarence's expletive-rich rant. He had no intention of paying the balance due and realized he may have to kill Mad Dog and his pint-sized helper. *I can do that,* he thought.

When the phone rang again, he decided to provoke Mad Dog. He was feeling indomitable. "I already told you why I couldn't talk."

"You better listen to me, you worthless little piece of shit. I *know* who you are. I *know* where you work, and I *know* where you live." Clarence calmly continued, "Think carefully. I see loads of excruciatin' pain in yo future if you make the wrong decision."

The Client started to panic. Due to the effects on his brain from his drug abuse, he hadn't thought things completely through.

"Listen to me, you little prick, if you don't pay what you owe me, plus five grand for expenses, plus another five thousand for hanging up on me just now, I'm gonna hunt you down, and when I find you, *and I will*, I'm gonna tie your little pecker to a trotline weighted with a lawn mower engine and drop your sorry, pasty-white ass in the middle of the Alabama River. You feel me?"

In a tone suggesting that this all had been a complete misunderstanding, he said, "I'll pay, man. All of it. I'm sorry. I've just been tied up with some unexpected business . . . that's all. I promise. Relax, dude."

"Don't tell me to relax. Just pay me all my freakin' money. Today! Am I clear?"

"Yeah, yeah, I . . . I . . . I just need a few hours, that's all. I'll call. I swear."

"You've got two hours, and then I'm comin' for ya."

"It's not a problem. By the way, great job with the media. I'm really impressed with your work."

"Shut up! You're wastin' time! Now you've got an hour and fifty-nine minutes," Clarence said angrily and hung up the phone.

Clarence wanted out. His back and kidneys hurt, and he needed to rest for a few days, without all the stress and worries. Nobody ever thinks about criminals having problems. He chuckled as he remembered a burglary he was committing where his cell phone rang at the worst possible time. It was an ex-wife calling to inquire about an old tax return.

The Client stared at the small phone and knew he had to think of something pretty quick. He had enough cash; he just hated parting with it. Turning the television volume up on a CNN report, his spirits were instantly lifted as he learned that the Montgomery police now considered Cooper Dixon a person of interest. This news energized him, although he hadn't slept in four days. Smirking as he admired his own brilliance, he grabbed a small travel bag and began planning to make it look like it was packed full of cash.

CHAPTER 74

Cooper didn't know where to go or how to get started, so he drove around aimlessly on side streets. He found himself close to the police station and struggled with whether he should see Obermeyer. He then drove downtown, past the Capitol building and the Southern Poverty Law Center, the Montgomery-based organization that helped bring down the Klan. Seeing the Law Center reminded him that he better get a good attorney.

Cooper couldn't go home, couldn't go to the office, and couldn't use a credit card. There was no doubt that in the next few hours everyone in Montgomery would know his face. Hiding in town was going to be nearly impossible, so he drove to the only place he felt secure. It was remote, and no one would think to look for him there.

When he pulled into Millie Brown's long gravel driveway, he felt the truck slightly shift as Dixie excitedly paced in the bed. *Shit, I totally forgot she was back there!*

Millie and Haywood Brown's home was a well-maintained, old shotgun-style house with a tin roof, located far off the old part of Wares Ferry Road. In the late fifties, prior to the tragic car accident, when their kids were just babies, the family moved from their farm—the property Cooper wanted to buy. The Browns sought to get their children into a good school system and hoped to find good paying work.

The area around the Browns' home was once part of a huge plantation that the expanding metro area of Montgomery was slowly absorbing. Most of the cotton fields had been replaced with subdivisions, but the suburban creep hadn't quite reached the Browns' property. Spanish moss was blowing in the breeze as the sun set across the field.

Walking slowly toward the house, Cooper eyed the large cur dog that walked a worn path and barked aggressively from inside an old chain-link fence. Both Millie and her husband were home. Their only vehicle, an old Dodge pickup was parked under the tiny carport. Cooper jumped back when he noticed a dead snake hanging near the gate. Giving it a wide berth, he also carefully watched the dog as he knocked on a raw wooden column. Dixie barked, too, but knew better than to jump out of the truck.

"Rolex! Hush up!" Millie said as she opened the door and swatted her leg with a rolled newspaper. "Lordy Cooper, whatcha doin' here?"

"Miz Millie, I . . . I don't have anywhere else to go," he said obviously stressed but managing a smile.

"They's saying all kinds of crazy things 'bout you on the TV."

"I know . . . but I didn't do any of it," he replied, watching the growling dog.

"Honey Child, I know that."

"Can I stay here tonight? I need to figure out what to do next."

"You sure can, Precious. Come on in here . . . shut up, Rolex!"

"First, is there someplace I can hide . . . I mean park my truck, so it can't be seen from the road?"

"Sure, pull it round behind the barn. Shut up, Rolex! She ain't used to white peoples."

"That's okay. Thank you, Miz Millie."

"Lord, child. I done raised ya . . . I'd do anythang for ya. You ain't gotta thank me. Go park that truck, and I'll fix you up some supper. You look hungry."

"Yes, ma'am. That sounds really good."

"I'll tell Haywood you's here. Lord have mercy, Cooper; you in a peck a trouble, but I'ze proud you's here."

Cooper hid his truck behind the old barn, between two bushy fig trees. He instructed Dixie to stay, promising to bring her some food and water later. Cooper shook his head, wishing he had noticed that the dog had jumped in the truck earlier—when he could have taken her back home. Dixie was always sneaking into his truck and rarely, if ever, obeyed him. The overweight Lab loved to smell the world as she rode in the back.

Walking slowly back to the Browns' house, Cooper knew he was safe for a little while and needed whatever time he had to plan his next move. By now, he expected that the media would be destroying him. *How'd my life get so crazy? Why in the hell would someone kidnap Kelly? Why hadn't they asked for a ransom? It's easier to get my head around her being off 'cause she thought I was cheatin'.*

As he opened the Browns' screen door, Rolex erupted into another outburst of barking.

"Hush up, Rolex, or I'm gonna knock ya into tomorrow with this here broom! Come on in here, Cooper," said Millie excitedly.

Cooper slowly stepped past the dog and was thankful when the door shut. The house smelled of fried foods. The furnishings were old and simple. Mr. Haywood Brown was sitting in a well-worn recliner, watching the news, shelling the last butter beans of the year. He stood up and shook Cooper's hand, welcoming him into their home. The floor shook and pictures on a wall rattled when Cooper walked inside.

The house was exactly how he remembered it from his youth: small, warm, and comfortable. Each Christmas Eve his parents would deliver gifts to the Browns, and Cooper always rode along. Since marrying Kelly, Cooper just gave Millie a gift at his house, which suddenly felt insincere.

"Good evenin', Mr. Brown."

"Evenin', Cooper."

"Guess you've heard about the mess I'm in."

"Them news peoples seems to think you been pretty busy," Haywood remarked with a sly grin as he rolled up the butter-bean hulls in yesterday's newspaper.

Cooper nodded at the newspaper. He knew his picture was in it, but he couldn't bring himself to read what was being said, so he asked, "Is it bad?"

"Well . . . I say they don't know you like we do, Son," he said with a comforting smile that Cooper appreciated.

"That's right. Now Cooper, come on here and sit down. I gots cream peas, cabbage, fried okra, and fried chicken," Millie said as she tied on a white cotton apron and continued, "and some biscuits with homemade fig preserves."

"That sounds mighty good, Miz Millie; I wish I was hungry," he said, sitting down at the worn oak table. The chair creaked under his weight. Millie was old and slow, but in the kitchen she floated with grace. She smiled, obviously enjoying preparing the meal. Cooper hadn't realized how hungry he was until he saw the chicken. He hadn't eaten a decent meal in days.

"Haywood and I ate 'bout thirty minutes ago, but I always makes too much," she explained, wiping her hands on her apron. "It's hard cookin' just for two."

"Rolex eats real good though," Haywood said from across the room, and then added, "The peas need salt. She don't never put enough salt on 'em."

"Now Haywood, you knows I's watchin' yo pressure."

Cooper smiled. The meal was a cholesterol-scale tipper, but he wasn't complaining.

"Here's one of them little Co-Colas you likes so much," Millie offered as she sat the six-ounce bottle on the table. "But they ain't from Mexico though."

"Thank you, Miz Millie."

"Haywood likes 'em too," she said, smiling at her husband. Cooper noticed the love in her eyes.

"I have a six-pack of Mexican Cokes in my truck that I'll leave with you; he'll love 'em," Cooper whispered to her.

"Oh thanks, Honey Child. He'll drink 'em all. Now here's ya food." Millie set the plate of reheated food in front of Cooper and smiled at him. "Now, I'm gonna tell you just like I'd told my own chirruns. Iffin you gonna eat my food, you gotta listen to me talk. I's been round a long time, and I's knows things."

Cooper nodded his understanding and consent, though he was mentally exhausted and didn't want a lecture. The food's aroma was too much to resist. He was now starving and would have agreed to any terms she demanded. But deep inside, he knew Millie had something worth hearing. He certainly didn't have the answers, and she was by far the happiest person he knew.

As he picked up his fork and scooped up some peas, Millie started saying grace. He set down the fork. After blessing the food and Cooper's health and praying for his safety, protection, and future, she nodded at his plate, indicating that he could eat.

Millie sat down and smoothed the tablecloth in front of her. Her hair was solid gray, and her hands bent from arthritis. She was overweight. Cooper had never seen her wear anything but a cotton dress, white stockings, and a sweater.

In a sweet, calm voice she began, "Now Cooper, let me ax you, what's goin' on wit you and Miz Kelly?"

Cooper chewed a second forkful of peas as he looked around the kitchen and then said, "Miz Millie, I don't have any idea what happened to her or where she is."

"Mmhhmm. You got to knows somethin'. Be straight wit me."

"Honestly, I don't know anything," he said as he salted and peppered his peas.

"Cooper, I knows you as well as anybody. I done practically raised you my ownself. I's been with you since the day your parents brung you home."

"Yes, ma'am." His mind flooded with images of growing up under her watchful eye and his earliest memory as a little boy, holding onto her leg when frightened, her gently stroking the top of his head. Tears welled in his eyes.

"Now tells me the truth. I's not gonna judge you."

"Miz Millie, our marriage has gotten stale. Boring would be the best word. I just feel like I'm goin' through the motions, and I'm sure Kelly feels the same way. It's like we went from being best friends to being too busy for each other. We're tired of each other."

"Hhmmuff," Mille grunted.

"The kids are great. They're what's holdin' us together, but it's gettin' tougher every day. We fight about every little thing."

"I know that's right. So where is she?"

"I don't know." Cooper exhaled. "I swear. On Sunday, I thought that she had run off, finally had enough of me and just left. You know? I was sure of it. But now the cops are sayin' she's been kidnapped, and they think I did it! I've just been standin' around waitin' for somethin' to happen, and now I'm about to be arrested. I can't believe this. Somebody's settin' me up!"

Cooper was stress eating now. He hoped that Millie didn't ask him a bunch more questions. He just wanted to eat, preferably in silence, but he knew that wasn't going to happen. He was wishing he had somewhere else to go. Her eyes were making him uncomfortable.

"Okay, Cooper . . . now you gots to listen to me." Millie paused and waited for Cooper to look at her. When he did, she continued, "You're a good boy. But you been so busy tryin' to get ahead, you missed out on livin'. Happiness ain't about how big your house is or what kinda cars you got or about wearin' all them fancy clothes. MMhhnnn. No, sir. And I knows you was raised better than that."

Cooper wanted to run, but he respected Millie too much to interrupt and leave.

"You ain't promised nothin' in this life. You ain't promised health, happiness, or money. You bustin' your tail workin', and she's bustin' her tail tryin' to be all Miz High Society—somebody y'all ain't. And what for? And I know you ain't got much money . . . you bounce checks to me all the time."

Cooper was taken aback. He had no idea they had ever bounced a check to Millie. Kelly kept the family checkbook.

"And I'll tell you another thang. That Gates fellow, he ain't no good a-tall, and he thinks of you like a rented mule. That's all you is to him: a rented mule. He's tryin' to get all he can outta you. You know 'bout rented mules, don't you?"

"I think so."

"You don't want to rent yours out. Ain't that right, Haywood?"

"Amen," Haywood answered, while watching a muted television show.

"Nowadays, most folks believe iffn you don't own it, you ain't got no reason to take care of it. Just work the hell out of it. Forgive me, Jesus."

Cooper stopped eating to listen. Her words were ringing true—each comment stinging a little more than the previous.

"You be Gates's rented mule . . . and Miz Kelly treats you 'bout the same way. But you listen here . . . you don't treat her no better. She needs you to talk and to listen to her. That's why she does all that she does . . . 'cause she don't get the love she needs at home. She's fillin' a hole in her life. Y'all done both screwed this up. I been watchin' and bitin' my tongue, but I can't no mo."

Cooper knew she was right about all of it, but hearing it was painful. He looked over at Haywood who was nodding his head in agreement. Cooper turned back and stared blankly at the tabletop. Millie touched his hands and smiled.

"Now, look here," Millie continued. "You can fix this. I don't know where she is, but you gotta find her. Y'alls need to get back to takin' care of each other, pillow talkin', plain cars, plain house, savin' money, workin' less; yeah, you heard me . . . ain't no need fo you workin' that many hours every week. You just don't wanna be at home."

"You're right. You're right. You're right about all of it." Cooper put his face into his hands.

"Me and Haywood done been married sixty years, and we love each other more now than when we's started. Don't mean we ain't never been mad, and Lawd know we had a hard time when them blessed chirrens died. But we talk, and we work on it. Marriage ain't always easy, Son. Problem is, you workin' harder at work than you is on bein' married. You hearin'?"

"Yes, ma'am."

"You need to get right with God, you need to get right with Kelly, and you need to start spendin' time with dem precious chirren. Don't matter hows much money yous got, you can't buy back time. You been worrin' 'bout all da wrong thangs."

"I had no idea we'd bounced checks to you, Miz Millie."

The quickness with which she pushed back and out of her chair and then stood caused Cooper to nearly choke on his biscuit.

Millie was wide-eyed. "That's the least of your problems, child! Ain't you listenin' to me?

"Yes, ma'am, I'm listening." Cooper let out a deep sigh. He knew that she was right. What he didn't know was if it was too late.

"And another thang, Cooper, now, it ain't none of my bidness, but I pray to baby Jesus you ain't got no woman on the side. That really complicates thangs. You can't be havin' no outside woman and be tellin' her 'bout your problems at home. She'll learn right quick what ya need to hear, and that's what she'll be tellin' ya. It ain't fair to Miz Kelly. You understandin' me?"

She's wise, he thought and said, "It may be too late, Miz Millie."

"I hope it's not. Dear Lord, I pray it ain't."

"Cooper? CNN's goin' live from the Montgomery

po-lice station. You may wanna watch this," Haywood said, turning up the volume.

"And I gots one more thang to say," Millie declared, running her hand over her worn Bible. "I ain't so sure you oughta be buyin' my land."

CHAPTER 75
WEDNESDAY–DAY 4

"O, have you established a motive?" the commander asked as she nervously sipped coffee and handed the district attorney a package of cream.

Detective Obermeyer was not a fan of the DA. They had clashed many times. The attorney thought the detective was too hung up on following procedures, and the detective thought the DA was using certain cases to climb his own political ladder.

Obermeyer chose his words carefully, "Yes, ma'am, I think so . . . I need to make a few phone calls to solidify it. Driving back to the office . . . I remembered something his secretary had said, and I followed up on it. A Realtor tried to call Mr. Dixon. Apparently, Cooper's trying to buy an expensive hunting property."

"How much money are we talking about?" she asked.

"Dixon told the guy that he needed it to appraise for $1.1 million or more for the loan formulas to work."

"If he had a loan in place, why all this?"

"He didn't have the loan. At least two banks denied him. I found the papers in his desk."

"You really think that's the motive?" the commander asked, shaking her head. "I don't buy it."

"It's the only angle I have so far. We know folks who have done a lot more for a lot less."

The district attorney weighed in, saying, "That's kinda weak. People invest in land all the time. You gotta dig deeper. I'm not arguing something that thin in front of a judge. We don't actually have proof that she's been kidnapped. And if we get that, then the FBI steps in. Let's keep this in the family for as long as we can. For now, the only indisputable fact we have is that Kelly Dixon is missing."

"You've seen the e-mails."

"They're very incriminating, but they are not evidence of a crime. I need facts and a *plausible* motive to build a solid case."

"We may never know the *exact* motive, but what I'm offering is *plausible*," Obermeyer explained.

Silence filled the room for a few seconds as they tried to ascertain Cooper's motivation. Both the commander and the DA wanted to comment that being married to a nut job would be a sufficient motive, but neither did. Obermeyer lacked a point of personal reference.

The commander, shaking her head, said, "So he's too cheap for a divorce or didn't want the embarrassment at church or whatever, so he hires some criminals to kidnap his wife? It doesn't pass my smell test."

"Go back through your notes, Detective. Maybe you missed something," the DA requested.

Detective Obermeyer said, "Look, think about it. Cooper Dixon doesn't have the money to buy this land that he wants bad—he's been eyeing it for years and has already fixed up one of the shacks as his huntin' camp, and for years he's been managing the land for big deer—but he now has a new million-dollar life insurance policy on his ole lady. A million dollars goes a long way toward paying off this place. I'm tellin' y'all, I know it sounds crazy, but this is his motivation. Also, consider this: If he didn't have his ball and chain of a wife hangin' around his neck and he owned that property free and clear, he'd sell the Wynlakes house and haul the kids out there to live in a heartbeat. Plus, with his take from his business sale, he'd be set for life."

"He kills the mother of his children for a piece of property? No way. I mean, I don't buy that at all. Is he having an affair? That smells right," the commander offered as an alternative theory.

"Killed? You don't think she's alive somewhere?" the DA asked, watching CNN reporting live from the Dixon home. He was deciding if getting in front of the camera would further his political aspirations.

"I don't know. Probably. I do know that we need to get Cooper in here and interrogate the hell out of him," the commander stated.

"I just spoke to him, and he's not coming in on his own."

"Any idea where he is?" the DA asked.

"No, sir."

"Well, O, what about the possibility of him havin' an affair and wantin' his wife out of the way to keep from gettin' drained in a divorce? This I can see . . . it's almost predictable," the commander offered as though she had firsthand experience.

The big detective shook his head. "I'm diggin'. I did learn that he's been spending some time with an artist who doesn't work there. If he is, I'll find out."

The DA said, "Okay, let's make Cooper Dixon's world

a lot smaller. Leak that we're convinced he's responsible for his wife's disappearance, trace his phones, monitor his credit cards, and ask the public for assistance. I want him off our streets right now. I'll use the detective's theory to get the necessary warrants, but I'll probably have to call in a few favors to do it."

The detective nodded his understanding and was relieved that the conversation was ending.

The commander added, "Dig into Dixon's greasy partner. He may be involved. The FBI's lead investigator for their Racketeering Task Force is on his way over. He said he has some information we need. He mentioned Gates Ballenger by name. I'll let y'all know what he says."

"Let's find Mrs. Dixon. With any luck, she's still alive," the DA said as he started out the door, heading to his hair stylist.

Detective Obermeyer said aloud but mostly to himself, "It's been three days already. Statistically, this won't end well."

CHAPTER 76

The blonde national newscaster stared into the studio camera with a frustrated, disbelieving look. Countless times she had seen the details slowly unfold, revealing suspects, who, despite overwhelming evidence to the contrary, continually deny guilt or involvement. Shaking her head slowly, she began what she did best—asking questions, holding on tenaciously for truthful answers. More times than not, that pressure ultimately helped reveal the truth, serving justice and her ratings. The newscaster often used her platform to speak for victims. Tonight was no exception. She was repulsed by the facts as she spoke with the field reporter.

"Now, let me get this straight. You're telling me that this guy, a business owner, possibly kidnapped and probably killed his own wife, the mother of his two young children, for her insurance proceeds? And he planned to use that blood money to buy some hunting land? Did I understand you correctly?"

"Yes, that's correct. That's what our anonymous source within the Montgomery Police Department confirmed this afternoon," the male field reporter answered over the constant drone of dog-day cicadas.

"Do they have any idea where his wife is now or even if she is still thought to be alive?" she asked, rolling her eyes in disbelief.

"No, in fact, that's the big question. Kelly Dixon has been missing since the weekend and her husband, Cooper Dixon, has been named a person of interest. But the police are not going as far as to formally announce that Kelly's been kidnapped. Mr. Dixon, apparently, is on the run, and law enforcement is reaching out to the media to get his face on TV in hopes that someone will recognize him and turn him in," the reporter replied, glancing down at the small monitor, noticing with satisfaction that Cooper Dixon's driver license photo covered the screen.

"When we had Mr. Dixon on our show just a few days ago, he seemed sincere and genuinely concerned. It just goes to show that you have to trust the facts, *not* what someone tells you," she replied with disgust. "Typically, when we learn that a woman is missin' . . . isn't it almost always her husband or boyfriend who's involved?"

The reporter held the earpiece in place and shook his head as he waited to respond to what was a sarcastic comment rather than a question. The actual reason he was shaking his head was because he was thinking, *Not all men are bad.*

"One more question, before we break, is there another woman in this crazy scenario?" the newscaster asked with a cynical sigh.

"Yes, there is rumored to be 'another woman' as you put it," he said with a smirk. "Every day we are learning something new about this guy. As you can imagine, these are things that people go to extremes to keep private."

"Well, those details won't be private for long! Okay, America, let's have another look at this questionable character, Cooper Dixon. This is his DMV photo. He hasn't been seen in several days, and the police really wanna get their hands on him. Pretty normal-looking guy, but who really knows what's in his cold, dark heart or head. He has two wonderful children, who he evidently doesn't care about, and his beautiful wife has been missing for at least three days now. We do know that the longer she's missing, the less likelihood we have of her surviving this nightmare. Here's her photograph. She's close to my age, a beautiful soccer mom who's active in her community."

She added, shaking her head, "This is just sad. It's really unbelievable. All for a place to hunt and fish when there's thousands . . . literally hundreds of thousands of acres of public lands available to this guy for free. America, help us find Cooper Dixon."

"Our thoughts and prayers are with Kelly Dixon and her darlin' children. We pray that she is alive and well and that soon she will be reunited with her kids. We'll be right back."

CHAPTER 77

Gates sat at his desk, knowing that his world was on a razor's edge of collapse. All his life, he only did enough to get by; he never developed any strength of character through hard work. He had bribed several of his high school teachers in order to graduate. He even counterfeited his college diploma. Gates had never done anything that required persistence or honest work. He had managed to get everyone else to do the heavy lifting. He considered Cooper a brother, but this time Gates had crossed a line that he never knew was there, and he needed money, no matter how it came or who it hurt. However, with all the drama surrounding Cooper, the sale was slowing and could possibly be derailed. Gates hadn't fully considered that scenario.

Earlier in the day, Don Daniels told Gates that he was waiting to see what happened with Cooper. Gates knew that his days were numbered. He was tired of looking over his shoulder. He tried not to think about it, turning his attention to the newspaper and the lines for the weekend games.

"Gates, you have a call on line three. It's CNN!" Mrs. Riley paged excitedly.

"Okay," he answered as though CNN called every day.

He sat up straight, cleared his throat, and punched the blinking telephone line button, "Ballenger."

He listened to the voice on the other end and finally said, "Yes, yes, of course, I know him well. We're business partners. Yes, you could say 'best friends.' Okay. I'd be happy to be interviewed tonight. What time and where?"

He jotted down the details, smiling at such a fortuitous opportunity. He wondered if he had enough coke in his cigar tube to help him through the interview.

CHAPTER 78

Classic rock pounded as the Client sat inside the shrine. He stared meticulously at the images of the endless slide show, slowly fueling his desires. A strobe light helped amp the mood.

The various illegal drugs he'd been enjoying for several days made him feel invincible, which was being counteracted by his natural psychotic state since he stopped taking his prescriptions. His face, still stained with the purple cattle medicine, added to his crazed appearance. He was running on meth-fueled adrenalin from his latest heinous crime, the imminent elimination of Cooper, and his orchestrated opportunity to have the object of his demented mind's desire. He was on the cusp of full-blown mania.

His mind was racing with ideas, all of them bad and completely out of sync with the plan he meticulously worked through months ago. Hearing Cooper on TV begging to pay whatever ransom was asked gave him fresh ideas about monetizing this unanticipated development. *Hell, I might as well make that final payment to my hired boy.* He chuckled. *I won't hafta worry about his big ass gunnin' for me. I'll just squeeze Cooper for five hundred large. Halfa-mill has a nice ring to it . . . and that's a damn fine return on my investment.* That thought made him laugh out loud.

He devised what he thought was an ingenious improvisational second act. Smiling as he sipped a cold beer, he slowly closed his eyes and envisioned exactly what he wanted, needed, and felt he deserved.

Picking up the small cell phone the kidnappers had given him, he looked at its call history. Only one recent incoming call. With the remote control, he turned down the music and then hit Return Call. As he put the phone to his ear, he bounced both feet to a beat only in his mind.

Clarence was lying on the couch with the old air conditioner blowing on him when his cell phone rang. He sat up, noticed the number, and swore under his breath. He hit the button to accept the call.

He thought before he spoke, not wanting to say anything incriminating in case the Client was recording the conversation: "Speak to me" was all he said.

"I'll add an extra five grand if you'll wait till tomorrow night around eight."

Clarence didn't say anything after the Client paused, so he continued, "Okay, here's the deal, I'll bring you all the money, and then y'all leave immediately," the Client said rapidly. "Take all your shit and get gone."

Clarence thought for a few seconds. "Deal. Just bring cash. All of it, or I swear to you, I'm gonna stomp the dog shit outta you on the spot."

"Don't worry, you'll get what's comin' to ya," he replied and hit End Call.

"That crazy-ass redneck!" Clarence exclaimed. "Hang up on me! I swear I'll . . . Jenny! Jesse Ray! We're outta here tomorrow night."

"Hell yeah . . . that's what I'm talkin' 'bout!" Jesse Ray yelled, looking up from his laptop.

"We get paid and turn this haunted house over to him."

"That's the best news I've heard since we started this job. I hate this place," Jesse Ray added.

"I don't like it . . . he could be settin' us up for something," Jenny said with suspicion.

"Yeah, you're right. Regardless, Jesse Ray, get Maynard to help you start getting organized and cleaning up and wiping the place down."

"Anything to get outta here. I need some sleep. This spooky-ass place is wearin' on me!"

CHAPTER 79
THURSDAY—DAY 5

Dawn cracked as Cooper sat on the tailgate of his truck, parked behind the Browns' barn. With tears in his eyes, he rubbed his dog's head resting in his lap. He hardly noticed the squeals of a small group of wood ducks that came in low to his left to land on the oxbow lake behind the house.

Millie had talked to him until well past midnight, probing and preaching. She knew he was wanted and that he didn't have many options for cash. He explained that he couldn't go home, his bank accounts were closed, his credit cards weren't working, and he had less than eighty dollars in his billfold. He explained that he wasn't going to allow himself to be arrested, and he was going to find Kelly himself. He had planned to hire a private investigator and seek the volunteer assistance of Texas EquuSearch—the Houston suburb–based search-and-rescue outfit best known for its involvement in the searches for Caylee Anthony and Natalee Holloway. He was grasping for whatever straw might hold some hope.

Earlier, Cooper had been watching a repeat of the news story about him when Millie and Haywood walked into the room. In Haywood's hand was a large Mason jar filled with cash. Without hesitation, Millie took the jar and then handed it to Cooper. She stated that they wanted him to have it, to use it to find Kelly and clear his name. It was their life savings—everything they had, and they offered it to him. He was stunned and touched by their heartfelt generosity. Millie's eyes shone with love; Haywood's with resolve and support.

Cooper had protested that he couldn't take their money, but the fact was it presented his only lifeline to Kelly. Operating under the radar required cash. He needed cash to pay for assistance or to at least make down payments.

Reluctantly, he agreed to take $3,000 and insisted that they take, for collateral, his Rolex Submariner—a generous and grateful client had given it to him for his stellar work when her company successfully went public.

"This is just a loan. I promise, you'll get it back," Cooper said as he stood to leave.

"You go get Kelly," Millie said, giving him a big hug.

Haywood shook his hand and then pointed at Cooper's heart. "You gotta do whatja need to do to make this right or you'll be regretin' it fo the rest of your life." Haywood continued after a moment's pause to let that sink in, "And you're welcome to all the rest of da money iffin you need it."

Cooper was deep in thought about last night when Dixie suddenly sat up next to him to watch the ducks pitch in behind the cypress trees. As the sun shone through the trees, Cooper began to feel energized. He decided to call his attorney, to have him communicate on his behalf with the police. Regardless of the risk of being located by his BlackBerry, he knew whom he needed to call.

Rubbing Dixie's head, he waited for the device to power up. Within seconds it vibrated, alerting him to awaiting text messages and e-mails. Clicking on the icons, he saw his usual daily e-mails and at least a dozen others offering support or wanting details. Sandwiched in the middle of the list of text messages was one from a south Alabama area code and number that he didn't recognize.

Scrolling down and clicking on the text, he opened it and read aloud: "having fun yet asshole!!!!"

Cooper read it twice and then looked again at the number. His heart raced as he punched in the number and hit Send. Listening to it ring endlessly, he ended the call and then clicked on the number to text a reply message. Pissed off, he quickly typed, "You're the asshole! When I find out who you are, I'm going to kill you!" He stared at the screen, breathing heavily.

Dixie nudged Cooper's hand, looking for more rubbing. Cooper did so and said, "Thanks, Buddy," and then deleted the text before it sent. As his heart rate returned to what was passing for normal since Sunday morning, he composed his thoughts and typed, "Who is this? I want my wife back! Please! Tell me what you want," and hurriedly hit Send.

CHAPTER 80

Detective Obermeyer stood in the corner like a marine awaiting orders. Several other officers and local governmental officials slouched in chairs, drinking coffee.

Obermeyer's commander read an update on the night's events and then turned the meeting over to the DA.

"Okay, people, let's settle down. Thank you. I wanted to address y'all regarding the Dixon case. As you know, the media's in a feedin' frenzy, and I don't want them turnin' their scrutiny on me, the city . . . or the police department," the well-dressed district attorney explained, obviously overwhelmed. He had his smartest, most trusted advisors in the room, even those he didn't like.

Initially he wanted the television coverage and the potential glory, but he quickly realized the media groups were going to be relentless in their pursuit of a story. His interactions with the national contingent had left the distinct impression that they had no qualms with regard to creating a sensationalized version of the Dixon case. They were not going to let the facts get in the way of a good story. So he decided it prudent to lay low from then on, focusing on actually solving the crime and getting convictions of the perpetrators rather than leveraging the exposure.

The DA, not able to turn off the politician within, continued, "This case occurred here, but it does not define us. It is not what Montgomery's about . . . we've got such a great city, with air force bases, the state's Capitol, with all types of industry, and we're ground zero for the civil rights movement. We're not going to be portrayed as a city of delusional men kidnapping and killing their wives to collect insurance monies in order to buy huntin' land."

Obermeyer was gritting his teeth in anticipation of where the DA was going with this line of comments.

"I never thought this was a 'real' kidnapping from the beginning, but the more it unfolds, we have to give the Vaughn Park event credence. I called a friend at the FBI. Until we know for sure, they'll be assisting, in a supportive capacity . . . only. The problem is the media has—"

"Made this a national spectacle, and it's an election year?" Obermeyer interrupted, with no attempt to mask his contempt.

Glaring at the detective, the DA took a deep breath and then pointed at him, saying, "Thank you, Obermeyer. I wish we all could be so freakin' perfect, like you. But we aren't, and yes, this could ultimately burn my ass. It could also burn all of us. I'd like for y'all to remember that.

"Detective Obermeyer, I know we've had our problems. You do everything by the book. I respect that. I'm just simply askin' that all of you keep me informed and help protect all of us. No one in this room wants any of us to be made fools by those media vultures."

Obermeyer said, "Play by the book and make good choices, and you won't have any issues with me."

"That's enough!" the commander yelled, looking at both of them. She stood and then said, "Let's worry about finding Kelly Dixon. The first step in doing that is getting her husband in here. Then we can put the heat to him and find out what he's done with her . . . and to her."

Every officer in the room nodded in agreement, and there were more than a few, "Yes, ma'ams!"

The DA interrupted by asking, "Do we have any additional facts since our last meeting?"

"Not really," replied Obermeyer.

The DA let out a deep breath. "What about an alibi?"

"It's weak. He says he was at his hunting camp by himself. Nobody can substantiate his story or refute it, actually. There are about twenty hours that are not accounted for to my satisfaction. His business partner's lying his ass off, covering up something. He did finally admit that he was surprised when Cooper didn't show up for the Auburn game. They had important clients to entertain. Cooper was aware of this, and the day before said that he would be there."

"What's the latest on tracking Dixon?"

The lead tech officer stood and said, "Sir, we've been monitoring his phones—no pings on his cell, and he hasn't called home. All of his personal credit cards and his wife's are inactive as of Saturday, so no real leads there. We know that Mrs. Dixon's attempt to charge clothing on Saturday was denied by the credit card company. And as soon as the company replies to our subpoena, we'll know exactly why those charges were declined—whether they are maxed out or failed to pay their bill. We're also monitoring his business cards. No activity there. There has not been any banking or ATM activity either."

The commander let out a deep sigh and reluctantly asked, "Obermeyer, got any ideas on how to find this guy?"

Obermeyer nodded, and then held up a hand.

"What?"

"Stand by."

"Dammit, O. What the hell's on your mind?"

"What if we tricked him into believing that we found his wife?"

The group was silent.

"If he's innocent, he should come racing in. If he's guilty, he'll smell a rat and run. At least we'll know."

Everyone turned and looked at the DA. Exhausted from the stress of the kidnapping, rapes, and relentless media attention, he exhaled deeply and after a moment's thought, said, "It's actually not a bad idea. If you don't have a handle on his location by dark, we'll consider it."

He then looked over at the commander and said, "Better inform the top brass what we're up to. The chief will back us up."

CHAPTER 81

James Longstreet had survived a hard night at the Montgomery Country Club, drinking Highland Park eighteen-year-old single malt scotch with his poker buddies. When the phone rang at 6:05 a.m., he couldn't fathom who would be calling him. All his kids were grown, and his wife was on a trip to Greenwood, Mississippi, for a cooking class at Viking. He had planned to sleep late and then for the rest of the day watch a *Through the Wormhole* marathon on the Science Channel. He was one of the finest criminal defense attorneys in the city, and he had been a personal friend of Cooper's for many years. At this stage in life, he basically did only what he wanted, when he wanted.

He cleared his throat before answering the phone, "Hello?"

"Mr. Longstreet? It's Cooper."

"Cooper Dixon?" he answered, shaking himself awake.

"Yes, sir. I need your help. I know now that I shoulda called days ago."

"Is this your one phone call, son?"

"Not exactly. But that's why I'm callin'. The cops wanna arrest me. They think I did it."

"That's all everybody in town's talkin' about. Shit fire, it's all over the news. National news. I was wonderin' if you had counsel and hoped that you'd call. You're a hot item."

"I know. It's crazy. I'm being framed, and I need a lawyer."

James Longstreet swung his feet to the floor, stood up, and began pacing with his cordless phone.

"Okay, now, you got one. Where are you?"

"I don't want to say over the cell phone. But I'm not comin' in to get arrested."

"We have to meet."

"I gotta move carefully. I don't know who to trust. Somebody's frozen my bank accounts, none of my personal credit cards are working, and I'm not gonna get locked up and railroaded for somethin' I didn't do."

"Cooper, listen. We have to meet. You know that you can trust me. Don't you?"

"Yes, sir. We can meet, but first I need you to speak to the police for me. There's this detective. Detective Obermeyer. I need you to talk to him and tell him that I didn't do it and that I'm tryin' to find out who did, and the cops need to do the same. They need to quit wastin' time lookin' at me for this."

"I'll do that, but you really need to cooperate with them. The news has put forward a good case of your guilt. I'm not asking . . . I actually don't want to know . . . but I tell ya, Cooper, you're lookin' damn guilty. I don't believe it. I'm just tellin' you how it looks."

"I know, Mr. Longstreet. I'm bein' set up for some reason. That's why I can't come in. I just got this text, and I think whoever kidnapped Kelly is about to start communicatin' with me."

"Are you serious? If you have any information, we need to go to the police with it. They really do know how to handle these situations. I have friends down there."

"Not until I know more. Somebody who knows me very well is behind this. I have some e-mails you need to see."

"Okay, but Cooper, they'll find you if you keep your cell phone turned on."

"I know. Look, just buy me some time. I've got a phone number I need you to track down. I'll call you every two hours on the hour and check in. Until then, I'm turnin' it off."

"How are you gonna do this? How are you planning on hidin' at the same time?"

"I don't know yet. I'm just doin' the best I can."

"I understand. Be careful. Can you get to a landline and call me back? They wouldn't tap my line even if they knew I was your lawyer. Find one and take a few minutes to bring me up to speed. Then go do whatever you need to do. I gotta know a few details first, and I'll make arrangements to drop you a prepaid cell that we can talk on anytime. You gotta get off that one. Pull the battery. It's not gonna be easy defending a man on the run, particularly one who's bein' persecuted by the media, by the national media, like you are, and when they learn, and they will, that you now have counsel, it'll get much worse because you're refusing to come in."

"Yes, sir, I understand. I'll call you in a few minutes."

"And Cooper, listen to me, they are *crucifyin'* you."

"I've seen some of it. That's why I need you and need to be free, so I can fix this." Cooper broke the connection but, ignoring the risks, left the phone on for a few more minutes, hoping for a response to his text.

CHAPTER 82

The key rattling in the padlock woke Kelly. She knew that they were coming down to administer more drugs. She had the port pulled out again and prayed that this time it worked. They never suspected she was responsible for the other times it was loose. The mental fog was still thick, and her muscles ached from inactivity. The cool, musty air of the cellar now had undertones of human waste.

Her captors had not hurt her and had, in fact, worked to ensure that she was well cared for. Whenever possible, she attempted to talk to them, but they never answered her questions. The more she asked, the faster they worked to put her back under. No one ever made eye contact.

A skinny white man sauntered down the basement steps wearing a Sammy Davis Jr. mask. This was the first time she had seen this guy, and she began shaking. She was humiliated, her spirit almost broken. Being tied up for days, uncertain of her future, and thinking of Cooper, her children, and her life had taken a significant toll.

Sammy Davis Jr. stood at the bottom of the stairs, looking around the room and finally at Kelly, making eye contact.

"Please help me . . . please," she begged with fear in her voice and tears in her eyes.

"Are you hurt?"

Kelly sobbed and nodded her head. "Yes, and I wanna go home. I have kids. Please."

Maynard took a step toward her and quickly glanced up at the top of the stairs.

"Why are you doin' this?" she asked.

"Money," he whispered back.

Kelly tried to understand. *Money? What money?*

She said, "Please help me. I'll die if I keep lying here. I'll pay you if you help me."

Maynard carefully watched her eyes, studying the depths of her suffering.

She continued in a soft voice, "Is my husband doing this?"

Maynard looked intently at her. He knew that she wouldn't be hurt with his cousin's crew—they weren't murderers or rapists—but he didn't know the Client's intentions. Maynard could steal and sell anything without remorse, but seeing this helpless woman bothered him, the tug of conscience getting stronger the longer he was with her. *My momma raised me better than this.*

Maynard began thinking through potential scenarios of how he could help her. He noticed her necklace with a small, shiny aluminum duck band hanging on it. Maynard hunted ducks when he lived in Arkansas and immediately recognized it as a rare and highly prized Jack Miner band.

"Whereja get this?" he asked, reading the short Bible verse inscribed on it, *Have faith in me.*

"My husband shot the duck and told me the story about this missionary from Canada who bands wild ducks. I loved the story," she whispered, frustrated to be talking about duck hunting, but realized that she was making a personal connection with one of her abductors, which couldn't hurt.

"I've only heard of these, and I've seen dozens of federal duck bands, but this is a real honest-to-goodness Jack Miner," Maynard reverently responded as he held it.

"Help me get out of here, and you can have it," Kelly offered with hope in her eyes.

"No, no, I don't want it . . . it's yours . . . it's special. Your husband must love you very much to give it to you. Most guys would keep it and show it off on their call lanyard. Believe me, I know. I'm a duck hunter."

"Please, I have a family," she begged. "Help me."

"Where you from?" Maynard asked quietly.

"I grew up in Union Springs."

Maynard's eyes grew wide. "Who's your daddy?" he spat out, surprised.

She told him.

"No shit!"

Maynard knew her father. He had worked for him at Bonnie Plant Farm until they caught Maynard growing marijuana in the corner of a greenhouse. Kelly's father did not have him arrested, and Maynard knew that he could have. Maynard owed him.

Kelly said, "Small world, isn't it?"

Her eyes had hope in them as she watched her captor processing this information. She watched him pick up a syringe of drugs and then squeeze it out onto the floor. He looked at her and then walked over beside the cot. He quickly glanced up the stairs to see if anyone was coming down or standing and listening. He turned to her and whispered, "I'm gonna help you get outta here tomorrow. You can trust me. Okay? Nod if you understand."

Kelly emphatically nodded her head.

"Here, drink some Gatorade. No more drugs. But you gotta promise to be quiet. If someone else checks on you, you gotta act drugged and asleep. I'll do my best to make sure I draw the straw to treat ya next time. We're leavin' tomorrow . . . and I'll think of something. Okay?"

"Tell me the truth, is my husband responsible for this, and where are we? Tell me, please," she whispered.

"We're 'bout an hour north of Montgomery, and all I know is that somebody really wants to destroy your husband, and they want you to think he's responsible for all this," Maynard explained and inserted a teeth-whitening strip to soothe his frayed nerves.

Kelly's mind was sluggish from the effects of the powerful sedatives she had been receiving for several days. *Someone wants to hurt Cooper?* She started shaking and crying. After a moment she quietly asked, "Is my husband all right?"

"Don't know. The cops can't find him."

"Oh God!" She whimpered and started crying.

"Shh . . . be quiet. You gotta be quiet, or I can't help ya. Look, you gotta trust me and don't do anything crazy, or you're on your own."

Maynard looked toward the top of the stairs again and then leaned down to her ear and asked, "What's your husband's cell phone number?"

Kelly whispered it to him. Her eyes reflected an odd combination of fear and hope. Maynard swallowed hard and then put a finger to the plastic lips of his mask to signify silence. She nodded her understanding and then closed her eyes, saying a silent prayer of thanksgiving.

When Sammy Davis Jr. went upstairs, she lay still and tried to think of who would want to hurt Cooper so much that they would go to this extent.

CHAPTER 83

By late afternoon, Cooper had endured the toughest day of the ordeal—each was actually getting more difficult than the day before.

Earlier, at 12:27 p.m., Cooper received another text from the captor, explaining that Cooper wasn't allowed to ask any questions and that this person had "ALL the answers." Cooper sent several replies. Not one was answered. He was enraged and frustrated.

Cooper sent Millie to discreetly talk to Donna, his family, and especially the kids, to try calming their fears about his absence. He knew they all had to be worried sick and confused.

At Millie's, Cooper watched one of Kelly's uncles, who Cooper hadn't seen in a dozen years, claim on CNN that none of this surprised him. He said that he always suspected Cooper was capable of anything.

Cooper's midafternoon conversation with James Longstreet revealed that Gates had been arrested on charges of illegal gambling and possession of a controlled substance.

According to Longstreet, who had contacts inside the FBI feeding him information, Gates was singing like a bird to avoid prosecution and was asking for protective custody. He also learned that Gates believed his gambling debts were responsible for Kelly's disappearance.

"Gates is responsible?!" Cooper asked, stunned by this turn of events.

"Apparently. The Alabama Bureau of Investigations and the FBI have been watching Gates's bookie and wiretapping his telephone and office conversations for months. They arrested everyone involved a short time ago. When asked a question about the bookie, Gates started talking and wouldn't shut up. Turns out, handcuffs were a real buzzkill for your boy Gates."

"Good grief," Cooper replied, staring out the windshield. "Get to the part about Kelly!"

"When they busted into his office, he was in the middle of a line of coke. That may have encouraged his mouth to outrun his brain," James Longstreet replied incredulously.

"I'm gonna kill him!"

"Remember what I told you when you wanted to enter this partnership?"

Cooper sighed audibly.

James Longstreet continued without waiting for a response, "You only need a partner if you have a bucket of shit to eat."

"Look, I really don't need a lecture right now. I need to know about Gates!"

"Okay. The bad news is that the cops aren't puttin' much stock into what Gates is saying because of what they discovered in your office. They still think you're their man. Apparently, Obermeyer lost his composure when he found out I'm your attorney. He wants you bad. I mean real bad.

Pressure is coming down hard on him from high above. Anyway, the good news is that they're checking into Gates's story because there's a taped conversation about screwing you out of your interest in the Tower Agency so that when it's sold Gates would use that money to pay down his gambling debts. This is all good. It's ammunition for us."

"It's unfreakin' believable is what it is!"

"They're about to put Gates's bookie through the ringer to see what comes out. The FBI's going to interrogate him."

"I can't believe this. Gates has been my partner and friend for years."

"Cooper, he's basically broke, and his family quit supporting him financially. I don't think that they are going to make bail for him either," James Longstreet explained.

"He's always had money issues."

"It's more than that. Gates got cut off from any family money months ago, and with the sale of your business pending, he had to quit milking the agency too. But he never stopped gambling or drugging or anything."

"So how does Kelly's kidnappin' help him? I don't have big money, and they've not even asked for money yet." Cooper paused a moment, trying to think. "I'm gonna kill Gates myself."

"Whoa, son. Just hang loose for a little while, let me get some answers. I'm working on some theories, and the Feds are about to put the heat to these boys."

"What about this son of a bitch who's been textin' me?"

"No word yet. I have people on it though. Please try to calm down. We'll get this straightened out."

"Calm down?! The cops are after me. The media's rippin' me a new one. I'm worried sick about Kelly. My kids are freakin' out, being told by folks on national TV that I kidnapped their mother and probably killed her, Gates is screwin' with my life. I've got too much to think about . . . and to do. I don't have time to be calm."

"Just don't do anything stupid. They know you'll be gunnin' for Gates once you find out he's involved. He's in jail. You couldn't get to him anyway, and you gotta stay away from his house and your office. Just do your best to sit tight and wait for me to get some answers. Check back in a couple of hours. I'll have more information then. I gotta take another call." James Longstreet hung up without another word.

CHAPTER 84
FRIDAY—DAY 6

Jesse Ray was giddy to be leaving the old house. While packing his electronics, he sang out loud to keep from thinking about all the paranormal activity since they arrived. At night he thought he heard footsteps and had experienced many events that he believed were otherworldly. Once, while sleeping, he was convinced something grabbed his leg and tried to pull him from bed. Another night, while medicated on over-the-counter-pain meds, he thought he saw an old man walking slowly across the yard, carrying something. He kept this to himself and had not slept soundly since.

Clarence, too, had scarcely slept. He didn't know what to believe, but did know that something to do with this house had him on the edge. He tried to shake it all off and act unbothered. But the fact was from about midnight to dawn each night, he thought he heard voices and stayed freaked out. So much so, he had decided he just wanted out of this deal. This desire figured strongly in his decision to drop the pursuit of a more profitable angle for this job. He had blamed the painkillers, but what had pushed him over the edge was an apparition he saw in the yard around two in the morning. A pale man wearing a black hat and overcoat was standing in the trees, looking at the house, and then it suddenly vanished. Clarence assumed it was his imagination, the drugs, exhaustion, or most likely a combination of all these. But it seemed too real to discount offhand. The man was gaunt with the appearance of someone straight out of the mid-1800s. The apparition seemed to be in black-and-white, not in color, which further confused and fueled Clarence's wild thoughts. He didn't tell the others, but swore to himself that he wasn't spending another night in the creepy old house.

When the Client called, Clarence was jubilant. He and the rest of the crew were eager to get back to their relatively mundane criminal activities—robberies and burglaries, or really anything that didn't bring to mind a haunted house.

"Jesse Ray, shut up singing and listen. You and Jenny gather up all your shit, wipe down your rooms, and get back to the hotel," he directed with authority.

"Maynard, you clean up the den, wipe down *everything* . . . even if we didn't touch it. We'll take all the trash with us. You're stayin' with me until the Client gets here with the money."

"What's next?" Jenny asked. "Got any ideas?"

"Somethin' that's more our style. I'm open to suggestions."

"That Florida home-shopping warehouse!" Jesse Ray exclaimed.

"Plan it out, and present it to me."

"No problem. I am so outta here. I'm never staying anywhere old again."

"At least you don't have a ghost leaving you flowers," Jenny added. Everyone wanted to laugh but didn't.

"Larry and I will be there as soon as we get the cash. Okay, let's get busy."

Jesse Ray looked at Clarence and winked. His facial expression said that he had everything under control. Maynard took this chance to plead his case to stay a part of the group.

"You gotta keep me on, Dog. I'm multitalented!" Maynard added with a toothy smile.

"Show me some cleanup skills, and we'll talk later. I'm ready to get outta here. The water's even freakin' me out. Smells like an animal died in the well."

"That's just sulphur," Maynard explained. "Y'all obviously ain't ever lived in the country and drank from a well."

While gathering his things, Clarence remarked, "And I can't wait to be someplace where the lights stay on till you turn 'em off."

"That's happenin' to you too?" Jenny asked, with a bit of relief in her voice.

The crew glanced around at each other.

"At first I thought we were blowin' fuses," Jesse Ray added.

"I thought it was Larry King," Jenny said as she crossed her arms.

"It ain't me!"

"And we ain't blown a fuse," Jesse Ray said.

"Everybody just shut up and get your shit together so we can get the hell outta here," Clarence ordered, glancing out the window, hoping *not* to see a haint.

CHAPTER 85

Cooper had been driving around and periodically turning on his cell phone to check for text messages from the kidnappers. EquuSearch turned him down since he was a prime suspect. He tried explaining about Gates, but they weren't buying it. They did promise, however, to verify his story with the Montgomery police, and if the police gave consent for EquuSearch to become involved, they would contact him to get a recent photograph of Kelly and to have him fill out their missing person report. Cooper gave them Detective Obermeyer's cell phone number.

Twice he had seen police cars, but since he was driving Haywood's old truck, he didn't rouse any suspicions. He was worried about being pinged but didn't know of any other options. He glanced at his cell phone screen: 5:55 p.m. He let out an anguished groan. Darkness was falling across the city, and he was as low on options as he was hope. Cooper missed his family.

He was just about to turn off his phone when it rang. He recognized James Longstreet's number and immediately mashed the green button.

"Yes, sir."

"How you holding up, son?"

"Not great. Tell me you have some good news."

"I wish I did. I just got a tip that the cops are planning to trick you into thinking they found Kelly."

"What! Why?"

"So you'll come out of hidin'. They keep thinking they have you located, but then you turn the phone off. They are chasing you pretty damn hard. They've got all their high-tech tools in play."

"Shit!"

"Look, if you can't trust the police, it really complicates the situation."

Cooper let out a deep sigh that could be heard over the phone.

The attorney continued, "The consensus, right now at least, is that neither Gates nor his bookie is involved. My sources say the bookie looked and acted genuinely shocked when they questioned him. But he is a cold, hardened criminal, so we don't know for sure. He'll be tough to crack, but they have their best guys workin' him hard. They'll know one way or the other soon."

"Hell, if he wasn't at the police station, I'd interrogate the sonofabitch myself. I can make him talk. I keep thinkin' about Gates, and I just can't believe he's behind this because he doesn't have the balls or the brains."

"I'm getting the facts as fast as things are happening and as soon as my source can safely relay any info, I'll pass it on. Just stay low . . . and don't get tricked."

"I'm tired of waitin'. I've been doin' nothin' too long."

"Just calm down. I keep saying this, but don't do anything crazy. I did find out that the number texting you is from a prepaid cell phone. No way to trace it. Speaking of, I need to get you one. Where's a discreet place we both know so that I can leave it? Don't say any specific name. In case the police have been able to tap your phone. Just give me a detail that I'd know."

Cooper exhaled, his mind racing; after a moment he asked enthusiastically, "How 'bout where you helped me train my first bird dog? Remember him?"

"Of course. Perfect. It'll be behind the right-hand gatepost in an hour."

CHAPTER 86

The Client's iPhone was cradled on the dash, displaying a near eye-level portable version of his electronic shrine. Knowing that driving under the speed limit was much more suspicious to law enforcement than slightly over it, he set the cruise control at exactly three miles per hour over the limit and tried to relax. He grew excited with each passing mile marker as he headed to his family's abandoned homestead in rural Coosa County, Alabama.

He would pay the gang with embezzled funds from the bank. It was so easy to spend stolen money. He had decided to take over the hostage and change the plan by asking for a ransom. He had to do something. The bank examiners had begun crawling all over his files and would soon learn that he had made dozens of spurious loans and kept the proceeds. His crime forced him to make additional loans to bogus companies to pay down the earlier ones, and now the cycle was catching up to him. It had just about run its course . . . unless he infused some serious liquidity, quickly. The Client had expertly painted himself into a corner, but milking Cooper would buy him some much-needed time.

The Client had lost focus. All he cared about now were his insatiable desires and fantasies. He was spiraling out of control. He wanted dominion over Brooke. He knew of her interest in Cooper. He read it in her diary that he had stolen months ago. His mind burned with jealousy and resentment when he read it. He was determined to annihilate Cooper, and he was willing to pay any price for his desires. Brooke would come to him when he had control of the bank and the Tower Agency. The focus was coming back, and it was all so clear. He would have two things she wanted.

Glancing down at the passenger's seat, Grayson, wearing pajamas, was silently sobbing. The little boy dared not look up. The Client had terrified him when he stormed the house. A shock collar designed for a one-hundred-pound dog was fastened tightly around his neck, guaranteeing obedience.

The Client said, "Grayson, when I tell you to, get down on the floor and stay there. If you don't, I'm goin' to shock the shit out of you."

The Client then smiled, thinking of the future and the woman in the trunk of his BMW. He wondered briefly if she was comfortable. He loved the silky Victoria Secret lounge-wear he found her wearing. *This is my lucky night.*

CHAPTER 87

Clarence felt unprepared, which was distressing. As he stood on the front porch of the shadowy old mansion, all he could think about was getting his money, and then getting home. He glanced at the area next to an old privet hedge where a few days ago he thought he saw the apparition. *Must have been the painkillers.* The old house was full of antique pictures, and Clarence had studied all of them. They gave him the creeps. He was ready to leave.

Maynard was positioned inside the edge of the woods with a pistol in his hand, nervously refreshing his teeth-whitening strips like a chain-smoker. Clarence had faith in Maynard's ability to cover him, and it occurred to Clarence that there was a need to have Maynard on the team full-time. For one, he had weapons skills the others didn't possess, and at times like these, they could prove very handy. Clarence was assembling a team the way a college football coach recruits to meet his current and future needs. Since Clarence had grossed nearly $800,000 in the last year, he could afford more talent.

Clarence was focused on the sweating of the old concrete walkway, which meant that it was sure to rain, when suddenly gravel popped and headlights rapidly approached the house. He watched Maynard disappear behind a giant oak just inside the tree line. Taking a deep breath, Clarence adjusted his black sweatshirt over his bulletproof vest and transformed his demeanor into Mad Dog.

The car stopped in front of the house. The driver kept the high beams shining in Mad Dog's face.

"Hey, Bro!" the Client casually commented as he stepped out of the car and gently shut the door.

"Don't call me bro, asshole. I ain't yo brother, and you ain't black!"

"I'm jus tryin' to get along," the Client remarked with an overzealous laugh.

"You got my money?"

"Yeah, I got it. Is she in the cellar?"

"Sleepin' like a baby."

"You've done a fine job. A. Fine. Job. I've never enjoyed the news like I have these last few days."

"Where's my money?"

The Client smiled and then opened the car door, reached in, grabbed a duffle bag and then tossed it at the feet of the big man. "As promised."

Clarence unzipped it and saw a bunch of bundles of twenty-dollar bills and asked, "It's all here?"

"Count it," he said as he leaned against the car.

"It better be." Clarence reached inside, pulled out a bundle from the bottom of the bag and began inspecting it. He touched a random bill with a counterfeit detector pen.

"And here's your phone," he said, tossing the small phone to Mad Dog. "I texted Cooper a few times from it—just to mess with his head."

Clarence stepped out of the bright headlights and focused on the wild-eyed Client for a moment. He recognized the signs of drug abuse. The Client was as high as a kite and appeared capable of doing anything, at any moment.

"That does it for us," Mad Dog said, zipping the bag shut and feeling the relief of being paid.

"I didn't plan on sending you a ten-ninety-nine."

"That's mighty white of you," Mad Dog said sarcastically and glared at the man. He could see his eyes were flashing wildly, and he had an odd purple stain on the side of his face and neck.

"You're on your own," Mad Dog stated and started toward his Escalade, looking away from the BMW's bright lights. He felt himself gritting his teeth with each step. The weight of the money helped diminish his nearly overwhelming desire to kill the Client, cleaning out the gene pool of one worthless contributor. He motioned for Maynard to meet him. Slinging the bag over his shoulder, he tossed the phone to Maynard. Stopping in the shadows, Mad Dog looked back at the Client, "What are you fixin' to do with her?"

"Make everything right. Don't worry, she's in good hands."

"We've covered our tracks, so don't even think about tryin' to contact us again or it will be very painful for you. Is that clear . . . brother?"

"Thank you, Mr. Mad Dog. I appreciate your good work," the Client replied calmly as though he had just paid to have his grass cut.

CHAPTER 88

Cooper had just turned on his cell phone, checking for texts, when it rang. He recognized the number as Obermeyer's. It didn't surprise him, but this was the first time he had called when the phone was actually on.

"I'm innocent, Detective," Cooper answered.

"I know . . . that's why I'm calling, to let you know we found Kelly. We have her, she's safe . . . we need you to come immediately to the station."

Cooper didn't respond. From Longstreet's heads-up, he knew Obermeyer was attempting a deception, but he now wasn't sure how to play it. *What if it's true? What if they really found her?* The thought was causing him to panic.

"She's askin' for you, Cooper. Come on in. I'll meet you at the back door, or better yet, just tell me where you are, and I'll have a patrol unit pick you up."

"Prove that she's there. Let me talk to her. Where'd you find her? Was Gates involved?" Cooper asked excitedly. He wanted to believe, but he couldn't risk it.

"I'll fill you in on all the details when you get here. What's your location?" Detective Obermeyer said by way of not answering. He was looking back and forth between the DA and his commander and shrugged to indicate that he didn't know if the subterfuge was working.

"Does the media know?"

"No, not yet; we wanted to let you know before we went public. It's SOP in situations like this to notify the family first."

"I'm gonna have my attorney come down there."

"Cooper, look, I'm on your side, but you're actin' guilty. If you won't come in right now, it will pretty much seal your fate with us." The DA was waving his hands and shaking his head at Obermeyer, hoping that he hadn't just tipped their hand. Obermeyer immediately looked out the window.

"I know that you're just doin' your job. It's just that you're not doing it worth a shit!" Cooper answered angrily and ended the call, tossing the phone on the seat beside him. He pulled down his baseball cap, low over his eyes, and paid the toll to cross the Tallapoosa River.

"Cooper. Cooper! Damn it. He didn't buy it," the detective said, deeply exhaling.

Cooper was headed back to the security of the Browns' home. He tried to run through all the scenarios that could be unfolding, and he worried about what Gates had done. He really wanted to talk to Gates and considered calling his cell.

Cooper jumped when the phone rang again and he saw the number. It was from the same area code but a different number from whoever had been texting him. He quickly pulled to the side of the road and hurriedly answered the call.

"Hello! Who is this?"

"Is this Cooper Dixon?" Maynard asked from the passenger seat as he watched Clarence drive.

"Yes, who the hell is this?"

"Listen carefully. I know where your wife is, and I'm willing to help you get her back, but only if you'll do exactly what I say."

A chill shot down Cooper's spine as he listened to the audacity in the voice on the phone. Controlling his emotions, he simply said, "Okay."

"She's fine . . . for now. She's being held in the basement of an old house in the country. I can tell you exactly—"

"How do I know I can trust you? How do I know you've actually seen her?" Cooper interrupted, shocked by what he was hearing.

Maynard realized this was a legitimate question and thought about a response as he watched the lights of Montgomery off in the distance. Clarence's furrowed brow suggested that he wanted to know what was being said.

"That's fair. She's wearing a Jack Miner duck band on a silver necklace. Remember the verse?"

Cooper's mind raced. He was surprised to hear him mention the duck band. He had killed the banded mallard several years ago on the Tombigbee River. Kelly wore the band almost every time she had on any other silver jewelry. She said it was a conversation piece that no other woman had. *This guy knows something. What's that verse?*

"I can't remember the verse! Just tell me where she's at!"

"Come on, think," Maynard replied casually, toying with Cooper. "The verse says what *you* need to do."

Cooper racked his memory . . . it had been too long since he killed that duck. His mind was spinning. He finally blurted, "Have faith in me!" Cooper was breathing hard and continued, "Okay, you've got my attention. You couldn't have known that without seeing her."

"That's right. Now, you can have faith in what I'm about

to tell ya. There's one guy with her, and he's pretty screwed up. You oughta be able to figure out a way to get her out. She's been drugged, but she can probably walk by now."

"Drugged? Is she okay?"

"Yeah, she's fine. You got some paper? I'll give you directions."

"Tell me!" Cooper answered excitedly as he reached for a pen and paper.

Maynard explained in great detail how to get to the house and exactly where Kelly was being held. He also suggested where Cooper should park to avoid detection. Cooper tried to ask questions but was stonewalled on most of them.

"If you gotta pistol, you better take it with you and let me stress this: Do. Not. Call. The. Cops. Things will go to shit real quick if this dude's confronted by the police. He won't be expectin' *you*, believe me. Get the drop on him, shoot that sonofabitch in the head like the rabid dog he is, and get your wife back."

"Who is he?"

"Don't matter. Now, listen to me. You can surprise him if you do exactly what I said."

Maynard explained, watching a wide smile develop on Clarence's face.

"Who are you?" Cooper finally asked.

"Can't say. Do exactly what I said, and it will all work out," Cooper heard a muffled voice in the background.

"Look, I'm not some kind of superhero. Why can't I just call the police and then they can send in SWAT or someone who knows what the hell they're doin'? I don't know shit about this kinda stuff," Cooper begged in frustration.

"Because . . . it's complicated." Maynard replied, noticing Clarence was shaking his head vehemently.

"No pigs!" yelled Clarence, using his Mad Dog persona,

and continued, "or every last one of ya dies. We be watchin' you *and* them kids of yours. Ain't nobody we can't get to . . . when we want to!"

Clarence knew that it was unrealistic to think that Cooper wouldn't eventually get the police involved, but he also knew that instilling this level of fear in Cooper would buy them enough time to get out of the area.

"Who was that? Who are y'all?!" Cooper asked, losing his patience.

Maynard eyed Clarence suspiciously and then grinned at the bluff and said, "You're wastin' time. Look, if you don't want her back, then that's cool with us. We can sell her."

"No! No! No! No! Wait! Of course I want her back!"

"Good. Then shut the hell up and pay attention. I'm only gonna say this one more time. Do. Not. Call. The. Police," Maynard stressed.

"Shit! What's all this about?" Cooper exhaled.

"Are you retarded? You're wasting your wife's time to live . . . again."

"This is beyond crazy!"

"Just shut up and pay attention! I'm gonna talk real slow, so maybe it sinks in to that thick head of yours. Here's the deal, first, you . . ." Maynard carefully explained again in detail what Cooper should do and then without waiting for a reply hit End, terminating the call.

"Wait!" Cooper yelled into the phone. "Shit!" Staring at his BlackBerry and knowing it probably had just betrayed his location, Cooper immediately turned it off. The call had floored him. Knowledge of the duck band proved to him that the caller was for real.

He punched the accelerator and headed for the Browns' house. He tried to remember what all he had in his truck that could be useful.

Cooper grabbed his BlackBerry to call Detective Obermeyer but paused. His rational mind was screaming "call the police," but the words of the kidnappers haunted him. As he drove, he kept glancing at the phone in his hand.

As Maynard put his cell on the console, Clarence smiled with satisfaction and said, "That'll teach that crazy cracker."

Maynard replied, "That was kinda fun, and it sure felt good to turn Cooper loose on the Client. Man, he reminded me of some dudes in prison that you knew just weren't right in the head and that guy *definitely* ain't right. He's about to cross over some boundary line to the dark side . . . iffin he ain't already there. And he had some wicked drugs in the frig, too, according to what Jesse Ray learned from searchin' the Net."

"Yeah, well, he's gonna be disappointed when he goes lookin' for 'em, cuz I got 'em," Clarence said.

"What are you gonna do with 'em?"

"I don't know. Nothing, probably. I just didn't want him to have 'em," Clarence replied.

"I'm sure the Client's gonna hurt that woman. Probably kill her when he's done with her. May do it anyway, if her husband screws up," Maynard added, sucking his teeth.

"We'd go back and help Cooper if I knew that it wouldn't get our asses thrown in jail. I'm allergic to prison," Clarence said.

Maynard said, "If he's any kind of decent hunter . . . he knows how to be sneaky."

Clarence hoped Maynard was right about Cooper. Now that Clarence had full payment, he tried to think of this as just another completed job, but it didn't feel finished.

Maynard had helped Clarence scrutinize the decision to call Cooper and how to play it out with him. Thinking about that, Clarence looked over at Maynard and said, "You know, Larry, you're all right."

"Call me Tim," Maynard replied, inserting a whitening strip. "Jenny really likes Tim McGraw."

CHAPTER 89

Huddled in the Situation Room at the police headquarters, twenty different officers from various
departments argued about what to do next. It was
organized chaos—their way of fleshing through ideas and
scenarios. For the uninitiated, it looked as though they were
fighting, but most law enforcement officers would recognize
it as a typical exchange.

"He didn't buy it," Obermeyer said. "But as much as I
like him for this, it doesn't mean he did it."

"What the hell are you thinkin', O? If he thought there
was even a chance that we found his wife, he shoulda broke
the sound barrier getting his ass down here," a cocky young
detective remarked.

Obermeyer disagreed, and his face turned red. His spastic colon was about to go into overdrive. He said, "Y'all can
think what you want, but it doesn't prove his guilt. Think it
through. You'll see the logic."

"Okay, everybody, let me have your attention. We are
about halfway through the list of his friends and associates.

I'm authorizing overtime. See what every one of these folks knows. Maybe we'll get lucky and find him hidin' in somebody's tree house," the weary commander said. "Let's tighten up."

Suddenly, the door flew open and a young officer waved her hands at Obermeyer and then looked at the commander. She said, "We just pinged him. He's movin' and two different towers juggled his call. We triangulated him; he was movin' out Wares Ferry Road. Way out on Wares Ferry Road. In the boonies, before he turned it off."

Obermeyer jumped up to grab the sheet of paper with the details. This was the break they needed.

"So we have his location?" the commander asked, not wanting to continue the chasing of moving pings.

"Well, at least we know what part of the county he's in. If we could get him one more time, it would help. But he could move miles before he turns his phone on again. He's been so sporadic. Anyway, I thought y'all would want to know. This is the longest his phone has been on since we flagged it."

"Thank you. Let us know the moment you have anything else," the commander politely ordered; then she turned to another officer and said, "Put out a radio alert for his twenty. Watch all roads in and out of that area. Stop every white male even close to his description. Don't focus on the vehicle. Go! The rest of you, just stay the course. Let's find this guy."

"Stand by," Obermeyer said as if in a trance. He was staring at a television monitor in the corner. Gates's interview was being replayed by CNN. The camera cut to Gates sooner than he expected, catching him drinking a small bottled Coca-Cola with an odd-looking label. The shot was gone just as fast as it happened. Obermeyer tried to comprehend what he had just seen. *Where have I seen one of those bottles,* he thought, while listening to Gates ramble.

CHAPTER 90

Driving his pickup as fast as he dared, Cooper thought about the Jack Miner Migratory Bird Foundation band. It was from his first banded duck. At the time, he didn't know the significance of this particular band. And now, that band had greater importance—it was conclusive proof that the caller had been with Kelly. Whether or not she was still alive was another question. *I just gotta have faith!*

Prior to leaving Millie Brown's house in his truck, he rapidly inventoried his resources. In the truck's console he had a Browning Hi-Power 9 mm, semiautomatic pistol with a full magazine and one in the chamber. He also had a Browning .22 semiautomatic rifle with plenty of cartridges.

In his hunting pack, he had a small LED flashlight, a fifty-foot pull-up rope made from Dynex Dux 75 that he had gotten from a sailing buddy in Fairhope, and the typical accessories a hunter normally carried.

Behind the backseat were a couple of spring-operated beaver traps. He tossed them into his pack without much consideration as his mind raced to think what else he had that might be helpful.

Cooper grew excited when he remembered that he had stowed his scoped Thompson Center .243 under the backseat. He slid it back into its case when he realized that he didn't have any ammo for it.

Looking at his pack, he knew that his main assets were the pistol and the element of surprise.

Cooper knew the general area of where he was going. It shared a property line with the land that he was trying to buy. He didn't know who the owners were specifically, only that the estate never allowed any trespassing. The land was rolling hardwoods, with a few pine plantations, and very remote. The caller's instructions would place him where he could sneak through the woods to the house and survey the situation.

Millie had fussed at him for leaving without any explanation as to where he was going and why he was in such a hurry and for not taking Haywood with him.

Cooper heard Millie holler, "Be careful!" from her front porch as he drove past.

If she only knew, he thought, doing a quick visual check of his 9 mm pistol to ensure that a round was in fact chambered.

CHAPTER 91

The Client was walking around the outside of the house, remembering his ugly past when he saw Grayson running toward the barn. He felt in his pocket for the shock collar remote. It wasn't there. Hurrying to the car, he grabbed the remote and then jogged toward the barn to discipline his defiant little hostage.

Through clenched teeth, he said as he neared the barn, "Grayson. Grayson! Get your ass out here!"

Grayson's silence mocked him, making him furious. "Grayson, I swear to God, I'm gonna hurt you if you don't come out. I'm countin' to three. Do you hear me? One, two . . . I mean it!"

The Client paused for effect, placed his finger over the red button, and smiled as he punched the shock button and whispered, "Three."

Instantly Grayson screamed in agony at the top of his lungs and then started crying. Brooke was shrieking obscenities at him while beating and kicking the inside of the trunk.

The Client grinned and hit the button again, causing the desired response from both mother and son.

The evil man stood, feet spread shoulder-width apart, arms folded across his chest. "Okay, Grayson. Come out here this instant or I'll shock the shit out of you again!" He felt in total control of everything.

"No! Please. It hurts. I'm comin'!"

When Grayson walked out sobbing, the man held up the remote and warned the boy, "I brought you here to teach you a few things. The first is to respect me. I don't expect you to understand everything that's goin' on just yet, but I do expect you to obey—"

"You're hurtin' me," Grayson interrupted, pulling at the zip ties preventing the collar from being unbuckled.

"I'm helping you . . . not hurting you. You've got to learn to embrace pain in order to grow. With time, you'll like it, and then one day you'll enjoy inflictin' pain. I can't wait for you to experience *that* for the first time! There's an art to inflicting pain. I'm trying to teach you. It's in your genes. You can't resist the pull of your blood heritage. I know."

"Please, Dad, take this off me," Grayson begged while struggling with the collar.

"Quit whinin' and pay attention. You and your mom will soon understand me, fear me, respect me, and love me," he explained calmly as he walked toward his car.

Brooke's screaming and pounding had not waned. He briefly considered letting her out, but was too anxious to check on his prize in the cellar. He quietly walked up to the trunk of his car and without warning slammed down his fist on the top yelling, "Shut the hell up, you crazy bitch!"

CHAPTER 92

Detective Obermeyer was exhausted from interviewing Gates Ballenger. All that it had accomplished was to make the detective more confused and frustrated. Gates could not tell the same story twice. Obermeyer quickly figured him for a pathological liar.

The detective knew that Gates had called Kelly on her cell phone two days before she disappeared and that was troubling to him. Obermeyer was trying to unravel the truth, and Gates didn't seem to have it in him. Neither the FBI nor the Alabama Bureau of Investigation had any luck either. The question swirling around the investigation was whether Gates was really bright or a complete idiot.

And this was not Mitchell Holmes's first rodeo. He was cool as ice and took the Fifth when questioned, until they mentioned Kelly's kidnapping. At that point, he cooperated fully and offered more information than was required to make certain that they believed he wasn't involved.

For the last few minutes Obermeyer had been meeting privately with his favorite newspaper reporter. In his mind, she smelled like heaven and was built to match. Obermeyer wanted her to appreciate his superior intellectual skills. He was suddenly aware of his extra weight and the plainness of his sport coat and shoes. This morning they had seemed conservative, durable, and efficient as he dressed. Now he was second-guessing his choices and also wishing that he knew about wine and fine foods so that if they went on a date, he could impress her.

Casually allowing his jacket to open, he hoped that she would notice his pistol, and that seeing it would make a positive impression. His firearm and leather shoulder holster were expensive and looked it.

She asked good questions, which he answered carefully. Her spectacular cleavage made concentrating difficult for him. They each stopped talking and acted busy—looking at their notepads and periodically writing—when another officer walked into the break room where they were sitting in metal chairs on opposite ends of an old six-foot-rectangular folding table.

She thought she was getting the skinny and would exploit her assets for an exclusive. Obermeyer promised to tell her more when he could. Her beauty was his weakness.

"So, basically, you think Cooper Dixon did it?" she asked under her breath when they were alone again.

"Sure looks that way, but I have this gnawing, uneasy feeling that there's way more to this story that's yet to be revealed," he replied, paused for a moment, and then willfully struggled not to ask her to "stand by." Then he said, "It's a gut feeling. I'm also trying to understand Cooper's motive, *and* he doesn't have shit for an alibi. Excuse me."

"That's okay. I'm used to it. I guess crimes like these must put you under a lot of pressure," she commented, slowly leaning forward.

Obermeyer struggled to look her in the eye. "You just don't know what kind of pressure I'm under."

"Here," she said, handing him her business card. "My cell number's on the back if you get anything else you wanna tell me."

This card was a trophy to the detective. He held it tightly with his right hand. "You'll be the first to know." His cell phone started ringing, but he seemed to not notice.

"Aren't you going to answer that?"

Obermeyer saw that it was his commander calling. "Yeah, I need to. I'll call you."

The reporter whispered, "Thank you," before grabbing her notebook and standing up. The big detective melted at the sight of her tight skirt.

"Detective Obermeyer," he said before the phone touched his ear. He watched her glide out of the room.

"We just got a reliable tip from someone who works at MidState Bank."

"MidState?"

"Yeah."

"Stand by." The detective was trying to connect MidState with Cooper.

"Damn it! Don't start that shit now; I don't have time! This guy's had several conversations with a Mark Wright about the bank buying Cooper's business. Mark told our informant to 'watch Cooper's world implode.' He said it like he was braggin'."

"What's Mark Wright's involvement?"

"He works for the same bank, but what's interesting is that Mark Wright's ex-wife does a lot of work for Cooper's agency."

"That is interesting."

"He said Mark's a real oddball. He's not suggesting that he did it, but he said Mark was positive something was gonna happen. Like he knew."

"Stand by," Obermeyer said, staring at the tabletop, soaking in all of this.

"Obermeyer, if you tell me to stand by one more time—," the commander said immediately.

"Is his ex-wife's name Brooke?" Obermeyer asked, looking back through his notes.

"You're the detective; you tell me!"

"I see a connection. I need to talk to Mark Wright!"

"Go pick him up," the commander directed. "Immediately!"

"Yes, ma'am."

"One more thing. The couple that witnessed the kidnapping found an unusual Coke bottle in their yard right where the incident occurred. They'd never seen one before until they saw Gates Ballenger on CNN with one. They just called and told me."

The big detective was silent as his mind recalled everywhere he had seen the bottles.

"O? What are you thinkin'?"

"The only place I've ever seen those bottles was at Cooper Dixon's house and office. They're from Mexico."

"Find out whose Mexican Cokes those are. If they are Cooper Dixon's, then it really is beginning to pile up against him," the commander stated.

"Yes, it is."

CHAPTER 93

When Cooper was less than three miles from the point where the caller had told him to enter the woods, he checked his cell phone signal strength and then called James Longstreet, his attorney, to tell him what he was doing. That conversation didn't go too well. Cooper gave details of his plan, but before he could tell him where he was, James Longstreet freaked out to the point that he was yelling at Cooper and then pleading with him. Cooper listened and tried to clarify, but there was no changing Mr. Longstreet's opinion that this was a monumentally stupid idea. Cooper had to agree, but stated that he had to do it and hung up before he changed his mind.

Cooper slowed as he neared the location where he was to find the landmark mentioned in the directions—a new plastic wreath hanging on a white cross on the east side of the road. While he searched, a misting rain began to fall. When Cooper read Shynequa Riggins's name on the cross, he knew he was in the right place. He hadn't passed a house in several miles. The trees were tall and mature on both sides of the two-lane county road. The mist made the night feel even darker and obscured the moon and stars. He had been instructed to walk a half mile through the woods, due east from the cross. By so doing, he had been assured that his approach would not be noticed.

Cooper parked his truck in a flat spot just off the road. With shaking hands, he grabbed his hunting pack. He quickly checked his gear. Before zipping it shut, he noticed something Kelly had given him for Christmas the year before—a SPOT satellite personal locator beacon used to alert authorities of your position should you need emergency assistance. He slipped it into his back pocket.

Slinging his pack onto his back, he grabbed his weapons and took off through the dark in the direction that his rearview mirror compass indicated was east.

The early fall woods were thick with briars. He struggled through, hoping to pick up a game trail. He stopped briefly to listen. The forest was silent except for a distant owl hooting and dark with the exception of the rare lightning bug. When he started moving again, the damp leaves helped silence his steps. Cooper was anxious and prayed that he wasn't walking into a trap. The image from the caller's description of the house and of Kelly being tied to a cot in the cellar fueled his resolve that he was doing the right thing.

Periodically clicking on his small flashlight, he picked his way through the thick woods until he noticed red spider lilies blooming in a small cluster. He slowed his pace. The unique lilies were often found around old Southern homes and bloomed only in September, after rain. He knew these must have migrated down the hillside from an old home place.

As he went into a low creep toward the house, the unique scent of wet woods filled his nose. Briars entangled him as he crawled close enough to the ancient antebellum mansion to see dim lights burning in a few rooms. After several more feet, the drizzle let up enough for the moon to glow through the clouds. He could now see that the house was in terrible disrepair. Giant oak trees older than the home surrounded it. Bushes near the house were overgrown. Ivy grew around and up the huge columns and onto the second floor balcony over the entrance. The mansion appeared abandoned long ago. The incongruity of the new BMW parked in the tall weeds in front was stark.

Cooper quietly did another quick visual check of his pistol to ensure a round was chambered. He leaned the small rifle against a nearby tree and studied the house, searching for movement. The place appeared to have been built in the mid-1800s, most likely by a timber baron or wealthy planter. Any other day, Cooper would have been interested in the backstory of the mansion, but tonight he feared Kelly was suffering at the hand of a psychopath in the basement of the old place.

He was hunting—just like the mystery caller had suggested he do, and the stakes could not have been much higher. He crept through the underbrush toward the back of the mansion. Near the rear of the house, about thirty yards from the side opposite the barn, he bumped into a wrought iron fence. A moment later a dozen headstones came into focus. He squatted next to the one closest. Not wanting to use his flashlight, he couldn't read the worn names or dates, but they were obviously very old. As he pushed a little further, he fell into a low spot. Looking around in the faint moonlight, he saw several sunken areas and realized these were unmarked graves. A chill went up his spine. Wiping sweat from his eyes, he continued around the house until he saw the old barn described by the caller. *So far, so good.*

Now, he had to slip undetected into the kitchen. Cooper stood, swallowed hard, and eased toward the house, squeezing the pistol in his right hand. *I've not shot this thing nearly enough.*

CHAPTER 94

The thudding of heavy, purposeful footsteps caused Kelly's heart to race. Someone different was in the house. When she heard a child's frightened muffled voice, she began to hyperventilate. Straining to recognize the voice, the jolting rise in blood pressure gave her a splitting headache.

She was terrified by the metallic sound of the lock as it keyed open. She immediately closed her eyes to feign unconsciousness from the drugs. The new footfalls were timid as though the person was trying not to be heard for some inconceivable reason, which was a terrifying thought. Kelly tried to be calm as the bare seventy-five-watt lightbulb clicked on. Through closed eyes, she could tell it was swinging and could hear the soft padding of feet stop beside her. She sensed being stared at. Her heart was in her throat. The thought of pleading with this captor raced through her mind, but something about his pace, smell, and demeanor terrified her. She silently prayed, thought of her family, and tried not to tremble—innate warning sirens were screaming that her life depended on it.

The Client stared down at Kelly, relishing what he had carefully masterminded. He gently brushed a strand of hair from her forehead with his left hand. She looked gaunt and haggard. He didn't care, as long as she stayed alive long enough to get his cash. He could see her shallow breathing and then noticed how chafed her skin was under the restraints. The thought of her struggling aroused him more. He considered exploring her body but knew he had too much to do and there would be ample time later. He would wait until she was awake, so he could see the fear in her eyes and enjoy her frantic, futile attempts to escape.

He walked to the far end of the room and slid the armoire about three feet to the right, exposing a dark, narrow dirt passageway. He checked the condition of the nearly invisible lightweight thread that he had installed to indicate if someone ventured down the tunnel into his family's secret. *Perfect. Just as I left it.*

CHAPTER 95

Outside the Dixon home the media encampment had grown. Satellite trucks and reporters were everywhere. The neighbors were weary of the attention and worried for the family. The mainstream mass media was doing its job—making Cooper appear guilty without having all the facts and sensationalizing the entire matter. Kelly's disappearance was the talk of the town, from gossiping housewives to the many state office buildings to the local AM talk radio station. Cooper Dixon was prosecuted and persecuted in the court of public opinion.

Inside the house, Donna was running the show, doing her best to hold her sister's family together. Piper and Ben had not gone to school since Tuesday. They could not concentrate with the other kids asking millions of questions that obviously came from their parents. School was too stressful for Piper and Ben and too distracting for the other students . . . and faculty. The principal recommended that the children stay home until the situation was resolved. Kelly's parents were also staying at the house. Cooper's parents came early in the mornings and didn't leave until late. The kids were rarely allowed outside. Everyone avoided the Dixons, except immediate family. The respective families were civil to each other, but with each passing day tensions increased and opposing claims of culpability were beginning to surface.

Millie did her best daily to comfort all of them, without revealing too many details, wisely telling them just enough to keep hope alive. Between her domestic duties, she helped the children wrap all the trees with yellow ribbons.

James Longstreet had called numerous times to let them know he was communicating with Cooper. He vehemently expressed his belief in Cooper's innocence. Both sets of parents appreciated that he always called in advance of appearing on any news shows. It was obvious that Cooper's best interests were of utmost importance to him. He considered the entire family his client.

Piper desperately wanted her life back. For a thirteen-year-old girl, isolation from her friends, even for a day, was tantamount to an excruciating, slow death. She traded daily texts and one brief cell phone call with her dad. She believed in his innocence. She had fought bitterly with both parents just days earlier, but now she wanted to show them how much she loved and respected them.

Fortunately, Ben couldn't truly grasp the significance of the situation, but he did badly miss his mom and dad and Dixie.

CHAPTER 96

Before making a move for the kitchen, Cooper decided that he should determine if there was anyone he could see inside the house. He stealthily moved toward the front and then slithered through the giant camellia bushes to peek inside. As he positioned himself to look in the first window, he stepped on a nail that pierced his boot and foot. Pain flashed through him as the board stuck. He screamed in his mind. Looking down, he realized that someone had intentionally placed the nail-studded board there.

He yanked the board free, threw it aside, and ignoring the pain, stood on his toes to look through the window. He could only see a few pieces of old furniture and several boxes stacked against the far wall. This time, he carefully eased to the next window, taking extreme care where he stepped. He looked in, and from this vantage point he could see that the living room furnishings consisted of an old couch, a few chairs, and a television set with an aluminum foil–wrapped, rabbit-ear antenna. Oddly, on the coffee table was a jar of fresh-cut flowers. Cooper wiped the rain from his face and then carefully moved to the next window. This room was dark, so he kept moving toward the back of the house.

When he got to the back of the mansion, he noticed that the kitchen door was slightly ajar, so he quickly went past to a window so that he could determine if anyone was inside. On the inside wall, he noticed a small door that was closed, but the lock hasp was empty. *That's it! He must be down in the cellar right now.*

Cooper took a deep breath and then squatted down. He turned to lean his back against the side of the house while he thought of exactly what to do next. He felt an intense urgency, yet recognized that he needed to be careful and exact in his actions. The element of surprise at the moment was his most valuable weapon. He silently prayed that he had it.

Pulling out the personal locater beacon, he held it close to his eyes. He knew that once he set off the distress signal, Emergency Response Officers monitoring the system would know who needed assistance and exactly where he was located. Cooper figured that it would take at least twenty minutes for a response team to arrive, and based on his popularity in the media, more than just first responders would be arriving, loaded for bear. Hopefully, he would have time to surprise Kelly's captor and hold him at gunpoint until the cavalry arrived. Cooper also decided to call Obermeyer to alert him. As he fumbled for his phone, he heard a blood-curdling scream. *Shit!*

He immediately stuck his phone into his pocket and quickly punched the 911 button on the orange beacon and then set it on the windowsill. He took a deep breath, quickly made his way to the back of the house and slipped quietly through the kitchen door. He noticed the pungent, musty smell of the old house right before he stepped on a wide pine board that creaked. He froze for a moment, expecting violence. There wasn't a sound, so he carefully tiptoed across the kitchen to the cellar door where he heard muffled voices rising from below. He cautiously turned the glass knob until the hardware retracted enough for him to quietly pull it open. His heart was pounding so intensely that his vision was blurry.

Cooper pointed his pistol inside the stairwell as he followed the growing slice of light that the moving door created. One bare bulb illuminated the bottom of the stairs and a half moon of the dirt floor for a few feet out. Before he could see anything, he could smell urine and hear the thumping of music that appeared to be coming from some distance. Blinking his eyes to adjust to the darkness, Cooper was shocked to see Kelly strapped to a cot and Brooke bound to a chair. *What the hell!*

He dropped his gun to his side. He couldn't believe what he was seeing. *Nothin' makin' sense. Somebody's really screwin' with me!*

Cooper's first instinct was to dash down the stairs, grab the women, and get the hell out of there as fast as possible. On his first step, a thought brought him up short—the guy behind all this was down there, somewhere. He quickly raised his weapon as he surveyed the room again as best he could and then hurriedly slipped down the stairs.

When Cooper got to Kelly, he said softly, "Kelly, it's me. Cooper. Are you okay?"

Brooke's eyes were wide, unblinking. She was trying desperately to speak but couldn't because her mouth was duct-taped shut.

Cooper easily cut Kelly's restraints with his pocketknife. He helped her to sit up and then hugged her reassuringly. He whispered again in a panicked voice, "Are you okay?!"

She struggled to faintly say, "Cooper!" Tears were streaming down her cheeks.

"Are you all right?" Cooper asked, trying to look into her eyes while scanning the room for threats.

"You came for me. I'm so sorry about everything! I love you!" Her voice was weak.

"I'm here, baby. I love you too. Don't talk now. SShhhhhh . . . I'm gonna get you outta here. Can you walk?" he asked, helping her turn to sit up on the edge of the cot. Cooper was horrified at how weak she looked.

Once she was sitting up. Cooper looked around the room again, noticing the dark tunnel with a hint of light at the edges. The pounding bass was coming from it.

He touched Kelly on the shoulder. She looked up at him. He said, "Can you sit for a second?" She simply nodded.

Cooper moved quickly to help a frantic, distraught Brooke. He pulled the tape off her mouth. "It's my ex-husband, Mark . . . Mark's done all this . . . the bastard's got Grayson down in that hole! I gotta get my son!"

"Mark? Mark Wright? Mark Wright's your ex-husband? Shit! Okay! Okay! I'll get Grayson," Cooper said, looking at the tunnel.

The U2 song "Bullet the Blue Sky" was thumping through the earth and out through the tunnel, permeating the cellar.

Cooper couldn't understand how or why Mark Wright was responsible. But that didn't matter—seeing how Kelly suffered made him wild. He quickly cut the tape binding Brooke's arms and legs. She immediately took off running toward the tiny tunnel. Cooper caught her by the arm and wheeled her around toward him. He held both of her arms and in a forceful whisper said, "NO! Listen to me . . . get Kelly out of here and call the police! Tell 'em where we are.

I just sent an SOS through an emergency beacon, so somebody's gonna be comin' soon."

"No! I'm goin' after Grayson!"

"Listen to me! I'll get him. Brooke, look at me! I will get him. You and Kelly hafta get outta here. Take care of Kelly, and I'll take care of Grayson. Okay?"

Brooke nodded and started crying.

"Does Mark have a gun?"

Through sniffles, she said, "Probably." She paused a moment and then continued, "That son of a bitch's crazy! He's off his meds. He planned all this . . . and only the good Lord only knows what he's . . ." Her voice trailed off as she looked into the tunnel.

Cooper could see something primal in her face—fear or horror or worse. Whatever was on the other end of that passageway, she believed it evil.

"Okay listen . . . get outside and call the police; then y'all go hide in the barn until the cops get here. Here, take my phone. Get help here fast," he said, placing his phone into her hand.

"But Grayson!"

"Look at me. I'll protect Grayson. You gotta trust me, and you've gotta take care of Kelly. She's in bad shape. Okay? Okay, Brooke?"

Cooper didn't know what to do other than directly confront Mark. What he really wanted was a few pounds of flesh and some answers. He helped Kelly to her feet and then Brooke helped Kelly climb the stairs. Kelly was very weak, and Brooke was terrified.

As the women neared the top of the stairs, the music stopped. They froze and looked expectantly at Cooper. He was signaling for them to continue when they heard Grayson scream and a grunting sound from the tunnel. Brooke wheeled around, causing the stair tread to creak loudly. The trio froze.

"Brooke, you bitch! You better get your ass back down here!" Mark yelled and then cranked up the music again.

Cooper gestured wildly for Brooke to get Kelly out of there. He started toward the tunnel, his pistol aimed at the opening as he moved.

Cooper screamed over the music, "I don't know what the hell's goin' on, but it's over. Let Grayson go!"

Mark didn't immediately respond—obviously surprised to hear his nemesis—then confidently yelled, "Boy, this day just keeps gettin' better and better! How lucky you came to me. Did ya bring your checkbook?"

"I want Grayson. I just wanna get him outta here."

"I don't give a shit what *you* want! By the way, how's life been treatin' ya lately?" Mark replied boldly and laughed.

"I'll write you a check . . . how much!"

"Actually, I'm gonna need cash. I don't think your credit's good anymore," Mark said, laughing.

"I can get cash! Whatever you want! Just let me have Grayson, and I'll personally get you anything you want," Cooper said while still holding his shaking pistol in Mark's direction.

"You don't know what I want?"

"No, no, I don't, but I think you'd rather have me than Grayson. Think about it. He's just a kid."

"Brooke, get your ass back here or you'll never see Grayson again!" Mark screamed from the darkness.

"Brooke's gone. It's just you and me!"

"You're trustin' her?" Mark laughed wickedly, "She's part of this; don't ya see?"

"What?" Cooper asked in obvious confusion. While keeping his pistol pointing in Mark's direction, he quickly glanced toward the top of the stairs.

From the kitchen Brooke yelled loud enough for Mark to hear, "I don't know what he's talkin' about!" Quietly she said, "He's insane."

"Dixon, you're such a fool. You tryin' to have her just proves it," Mark said with another laugh.

"Give me Grayson!" Brooke shouted, almost in hysterics.

"I'm only gonna say it one more time: get your pretty little ass down here!" Mark screamed.

Cooper inched closer to the tunnel opening. He couldn't make out Mark's outline against the rough tunnel wall. A few more inches or a different angle and Cooper might have a clear shot. He heard Grayson crying. Cooper was confused by Mark's comments. He wanted this to be over, but he knew that there was a small boy who desperately needed his help.

"Look, Mark, it's over. Whatever's going on, it's over. Just let me have Grayson. He's scared. He's just a boy. Let me take him outta here," Cooper pleaded in the calmest tone he could muster.

Mark screamed, "If you leave this house, you'll never see Grayson alive again!"

"Mark! Mark?" Cooper yelled.

"What?!"

"You're wrong about me and Brooke . . . there's nothin' goin' on between us!"

"Bullshit! You're keepin' me from gettin' her back. Don't you understand? I want *her*, but she wants *you*."

"This is ridiculous; let Grayson go, and you and I can talk about it . . . this doesn't have to go bad. I can help you."

"Oh, it's going bad, and you're going with it."

"Mark, the police are on their way! It's over!"

"Well then, looks like we better get this party started before they get here."

"I'm sick of this! Give me Grayson, now!"

Brooke and Kelly could be heard faintly sobbing. Kelly was coherent enough to know what was going on but couldn't walk without assistance.

Mark said, "Whatja gonna do, Cooper? Shoot me?"

"I will if I have to!"

At that moment, Brooke and Kelly knew they had to get out of the house. Brooke yelled as loud as she could, "I hate you, Mark!"

Mark realized that she was leaving and became enraged. "Okay, bitch! You've made your decision," Mark yelled, pulling the shock collar control from his pocket. Smiling, he depressed the button, unleashing a piercing, excruciating scream from the tunnel.

After Grayson quit screaming, Mark yelled, "Cooper, if you want Grayson, you gotta come into my world and play."

"Stop, Mark! It's all over!" Cooper yelled as he tried to aim at the center of Mark's body moving in the shadows. Cooper didn't take the shot because he couldn't see Grayson.

Cooper watched Mark's shadow vanish. He knew that he had to follow him down the black hole. *I shoulda shot the sonofabitch when I first had a chance.*

His mind raced, trying to make sense of it all. Cooper looked at his watch—it wasn't there. He tightly squeezed the pistol.

"Shit. Here goes," he said softly aloud, sticking his head into the dark tunnel, preparing himself to kill Mark Wright.

CHAPTER 97

The minimally maintained house was dark. No vehicles were in the driveway. It appeared to the detective that no one was home, but he wasn't taking any chances. Obermeyer always did everything by the book. He carefully made his way onto the unlit front porch. He placed his left ear to the front door to listen for a while. He was on full alert.

After a long moment, Obermeyer pounded on the front door with his weak side hand, his strong hand was on the butt of his service weapon, announcing, "Montgomery Police! Anyone home?"

The door creaked open a half inch. Realizing that it hadn't been securely shut, Obermeyer quickly drew his weapon and without hesitation entered. Upon methodically clearing each room, he realized that he was standing in a psychopath's home.

The walls of the den were covered with clippings of hundreds of newspaper articles. One wall was nothing but the latest Montgomery rape articles. Another was Cooper's trials and tribulations. The detective recognized each story. He walked around slowly, absorbing every detail.

Scattered on the kitchen table and the living room couch were books on the Underground Railroad, bondage, sado-masochism, and aggressive interrogation techniques.

Obermeyer pulled on a pair of exam gloves as he walked down a hallway to meet an officer who was calling his name. The officer was standing outside a padlocked door. Tensions were high as the big detective walked up and pounded on the door while calling out to see if anyone was in the room.

Two assisting patrol officers were looking around the house. Obermeyer worried about entering the locked room and how to ensure that he wouldn't be in legal hot water. He didn't want anything he might find inside to be inadmissible at trial, but he knew that he needed to get inside that pad-locked room fast.

"Don't touch those," he stated emphatically to a young officer who was reaching to pick up some notes written on a yellow legal pad. The officer immediately backed away. Obermeyer relished the thought of what he would find on this guy's computer. He knew he had one somewhere. Obermeyer redirected his attention to the locked room. The hallway was too narrow to get a running start or to kick it in.

"Hey, uh," Obermeyer said, looking at the name tag of the officer standing beside him. "Officer Jones . . . run out and get me the tire iron from your cruiser."

The young officer looked at him curiously and then at the padlock. "Yeah, sure."

Obermeyer was concentrating on all he was seeing, attempting to understand Mark Wright. His trancelike state was interrupted when the uniformed officer handed him the heavy tire tool.

"Did y'all hear that?" Obermeyer excitedly asked.

Both officers looked blankly at him and shook their heads sideways in unison.

"Both of you need to get your hearing checked, probably from not wearing proper protection at the firing range," Obermeyer explained as he smacked the padlock with the tire tool. It held. On the third whack, the hasp tore from the door.

"Hey, man, don't we need a warrant for this room?"

"No. I told you. I thought I heard a cry for help. It's exigent circumstances. You might wanna write that down," Obermeyer explained.

"I heard it too," the other officer added, catching on.

Obermeyer smiled at him, nodded toward the door, and without a word among them, they stormed the room, weapons drawn. What they saw took their breath. Rotating electronic images and videos of a brunette woman were being displayed on the monitors. The dark walls added to the sensation that they were in a cave. Unlit candles caked with melted wax suggested someone spent a great deal of time in here. On one wall, various pieces of jewelry were strategically displayed. Obermeyer knew instantly that they belonged to the rape victims. They were prizes. All the rape victims had similar features to the woman in the shrine of photographs.

On the floor next to a credenza, Obermeyer saw several white rags stained purple. "Gentlemen, I believe we've found our rapist." Detective Obermeyer did a slow 360-degree turn in the room, amazed at what he was seeing.

"Whoa. This is some freaky shit, man!" one policeman replied nervously.

Obermeyer grabbed his cell phone and dialed. He kept studying the room while he waited for the commander to answer.

"Commander. Mark Wright is our rapist."

"You got him?"

"No, ma'am. He's not here, but he's our perp. Get out an APB for him right now! You are not going to believe this place. You must come see it for yourself to believe it."

"Okay, I'm on it, but hear this: it turns out that Cooper Dixon's longtime family housekeeper lives out on Wares Ferry Road."

"That's it, Commander! That's where we pinged him!" Obermeyer said as excited as he had ever been. Both of his major crimes had significant breakthroughs within minutes of each other.

"Have the patrol boys lock down Wright's place and keep an eye out for him. Stretch police tape around the whole yard. I'll get a warrant and a crime scene unit to your twenty to start processing, and I'll get out an APB immediately on Mark Wright."

"Don't let 'em touch anything in here. It's pristine. It's a gold mine of information and insight."

"O, I need you at the maid's house right now. Blue lights to the Walmart on the Atlanta Highway. We'll pick up a couple patrol units and go to her house. I'm getting a search warrant for her place as well."

"I hate to leave here, Commander," he replied, standing in the hall, looking into the shrine and wanting to dig deeper.

"You're the only one who's had dialogue with Dixon. If he's there, I'll need you to talk him out. I'll have our snipers in place before you get there, just in case it goes to shit. Don't worry, we'll find Mark Wright. He's been hiding in plain sight for months and unless he drives up, he won't know we're on to him. I'll have the officers seal the house and lock down the exits to the neighborhood. Nobody will be able to leave. Don't worry, O; we'll get him."

Obermeyer glanced down the hall toward the den and then turned and stared at the shrine. He had read about deranged criminals doing this, but this was his first to witness. *Normally, shrines are pictures taped to a wall and maybe a few extraneous things that remind the psycho of his obsession. This guy, though, turned it up a notch with his sophisticated electronics. This techno shrine was easily portable by downloading it to an external device, allowing him access anywhere there was a computer, modern television, or even on a smartphone. This is one kinky dude.*

His mind jumped to a thought about catching Cooper, hiding in his housekeeper's bathtub, behind a shower curtain. He wanted to stay to study the lair, but the commander was right. Cooper was a priority. Tonight was turning into a career-defining evening for him. His irritable bowel syndrome symptoms were beginning to kick in.

"Yes, ma'am. I'm on my way," he said and then hung up the cell phone. Detective Obermeyer was thrilled to be needed, finally.

"Y'all tape off the entire property. No one steps foot inside the tape except the crime scene guys." He excitedly explained and continued, "And keep your eyes peeled. He just might drive up, not expecting anything. Be sharp. This dude's an unknown, but at a minimum you should expect an irrational and disproportional violent response to us being here, disrupting his ritual. I'll be back as soon as I can. I don't wanna miss that!"

Detective Obermeyer sprinted to his car.

CHAPTER 98

Cooper touched the red dirt at the edge of the small tunnel, quickly peering into the void, and then tried to swallow the lump in his throat caused by his claustrophobia and loathing of the dark. The music pulsated, Mark yelled unintelligibly, and Grayson screamed in fear and pain. Cooper pushed his pistol in front of him as he squatted to get into the passageway. From what he could surmise, the tunnel was about three feet in diameter and had a fairly steep drop in elevation. He couldn't see the end of it. He quickly tucked the pistol into his waistband at his lower back in order to crawl on his hands and knees. The dirt ceiling touched his shoulders and scraped against his backpack. The tunnel seemed to get smaller the deeper he inched. To overcome his own fears, he focused on saving Grayson from his sadistic father.

As he progressed through the tunnel, he touched Romex on the ground. He stopped to feel it. *Must be the electrical supply for the lights and music,* he thought. He considered cutting it, but didn't want to get shocked or face Mark in complete darkness. He momentarily considered backing out of the tunnel, covering the opening with his gun, and just waiting for the police to arrive, but Grayson's screams shattered that idea.

Cooper was not trying to be a hero, but he couldn't leave—do nothing—knowing Grayson was down there, experiencing some unmanageable hell. He told himself that Kelly was safe and that if Grayson were his child, he would do anything—everything—to save him.

Cautiously exiting the tunnel, pistol drawn, Cooper was stunned at the size of the cavern that lay before him. The main chamber was the size of a modest three-bedroom house. He was having difficulty comprehending that this volume of space was deep underground. At first blush it looked like a Universal Studios movie set. Taking a deep breath, Cooper took stock of the situation. The two bare bulbs did little to illuminate the vast area. Mark and Grayson were nowhere to be seen or heard.

Cooper quickly climbed down the old wooden ladder to the floor of the cavern. The music was loud and reverberating from several directions. He crouched behind an old wooden table, searching the shadows for movement. He knew from state history in grade school that Alabama had more caves than almost any other state, some of them giant and stretching for miles, but he had never been in one. There were giant stalactites and stalagmites and other formations he had only seen in magazines. Among the beautiful, natural formations were rusted chains and shackles, neatly coiled and eerily ready . . . for something. There were two freestanding wooden stocks and a whipping post. Several boards with shackles attached were mounted to the cavern walls. Cooper realized that he was in some sort of torture chamber.

Given the age of the house, it probably dated back to the days of slavery.

The music was so loud that Cooper couldn't think clearly. Grayson screamed again. The faintness of the shrieks now indicated that they were traveling away from him, farther down into the darkness. Cooper saw the speakers, traced the wires to the sound system, and punched off the power. The stereo was sandwiched between two very large, empty terrarium containers.

The main cavern chamber appeared to have two large caves or tunnels branching off into the abyss. Cooper clicked on his flashlight to look for footprints. He hated the dark, and being underground, even in a large space, made him feel confined. He looked at the ceiling and swallowed hard.

"Thanks, Cooper! Now I can hear you comin'. I'm so glad you joined my party! I think you'll like the guest list: you, me, Grayson, and the five big-ass rattlesnakes that I just let loose. They make wonderful pets. Kinda mean though," Mark shouted in a suspiciously calm voice. "They don't move real fast down here in the cool . . . but they're still active and surprisingly nasty. I've got on snake chaps that will come in handy. Sorry I don't have any for you or Grayson."

Cooper stood, breathing hard. He really didn't want to respond. He squeezed his pistol and flashlight, while now searching the ground and walls for snakes.

He stepped carefully as he moved toward Mark's demented voice and yelled, "Give me Grayson!"

"You just don't get it. You're the problem, not the solution. I swear, how'd you get to be so successful being so freakin' stupid?" Mark shouted as he purposely led Cooper deeper underground.

He wanted Cooper in total darkness so that he could double back and get between him and the exit. From years of exploring, Mark had memorized every inch of the twisting half-mile-long cavern.

"Just let Grayson go. We can talk and work this out," Cooper answered, noticing hundreds of gray bats hanging from the roof of the smaller cave area. *Wonder why these bats haven't gone out for the night,* he thought.

Cooper could see fresh footprints in the dirt and bat dung. He used his light to follow them. His pistol at the ready.

"Oh, don't worry. I'm gonna talk with you . . . and you're gonna be begging me," Mark taunted. "You ever heard of Anectine? Wanna try some? My Uncle Don recently did, to his surprise, and I bet some of your huntin' buddies know what it does."

Cooper was freaking out at the mention of the drug. Years ago, when it was legal, he heard of bow hunters placing the drug behind their broadheads in tiny balloon-like bags, called poison pods. If a bow hunter arrowed a deer, even with a poor hit, and it drew blood, the poison would kill the animal inside sixty seconds. Those pods were deadly, and he wanted nothing to do with them or the drug.

After Cooper had traveled about 150 yards or so, he was ready to get out. Mark's comments, the fear of rattlesnakes, the darkness, and his claustrophobia were starting to overwhelm him. Other than the occasional dripping of water, the cavern was silent. Mark had quit talking, and Grayson hadn't screamed in several minutes. Cooper stood in complete darkness, thinking about what had brought him to this place, both physically and emotionally.

Utilizing a smaller tributary cave, Mark circled around Cooper. Grayson's mouth was covered with duct tape to ensure silence. Mark's intimate knowledge of the cave allowed him to move quickly in total darkness.

When Mark and Grayson arrived back at the tunnel to the house, Mark whispered to Grayson, instructing him to remain completely still or else he'd get shocked. Mark quietly opened an old wooden box and retrieved four sticks of dynamite. They were damp from nitroglycerin perspiring through the paper wrapper. He hurriedly inserted aluminum blasting caps and trimmed the fuses to a dangerous four inches, equaling about twenty seconds of burn. Mark knew that Cooper was in deep and smiled at the thought of what lay ahead.

Opening a newer box, Mark removed a pair of military-grade thermal imaging goggles. After twisting the fuses together, he calmly lit two sticks and tossed them into the tunnel leading to the house. He grabbed Grayson and quickly moved to the far side of the cavern, where they crawled under a giant wooden table. He placed his hands over his ears. Not knowing what was happening, Grayson sat unprotected.

Twenty-two seconds later the explosion collapsed the tunnel and blew out the lights. A fog of dirt and dust filled the air. Grayson screamed behind his taped mouth, and his demented father smiled. Mark stood up in the total darkness that he loved so much. Placing the thermal goggles over his eyes, he could see the heat from the explosion in the dirt where the tunnel had been. He looked down at the white heat signature form of Grayson on the dirt floor and heard him crying softly. The dirt showed where Grayson had thrashed about. Mark grinned at the thought of Grayson's fearful struggling. Somehow he had freed his bound hands because the silhouette of the shock collar showed where his warm little hands had attempted to remove it. The tape he took off his mouth was lying on the ground beside him.

"Man, I love these things," Mark said aloud but mostly to himself.

The cave's ambient temperature made the goggles particularly effective at displaying body heat and remnant warmth from recently touched surfaces. As Grayson got to his knees, Mark backhanded him flat to the floor. Grayson screamed.

The ominous detonation at a distance echoed through the cavern like no sound Cooper had ever heard. He had no idea that the tunnel had been blown shut, but he knew whatever had just happened was not good. The entire earth seemed to shutter. Hundreds of bats were flying erratically.

Cooper clicked off his flashlight, squatted down, took a deep breath, and said a prayer for Grayson and himself.

CHAPTER 99

Brooke was feeling guilty. If it weren't for Grayson, she'd be gone. She wanted to go back inside the house to kill Mark with her bare hands, in front of Grayson. She hated Mark—actually "hate" really wasn't quite strong enough of a word to characterize how and what she felt for him. He had become a nightmare since they divorced. He had changed drastically. Shortly after they married, Mark admitted to a family history of mental disease and that he had been diagnosed bipolar. As long as she kept him on his medications, he seemed fairly normal. But it would take only a few days of being off them to flip his personality switch. Had she not been pregnant, they would have never married. At the time, she thought it the best option for her and her baby. Within a few months, however, she became acutely aware of her error in judgement. Dealing with Mark got much worse after the divorce because among other things, she could no longer monitor his medications. She suspected that he stalked her, but she couldn't prove it.

Kelly needed Brooke's assistance to walk, and once outside Kelly started to shake uncontrollably. Brooke tried to comfort her and realized her own arm was injured as she tried to hold Kelly up. Kelly was so relieved to be free, but she was weak from several days of constant sedation, immobility, and lack of proper nourishment.

Brooke dialed 911 on the cell phone given to her by Cooper. She rapidly told the operator who she was, that she had Kelly Dixon with her, and that Mark Wright was holding her son hostage. The stunned operator had her repeat everything three times to make certain she understood. Brooke did her best to describe where she was, but she didn't know exactly. Unfortunately, Coosa County had not installed enhanced 911, so the operator asked Brooke to stay on the line so that they could triangulate her location. "It's going to take a few minutes," the operator explained.

Brooke leaned Kelly against the car and searched the inside for keys. They weren't anywhere she looked. Brooke wondered if they were inside the house, maybe lying on the kitchen table. She turned her attention to Kelly and saw her eyes rolling back in her head.

"Hurry, please! I think she's goin' into shock," Brooke screamed into the cell phone.

"Make sure she's warm, wrap her in a blanket. We're doing the best we can, ma'am. I promise," the operator responded professionally.

Brooke tossed the phone down and grabbed Kelly, wrapping her arms around her. "Kelly! Kelly! Hang on now, you're safe. Please stay with me. I'm gonna get you a blanket. You gotta stay warm."

"He came for me," she mumbled.

"What? What didja say?" Brooke frantically asked.

"Cooper came and rescued me. He said he loves me."

Brooke was being inundated with conflicting emotions. Grayson was in Mark's evil hands; Cooper was in grave danger too; and the wife of the man she desired was deliriously talking about him and clearly moved by his efforts to find her. Even in Brooke's fragmented mental state, she could tell that this woman was not the Kelly that Cooper described. Brooke believed that the events of the past several days had changed everything, and the events of tonight would cement the directions of everyone's lives—that was the only certainty in her world. Since Cooper was protecting Grayson, she needed to help and comfort Kelly.

"He does. He loves you very much," she said rubbing Kelly's head.

"How do you know Cooper so well?" Kelly asked in a weak voice.

"I do design work for his agency."

"I didn't think he would come for me. I didn't think he loved me anymore."

"He does. He loves you and your kids very much."

"I've made a mess of my marriage," Kelly cried.

"Marriage is tough, I know. I've had the worst one imaginable."

"I wanna have our love back. I miss Cooper."

"Kelly, you will. You'll have your marriage back. Just hang on. The sheriff's trying to locate us," Brooke replied, letting out a deep breath. Kelly's words about Cooper were difficult to hear. She continued, "Cooper's been going crazy this week with worry . . . I know he misses you terribly. Do you hear me? It's true, I promise." She wiped a tear from Kelly's face, "Listen to me. Cooper loves you. I can tell. You *can* have your love back. I'm gonna sneak back in the house and see if I can find a blanket. Please, stay right here. Okay?"

Kelly nodded and with tears in her eyes worriedly looked up at Brooke. Brooke watched Kelly's faint attempt at a smile. Brooke let out a deep sigh and then put the phone to her ear and asked, "Have you found us yet?!"

"Yes, ma'am. We're dispatchin' all of our deputies and the sheriff. We've notified the Montgomery Police Department and volunteers from the fire department are en route. Get in a safe place, and stay put!"

"Please hurry!" Brooke exclaimed. She glanced at Kelly, threw the phone onto the hood of the car, and then ran as fast as she could toward the old mansion to find a blanket. *Please God, please bring Grayson and Cooper out alive. Please!* She prayed.

As Brooke entered the front door, there was a loud explosion, shaking the house. The old mansion rumbled in response, pictures fell from the walls. Brooke fell to the floor. She couldn't imagine what had just happened. She stood and then raced toward the kitchen and into a billowing cloud of red Coosa County dust.

CHAPTER 100

Detective Obermeyer and his commander led two patrol units into the yard of Millie and Haywood Brown. The last unit pulled immediately to the back of the house as planned. The tension among law enforcement over the last few days had reached a crescendo.

With skill and precision they surrounded the house, and the commander, who rarely left the comfort of her office, led the charge to the front door. Obermeyer lived for these moments, while hoping his bowels didn't cause problems. The police had not expected a pissed-off dog, which went into a barking rage, alerting everyone inside that something urgent was happening. The porch light suddenly illuminated the front yard, and Millie Brown cracked open her front door to see two well-dressed people trying to talk the toothy dog into calming down.

"What's going on out there?" Millie hollered.

"Montgomery Police! We have reason to believe you may be hiding Cooper Dixon."

"I ain't got Cooper!" she answered incredulously.

The dog had taken her barking up a notch with Millie present.

"Ma'am, we have a search warrant and intend to come into your house and search the premises. Please call your dog off, before something bad happens," the commander nervously yelled back, noticing a dead snake hung on the fence.

"Y'all's welcome to come on in. You don't need no papers. Sorry 'bout Rolex, she ain't so welcomin', but she ain't gonna bite nobody less'n they try to hurt me."

The officers slowly walked to the front porch. Millie threatened a swat at Rolex with her broom, "Hush, Rolex!"

In a whispered voice, the commander inquired of Obermeyer, "Rolex?"

"She's a watchdog," he replied with a smile, while studying Millie Brown.

"Oh. Okay. What's with the dead snake?" the commander quietly asked Obermeyer.

"I's killed it yesterday. If'n you hang one up likes that, it'll rain in three days. We needs the rain, ma'am," Millie explained. Both officers were surprised that she had heard their whispered words.

"Okaaaay," the commander responded as she passed the snake carcass.

"You officers come on in."

"Thank you, ma'am," they said in unison, holstering their weapons.

"I do needs to see your badges first, I reckon," she said with a serious look.

Obermeyer had his out first, and she studied it until satisfied. The commander then handed over her shield for inspection. Again Millie studied it for authenticity.

"Ummhunh. Y'all come on in. Excuse my ironing board. Gettin' ready for church on Sunday," Millie explained, discreetly sliding a small object into her apron pocket.

The detective and the commander both noticed.

"Ma'am, I need to see whatever it was that you just put in your pocket," the commander stated, suspiciously.

Embarrassed, Millie reached in and pulled out a small silver can. She held it in her hand for the police to see. "Dat's just my snuff. I's embarrassed for y'all to see it," she answered bashfully.

Millie's simple demeanor and willingness to cooperate relaxed both the detective and the commander. They both noticed an older man rise from his chair as they entered the room.

"This here's my husband, Haywood. He's watching tee-vee. Don't move much on Friday evenin's."

Both officers took steps forward and shook Haywood's hand. He was quiet and seemed more interested in the television than the police officers.

"Evening, it's nice to meet you," the commander offered.

Haywood nodded and remained standing though clearly wanting to sit back down.

Obermeyer noticed Haywood Brown's Coca-Cola bottle next to where he had been sitting.

"You like those small Cokes?"

"I do," Mr. Brown answered curtly.

"It looks different. Is that Spanish on the bottle?"

Mr. Brown looked at the bottle, and then at Millie, and finally to the detective. "Um, well, yeah, I guess it is. I don't know where she gets these."

Obermeyer thought about the Coke bottle while the commander turned her attention to Millie Brown. "Mrs. Brown, we're looking for Cooper Dixon, and we have reason to believe that he might be here."

"Lord no, he ain't here."

"Has he been here or do you know where he is? We want to help him," the commander explained.

"I don't have no idea where he's at," she responded carefully so as not to lie but not offer too much truth either.

"Mrs. Brown, where were you late this afternoon?"

"I went to my friend's house and got my hair did."

"Where does she live?"

"She stays about a mile up the road."

"Has Cooper been here or there today?" Obermeyer asked.

"Damn it!" Haywood yelled before Millie could answer.

"Haywood, we's got company," Millie scolded.

"Even I's knew da answer to that puzzle," he replied, without looking up.

"Ma'am, we need to look around. We believe Cooper is not here, but we can't leave any stone unturned. I'm sure you understand," the commander offered.

"Yes, ma'am, go ahead, but you ain't gone find nothin'. Somebody's settin' that poor man up to look bad. I knows he ain't done all that the TV folks says he has."

"You've known Mr. Dixon a long time?" Obermeyer asked.

"All his life. Practically done raised that boy myself. I shelled many a pea with that child settin' in my lap."

"Ma'am, may I use your bathroom?" Obermeyer asked politely. The events of the day were having their usual effects on him.

"It's right there," Millie replied, pointing at a narrow door.

The commander instructed the patrol officers who had just entered the house to spread out and look through the house and barn. She sternly told them not to make a mess of anything. As soon as she finished completing her orders, her cell phone rang, and she answered quickly. Her eyes widened and her gaze met Obermeyer's before he shut the bathroom door. With several nods of her head, she confirmed her understanding and slapped the phone shut. She said, "That's it. Emergency Response monitors have a personal locater beacon with Cooper's name coded into it going off in Coosa County!"

"Coosa County! That's where Cooper's hunting property's located! Stand by!" the detective said excitedly.

"We also just got a call from the Coosa County sheriff's department saying they just received a 911 from a woman claiming she just escaped from a cellar with Kelly Dixon! She also said that a Mark Wright is in the house holding a boy hostage and that Cooper's trying to rescue him!"

"Mark Wright!" Obermeyer exclaimed, quickly walking away from the bathroom. Obermeyer wanted to think and not react.

"That's what they said, and that's all I know."

"Holy shit!" Obermeyer exclaimed and then remembering Millie, said, "Sorry, ma'am."

"Das all right, young man. We've heard worse," Millie replied.

"Commander, we need to roll."

"We are, but hang on, slow down. Stand by!" she said with a twinkle in her eye.

The commander looked at Millie Brown and then around her house. She said, "Miz Brown, I'm gonna have two officers stay here in case this is a trick."

Turning to Obermeyer, she said, "You and I take separate cars. I'll relay details by radio as I learn 'em. Let's go!"

As they quickly left the house, Rolex broke into another tirade and chased the commander all the way to her vehicle. She hurriedly shut the door and sprayed gravel as she pulled to the edge of the road, waiting on Obermeyer.

Obermeyer jogged to his cruiser. He yelled and waved

for the uniforms to follow him. As he was buckling his seat belt, the passenger door flew open, and Millie Brown sat down and began pulling on her seat belt.

"Whoa! What do you think you're doing?"

"Comin' wit you."

"No, ma'am, you can't."

"Now you listen here, young man, if this has got anythin' to do with Cooper bein' in Coosa County, I'm goin', and I'm riding wit you," she stated emphatically, clicking the seat-belt buckle.

"What's that?" he replied, pointing to her lap.

"My iron. I's takin' it for protection."

CHAPTER 101

The loud explosion confused Cooper, and initially he feared that Mark had doubled back somehow and left him in the cave alone, blowing the exit tunnel shut, entombing him. But after a moment he could faintly hear Grayson crying. He didn't think Mark would have abandoned the boy—he was his bait, his leverage. Cooper believed that Mark was still in the cave, near what he surmised to be the destroyed tunnel, and he intended to hunt Mark down before he seriously harmed Grayson.

With the cave in total darkness, Cooper knew that using a flashlight would betray his location, but he didn't have a choice. Whenever he clicked the light off, he couldn't see anything. He had never experienced such black. Above ground, even in the deepest, darkest woods at night, there was always some source of illumination. Here, he couldn't see anything—not even his hand in front of his face. *At least Mark can't either.*

The silence after the near-deafening explosion, the darkness, and the enormity of the cave were suffocating Cooper's attempt to think clearly. He dropped to his knees, suddenly realizing he had his backpack with him. He took a deep breath, let it out slowly and started formulating a plan to rescue Grayson. By touch alone, he opened his pack and removed the steel traps. He wondered how to best use them. *If I could arm them, set 'em in that narrow part of the cave I came through, and then lure Mark to the area, he just might set one off. At that point, I click on my flashlight and shoot the bastard.*

After a few moments' consideration and not having a better idea come to mind, he quietly gathered up his gear and began feeling his way back toward the narrow passageway.

After moving only a few yards, Cooper heard the iconic warning buzz of a rattlesnake's tail. A cold chill shot down his spine, and in that split second, a wave of perspiration covered his body. The sound bouncing off the cave walls made pinpointing its location impossible. Cooper was shaking as he tried to locate the increasingly intense sound, finally deciding that the snake must be ahead of him or it would have already struck. He squatted to make himself as small of a target as possible, in case Mark was nearby, and then he clicked on his flashlight to search for the snake.

When the light came on, Cooper immediately spotted the snake. It was less than an arm's length away. The timber rattler, one of the largest species of rattlesnakes in the world, appeared to be as big around as his upper arm. Cooper wanted no part of it or its potent hemotoxin venom that would likely kill him before he could get out of the cave. Cooper headshot the snake. He briefly watched it twist in erratic spasms on the cave floor and then fall off a ledge. He clicked off his light. *One down.*

• • •

This cavern was Mark Wright's ancestral dark secret. Each generation worked diligently to keep it off the official known list of over four thousand Alabama caves. Doing so guaranteed privacy. Anyone exploring the cave would be horrified at what they would discover.

Mark's great-great-grandfather had been part of the Underground Railroad that helped funnel escaped slaves north. The truth, however, was that his great-great-grandfather was an opportunistic, malignant sadist. He helped many make the journey but solely as a front to ensure a fresh flow of victims coming through, from which he could carefully select the right specimens for his torturous pleasure. If a large group came to him, he would help most move to the next stop. A weak male or a single female would be culled. Allowing the vast majority of travelers to pass eliminated most suspicion, and since it was a dangerous trip that many didn't survive without the predilections of a demented old man, he enjoyed impunity.

Sickened by what her husband was doing, Mark's great-great-grandmother slipped away one night with most of the family cash, never to return. A month after she was safely several states away, she sent a man to stop her husband, but he never returned. Two months later, she was found at the bottom of a well. The old man continued his evil ways until his natural death many years later.

• • •

Mark's thermal goggles had been a present to himself last year. He dreamed of stalking one of his brunette victims through the cave. He had been working himself up to human prey. Experimenting with a few stray dogs and one cat, the clarity of the heat signatures were unbelievable. He could tell specifics about each animal before killing it.

Mark affixed his goggles and then checked his pockets for his old .38 caliber blued steel revolver and the two remaining sticks of dynamite. He looked at Grayson's white form and touched the shock collar remote. Grayson screamed in pain and pleaded for his dad to stop.

"Do you hear that, Cooper? He wants you to come help him! And by the way, you can turn around. We're back in the main cavern now."

Mark listened but couldn't hear anything other than Grayson's whimpering and sniffling. He knew that Cooper could hear his voice, but he was not close enough for Mark to see his heat signature. Mark would sit and wait. Over the years of stalking his rape victims, he had developed patience. Mark dangled his legs off the table's edge.

"So, Cooper, how do you like complete darkness? Can't see shit, can ya? I find it . . . invigorating. You gotta imagine everything. How do *you* imagine things? What do you want it to be like?"

Over! I want this to be over . . . and you dead at my feet, you son of a bitch, Cooper thought but held back from screaming it.

Cooper was slowly inching his way through the cave toward Mark's voice, making steady progress. He knew that he would eventually have to turn on his flashlight but was trying to cover as much ground as possible by touch, fearing snakebites with each step and movement of his hands along the rock wall.

After several minutes of silence, only periodically broken by the echoing drip of water, Mark stated loudly, "Oh, Coooooooper, I'm guessin' you killed one of my snakes. Seen any of the others?" Then he laughed sadistically. "You might as well talk to me. So how *are* you and Brooke doing these days? Better than you and Kelly? You don't know Brooke like I do. Has she put the moves on you yet? Answer me! You know, I can't believe you trusted your wife with that nut job Brooke. Now, *that* was a mistake you're gonna regret, my friend."

The constricted passage was obvious. Cooper had to turn sideways to fit through. When he reached the opposite end, he focused on blindly setting the traps in the center of the narrow trail. His hands were shaking as he realized he could easily be wearing one of these traps if he wasn't careful. Setting traps in broad daylight was difficult enough; doing it from memory, blind, with the fear of being bitten by a rattler at any moment or attacked by a psychopath was almost too much.

"Another thing . . . if you happen to find some funky sticks while you're fumbling around in the dark, they aren't sticks. They're bones!" Mark let out another disturbing laugh. "Nobody other than family's made it outta here alive in decades. I just thought you might benefit from that little piece of knowledge. And . . . in the spirit of being a good host, I've decided to share a few tidbits of family history with you and Grayson . . . and since you'll never have the opportunity to divulge any of it, I thought why the hell not?"

Mark continued as if in a casual conversation, "So anyway, this is family property—been in my family for generations. Before the War of Northern Aggression it was a big-ass plantation called Live Oaks. Do you see? Live spelled backward is evil. Live Oaks . . . Evil Oaks. Ironic, isn't it?"

Cooper didn't respond but continued setting the traps. As long as Mark kept talking, Cooper had a good idea where Mark was and how much time he had.

"Unfortunately, for me, they had to sell a chunk of the property to keep the family afloat. That still pisses me off.

During prohibition, they were gonna make this cave into a gambling hall like Bangor Cave in Blount County. Those owners made millions back in the early 1900s . . . but the family worried somebody would find out what all had gone on down here—just another missed chance at gettin' rich. Well, I decided to keep up the family tradition. Not much left of the family but me, Uncle Don—who, by the way most likely died yesterday—and a crazy uncle who lives up the road a little ways. Now that dude's pretty interestin'. The old bastard had a stroke and can't talk . . . and he thinks he's livin' at the turn of the century. He just roams the hills around here, scaring the shit outta everybody. Locals won't even come near this place or him because he's bat-shit crazy. You never know where he's at. Hell, he could be in here with us, right now. He could grab you by the throat and gut ya at any second. Everybody needs a crazy uncle, and mine sure has come in handy."

Mark continued with an eerie ease, "Maybe I'll get him to help with my little project. He'll do whatever I ask. All he's ever wanted was to see the Mississippi River—since he saw it in a *National Geographic* when he was a kid. Just wants to look at a muddy river. Not very ambitious, is it? You know, I could tell him where your family lives, and for the price of a bus ticket they'd disappear down here one night. So here's my proposal. How 'bout you come to me, and I won't tell him where you live? That's fair. Come on, Cooper, be a hero for your family."

Cooper listened to every word as he carefully finished locating and setting the traps where Mark would surely step on one. Taking a deep breath and saying a quick, silent prayer of thanks that he still had all his fingers, he momentarily clicked on his flashlight to find a place to hide. He quickly spotted a giant limestone formation that offered decent concealment, and it would help him steady his aim. He grabbed his pack and began feeling his way into position when he realized that he didn't have his rifle with him. *Damn it! It's leanin' against a tree.*

Mark taunted, dragging out each word, "Oh, Cooper? Where. Are. You? If you don't say somethin', I'm gonna shock the shit outta little Grayson here, and it'll be all your fault."

Cooper turned away from Mark's voice, cupped his hands, and yelled, "I can't walk. I think my leg's broke. For God's sake, don't shock the boy. You can have me."

Mark laughed out loud. He knew well how easy it would be to fall. The cave was full of holes, ledges, and loose rock, plus no small amount of slippery bat guano.

"Fine!" Mark yelled, jumping down. He turned around to look at the table to see his butt print. He could even see the heat signature from where his hands had gripped the table's edge.

He squatted down to whisper to Grayson, "I expect you to be right here, in this spot, when I get back. Don't move! If you do, the rattlesnakes will bite you and you'll die . . . a very slow and painful death. Ya hear me? You little pansy."

Grayson's only response was to curl into a tight ball under the table, whimpering. Mark knew he had broken him. Not that it mattered anymore. Without Brooke, Grayson was a burden. *Unless I could sell the little wuss.*

Mark stood up and yelled in Cooper's direction, "Hey, Coop, I got an idea. Let's play Marco Polo! I'll be Marco, obviously. You're Polo . . . since you wear those preppy shirts all the time . . . you faggot!"

"Whatever you want. Just leave Grayson alone!"

"Quit trying to be such a damn hero for Brooke. You won't even come out of hidin' to save your own family, and you're worried about *her*. What's up with that?"

"Why are you doing this to me?" Cooper asked, trying to keep him talking.

After a few steps, Mark stopped stalking Cooper, took off his night-vision goggles, and sat down on a ledge. He pulled a small glass pipe from his shirt pocket for a hit. With the last draw, he said, "Yeah, baby, that's what's been missin' from this party." After replacing the pipe and pulling on his night-vision gear, he continued talking conversationally as he eased toward Cooper's voice.

"Now, where were we? Oh yeah. This ain't about me and *you*, dumbass. Don't you get it? It's about me and Brooke. She's been workin' on you, seducing you, trying to get you to leave your wife. And she usually gets what she wants. Did you ever get a little taste of that? Doesn't really matter to me. Just makin' conversation. At any rate, if that didn't work, then she was goin' to make it so that Kelly would dump you, so then you'd come runnin' to her. The only thing wrong with her plan was that she wasn't countin' on me. I couldn't let you have her. If I can't have her, then nobody can. I swear, you've been so distracted by her for so long, you couldn't see that there's been a whole bunch a folks plottin' to take you down . . . and not just me and Brooke. The sweet thing is that I get to write the final chapter."

Cooper heard every word but didn't know what to make of it. He began worrying about Kelly. *Should I've trusted Brooke to take care of her? Is Mark makin' this up to distract me?*

Cooper quickly tried to remember everything he did and said with Brooke. *She never asked who was buying the business. That's strange, but it doesn't mean anything—maybe she was just being respectful of my privacy.*

The cave was closing in on Cooper. He could feel the crushing pressure of billions of tons of earth and hundreds of bad decisions.

Cooper's best guess was that Mark had to walk about forty yards before he got to the traps. The cave narrowed before that point and had a few twists, so Cooper couldn't be certain of the distance. The acoustics in the cave couldn't be relied upon to determine either the direction or distance of sounds. Every noise had a hollow echo. Kneeling behind a rock, with his pistol aimed toward the traps, Cooper waited.

Mark silently navigated the cave from memory, enjoying the hunt. After rounding a huge limestone outcropping nicknamed Devil's Forehead, he thought he detected movement. A white sliver of something vanished. He couldn't see or determine the object. Carefully, he surveyed the cave but did not see any heat signatures. Mark was confident that Cooper could not hide from technology, even though there were hundreds of cracks, crevices, and places that Cooper would believe provided adequate cover. Mark hoped that Cooper would seek out such a hiding spot because he'd be trapped like a rat before he knew it. *I love this. It's the ultimate game.*

Continuing several more yards, Mark spotted what appeared to be glowing handprints. *What the hell!* He quivered with excitement. Studying the slowly vanishing handprints, Mark bent down. "Cooper, I think you dropped something? What is this?"

Cooper knew Mark was close and readied himself. Other than the snake he killed earlier, he'd never aimed his pistol at anything alive. Now he was mentally prepared to place several rounds into the center of Mark's chest, but hearing him say that he could see was confusing. *How can he see? He's gotta be at the traps. How can he see? He doesn't have a flashlight turned on.*

Mark quietly laid down his revolver on the cave floor and then reached to touch Cooper's handprint. The trap tripped with a bone-cracking WHACK! Four fingers of Mark's right hand were crushed, nearly severing them. He wailed in agony, falling behind a giant rock.

Cooper immediately clicked on his flashlight in a desperate search for his target. He saw Mark's legs quickly receding behind a rock. Mark was screaming in pain. Cooper moved swiftly to take a shot.

Mark saw the beam of light and panicked. He reached for but couldn't grab his pistol because his right hand hung limply in the trap. He then struggled to pry open the trap and screamed, "I'm gonna kill you, you son of a bitch!"

Cooper rushed around searching for a place where he could take a shot, but none offered him the proper vantage. Either the rocks were too large to climb or he couldn't see Mark. Frustrated and worried about exposing himself, he retreated into the labyrinth of the cave to regroup. While Cooper stumbled and climbed, he wondered how Mark could see in the dark, but he couldn't tell it was an animal trap. *Night vision! No, night vision wouldn't work down here— zero light to amplify. What the hell's goin' on?* Cooper struggled to understand.

Shaking from fear and uncertainty, he forced himself to concentrate on his next move.

In the distance, Grayson could be heard faintly sobbing.

CHAPTER 102

The Coosa County Volunteer Fire Department was the first to respond to the emergency call, immediately springing into action. Several pickup trucks with small dash-mounted red lights roared into the yard of the old mansion. Within seconds, the volunteers were dressed in their yellow and gray firefighting protective gear. Ignoring explicit instructions to wait for law enforcement, they ran to Brooke and Kelly and started asking questions.

Minutes later, the first deputy sheriff arrived and took charge. Shortly after that, the county sheriff arrived, quickly surveyed the situation, and carefully noted the condition of the two apparent victims. Kelly, wrapped in an old patchwork quilt, was obviously in needed of immediate medical care. He explained that an ambulance was en route. Brooke was hysterical, and her initial attempts at explanation to the sheriff were incoherent. After a few tense moments, the sheriff was able to understand that her son and Cooper were trapped with her insane, drug-addicted ex-husband in a tunnel in the basement. She quickly showed them the cellar and the former opening to the tunnel.

Both the sheriff and deputy were speechless. After a long moment, the sheriff asked, "This the same guy that's all over the news? Cooper Dixon?"

"Yes, and he didn't do anything wrong. Mark Wright did it all. Cooper went in there to save my son! He's only eight years old. You've got to do something!" she pleaded.

"I got a shovel in my truck," a volunteer fireman offered.

"Get it," the sheriff ordered, without taking his eyes off the collapsed tunnel. A bit overwhelmed, he slowly turned to Brooke, searching for something he could do to take control of the situation.

He slowly said, "Ma'am, we'll get 'em out. It would be best if you go outside and wait on the ambulance. Your arm needs medical attention."

"I'm okay. Please, he's just a little boy," she said, running her shaking hands through her hair. "I have no idea if they're still alive!"

"Ma'am, I promise we'll dig to China if we have to. Now, please, let us get to work."

The sheriff turned to his deputy and said, "Get on the radio and see if you can find somebody who's got those devices that can listen underground—like they use in mine accidents. Somebody around Birmingham has gotta have one since they got coal mines up there."

"Yes, sir!"

"And," the sheriff looked around, "find somebody that knows about caves and get 'em here quick."

"Spelunkers."

"Right. I want the best one here A-SAP," the sheriff ordered calmly. "One more thing. Send somebody to get

Jubal. He was born and raised in this old house, he may know something that could help us."

"Jubal Daniels? I don't think he can talk."

"Get him anyway, and have Montgomery PD pick up Don Daniels and get him here as fast as they can. He owns the place."

The deputy said, "Ten-four, Sheriff," as he hurried up the steep stairs.

The sheriff turned back to the fresh dirt, picked up a handful, and then let it sift through his hands. He sighed deeply, "Buried alive. Lord, please bless their souls."

CHAPTER 103

Cooper was frustrated that he could not get a good angle on Mark to take a killing shot. Each time Cooper clicked on his light, Mark retreated farther behind the rock formation. Climbing high on a ledge, Cooper pushed his back against a wall where he didn't think he could be seen. He prayed that the police and search-and-rescue crews were working.

After several painful minutes of struggling with the trap, Mark finally pried it open. As blood rushed to the tips of his mangled fingers, a new wave of pain washed over him. He collapsed to the ground, writhing and swearing at Cooper, and then everything went black. When he regained consciousness, he thrashed about in a panic, knocking off his goggles. A long moment later, everything started coming back to him. He found and replaced the goggles and then looked down at his mangled fingers. The sight infuriated him.

Not knowing where Cooper was, Mark yelled loudly, "Dixon, you . . . and your entire family are dead, but not before I have several days of fun down here with your hot wife and that sweet young girl of yours. Just wanted you to know."

Mark struggled to his feet and then glanced down the cave, expecting to see Cooper's white form.

"Marco!" Mark said through gritted teeth as he pulled out his crack pipe. "It's no use. I'm gonna find you. You might as well play along."

Mark fell against a dirt wall and then clumsily tried to take a hit of his drugs with one hand.

Cooper laid flat on the rock and then peered over the edge, hoping to see something. Mark's voice was bouncing around, so he couldn't tell if he had moved.

"That big explosion was the tunnel being destroyed. Amazing what a few sticks of dynamite can do. We're all trapped. There's no way out. Marco!"

Cooper swallowed hard. Mark just confirmed his greatest fear. Just a week ago his biggest concern was cash flow analysis for a new computer system at the agency, now he was fighting for his life and preparing to kill Mark Wright, if the police didn't arrive soon.

Mark's voice was coming from Cooper's left, deep toward the main cavern. But Cooper thought he heard something to his right, so he momentarily clicked on his flashlight. At the far reaches of the beam, he thought he saw movement—a ghostly image of a person in a long coat. *Shit! What the hell's that!?*

"You don't have a chance, Cooper. I see where you've been. I own the darkness. Marco!"

Cooper could tell that Mark was now moving in the opposite direction, so he jumped down to check his traps. When he slowly approached the narrow passage, he momentarily flashed his light to make certain he didn't step on one.

He saw that one trap was missing, and one was still set. He slowly released it and then put it into his pack. With another quick flash, he noted a blood trail leading away and then Mark's pistol. By feel, Cooper quickly opened the cylinder and touched the round ends of six cartridges, confirming it was fully loaded. The gun seemed old in Cooper's brief glance and by the way it operated, which instantly gave him an idea. He quietly closed the cylinder and then pushed the barrel deep into the soft, damp limestone wall, thoroughly packing the barrel with dense damp dirt. Cooper used his shirt to clean off the outside of the gun. He shielded the flashlight while he quickly replaced it in exactly the same place he found it. He then picked up his gear and by feeling the wall as he inched along, moved in the opposite direction from where he believed Mark had gone.

CHAPTER 104

When the Montgomery police caravan arrived at the old house, there were dozens of emergency vehicles, lights ablaze, lining the paved roads leading to the drive and surrounding the house and barn. No one appeared to notice the drizzling rain. The media circus was close and trying unsuccessfully to get closer.

After brief introductions and thorough updates, it was obvious that the county sheriff had the situation under control, as much as that was possible given the circumstances. Deputies on cell phones were searching for caving expertise from North Alabama professionals. Several men were digging out the collapsed tunnel. The police commander, fully understanding and appreciating the sheriff's jurisdiction, graciously and generously offered support of the Montgomery PD's assets.

As soon as Detective Obermeyer turned onto the gravel road leading to the old mansion, Millie Brown became agitated. She said that she was terrified of the old house. All of her life she had heard that the place was evil. She was visibly shaken when she learned that Cooper was trapped inside. She explained that her great-great-grandfather had been a slave on this plantation and that it once sprawled for several thousand acres. Her relative had been tasked to accompany the youngest son of the landowner during the Civil War. Totally devoted, he stayed at his side while the young man's unit marched and fought all over the South. When the land-owner's son sustained a serious injury in battle, her family patriarch carried the wounded young man all the way home, across two states. The young man's father was so appreciative and grateful that he freed Millie's ancestor and deeded to him a substantial piece of property, which she now owned. One of the plantation owner's descendants had been trying for years to buy the land from Millie and from her father before she inherited the property.

Obermeyer got out of his car to walk around the old house, inside and out. He was absorbing but unable to make sense of all that he now knew, what he saw and sensed. This was it. This was where Kelly had been held. Two of the last three stops he had made tonight were pivotal in crimes yet to be fully understood.

Millie, seeing Kelly sitting in the ambulance, stepped to the door to comfort her. When Kelly saw her, she burst into tears. Kelly had refused to leave the site without Cooper. The paramedics were about to forcibly take her to the hospital when they realized that the ambulance had a flat tire, so they called for a backup. And since Kelly's vital signs stabilized when they administered IV fluids, they relaxed a bit.

Brooke was scared and ran from the ambulance to the house, demanding updates on the progress of the excavation. She prayed that Grayson could survive without any physical or emotional scars. She was consumed with remorse every time she looked at Kelly.

Obermeyer was in sensory overload. He absentmindedly tossed an empty Pepto-Bismol bottle onto the front seat of his car as he observed two county deputies attempting to talk to a gaunt old man who was wearing an outdated trench coat and a wide-brimmed felt hat. After an animated exchange, the annoyed deputies threw up their hands in frustration while the old man slowly wandered off into the dark woods, with an overweight black Labrador retriever trailing him. The dog looked vaguely familiar to Obermeyer. Out of habit, he muttered, "Stand by."

Brooke had given Cooper's BlackBerry to Obermeyer when he first arrived. He placed it in a jacket pocket and promptly forgot about it until he reached for his to make a note about Brooke's story and how it and she were connected to Mark Wright. He withdrew Cooper's BlackBerry and clicked the icon to open e-mails and text messages.

The EMTs put Brooke's right arm in a sling and sedated her. She was resting in their van. Since neither of their patients was in critical condition, they decided that they would wait for the arrival of additional ambulances. Unless it was absolutely necessary, the EMTs did not want to leave the scene with no source of emergency medical care.

Members of both law enforcement and fire and rescue were alternating between the arduous digging of the collapsed tunnel and carrying the dirt out of the cellar. Once a bucket brigade was established to remove the dirt, they started to make appreciable headway in their rescue efforts. The physical space constraints of the cellar, however, were now the principal limiting factor in how quickly they could either rescue Grayson, Cooper, and Mark or remove their bodies.

An excited deputy reported that underground listening devices were en route and that Don Daniels had been located and would be on-site in a little over an hour.

CHAPTER 105

As Cooper slipped deeper into the cavern, he decided that he needed to taunt Mark into aggressively hunting him. He assumed that Mark was injured badly due to the blood trail, but that because he was so high on drugs, it wouldn't slow him down too much. Cooper found an ambush site.

"Hey, Marco? Didja find my trap?" Cooper yelled, mimicking Mark's bravado. "Didja like it?"

"I'm gonna kill you!" Mark roared.

"You gotta find me first. Oh yeah, Polo!"

Mark chuckled at Cooper's boldness and complete lack of understanding or appreciation of who was in control. He calmly cut off the bottom of his shirt and tied it around his mutilated hand. Then he started using his goggles to search down the cave wall for Cooper's white form and down on the ground for another metal trap. Mark moved silently, relying on his now ragged memory and his thermal goggles to guide him. Cooper was about to be dead, and therefore, was the least of his worries.

Cooper yelled, "I think the score's me two and you zip. You know, I just may make some boots outta that pet snake of yours that I just killed."

Mark's pace quickened with murderous anticipation. After thirty yards he spied a small white spot on the cave floor. He approached cautiously and recognized the outline of his pistol. He smiled. The knowledge that the gun still retained heat from his hand was encouraging. He now knew that he could trust his goggles to locate Cooper's trail. Picking up the pistol with his left hand, he silently aimed it, thumb-cocked the hammer, and then slowly released it to get a sense for how he could handle it. Although he was using his weak hand, the gun felt good, bolstering his confidence as he continued his hunt.

CHAPTER 106

Cooper thought he heard movement deeper in the cavern and tightly squeezed the pistol's grip. He briefly flashed his light and tried to memorize the cave. He carefully positioned himself in order to be clearly visible to Mark. He squatted to wait. Cooper was counting on Mark's gun exploding when he fired it. It was incredibly risky and with each passing second, Cooper's doubts grew as to the wisdom of it. *What if it doesn't explode and the bullet has enough force to hit me? Will it kill me? Shit! I'm an idiot. I shoulda just kept the gun.*

Cooper didn't have many options now, and he needed to find Grayson. If he could shine his flashlight, he could avoid the rattlesnakes, but first he needed to neutralize Mark.

"Polo!" he yelled again loudly.

Mark smiled as sweat dripped from his nose. He could tell Cooper was close and in a few more yards he would be able to see him. The soft dirt and bat dung muffled Mark's steps.

"Hey, Marco. I said Polo! What's the matter? Don't cha wanna play anymore?" yelled Cooper.

Mark quickly moved past another large rock outcropping, and then he saw Cooper's full silhouette standing on a rock twenty-five yards away. *Perfect!* He didn't move for over a full minute as he methodically studied Cooper. He was confident that he could make the shot, and he was savoring the setup. The thermal goggles provided a near perfect image. His hatred and jealousy boiled.

He raised the pistol and took aim at Cooper's chest. The front and rear sight melted into one, hovering around the right side of Cooper's chest. Mark badly wanted to mock Cooper one last time, but he realized that he had exactly what he wanted. It was time to act. Cooper's upright stance told Mark that he had no idea he was so near. Mark slowly thumb-cocked the pistol.

Cooper heard the unmistakable sound of a pistol hammer locking back, and he wheeled to face Mark, clicking on his flashlight with one hand and aiming his pistol with the other. The moment Mark was illuminated, Cooper fired his weapon and dove to the ground.

Mark was too far into his trigger pull to stop and duck behind the rock. Cooper's Hi-Power flashed fire, the cave amplifying with the percussion of the shot. Simultaneously, Mark's .38, trained squarely on Cooper's chest, barked and exploded from the back pressure created by the plugged barrel.

Mark screamed in anguish as pieces of the destroyed pistol slashed his face and hands. Quickly dropping behind cover, Mark saw white dots splashed everywhere on the cave wall and realized it was his own blood. He continued to scramble backward, out of Cooper's line of site. Everything hurt. His face was warm with dripping blood. The goggles had protected his eyes, although the left lens was damaged badly. He was confused and furious.

Cooper's left wrist felt like it was on fire, but he ignored the pain as he carefully approached the rock he thought Mark was hiding behind. He was going to put a bullet into Mark's skull, find Grayson, and then get the hell out of there. By the time Cooper reached the rock, his adrenalin was surging. With his pistol drawn, he quickly stepped around the huge boulder and clicked on his flashlight. Mark was gone. *Damn it!* he thought. Before he turned off the light, he noticed that the cave walls were blood-spattered and there was a small piece of the pistol laying on the floor.

Cooper stood motionless, trying to listen over the ringing in his ears for any movement and struggling to quiet his breathing. After a long moment, the burning sensation in his left wrist and a warm feeling in his hand got his attention. He clicked on the flashlight and saw that his wrist was bleeding badly. Quickly cutting off a shirtsleeve, he bound the wound as tightly as he could. By the time he finished, the makeshift bandage was completely soaked.

CHAPTER 107

When Don Daniels arrived home Friday afternoon, he discovered his beloved female tabby curled up in his favorite chair. The frisky kitty typically would bound out from wherever she was hiding or sleeping outside to greet him at the door before he could open it.

Suspicious of the cat being inside and concerned that she wasn't moving when he called for her, Don eased over to the chair, knelt, and touched his limp companion. "Oh, God! No! No!" he wailed. "What happened?"

Don never left her inside the house while away because he feared that he would be called away on business and she would be trapped. The little feline was like a burglar, though, constantly sneaking inside unnoticed. But Don specifically recalled feeding her on the back deck before leaving for work that morning, without her going back into the house.

With shaking hands, Don gently checked her for injuries. As he lightly stroked her fur, he noticed something wedged into the crease of his old leather recliner. He tried to determine what it was without touching it. Leaning closer, he saw a needle sticking out of the fold. It was aimed straight at whoever sat down. He cautiously spread the seat cushion from the back of the chair to reveal a syringe that appeared to be glued to the leather. A piece of wood the size of a mousetrap was attached to the plunger. He carefully pulled it free. The barrel of the syringe still contained some liquid, presumably a drug. There was a single orange cat hair clinging to the tip of the tiny needle.

It was obvious to Don that this setup was meant to impale him. The needle would have stuck him in the small of his back, instantly surging the drug into his body. Apparently, the cat slunk in unnoticed with the intruder, and later, when she jumped onto the chair for a nap, the needle gave her the lethal dose intended for him. Don studied the syringe and then turned to his lifeless friend and screamed, "Damn it!"

Don had begun sweating profusely from the knowledge that he had been so very near death. He also knew who was responsible. There was one person who would want him out of the way. The thought of Mark Wright, his own kin, trying to murder him made his blood boil.

Fearful of Mark and more deadly traps around his house, and also likely at his lake cabin, he decided to check into the Renaissance Montgomery Hotel for a few days to think through the situation and his options. Calling the police wasn't a choice because Mark knew too much. Don realized that he had to handle this himself. He was never quick to react, but rather cold and methodical. His plans almost always worked, unlike Mark's. Don smiled at the thought of Mark assuming that he was dead and the added element of surprise that mistake would afford Don.

Don retrieved a small Ruger 9 mm semiautomatic pistol from his briefcase and checked the chamber and the magazine. Satisfied, he left it on the kitchen island while he retrieved a second gun, an old .32 caliber revolver, from his bedside table drawer. He palmed it thoughtfully as he walked quickly into the bathroom. A moment later he strode resolutely back into the kitchen, carrying a bag of cotton balls and the revolver. He laid both on the island and opened the refrigerator, taking out a half-full one-liter bottle of Diet Pepsi. He emptied the soda into the sink and then set the empty bottle next to the revolver. He opened a drawer and pulled out a roll of duct tape. Then he stuffed all of the cotton balls, as many as he could at a time, into the empty plastic bottle. Fitting the bottle opening over the barrel of the revolver, he ran several strips of duct tape around the bottleneck and gun barrel to secure the bottle to the weapon. The setup looked awkward, but he surmised that it would somewhat muffle the sound of the weapon should he need it.

The tired, old banker took a deep puff of his hand-rolled cigar, admiring his handiwork. He now had weapons for whatever situations he encountered. Don cursed under his breath as he loaded the weapons into a paper grocery sack. He knew what he had to do. Obviously, Mark was off his medications. Don had tried to help him in so many ways, but he knew that Mark had the genetic—and fatal—family flaw. He finished his cigar and then checked his watch.

One last time he punched a number into his cell and muttered, "Shit," when there was no answer.

Don's whole world was in jeopardy. He couldn't trust anyone, and after Mark's attempt on his life, he suddenly felt vulnerable, an emotion he had never experienced. He had to punish Mark and then kill him.

Grabbing his keys and the grocery bag, he walked out, slamming the door.

. . .

Don Daniels, bank president and CEO, looked every bit the part that night by the hotel's pool. He was enjoying an authentic Cohiba Coronas Especiales and two fingers of Macallan 18, neat, when he took the phone call from the Coosa County Sheriff's Department, informing him of the situation at his family estate. He stood stock-still in a controlled anger that matched his Cuban's slow, hot burn. Don gave the deputy his quick assurance that he would get there as fast as possible.

After hanging up the phone, he stared at the city lights, trying to envision what might possibly be happening. He hoped that this wasn't the loose thread that would result in the unraveling of his world. He now wished that he had confronted and killed his nephew earlier that evening.

With resignation, Don snuffed out his cigar, drained his scotch with a single swallow, and headed to his room to retrieve the paper sack.

CHAPTER 108

Cooper knew that Mark was injured, and he assumed badly because when he illuminated Mark with the flashlight beam, he saw Mark's damaged goggles and the blood splattered on them.

Trying not to think about being shot himself, Cooper concentrated on what he needed to do to stay alive. He had to assume that Mark was still armed. Cooper decided he had to find his way back to the main cavern and get Grayson. He knew there was another route because Mark had circled back with the boy. From there, he could force something to happen, or he and Grayson could wait for the police to dig through.

All Cooper had to do was locate Mark's tracks. He flashed his light briefly and set a course. The bat dung covering the cave floor was a double-edged sword for Cooper. It provided stealth for moving and easy tracking, and it contained deadly bacteria that could contaminate his injury. Inside the cave, Cooper's internal compass was spinning wildly, but he sensed that he was headed in the right direction and picked up the pace. As he padded softly through the dark, his mind was awhirl with worries—about Kelly, the police, and the quality of the oxygen levels in the cave. He knew that the police would arrive at some point, but it wasn't right now. Which meant that he was going to be the one who either killed or subdued Mark, and then he would have to find a way out for himself and Grayson. Feeling the blood drip from his hand, he knew he needed medical attention. His primary fear switched to bleeding out in the cave.

Mark saw fading heat signatures, and his pulse accelerated at the thought of Cooper hiding so close. Mark knew that about twenty yards ahead was an elevated ledge where he would be able to look down on Cooper. He climbed silently to the top and then slowly peeked over the ledge until he could almost see the rock he expected Cooper was hiding behind. The rock, still warm, glowed with Cooper's fading outline.

Mark wanted to scream in furious frustration but uncharacteristically controlled himself. The night wasn't going as planned, but he still had time to salvage it. He bounded down the rocks and resumed his soundless stalk.

When Cooper arrived at the main cavern and saw that the tunnel was destroyed, his heart sank. He needed a serious miracle. This cavern would be his grave if he didn't figure out something, and quick. Sweating and bleeding, he tried to estimate how long he'd been in there but couldn't. He could tell that his motor skills were deteriorating, and the stress was wrecking his reasoning.

Cooper sat down, put his head between his knees, and tried to think of his next move when he realized that Grayson must be near. He called out to him in a voice just above a whisper, "Grayson? Grayson? I'm here to help you."

In a little louder voice Cooper said, "Grayson, I'm a friend of your mom's . . . I'm here to help ya."

"I wanna go home," a tiny voice answered from across the space.

Cooper clicked on his flashlight, quickly spotting the frightened little boy huddled underneath a table. Cooper went straight toward him. When he got near, he whispered, "I'm gonna take you straight to your mom, I promise. Okay?" Cooper grabbed him up with his good arm.

Cooper could feel Grayson nodding and wiping a tear after he sniffed.

"Do you know where your dad is?" Cooper asked as he clicked on the flashlight, shielding the beam to create only a small amount of illumination.

Grayson pointed in the direction of a tunnel. Cooper realized that Mark could pop out at any moment.

"Let's get this collar off you." Cooper sat Grayson on the table and then carefully cut off the zip ties with his pocket-knife and unbuckled the collar. *I wish I could attach it to that son of a bitch and give him a little taste of his own medicine.* With disgust, Cooper tossed it to the floor.

"You gotta trust me and do exactly what I say, okay?"

Grayson nodded his agreement, with huge tears falling to the dirt floor as he whispered, "There's a bunch of rattle-snakes in here."

Cooper hadn't thought much about the snakes since killing the one but quickly shined his light around the immediate area. He saw dozens of old jars full of clear liquid. Some contained what appeared to be apples and some pears. Cooper assumed it was all moonshine. The sealed jars were stacked everywhere—on the ground, in vegetable and fruit crates, and on makeshift shelves along the walls.

Knowing that Mark could see with his goggles, Cooper

considered how to light up the place. Right now, Mark owned the darkness, but fire would level the playing field somewhat. Cooper decided that the cave's volume was big enough to support his idea. *Hopefully, the carbon monoxide doesn't kill us all.*

"I don't see any snakes around here. Go get in the corner behind that rock and close your eyes, okay?" Cooper shined his light for Grayson, who did exactly as he was told.

Once Grayson was in place, Cooper worked as quickly as he could. A swift pan of the cavern with his flashlight revealed several more wooden structures than he remembered. All he had to do was get the moonshine to ignite, and then it should burn like jet fuel. Lighting up the cavern should bring Mark running.

Cooper's hands were shaking as he quickly searched by feel through his backpack for something that might help. He found a can of bug spray and a Bic lighter. He busted a jar of moonshine and bent down over the liquid. He sprayed the bug repellent toward the moonshine on the floor and then flicked his Bic under the stream. The spray ignited, and then the alcohol. Satisfied with his experiment, he started breaking jars on anything that would burn. With his makeshift torch, he easily set everything ablaze, working his way around to the cabinets and wooden tables. He poured moonshine all over them and kept going. By the time he finished, fire was everywhere except in the corner where Grayson was hiding and at one entrance into the main chamber.

The main cavern was brightly glowing, thick black smoke pooling at the ceiling. Cooper prayed he had made the right decision.

Mark listened to the peculiar resonance of the moonshine erupting in flames. Terror shot through him as he raced toward the odd sound. The moment he rounded the last corner leading into the main chamber, he lost all vision. The goggles blinded him with retina-searing white light from the fire's heat. He had no idea what could be happening.

Cooper grabbed three jars of moonshine, tossed them into the hottest part of the fire, and then jumped behind a limestone outcropping. Then he trained his pistol on the cave entrance. The resulting explosion seemed to suck out all of the oxygen in the cave, and the heat generated from 190-proof liquor burning was intense.

Mark was knocked off his feet from the blast. Dazed and confused, he fought to get on his knees. He ripped off his goggles and fought to adjust his eyes to the intense light. He struggled to his feet and ran into the cavern just in time to witness the last tangible remains of his demented family history go up in flames. All he could do was stare.

Cooper could clearly see Mark about ninety feet away. He centered the pistol's sights on Mark's forehead and held a breath. As he squeezed the trigger, he yelled, "Polo!"

The muzzle kicked up slightly and a fresh round automatically cycled into the chamber. As Cooper tried to get back on target, he watched Mark spin and then fall to the cave floor. Mark quickly scrambled for cover behind some rocks before Cooper could get off another shot. Cooper knew that he had hit him. Anxiously looking at Grayson, who had his eyes tightly shut and his hands clamped over his ears, Cooper fervently hoped that the child had not just witnessed his father getting shot.

Mark's right shoulder felt like it had been hit full swing by a baseball bat. He lost almost all movement in his upper arm. His hand, face, and now his shoulder were in excruciating pain. His options were limited, but Mark knew what he had in his pocket would kill Cooper. The fire was raging all around, the ceiling of black smoke was dropping, and it was becoming difficult to breathe. Mark needed to act fast. *I gotta kill that son of a bitch right now and get the hell out of here.*

He quickly pulled out a stick of dynamite and pinched off the fuse. *That oughta be about fifteen seconds of burn time.* He got to his knees and peered over the rock. He saw Cooper kneeling in a corner, talking with Grayson and smiled.

"Acceptable collateral damage!" Mark said quietly as he lit the fuse. "The little shit should have listened to me."

With his good arm, he lobbed the dynamite across the room toward the corner where Grayson and Cooper were huddled. As soon as Mark released the dynamite, something black raced past him toward the lit stick of dynamite. Mark was too shocked to move.

Cooper turned to see Mark's head pop up over the rock. He snapped off two poorly aimed rounds. While firing, Cooper saw that the object Mark had thrown had landed close to Grayson. His heart nearly stopped when he saw the sparkling fuse so near the blasting cap on the dynamite. With no time to think of options, he dove to grab it, but before he reached it, Dixie appeared out of nowhere running full speed. Cooper hesitated, stunned to see her. She acted as though she was going to retrieve the dynamite, but the burning fuse perplexed her, and she, too, hesitated. Cooper knew that they were all dead if the dynamite exploded. He grabbed it, and with all the strength and speed he could muster, threw it toward Mark.

Dixie was reacting to Cooper's throwing motion the moment he started, anticipating chasing the stick. Cooper couldn't stop or change direction.

"Dixie! NO!" he screamed and then dove to shield Grayson from the blast.

Mark made a move to look toward Cooper's scream when the dynamite landed at his feet. He couldn't think.

Everything was happening too fast. All he could do was scream, "Noooooooo!" as he spun and ran.

Mark didn't get very far before the dynamite exploded.

CHAPTER 109

The old house and the very ground on which it stood shook and rumbled for a second time tonight, causing a collective gasp of horror. Then, for several seconds, there was not a sound. No words were spoken. A blanket of mist began falling. It was almost as if nothing had happened. The only tell was the palpable, permeating fear.

A CNN crew had slipped in and was interviewing the Montgomery DA with the old house as the backdrop when the explosion occurred. The DA wheeled around in astonishment. The camera operator, a veteran war correspondent herself, had the presence to keep rolling. She and her producer, who was watching live from inside the remote van and talking elatedly into her earpiece, knew they had just hit a highlight reel home run.

Brooke was the first to break the silence when she became hysterical and started screaming. She had to be physically restrained while paramedics from the second ambulance began searching for a stronger sedative to give her.

Kelly, already restrained and sedated, was being attended to in another ambulance.

Obermeyer and his commander stood motionless and slack-jawed. After a moment and without a word, the weary detective walked out of the house into the rain and stared in his characteristic standby mode. *What the hell's going on down there? Whatever it is, it's not gonna end well.*

When the initial shock of the explosion wore off, five minutes of pure chaos erupted in the on-duty ranks. Some kept hope alive by frantically returning to their tasks with renewed vigor. A few kept on but slowed down, with a dazed look. Some stopped altogether and just stood rooted to the spot as if afraid the ground might swallow them in the next moment. Others barked meaningless orders at everyone else.

The sheriff had been talking to Don Daniels when the explosion occurred, and he immediately raced inside the house and down to the cellar. Before Obermeyer had gone outside, through a window he saw Mr. Daniels nervously walk beyond the parked vehicles and slip into the woods, glancing back twice. In the mass confusion, no one else took note of him.

Obermeyer wiped the rain off his glasses as he thought of the effectiveness of Millie Brown's snake trick. He was about to follow Don Daniels when Cooper's BlackBerry vibrated the receipt of an incoming call. Without so much as a thoughtful "stand by," he clicked the green button and said, "Hello?"

CHAPTER 110

The cavern was filled with dust, smoke, and fire. Cooper's ears were ringing. His eyes and lungs burned. He grabbed Grayson's shoulders, turned him to directly face him, and gave him a quick physical assessment. He didn't appear to be injured. Without wasting any time, Cooper looked Grayson in the eye and held his right index finger to his lips, indicating that he should be quiet. Grayson's eyes were wide and wet with tears, but he nodded his understanding.

Cooper leaned down to Grayson's ear and whispered, "Hold on to my pant's pocket. Okay?"

Grayson again nodded and did what he was told.

Cooper pulled out his pistol and held it at the ready as they walked slowly toward what was left of the cave entrance. Fresh dirt covered the hole completely, leaving no trace of Mark or Dixie. *They must be buried.*

Cooper had no desire to dig out Mark and really didn't want to see Dixie after the trauma of a dynamite blast. He sank to his knees. Grayson did the same. *That damned dog would retrieve anything, for anybody.* Pausing before he stood, he realized there wouldn't be anything left of Dixie. That last image of Dixie running for the dynamite was seared into his mind, and he knew that it would haunt him if he survived. *I had to throw it; I didn't have any choice. Wait, Dixie didn't come in the cave with me.*

"Was that your dog, Mister?" Grayson whispered.

"I thought your eyes were closed?" Cooper asked, turning to the small boy.

"I peeked."

"Yeah . . . yes. Dixie. She is . . . I mean . . . it was. She was a good dog. A real good dog." Cooper's voice began to crack. Grayson put an arm around Cooper's shoulder.

With squinting eyes, Grayson looked through the heavy dust and smoke and into Cooper's heart. He said, "She musta been real smart too." He paused a moment and then added, "I'm gonna get me a dog one day, and I'm gonna name her Dixie."

Cooper realized that Grayson had been through an unbelievable ordeal and yet he was comforting him. *What an amazing kid!* Cooper then thought of his own son and gave Grayson a big hug, saying, "Every boy should have a dog like Dixie." Cooper continued, "Come on. Let's get outta here." Cooper knew that they were still in a bad bind because he had no idea how to actually get out.

Both Grayson and Cooper were shivering and covered in dirt. The fires were playing out. And the thick smoke was exacerbating Cooper's claustrophobia. He looked around, hoping to see it moving, indicating a way out.

Grayson mumbled something, causing Cooper to refocus and take a quick inventory. He still had his pistol and flashlight, and he knew how to get out of the main cavern, away from the smoke, to wait for rescuers. Shining his light around, Cooper glanced at the collapsed original tunnel he had crawled through to get into the cavern. He prayed that someone was digging toward them from the other side.

"Grayson, are you okay?" Cooper asked and watched him absently nod.

"Where's my dad?" he asked, without much emotion.

Cooper didn't know what to say. He wasn't certain what the boy had seen, so he decided it best to get to safety and then let a professional explain. All that he knew was that he didn't want Grayson melting down right now.

Cooper reached out to grab Grayson's hand. "I don't know. How 'bout we get outta here? Come on, big guy."

Holding Grayson's hand with his right and his small flashlight in his bloody left hand, he slowly started heading deeper into the cave in search of cleaner air and a safe place to await rescue. As they walked, his light reflected off a flying bat, and he immediately realized that there must be an opening to the outside. *That musta been how Dixie got down here!*

"Come on, Grayson," he said, picking up the pace.

As they hurried, Cooper began to feel that he was getting weaker, and it occurred to him that it was the result of blood loss. He knew that if he was going to survive, waiting to be rescued wasn't an option any longer.

CHAPTER III

Mark missed the brunt of the explosion because he had managed to scramble a few feet away as the stick rolled into a crack of solid limestone, forcing the main thrust of the blast up and away from him. The explosion caused a cave-in, cutting him off from the main cavern. He was in bad shape: bruised, bloody, shot, and confused. He stood slowly. His ears were ringing; his shoulder was throbbing with each heartbeat, and pain coursed through his body with each breath. As he wiped the blood from his face on his sleeve, he noticed blood pouring from the gunshot wound.

Slowly regaining his balance and composure, Mark started for the cave exit. He felt for the remaining stick of dynamite. He still had a chance. It was simple. Climb out the tiny fracture and then blow it shut, leaving Cooper and Grayson to slowly die in the dark of starvation, assuming the whole cave didn't collapse and crush them. He got his bearings and limped down the passage, wondering, *Where in the hell did that freakin' dog come from?*

. . .

Cooper stopped to let Grayson catch his breath. The kid was exhausted and seemed asthmatic, but he refused to be carried. Cooper suspected he didn't trust men and couldn't blame him, given who his father was and how he had been mistreated. Based on the little Cooper knew, he wondered what all the boy had suffered at the hands of that psychopath. He thought about Ben's innocent qualities and couldn't comprehend someone harming a child. *There's a very special ring of Hell for child abusers and molesters! I hope you enjoy it, Mark!*

Grayson and Cooper sat down on a rock to rest a moment. Again, Cooper looked at Grayson and held up his index finger to his mouth, signifying quiet. The only thing Cooper could hear was the ringing in his ears from the explosion. The flashlight beam was dimming, so he turned it off.

Grayson immediately cried, "No!" and began sniffling.

"It's okay, Grayson. Don't cry. I'm not gonna let anything happen to you," Cooper said as he clicked it back on.

Cooper looked around, wondering where to search for the bats' exit. His thoughts wandered to Dixie and how the hardheaded dog loved to retrieve everybody's birds, much to his frustration. The reality that his life was in chaos was hitting him hard. He didn't know if Kelly was safe outside with Brooke. He couldn't understand Mark's unbelievable anger toward him. He thought of his children, and then wondered what was going to happen to his business and to Gates. He started to worry that he would bleed to death before the rescuers arrived or before they found the way out, and then none of this would matter.

Cooper looked into Grayson's hollow eyes filled with tears, and he knew that he was going to die making things right by that child and everyone else, including Dixie.

Cooper rose, and without saying anything so did Grayson, who reached for Cooper's hand as they pushed deeper into the cave. Cooper was almost in a panic from the flashlight's dimming beam and sped up. After they had traveled about two hundred yards, Cooper noticed blood in the dirt and smeared on the cave walls. He tried to determine whether this was from Mark's earlier beaver-trap encounter or worse—if it was fresh, and Mark was somehow still alive. As Cooper pulled out his pistol, he whispered to Grayson to follow silently behind him.

Watching the cave ahead, Cooper worked the light into every crevice as his nerves began to unwind. Mark's blood spoor was becoming steady, and he also noticed his dog's tracks. Several times when he stopped short, Grayson bumped him, so again he put Grayson's small hand into his back pocket, hoping that he could tell when he was stopping. The cave was getting smaller and tighter the farther they went.

. . .

Mark smiled as he made it to the cave's opening, knowing that he would get away and that Cooper and Grayson were going to die in a few moments. Even if the cops were crawling all over the old house, Mark was safe. This unknown exit was almost half of a mile from the house, on the property's boundary line, and huge rocks on a hillside hid it. Brush was grown up around the fracture in the rocks, which was just large enough for a man to squeeze through. A long fuse would give him time to be well on his way before permanently sealing shut his past. Though he was physically feeling worse, mentally things were getting clearer and brighter.

Cooper thought he heard something up ahead and quickly turned off the light. Grayson began to complain, but

Cooper quickly shushed him. Though Cooper's ears were ringing, and he didn't fully trust what he heard, he listened intently. He thought he heard voices—one of which he did not want to hear.

Mark had pushed the goggles up on his forehead as he began crawling out the narrow slit. The air was heavy. Halfway out, he noticed someone's silhouette. Fear gripped him until his eyes adjusted, and he realized that it was his crazy uncle, Jubal Daniels, sitting on a stump, rubbing the head of a wet black dog sitting next to him.

"Damn it, old man, you scared the shit out of me, and that crazy dog almost got me killed!"

The old man, wearing his distinctive trench coat and wide-brimmed black hat, which drooped from the rain, stared back.

"Give me a hand, my arm's busted up," Mark commanded, reaching out with his good arm. "Help me, damn it!"

The old man sat motionless less than fifteen feet away.

"Besides bein' completely crazy, are you deaf too?" Mark said, continuing to struggle through the small gap. I'm gonna gutshoot that damned dog of yours if you don't help me!"

Mark looked around for something to grab onto when suddenly a boot slammed down on his injured hand. The pain was so stunning he couldn't utter a sound before momentarily blacking out. When he regained consciousness, he was looking down the barrel of a large pistol. As his glance shifted to the old man, he could sense a change in the man who Mark had abused since he was a teenager. The old man had been emotionless for as long as Mark could remember. He had silently endured beatings and emotional abuse, yet hung around like a spirit-broken dog, cowering in the presence of anyone, especially Mark.

"Look, old man. You better pull me outta here! We're family, and you ain't got much left," Mark said hatefully.

"I can't let you hurt that little boy no more," Jubal said in a tired voice.

Mark hadn't heard him speak in years. With clear determination and purpose, the old man thumb-cocked the revolver.

"Don't do it, Jubal," Don Daniels calmly commanded as he approached the scene. "That little peckerhead's mine."

The old man took a step back, his pistol still trained on Mark's head.

Don Daniels took pleasure in Mark's obvious shock at seeing him alive. "Surprised, aren't you?" Without waiting on a reply, he continued, "Do you know what you have done? Don't you have the ability to stick to a plan? Answer me!"

"I had to improvise!"

"Killin' me was your idea of improvising?" Don calmly asked, watching Mark's eyes.

Jubal looked back and forth between the men, confused.

"I . . . I don't know what you're talkin' about," Mark stuttered, struggling to say something.

"Mark, I'm tired of it. You have screwed everything up! Again. After all I've done for you and your momma. This is how you repay me?"

• • •

Cooper and Grayson slowly eased closer to the voices. Cooper could clearly hear Mark's voice and quickly turned around to Grayson, whose eyes were wide, and said, "Don't say a word or make a sound. Okay?"

Grayson obviously heard his father's voice, too, but simply nodded his understanding.

Cooper couldn't fathom how Mark was still alive. He listened intently, trying to determine what was being said and by how many. *I gotta get closer.*

Cooper instructed Grayson to sit quietly on a rock. He gave him the flashlight, telling him not to turn it on unless he told him it was okay. Grayson sat and pulled his knees up tight to his chest.

Cooper whispered, "Everything's gonna be all right. I promise." He then gave Grayson a hug before he stepped away.

The cave narrowed considerably as Cooper inched closer to the voices. His claustrophobia was in uncharted territory, but knowing that Mark was alive and still in the cave gave him something beside that panic on which to concentrate. The closer he got, the tighter he squeezed the grip of his pistol. His sweat poured.

Cooper stood hunched over, listening. Mark was close. Cooper could hear something scraping on rocks but couldn't see his hand directly in front of his eyes, so he decided he'd light his lighter. Aiming the pistol in the direction of the voices, he flicked on the lighter, illuminating the lower half of Mark's body sticking halfway through a small opening. *That's the way out!*

Cooper quickly extinguished the lighter. The fact that Mark was unaware of Cooper's presence gave him a moment to consider his next move. Hearing voices outside convinced him to be patient and to listen for anything that might help him understand what was happening. Cooper inched closer and decided that if Mark made even a slight move, he'd shoot him in the ass and take his chances with whoever was outside.

The closer Cooper got to Mark, the more confident he became. Watching Mark's legs slowly move reminded him of the rattlesnake he killed. The movement wasn't accomplishing anything, it was just nerves reacting to tension. As one of the voices outside became intense, Mark's legs frantically tried to find purchase.

. . .

The mist turned to rain as Don and Jubal Daniels stood staring down with disgust at Mark, half of his body was out of the small hole, and he was clawing in vain to pull himself free.

Don squatted down close to Mark's face and said, "If you'd just stayed on script and laid low, Cooper's land option would have expired, and I could have added that piece to all I've been buying up around here to sell to Toyota. You're a stupid son of a bitch! All I needed was this last piece of the puzzle. Once that old black woman learned that Cooper wasn't the saint she thought he was, I coulda got it for a song. The last piece woulda been in place. I already had the whole thing sold to the Japanese. I'da cleared twenty-five million! Don't you get it?! Everybody coulda had everything they ever wanted. I'da made a fortune and walked away, never to be seen again. You coulda been president of the bank, and you coulda lured Brooke back with the Tower Agency. I'd have given it all to ya. I never wanted that ad agency anyway. But I guess it was just too damn complicated for your jealous, drug-addled mind to comprehend. Don't you realize how much twenty-five-million dollars is and how rare of a chance this was? You're an idiot! You've destroyed my once-in-a-lifetime opportunity—my chance to get out. I'm so freakin' tired of the banking business—the shitty rink-a-dink ten-grand loans to some bubba who wants to open a bait shop, givin' mortgages to folks who can't afford a single-wide trailer much less a quarter-of-a-million-dollar mortgage that Freddie Mac and Fannie Mae force us to make, and all the bounced checks and the government auditors up my ass with a microscope! I was gonna get out! I had it all set up. Don't you see what you've done?!"

"Well, uh, I . . . I . . . I was, well, it's like this, Uncle Don, I couldn't . . . I just couldn't let anybody else have Brooke. She wanted Cooper, and it just makes me crazy to think about it!"

Lightning flashed. Don could see the fear in his nephew's eyes. He hated Mark for who he was and what he had done.

"I understand that. But hell, even Jubal followed the plan."

"It can still work. Nobody but us knows about this exit. We can blow it shut and maybe collapse the whole cave. I've got dynamite with me, right here in my pocket . . . if I could reach it."

Don paused for a moment and then said, "You're right. You're absolutely right. It can work out. That's the good news."

Don calmly reached into his coat pocket. "The bad news for you," he continued, "is that I intend to blame you for everything—with your mental illness and drug abuse . . . and fortunately for me, you won't be around to dispute a word of it."

Before Mark could respond, he saw Don withdraw a liter bottle from his coat pocket and point it at his head. For a split second, Mark wondered what was happening. Then, with horror, he recognized that the bottle was taped to a pistol, but before he could open his mouth, Don Daniels calmly squeezed the trigger.

The gunshot wasn't quite as suppressed as Don had hoped.

. . .

The sudden pistol report made Cooper jump. He lit his lighter just as Mark's legs went limp and his body slumped back down into the hole a few inches. It was obvious that Mark had just been killed when his bowels released.

Cooper stared at the motionless body, relieved that he was finally dead. He wondered who had killed him. The talking resumed, and Cooper was able to catch their last few sentences. Knowing it wasn't the police, he fell back to where Grayson was waiting, saying a silent prayer for Kelly's safety on the way.

Cooper's hands shook as he decided that he'd wait only a few minutes, pull Mark's body back into the cave, sneak out, and then shoot the men outside if they were still there. *I gotta do whatever it takes to save Kelly.*

CHAPTER 112

After he answered the call on Cooper's cell, Obermeyer had tried to pick up Don Daniel's trail through the woods. Along the way, he coursed a muffled gunshot and then took off running while nervously unholstering his Glock. Three times in one night he had drawn his duty weapon—a landmark day in his career. Slowing down to navigate the thick woods, the big detective never looked behind to see if any other officers were responding to the shot. Due to the effects of the homemade suppressor, the shot seemed farther away than it actually was, and as a result the unknowing detective almost ran into the thick of the action before he realized it.

About forty yards out he could see the old man who he noticed earlier and Don Daniels. He could see a pistol in the old man's hand. The wet leaves and falling rain allowed him to approach silently. He used trees to break his outline as he methodically but quickly closed the distance.

"Police officer! Show me your hands!"

The old man obliged and held up his hands. Don Daniels did not.

"Shoot him, Jubal," Don Daniels whispered.

"All the officers heard that shot, and I know the whole story. I know everything thanks to Mark. Apparently, he tried to have his hired help killed to tie up loose ends here, and they found out, so they dropped the dime on him!" Lightning flashed, and he had a brief look at everyone, instantly being replaced again by darkness.

"Shoot him. He's gonna hurt us," Don Daniels anxiously whispered to his brother, this time a little louder and with more emphasis.

"Put the gun down! And I need to see everybody's hands right now!" Obermeyer had his pistol trained on the silhouette of the old man holding the pistol. With his heart racing and adrenaline pumping, everything went into slow motion.

"Do it, Jubal!" Don whispered urgently, while holding his own pistol behind his back. He'd prefer Jubal make the move to distract the police officer.

Jubal glanced over at his brother and then began the motion of dropping his weapon.

Don Daniels cussed loudly, quickly aimed his pistol at Obermeyer, and fired a shot as the big detective simultaneously fired twice. Daniels's aim was true, striking Obermeyer squarely in the center of the chest, causing him to fall backward, landing motionless in the wet leaves.

Screams and shouts from the direction of the old house sent Don into a panic. He wheeled around toward Jubal with the intent of killing him and then escaping deep into the woods. Jubal was to be his new fall guy. But the old man was one step ahead, and when Don made the turn, Jubal was already pointing his pistol at him.

"Jubal, now think about this. I've always been there for you. I'm the only one who's taken care of you. I've got a plan for us to get out of this."

"The only thing y'all have ever done is hurt folks. That cave's evil. That house is evil. Mark was pure evil—evil as you can get—and you ain't no better. I ain't gonna be a part of this no more," Jubal said with a shaky voice.

Before Don could raise his own pistol, fire flashed in Don's eyes and a perfectly shaped round hole appeared just to the right of center of the tired banker's eyes. After wiping off his fingerprints and then cleverly placing his pistol in Mark's hand, Jubal ran as hard as he could into the dark woods, away from his past and into the future.

CHAPTER 113

The police and sheriff deputies converged on the scene, weapons drawn. Flashlight beams probed the area. The rain was intensifying.

Visibility was minimal, and when Detective Obermeyer was first spotted, they all feared the worst. Two Montgomery officers quickly knelt on either side of Obermeyer. A young deputy shouted, "Officer down! Officer down!" as loud as he could, immediately elevating the tensions and voices of everyone.

"I've got a pulse!" the other one screamed, which caused everyone to begin shouting louder and calling in for medical support.

Several officers spread out in the direction from which Obermeyer would have been shot. Upon seeing a mound of rocks and something oddly out of place, all talking and shouting stopped as if on cue. The four officers closest to the rocks spread out and moved in while the others set up to provide cover.

High intensity flashlight beams illuminated the head and shoulders of Mark Wright. His head was hanging backward with eyes open and mouth agape. One side of his face was stained from the purple cattle spray.

Don Daniels lay crumpled, faceup next to a stump a few yards away. A small trickle of blood had run down the side of his head from the bullet hole between his eyes.

"Looks like Obermeyer finally got to discharge his weapon," an officer kneeling next to the bodies said reverently.

"Yep, and he got both of 'em with headshots," another responded. "I'd heard he was a master marksman, but I wouldn't believe this if I wasn't seeing it with my own eyes. Dead-center accuracy!"

The first trained medical personnel to reach Obermeyer was a tactical first responder from the Montgomery Police Department's Special Weapons and Tactics Team. Both of the officers by Obermeyer's side stood when he approached and then stepped out of the way.

The first responder quickly opened a large, black tactical backpack with a trauma kit full of advanced life support medical supplies and went to work. Everyone held their lights on Obermeyer so that the medic could see. A few silently prayed. No one said a word.

Shortly, Obermeyer's commander arrived out of breath, took in the scene, and crossed herself. She was visibly upset. The commander watched the medic frantically searching the detective's body as if he were looking for hidden money. She looked at Obermeyer's face and forgot all of the headaches he had caused her; she saw a man, an officer of the law who loved his job and would be missed.

The medic sat back on his heels and placed his hands on his hips.

The commander interpreted his body language to mean that he had given up.

"Please don't give up!" she begged.

"This man's not wounded. He's got on a bulletproof vest!" He pulled open Obermeyer's shirt and stuck his finger into the hole in the officer's black vest. "See?"

"What!?" the commander exclaimed, kneeling down. "Are you certain?"

"Ma'am, I've examined him from head to toe; he's not shot."

"And his vitals are those of a sleeping man," said another medic who had joined in the assessment, taking the stethoscope out of his ears and showing his relief. "He's just unconscious, like he passed out. He may have some type of head trauma from the fall, though."

"So he'll be okay?"

"I believe so. We need to get him outta here to make sure. But everything indicates that he's not been hit."

"That's our O!" said the commander, smiling as she stood. "Everything by the book. He's my only detective who wears a vest . . . but I bet that changes now!"

Everyone let out a nervous laugh and sigh of relief. All of them knew that the jokes were sure to follow, but for now their focus was on getting him to an ambulance.

"Hey! Can y'all hear me?! I need some help over here!" Cooper called out.

Dixie appeared and immediately started barking. No one had even noticed the dog.

Everyone jumped from the surprise of the yell for help and the dog's barking.

"Identify yourself! Where are you?" a deputy called, not knowing where to look.

"I'm Cooper Dixon! I'm under Mark. I'm in the cave."

Almost all of the officers rushed to where Mark's body was sticking out of the ground.

"Are you all right? Do you have the boy?" the commander yelled back instantly.

One of the deputies began radioing for assistance. Two burly officers helped the commander pull Mark's body out of the crevasse.

"Get back, dog!" someone yelled.

"Yeah, I got him right here. Is my wife okay?"

"Yes, she is! Come on out," the commander hollered into the hole.

"I'm gonna send Grayson out first!" Cooper yelled. He could hear Dixie barking and smiled.

Realizing the carnage just outside the cave entrance, he paused before handing Grayson up.

"Hey, Officer?"

"Yeah, Cooper?"

"Be careful what you let him see. Okay?"

"Copy that. Send him through," the commander answered, reaching down to help pull out Grayson.

When she had Grayson in her arms, she quickly turned him where he couldn't see his dead father. She handed him to a deputy who wrapped him in a jacket and quickly carried him away.

The commander was extremely excited and relieved to see Cooper. She helped him out of the ground and onto his feet. They almost shook hands but hugged even though they didn't know each other. Dixie immediately jumped on Cooper, demanding attention.

"Hey, girl. You saved our lives," Cooper said, dropping to his knees as he grabbed her head, looking straight into her eyes and then hugging her. Dixie's tail wagged at hyper speed. Portable search-and-rescue lights now illuminated the entire area where the detective was found. Cooper stopped rubbing his dog and stood. Seeing Detective Obermeyer being attended to by several people, Cooper exclaimed, "Oh my God! Is he okay?" Cooper watched the detective being carried through the woods on a backboard.

"Yeah. Apparently, he got knocked out or something, taking care of these two," responded the commander, pointing at Don Daniels's and Mark Wright's bodies.

Cooper didn't respond to that observation but asked, "What about Gates; is he involved?"

"No, he isn't. At least it appears that Gates is not involved. It's complicated, and we don't know all the facts yet. But I know that Obermeyer is gonna hate that he missed seeing you climb out of that cave. He received a phone call a few minutes ago explaining almost everything. We know you're innocent."

Pointing at Mark, the commander said, "It seems that fine pillar of finance tried to clean up loose ends by contracting the wrong person to kill his hired kidnappers. The details around that are sketchy, but obviously the hit didn't go down—who knew about brotherhood among thieves?— at any rate, they knew who put out the contract, so they dropped the dime on their former employer. They called your cell phone, which Obermeyer had with him, and told him the whole story."

When the commander paused, she noticed for the first time Cooper's bloody, bandaged hand and asked, "Are you okay?"

Cooper looked at her, confused by all that she had just conveyed. "Ugh, yeah, I think so. I overheard a piece of what happened here, and I think I may know why they did it."

"That'll be helpful. We'll compare what you know with what Obermeyer learned and maybe it'll all add up to a motive."

"So you caught the kidnappers?"

"No. Not yet. We'll worry about that later. But we've got the masterminds," she commented, pointing at the bodies of Don and Mark.

"I heard voices, and then a gunshot outside the cave. I tell ya, I was relieved when Mark's boots quit moving. I . . . I . . . I just wish I coulda been the one—," Cooper held up his pistol.

"Ah, okay, whoa . . . here, I'll take that," the commander said, holding out her hand for Cooper's pistol. She dropped the magazine, unloaded the chamber, and then placed the ejected round into the clip. She handed Cooper's weapon to one of her officers. "You'll get it back when we finish our investigation."

Cooper nodded his understanding.

"Come on. Let's get outta here. Your wife's waitin' on you. Plus, it looks like you're gonna need a medic to look at that hand."

"How's Kelly? Was she raped? She wasn't raped, was she?"

"No. No. No. She's gonna be fine."

Cooper bent over and put his hands on his knees. "I really need to see her." He was obviously exhausted from the ordeal and looked as though he might vomit.

The commander put her hand on his shoulder. "That's good because she wouldn't leave here without you."

CHAPTER 114

Detective Obermeyer had regained consciousness by the time the first responders got him to the yard of the old house. He was too embarrassed to allow them to treat him on the stretcher. After they unstrapped him, he stood and tried to act as if nothing had happened.

He was secretly enjoying all the congratulations for stopping the bad guys' escape, though he acted as if it were no big deal.

"All in a day's work," he commented and patted his service weapon.

He couldn't remember actually aiming at the perps, and he was frustrated that he didn't remember the gun battle even though the whole exchange had gone into super-slow motion. He was confident that his training and instincts had gotten him through the ordeal.

The rain had let up by the time Cooper walked into the crowd of law enforcement and rescue crews gathered in the yard of the old mansion. Applause erupted, and the questions flew as he pushed his way through to the back of the ambulance. Fortunately, the media was kept at a distance, for the time being.

When Cooper saw Kelly, tears welled in his eyes. He didn't know what to say—too much needed saying. Kelly reached out for him, and they hugged the longest, tightest hug they had ever shared. Weeping openly, they clung to each other.

After several minutes, Cooper felt a hand on his back. He turned to see Millie. She had tears in her eyes and slightly nodded her head approvingly.

"I hope you got that devil that did all this to your family," she said emphatically.

Cooper nodded. "He won't be botherin' us anymore."

"That's good, Cooper," she said holding up her iron, "'cause I was gonna smite him."

"Smite him?"

"Smite or smote, I gets confused. It's what the Good Lord used to do in the Old Testament. But he ain't much in da smitin' bidness no more, which is just too bad if you axe me."

"I tell you what," Cooper said, "I feel like I've been smitten pretty good this last week," he said, looking at Kelly who smiled.

An EMT forced Cooper to extend his arm, and he started unwrapping the bloody shirtsleeve bandage. His face showed concern about the wound as he began treating it.

Inside the next ambulance, Brooke was ecstatic to see Grayson. She hadn't stopped holding him and didn't plan to anytime soon. She was distraught that her own husband had been responsible for all this pain, anguish, and death. Deep down, however, she wasn't very surprised.

Sticking his head inside Kelly's ambulance, the sheriff smiled at the scene and said, "Okay, folks, here's the plan.

The district attorney has gotten the governor's approval to use a helicopter from the Alabama DPS Aviation Unit to get y'all to the hospital. It'll also help y'all avoid the media circ—"

"I ain't gettin' in no helicopter," Millie interrupted.

"That's fine, ma'am. I promise we'll get you home," replied the sheriff.

"Can I have a minute alone with my wife first?" Cooper asked, his hand still being bandaged.

"Sure. As soon as they're done here, get to the chopper. It's about to land in the field behind the house," the sheriff commanded, looking at the paramedic working on Cooper's hand.

Before Kelly climbed out of the ambulance, Cooper touched her face and said, "I've made some serious mistakes. The biggest is havin' my head so far up my ass I couldn't see what's truly important—what matters. This week's shown me how much I love you and how badly I want us to have a great marriage. Baby, I know I'm broken, and I'll do whatever's needed to make this right. I love you so much! I'm so sorry. Can you forgive me?"

Kelly had huge tears rolling down her cheeks. She was almost too emotional to talk but managed, "No, honey, it's me. It's been me. There's nothing to forgive. I love you, honey. I'm so sorry. I don't care about the house or cars or anything but you and the kids. Please forgive me."

They looked at each other—really looked for the first time in years and saw in each other the person they fell in love with years ago. They smiled, hugged, and cried some more.

"The other night, last Saturday night, I almost made a huge mistake but . . . but I didn't. I couldn't. I came close, but I realized that I still love you, and I could—"

"I know," Kelly interrupted. "Don't say anything. I know. Brooke told me all about it. How you didn't show up." Shaking her head, she continued, "It doesn't matter. The important thing is we're together now. Really together."

Someone pounded on the side of the ambulance and hollered, "Chopper's ready!"

"Let's get the hell outta here," Cooper said. He then noticed the digital clock in the ambulance and pointed it out to Kelly. It read 1:11 p.m. She smiled, her bottom lip quivering. He kissed her affectionately.

"Is he gonna be okay?" she asked the paramedic, looking at the fresh white bandages.

"He'll live, but we need to get the wound flushed and better debrided," she responded with a warm smile and then deposited her bloody surgical gloves into the biohazard waste receptacle.

• • •

With relieved expressions on their faces, Obermeyer, the district attorney, and the commander stood outside the helicopter's rotor wash, watching the players in the week's drama. As Kelly was helped into the helicopter, Obermeyer stared off into the night sky.

"What is it now, O?" the commander asked with a sigh.

"Well, ma'am . . . we've still got Sammy Davis Junior, Oprah Winfrey, and Larry King to deal with, and I've got this naggin' feelin' there's something I'm missin' or forgot."

"Obermeyer, for goodness's sake, please don't tell us to stand by," the commander said, smiling wryly.

The district attorney was listening and couldn't help interjecting. "The way I see it, MPD's best detective here just won a gun battle with the brains behind a kidnapping that made national news and an established serial rapist . . . and he did it on his terms, by the book. Let's be thankful for what we have now—what's been accomplished here today. O can work on the rest of it tomorrow," the DA proudly stated and placed supportive hands on each of their backs. "And why don't y'all go meet with the press. You both deserve it."

CHAPTER 115

The medical techs carefully loaded Kelly into the helicopter and buckled her harness. Brooke and Grayson were already seated, holding each other's hands. Cooper carried Dixie, who was quivering, and climbed into the seat next to Kelly. The rotor noise was so loud in the Bell 206L that he could barely hear what anyone was saying.

"I'm Joe Wilson. I'll be flying y'all to the ER. Glad to have you aboard," the helicopter pilot said, looking over his shoulder at the group.

"Hope you don't mind having a dog on board," Cooper asked as he put his good arm around Dixie, who was still shaking but calmed down some once the door was shut. Cooper wasn't leaving Coosa County without her.

"No problem. Man's best friend. If you don't believe it, lock your wife and your dog in the trunk of your car, ride around for about an hour, and then see who's the most excited to see you."

"I'm bettin' the dog!" Brooke said with a smile and a wink at the pilot that made everyone laugh.

"You got that right!" Joe Wilson responded and then gave the thumbs-up signal, saying, "Y'all ready?"

Everyone nodded or said, "Yes, sir!"

With all that had gone on in the last week, and having actually been locked in a trunk, Brooke smiled and chuckled with relief. The joke served to break the tension of the events for her. She looked across at Cooper who made eye contact. They knew what almost happened between them. Cooper's thoughts drifted to all that Mark had said about Brooke, but looking at her, he was having a hard time believing that she was involved. Obviously, she said something comforting to Kelly, and that's all he cared about at the moment. Brooke appeared to be genuinely happy for them. She kissed Grayson on the forehead and then reassuringly looked at Cooper, smiled and mouthed, "Thank you." She began to cry.

Cooper nodded and squeezed Kelly tighter as Dixie licked his hand.

Obermeyer had given back Cooper's cell phone before he climbed inside the helicopter so that he could call his family. It buzzed at the receipt of a text. It was from Gates. The text read: "great news don't have to sell tower bookie n deep shit w feds will forgive debt if i help explain later"

Kelly noticed him reading the text and asked, "Everything okay?"

"Yes. Yes it is. Everything's gonna be just fine."

The helicopter slowly started its ascent. Cooper saw Kelly's bottom lip quivering as she looked down at the antebellum house, the various pockets of people, the news vans, and the flashing lights of the medical and law enforcement vehicles. She held the duck band on her necklace with one hand and Cooper's good hand with the other. She smiled when their eyes met as tears welled once again.

Once the helicopter reached a safe altitude, it banked hard to the south and accelerated. Instantly, the scenery changed. Cooper was leaving behind the past, racing toward his kids, waiting at the hospital, and an almost unspeakable gift—the opportunity to get right.

EPILOGUE
ONE YEAR LATER

Clarence "Mad Dog" Armstrong had vowed to never again work outside his area of expertise. That was until the oil spill in the Gulf. Soon after it happened, he bought two of the oldest trawlers on the coast and became an instant shrimper and eventually a spillionaire. It didn't seem to matter that he had never dragged a net. The tag on his restored vintage, full-size Hummer read: THX BP. He and Jesse Ray were planning their next big job.

Jesse Ray made a small fortune helping Clarence with the spill boondoggle and planned to purchase a Radio Shack franchise. He continued working e-mail and Internet scams— his latest for bogus virus-protection upgrades. Chances are you've received an e-mail from him or have been redirected to one of his web pages when trying to visit one of your favorite Internet sites.

Jenny and Maynard dated for a few months, and then married in a simple ceremony. He hasn't dressed like Larry King since the kidnapping job but is still addicted to teeth-whitening strips. The newlyweds recently closed on a run-down twenty-acre horse farm in Okaloosa County, Florida. Jenny is happier than ever, busier than ever, but she often misses her partners in crime. Maynard is happy just to be with Jenny every day. To Jenny's utter delight and amusement, he dresses like Tim McGraw.

Detective Obermeyer's legend and career were cemented after solving the kidnapping and serial rapist cases. Actually, there were a number of inconsistencies and much confusion during the forensic examinations of the bodies and crime scene with respect to who actually shot whom. The Powers That Be decided that it was in everyone's best interest to keep it all quiet. Obermeyer became the public beneficiary of the closed files. He continues to fight crime locally and occasionally teaches detail management courses at municipal police academies around the South. Frequently he pauses and "stands by" while he tries to determine who actually kidnapped Kelly Dixon. That mystery still bothers him.

As a condition of his plea agreement, Gates Ballenger checked into rehab. He was clean and sober for three months. Work became his new addiction, doing twelve-hour days securing and maintaining clients for the Tower Agency. He can be heard weekly, calling into the Paul Finebaum radio show, expressing his opinions on college football. His analyses are seldom accurate.

Mitchell Holmes was due in court for multiple counts of racketeering and money laundering. He was facing significant prison time if convicted. The odds, however, were better than even that he would get the minimum sentence since the judge hearing the case owed a favor to the elder Mr. Ballenger.

Brooke Layton was humiliated by her ex-husband and embarrassed at her own intentions. So as soon as she could, she and Grayson moved to Tallahassee, Florida, where she works for a large graphic design firm. Grayson saw a counselor once a week for a couple of months and made remarkable progress. The neighborhood they moved into has three stocked lakes, so Grayson, accompanied by his new dog, Dixie Girl, fishes almost every day.

Millie and Haywood Brown sold the biggest part of the property to a conservation organization and retired. They kept enough money for them to live on comfortably, set up a trust fund for the children at their church, and gave the balance to the Southern Baptist Convention missionary fund. Unbeknownst to Cooper, Millie retained two hundred beautiful, wooded acres of her home place, with an excellent pond site, for him. The Browns planned to surprise Cooper and Kelly with the deed to it in five years, on the Dixons' twentieth wedding anniversary.

Cooper and Kelly Dixon worked hard at their marriage and were both surprised at how easy it actually was once they both made the effort. They can be seen around Montgomery each Thursday evening on their date night. Kelly has been seen fishing with Cooper, and he was recently spotted under an umbrella at the beach with her, although he was nose deep reading *Gamekeepers* magazine. Their friends say that they look happier than ever.

Dixie never stowed away in the back of Cooper's truck again. Nowadays she can be found lying on a therapeutic dog bed inside the comfort of the Dixon home.

Jubal Daniels inherited Don Daniels's estate and Mark Wright's by default. He kept the old home place but immediately sold all remaining assets. The bank went to a large, regional financial institution based in Louisiana. With several *National Geographic* magazines as travel guides, he purchased a bus ticket to New Orleans for a seven-day paddle-wheeler cruise up the Mississippi River to St. Louis. He then hopped on Amtrak to see the giant Redwoods in California. He hasn't been seen since.

ACKNOWLEDGMENTS

I love the idea of engaging and entertaining readers enough that they keep turning pages past their bedtimes. That's why I write, and I'm humbled when they take time to contact me or post a review on Amazon. It's also equally humbling to have so many people promote my stories and do what they can to help advance my writing career—some barely know me; others go back many years. All are very much appreciated. Thank you!

Kyle Jennings and his wife, Jill Conner Browne, liked what I had to say from early on and encouraged me to write before anyone was willing to read the stories. Kyle is an excellent editor and business manager and, thankfully, he handles all the gritty details, allowing me to concentrate on storytelling.

Terry Goodman and the entire Amazon and Thomas & Mercer team are simply amazing. I can't thank them enough for all of their support here and abroad.

My wife, Melissa, and daughter, Jessi, have been constant and consistent supporters. They both allow me to bounce random ideas off them, and they give me honest critiques, along with no small amount of concerned looks. And I'm grateful to them for allowing me to disappear many nights and weekends while I try to piece together a cohesive story. My wife wishes that I'd write love stories, and Jessi would prefer something with vampires, but both seem to have come to grips with my preferred genre. Thank y'all. I love you both more than I can express here.

I'll never forget taking my mother, Peggy Cole, to the Pike Road Library book signing near Montgomery, Alabama, and how happy she was to listen to me talk about my books.

I thank you, Mom, for your unwavering love and for your many Montgomery area friends and their support. And a special thanks to Barbara Bryan and Deborah Speigner—as far as sisters go, I can't imagine any better.

A profound and extraordinary thanks to my Mossy Oak family, who have always been incredibly supportive of my writing. A man couldn't ask for a better place to work or for a better employer than the Haas family. Both are truly special. My friends at Alabama Farmers Co-op have also been very supportive, and for that I am genuinely grateful.

To the exceptional folks of West Point, Mississippi, a heartfelt thank-you for the enthusiasm you have displayed for my stories, especially Ginger and Randy Weimer and Connie Hudson.

Thanks again to those who have suffered through very rough drafts: Dr. Bill Billington, Robbie Speigner, Art Shirley, Traci LaChance, Jon Sverson, Tim Brooks, Norman Snead, Jesse Raley, and Page Todd. I appreciate all of the great feedback.

A particular thank-you to David Housel: a voracious reader, who discovered my stories by word of mouth years ago and now may be my most ardent supporter.

Thanks goes to the countless readers of *The Dummy Line* and *Moon Underfoot* who made the effort to find my e-mail address and contact me. Now you can reach me on Facebook at Bobby Cole Books.

Finally, a big thank-you to all of you who told friends and family about my writings and who e-mailed links, gave books as gifts, invited me to book clubs and book signings, and, in general, encouraged me at every opportunity. I could never name everyone, but you know who you are. It's my sincere hope and prayer that you enjoyed this story too.

AUTHOR BIOGRAPHY

Bobby Cole is a native of Montgomery, Alabama, and president of Mossy Oak® BioLogic®. Additionally, he is an avid wildlife manager, hunter, and active supporter of the Catch-A-Dream™ Foundation. He lives with his wife and daughter in West Point, Mississippi. Bobby is also the author of the novels *The Dummy Line* and *Moon Underfoot*.